JUST ONE MOMENT

RONNIE MATHEWS

Cover Design by Melissa Doughty at Mel D. Designs

Editing by Paisley McNab at Perfectly Write

Proofreading by Caroline Palmier at Love & Edits

ASIN: B0DJSQ5LYM (Ebook)

ISBN: 978-1-0683210-0-9 (Paperback)

Find the people who love you for exactly who you are.
And remember to love yourself.

Thank you so much for deciding to read Just One Moment. I hope you love Graham and Quinn's story and find all of their moments are as beautiful as they are.

Just One Moment is the second book in the Sutton Bay series and can be read as a standalone. All books in the series will be interconnected standalone stories, but I suggest reading them in order to get the full feel of the stories.

This is an open-door romance and intended for readers who are eighteen years or older. All characters written are consenting adults and you will find explicit, on-page sexual content, explicit language, and real life situations. I ask that you always look after yourself, and if you wish to see a full list of content and trigger warnings, please visit: www.ronniemath-ews.com

playlist

hey, honey - The 520s, hey, nothing
Northern Attitude - Noah Kahan
Grew Apart - Logan Size, Donovan Woods
Iris - The Goo Goo Dolls
No Right To Love You (Acoustic) - Rhys Lewis
Hey Girl - Stephen Sanchez
Too Sweet - Hozier
Falling in Love at a Coffee Shop - Landon Ping
Sailor Song - Gigi Perez
So What - Jillian Rossi
Skin and Bones - David Kushner
Apple Pie - Lizzy McAlpine
Feels Like - Gracie Abrams
Lost & Found - Darren Kiely
Searching For A Feeling - Thirdstory
I GUESS I'M IN LOVE - Clinton Kane
Stay With Me - Live at Abbey Road Studios - Sam Smith
Nobody Knows - The Lumineers
Some People - James Bay

Only Us - Laura Dreyfuss, Ben Platt
I'm Gonna Be (500 Miles) - Sleeping At Last
First Day of My Life - Bright Eyes

Scan QR code below to listen on Spotify.

graham

MARCH

I'M ENVIOUS OF MY TEN-POUND DACHSHUND.

No one expects Curly to show his face at social gatherings. But they expect it from me.

I knew coming here tonight was a mistake and a total waste of my time. Somewhere, deep, deep down, there is a tiny, extroverted version of myself living inside me, who takes over my decision-making on occasions and leads me astray from my introverted ways. That's the only explanation as to why I'm standing in an overcrowded, loud, and stuffy bar.

It's barely spring and already tourists have found their way into the local drinking hole, hoping to experience that small-town way of life. All they're going to find here are sticky floors and an owner who would rather they fuck off back to the big city, which is putting it politely.

Our family's restaurant, Our Place, is holding a team bonding night this evening. My brothers have somehow convinced Lenny—said owner—to allow them to host a pool competition here. He's probably grateful we're filling the room with townsfolk rather than tourists, but his attitude says other-wise. Shirley's is one of Sutton Bay's oldest establishments, having spent the last thirty years as every local's favorite hangout spot.

My eyes scan the sea of people as I take a sip of club soda. It's the same one I've been nursing for the last hour, and I grimace as the flat, lukewarm liquid glides down my throat. When I spot my brothers from across the room, what I see doesn't surprise me.

Booth, my younger brother, has been floating around like the social butterfly he is. He's currently chatting up a couple of doe-eyed tourists in the corner. They won't be in town long enough to catch feelings, which helps with his affliction to rela-tionships. My oldest brother, Patrick, is trying his hardest not to drool at the sight of Johanna, his childhood best friend, as he not so subtly watches her bend over the pool table. They've been doing this dance for years, right up until Jo left town six years ago. It's no surprise to anyone that they picked up right where they left off when she returned.

They're perfect for each other.

That notion leaves an acrid taste in my mouth.

I want him to be happy; he deserves it after years of looking after everyone else. A little over a year ago, I was in a long-term relationship and with my life in order. Now, I'm single and the idea of meeting new people, let alone entering the dating pool again, makes my skin itch. My bitterness doesn't stem from a place of what could have been, but from what I ignored for so long simply because it was easier.

Twelve years wasted.

Slamming my glass down on the high-top table and pushing up the sleeves of my sweater, I'm about ready to call it a night when something soft and warm lands on my forearm.

Looking down, I find a petite hand with bright pink nails and a pinky ring with a smiley face stamped into the silver band. My eyes trail higher, following the path of smooth, sun-kissed skin until it reaches the short sleeves of a denim dress. When I'm met with the most spectacular smile I've ever seen in my life, does my journey stop. Along with my heart.

A row of pearly white teeth dazzle me, framed by two plump, glossy lips.

But it's the woman behind the smile who steals the show and leaves me speechless. Though, most would argue that's normal for me. Bouncy curls frame her heart-shaped face. I couldn't tell you what color her hair is. It's a mix of so many earthy tones: dark brown, caramel, honey, and a few strands of auburn. Her eyes aren't just hazel either. No. Because that description is too simple for the molten copper irises that glow and shift, they're so iridescent.

She barely reaches my chin and the quick sweep I do of her body reveals soft curves that I want to trace with my palms, to follow the luscious slope of her hips and waist. Denim has never looked so good.

Her head tilts and the realization that I've been staring at her without uttering a word hits me. Words would be helpful and stop me from looking like a voiceless moron. I finally open my mouth to speak, only for my breath to get caught in my throat, turning me into a sputtering mess.

"Oh god, are you okay?" the woman asks as she reaches behind me to lightly pat my back. I don't know if she's singing or if her voice always comes out like the soft chime of bells. It's something close to how Snow White sings to the herd of animals she keeps in her kitchen. I know this because my niece has forced me to watch it an illegal amount of times.

It's been minutes, yet no one has captivated me like this before.

Otherworldly comes to mind. Which makes sense, because she seems to have appeared out of nowhere. I take in everything about her, let it run through my mind, so I can process her unparalleled beauty. When it's finished processing, it's clear I'm malfunctioning, because I still haven't spoken.

My mouth opens and closes like a goldfish as I try to find my voice. I'm not usually one to rush to get my words out; I like to think them through before blurting the first thing that comes to mind, but with her, the need to speak is oddly overwhelming.

She giggles and, fuck, it's a nice sound. Better than nice.

No, concentrate. Words are what you need right now.

"You must be Graham. Jo said you weren't much of a talker. And well, I am. Sorry not sorry." She shrugs, her smile not faltering. "I'm Quinn."

The angel has a name.

Quinn.

Never has a one syllable sounded so glorious. I want to say it aloud. Taste her name on my lips and let the letters roll off my tongue.

"Graham." My voice is stiff, and I immediately wince, because she knows who I am. Take two. "Graham Sadler. Patrick's brother. Accountant." Only when the words leave my mouth do I hear how robotic and awkward I sound. The room is dim enough, so maybe she won't catch the reddening of my face.

"I hope there are just three of you Sadler brothers. God help the women of this town if there are more." It's fair she looks me over, too, and she doesn't shy away from scanning me from head to toe, lingering on my face the longest.

"Only three of us," I confirm.

She swipes the back of her hand across her forehead dramatically with a *Phew*. "You're nothing like Patrick or Booth, which is good, it might be hard to tell the three of you apart."

I'm definitely nothing like my brothers.

I'm just Graham or *Gray*.

Like the color.

"Well, Jo already mentioned that you're an accountant and it just so happens I'm in need of some help." Her voice is equal parts nervous and excited. "I'm still what you'd call a newbie to Sutton Bay. I own the bakery in town, Just Brew It? I don't think I've seen you in there, but you should come in sometime."

She's vibrating with excitement, eyes wide as she talks animatedly, hands flying left and right.

Fuck, I can't believe I almost missed out on her. If I had ignored that annoying voice in the back of my head telling me I needed to socialize and hang out with my brothers more, I wouldn't be standing here and listening to her passionate rant about brioche and muffins. She wasn't wrong—she loves to talk and I'm a little lost, but it simply adds to her charm. I could listen to her all night.

After a few more minutes of adorable rambling, she slaps a hand against her forehead and gasps. "Oh my god, listen to me. Seriously, just tell me to shut up next time."

Highly unlikely.

"Anyway, I came over here to see if you'd like to meet for coffee?"

I go to respond, to tell her I'm very much interested and ask if tomorrow works for her—deciding right this second is being overly eager—when a much larger and unwelcome hand claps me on the back. I've been so hypnotized by her, that it's interfered with my annoying little brother detector.

"Gray! One of my chefs had to leave early. Will you fill his spot in the next game?" Booth says from behind me. With a quick glance over my shoulder, I find him beaming at me, brown shaggy hair flopping over his head, looking like a happy puppy.

Usually, I'd be grateful for him butting into conversations and saving me from having to make awkward chitchat, but not this time. I wish he'd fuck off, because the longer he stands here, the more my nerves start hammering around my body and my voice drifts farther away.

"Good to see you again, Quinn. Having fun?" he asks while waiting for my reply.

Of course he knows her. It appears I'm the last person to know she exists, and for whatever reason, that pisses me off.

"Hey, Booth. I'm having a great time, thanks for letting me tag along."

They talk back and forth easily, while I stand there like an intruder. Turns out she's good friends with Johanna, who lives in the apartment above the bakery.

Booth turns his attention to me, but my eyes are still on Quinn. I haven't looked at anything or anyone else since she skipped over to me. "Are you playing then?"

"Nah."

"Don't be like that. Quinn, you'll play, won't you?" Booth asks.

"I'm as hopeless as Johanna, so I'll stick to the sidelines." She laughs.

"Ugh, you two suck." He locks eyes with Lenny and heads toward him. "Lenny, my fine man, you down for a game of pool?"

We're alone again, and I still have no idea what to say. *You're pretty*, seems too forward. Hesitation and unease have sucked up all my vocabulary. She doesn't make me feel awkward, it's just how I am, especially when the silence is begging to be filled.

What surprises me, though, is Quinn's calm tolerance toward this entire encounter. She stands there, rocking on the balls of her feet, smiling up at me like she's happy to be here.

Clearing my throat and pulling at the neck of my sweater, I swallow my nerves and stick to safe territory. "How are you liking the town?"

She smiles wider at that question, and my chest swells with

pride that I somehow said something right. "Oh, it's the cutest. Jo took me out to Anakiwa Lookout the other week, and, wow, what a view. You've lived here your whole life?"

"Yeah. Well, I moved to New York for college. You? I mean, not here, you're clearly not from here. Fuck, not that you look like you don't belong here." My skin reaches dangerous temperatures, and the more I fumble over my words, the worse it gets. My eyes fall, because I don't want to see what no doubt is a weirded-out expression on her face. A grown man who can't hold a conversation. How appealing.

"Oh, New York, I've always wanted to visit. You studied accounting, I presume? A man good with numbers." Her ability to overlook my timidness surprises me, plus, she doesn't appear put off. I chance a look at her and the one thing I don't expect is for her to wink at me before her lips pout to the side in contemplation.

In the next beat, her hand is on me again, and I don't know what I did to even deserve her attention tonight, let alone her soft, warm touch, but here I am. Opening up her clutch with her other hand, she pulls out a pencil and uncaps it with her teeth. She tugs me closer, I go willingly, and as she bends over my arm, the hair at the top of her head tickles my chin.

Something sweet fills my nose. It's not overpowering or floral, something rich and inviting. Like brown sugar and vanilla.

The tip of the pencil glides across my skin in quick strokes and I peer down at what she's doing, only to realize it's one of those black eyeliner pencils. I remember my little sister, Florence, explaining something about smoky eyes, which sounded painful. When she's done, she pulls back and admires her artwork. Or the ten digits she's marked into my skin.

"I promised Jo I wouldn't leave her for long. That's my number..." She trails off and her eyes go wide as she spies the stack of napkins next to my glass. "Oops. Guess I could have written on one of them. But text me, and we can arrange that coffee if you like. Or come by the bakery, I'm easy. Anyway, what I've been trying to say is that Jo mentioned I should speak to you about the bakery and the restaurant working together. I could provide you guys with freshly baked bread and pastries."

My heart drops like a pebble in a well. She's not here to get to know me; she's here because she wants me to set up a business contract.

My eyes dart from her and the numbers on my forearm. If this were Booth, he'd somehow turn this around. Heck, he'd be the one writing the numbers on the girl's arm. Why can't I talk to a woman like a normal guy?

Much to my disappointment, Quinn's eyes leave mine as she waves at someone across the room and gives them a wide grin I'd stupidly hoped was only for me.

"I'm really glad I met you, Graham." Her smile and tone are so genuine, I question if she's still talking to me. Before I can tell her *It was amazing to meet you*, she gives my arm one last squeeze and walks away.

The moment I lose sight of her, the room turns cold, like her presence was the only warmth in here. Hoping no one sees me, I quickly type her number into my phone, before some drunk idiot spills a drink on my arm and washes away the evidence that she was actually here and wasn't a figment of my imagination. I'm desperate to leave, but I stick around a little while longer.

About an hour later, when I spot a tipsy Quinn taking unsteady steps into the cool night alone, my goodbye barely passes my lips as I abandon Patrick at our table. I need to make sure Quinn gets home safe. Selfishly, I hope it means I get to spend another five minutes with her, even if it just ends up with the silence being filled with her chatter. Without curious eyes around us, maybe I can take her up on her offer for coffee, even if it is to discuss a business relationship.

Since I've been single, no one has caught my eye the way she has.

My hope of getting to spend more time with her is desecrated when I watch her climb into the back of a truck along with two other people who were at the bar tonight. Her laughter echoes across the parking lot; carefree and bright. Maybe it's a good thing I didn't find the courage to ask her out. There's no chance in hell someone so quiet and awkward could make such a vivacious woman like her laugh. I wish I could be that person, though.

The driver is one of the restaurant's servers, who I trust to get her home safe. It doesn't stop me wishing they'd get a flat as they drive out of the parking lot. I know I didn't say much, and that would normally bother most people, but Quinn seemed happy talking to me. And I liked listening to her. She made the silence I usually leave in my wake a little less lonely.

I wait for the taillights to disappear before I drag my feet over to where my Jeep is parked. Disappointment in myself like lead in my boots. Had I not been a nervous wreck, I would have asked her out there and then. Typed her number into my phone and called her, so she had my number too. I would have insisted I drive her home and waited until she was safely inside before driving away.

Only, I'm not that guy, and a girl like Quinn is best matched with someone confident and outgoing.

Later that night, after I've let Curly out and locked up, I can't stop overthinking tonight's interactions. As usual, I put my thoughts down on paper before heading to bed, letting the words I couldn't find flood the pages. All my worries, doubts, and frustrations inked for my eyes only.

Tonight I met beauty incarnate.
Quinn.

How I hadn't heard about her before has an odd sense of anger bubbling in me. I was aware of the bakery that had opened on Robin Road, but I'm hardly ever in town. Maybe if I didn't have such a dislike for sugary snacks, I would have met her sooner.

I was so enthralled by her that I almost forgot what a fucking mess I was making of our meeting. Almost.

Who am I kidding thinking she would ever be interested in me. It's a good thing I couldn't string a coherent sentence together. I would have bored her to death. I watched her laugh and dance all night. So full of life.

And I'm just not anything that would interest her.

I just wish I could be.

I always feel lighter afterward, but something still niggles in the back of my head, scratching to get out. Before I overthink it, pen meets paper, and I find myself doing something I haven't done for a long time.

Etched into a fresh notebook, sit three short lines.

A prism of colors
Her beauty outshines us all
Too bright for dull gray

CHAPTER TWO

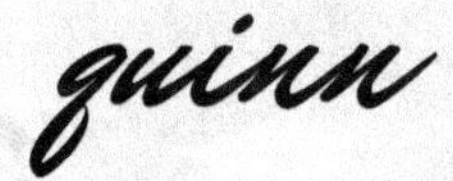

OCTOBER

"Hey, Siri, how are you today?"

"Hey, I can't complain. Thanks for asking," the automated voice from my phone responds.

"Well good for you."

The weight of my arm increases with each pass around the ceramic mixing bowl. I'm certain it's going to fall off if the clumps of flour don't disappear soon. Sometimes my KitchenAid doesn't give me the consistency I want, so I have to revert to the old-fashioned way. Blisters be damned, I will get a lump-free cake batter.

"Hey, Siri, what's the weather like today?"

My phone dings, prompting the voice of my robotic friend again. "Expect clear skies, with daytime highs of seventy-one degrees and lows of forty-nine degrees Fahrenheit."

"Fall is definitely here," I singsong, though it's a little breathless.

When I glance down, the greenish-yellow batter looks well combined. I place the bowl back on the worktop with a big sigh, reach up to the ceiling, and stretch out my aching muscles.

Who needs a workout when you attempt to beat at one hundred and fifty strokes per minute?

Pun intended.

Before the screen on my phone locks, I see that it's almost seven a.m. I came into the bakery early today, eager to try out some fall-themed recipes. When inspiration hits, I grab it by the horns, no matter how bad my bed head is. Which is why I've been here since five.

There are currently several sponge cakes lined up in front of me: spiced apple and pecan, maple butternut, and cranberry-orange. All flavors of fall, and the spicy, buttery goodness that comes with it. The batter I've just finished is for pistachio and cardamom muffins, which I'm planning to pair with a cream cheese frosting. And, of course, there will be something pumpkin spiced, I'm not a monster.

Once I transfer the batter to the muffin tins, I pop it in the preheated oven and move the finished cakes to the large refrigerator behind me. I slap my hands together—the excess flour clouding in front of me—and switch my raggedy, denim apron for one of the newly branded ones I had made for the bakery.

They're peach with the bakery's name embroidered on the front. Just Brew It. *My bakery.* I'm a sucker for a good pun, so when the name came to me on the long drive to my new home, it was meant to be.

It's been ten months since I opened the doors, and the need to squeal every time I'm reminded that I'm my own boss hasn't lessened.

How does one decide to open up a bakery slash coffee shop in coastal New England? Easy. A few too many margaritas, a dart, and a map. A week later, I'd packed up my van, and it was goodbye, Golden, Colorado, and hello, Sutton Bay, Maine. Trading snowy mountain ranges for crisp, salty air. It's the first time since I was eighteen that I've lived near the ocean.

Oh! Sea salt and rocky road cookies. The idea suddenly pops into my head, and I jot it down on the pad stuck to the cork board before I forget.

The quaint little fishing town is hidden away next to the state's beautiful natural habitats, Acadia National Park, and since moving here, I totally understand why tourists flock to this corner of the world every year. The moment I parked my orange VW van up along the beach, I was furious at my past self for having never been to New England.

While I had the funds to rent a small commercial space and open up my very own bakery, I hadn't expected for it to happen so soon. I'm certain fate had a part to play in where that dart landed. Within my first hour in town, I'd come across this very building, and by the end of the week, I'd secured a three-year lease agreement. Hey presto, Just Brew It was born.

A tapping noise from the front of the bakery gets my attention. I peek my head around the partition wall, separating the kitchen and seating area, and see Jo waving through the window, her blonde hair shining in the early morning sun. Padding over to the door, I unlock it and let her in. Without her needing to ask, I'm already making my way over to the coffee machine and starting up her usual order.

Johanna Thomas was born and raised in Sutton Bay but lived in Tennessee with her sister until earlier this year. Maybe fate had a part to play in her return, too, because she ended up getting her second chance with her childhood friend, Patrick. She moved out of the apartment above the bakery and into Patrick's house last month, but she still pops in most mornings for her daily fix of caffeine.

She makes grabby hands toward the fresh coffee pouring out of the machine. "Oh god, I need that so bad today. Lottie had us both up before the ass crack of dawn. She's had a thing about being late for school ever since she started kindergarten."

Chuckling, I pour the double shot of espresso over the ice I've already scooped into a plastic take-out cup, add a pump of syrup, and top it off with coconut milk. Lottie is Patrick's young daughter, and despite not being with her mom, Carrie, they make a really good co-parenting team. Lottie is obsessed with Jo, as is she with the five-year-old. I wouldn't be surprised if they started popping out their own little gremlins soon.

"Here ya go." I hand over the cup and she presses her nose to the lid with a deep inhale. "You need help." I laugh.

"I know, I know. Patrick dared me not to drink any iced drinks once the temperatures drop below forty. That's, like, next week, Quinn!"

I shake my head and start flipping the chairs over from the tops of the tables. The small space has six two-seater tables, allowing people to sit in with their coffees or pastries if they wish. Most take their orders to go, but it's always nice to meet someone new and hear about their life story or what their plans are for the day.

"Where has this year disappeared to?"

"It's really gotten away from us," she answers. A wistful smile pulls at her lips, and I know she's thinking about the last few months and how much has changed between Patrick and her. I'm happy for them. They're obviously soul mates and I'm a big enough girl to say I'm jealous. Heck, I tell Jo I'm jealous of her all the time.

"How are things with the new owner?" I ask hesitantly.

She looks as fed up as the last time I asked her this. "Their lack of involvement is really starting to grind my gears. Each week, we wait for some life-changing email from the buyer, but all they ask for are the same boring updates or to boss Booth around. It's bizarre. What kind of owner doesn't even show their face or reveal their name to their new employees?"

George and Ted, Jo and Patrick's dads, founded and co-owned a seafood restaurant down the road called Our Place. Patrick's dad sadly passed away almost seven years ago, leaving his eldest son to take over the family business. To the shock of everyone earlier this year, Patrick's mom and Jo's dad broke the news that the restaurant was struggling, and despite months of trying to save it, they had no choice but to sell. Oddly, the new owner is very hands-off. So hands-off, in fact, that no one knows their name or what their future plans are. The silver lining is that everyone who works there got to keep their jobs, and nothing has changed.

"What does Graham think of it all?" It's a hard task to keep my face neutral as I wait to hear about Patrick's brother.

"Tight-lipped as always. He's taken a step back from his firm, even dropped a few of his big clients to spend more time at the restaurant. He's just as worried as we are, though less vocal. The uncertainty is starting to get to Booth too."

Graham and Booth are polar opposites. Booth reminds me of a hyperactive golden retriever who hasn't been neutered yet, and he's quite the ladies' man. Graham, however, is an enigma. A shy, handsome, and serious nut to crack. He always looks deep in thought behind his glasses, which makes the brooding stare even hotter. They're tortoiseshell glasses, for Pete's sake.

"I'm sure it's a good thing he's close by now," I supply.

"Absolutely. Lottie loves him, Claire is happy he's not traveling into the city each day, and it's nice having him around more."

Claire is the matriarch of the Sadler family, and she's always been sweet and welcomed me to Robin Road when I opened the bakery. She comes in with her sons on occasion, but just once with Graham. Thinking back to that particular afternoon when Graham calmly, yet sternly, warned his older brother has me biting my bottom lip. Poor Patrick was in a bit of a panic when he stormed in here looking for Johanna after they found out the restaurant was being sold, so I don't blame him for his abruptness.

"*Watch it*," he'd said. Voice all deep and gravelly. It was only our second time meeting, but it was certainly memorable...

"Did you ever speak to him about working with the restaurant?" Johanna's question interrupts my daydreaming.

My grimace is hard to hide. In March, Jo had suggested I speak to Graham about us partnering up. To my surprise, I found out he's the restaurant's accountant as well as being in charge of supplier relations. When Jo first mentioned it, the ideas I had for the restaurant were endless. Lobster-shaped croissants. Fresh brioche rolls. Sourdough bread.

After a couple of shots at the local bar, I accosted Graham, who also happens to be a brooding hottie. I quickly realized a bar wasn't the place to build a working relationship, so what did I do? I scribbled my number on the poor guy's arm—a very nice forearm, I might add—with eyeliner and practically begged him to call me.

Only, he never called, and that was seven months ago, and he's a hard man to "bump into." Sure, I could reach out to him, but soon after that night at the bar, I realized what a shit show my financials were in. There was no chance in hell he would want to work with me and my shoe box full of receipts and invoices. Numbers are not my forte, but I've done enough research to know I won't be dealt a hefty fine at the end of the tax year.

It was the responsible thing for me to get my bookkeeping in order first, before starting up any business arrangements. Especially with Our Place, where I presume I'll need to get approval from their faceless owner.

"Oh. Do you know what? It totally slipped my mind." I'm a terrible liar and from the quizzical brow Jo raises, she sees right through it. Most people say they can read me like a book, but right now I'm trying my best to keep my pages tightly shut.

"You forgot?"

"Mm-hmm." Spinning around, I give her my back and hope she doesn't see me gnawing away at my lip as I wipe down the milk steamer.

"Quinn. If I've overstepped, you'd tell me?" Her voice is cautious and my stomach drops.

"No! No!" I rush out, spinning around, and almost send the rag in my hand flying. "It's not that, I just...I think I need some accounting help first." Embarrassment floods my cheeks.

"Well, it's a good thing Gray is an accountant. Let me speak to him."

"Gray?"

"Yeah"—she shrugs and takes another sip of her drink—"that's what we all call him."

"Oh." I make a mental note of the nickname, but I think I prefer Graham. "You don't need to do that." If there's one thing I hate, it's favors. Maybe it's juvenile, but after years of being told how lazy and what a burden you are, you start to see handouts as the easy way out.

She studies me for a moment, sensing my discomfort, then gives me a gentle smile. "Well, when you're ready, talk to Graham. He'll have to speak to the owner, but I know he'd love to work with you. No pressure. He's not as big and scary as he looks."

Nodding my head slowly, I suck my bottom lip between my teeth, holding in my rebuttal. The last thing I want anyone to think is that I'm not serious. And despite only speaking to Graham on two occasions, he's someone I don't want to disappoint.

I'd hoped to make another friend in town, but when he didn't text or call, I put it down to the fact I came across as unprofessional or annoying. Without sounding narcissistic, I have an innate need for people to like me.

My mind wanders back to the evening at the bar seven

months ago. When I spotted a man in the corner, standing by himself, I asked Jo who the "tall, moody drink of water" was, and it just so happened to be Graham.

Short, neatly styled hair the color of sand right after the tide has gone out. Dark, thick eyebrows hidden behind his tortoise shell glasses, that do all sorts to my insides, frame vivid green eyes. Reminding me of the moss growing in the lush forests in the park. He's always wrapped up in a knitted sweater or cardigan that does nothing to hide the strong muscles that stretch the wool around his shoulders and arms.

Yes, I wanted to butter him up, however, something else drew me toward him. The slight crease between his brows as he studied the room deepened when the music got turned up, which made me giggle. He was tall, very tall. Mysteriously alluring. He didn't demand the attention of the room, but he had it—or mine, at least.

I remember feeling like I'd found a hidden treasure that night.

Fueled by a questionable shot of liquor I thought was a lemon drop, but most definitely wasn't, I skipped over, introduced myself, and dove right in. There was something fascinating about him. Most of the guys I've dated have been immature and stare at my breasts rather than listen to what I have to say. Graham was different. Maybe it's because he's a little older, but during our short interaction I knew he was listening intently and something about his quiet, considerate demeanor had me forgetting why I approached him.

People around town describe him as intimidating or stand-offish, but I disagree. I could chat to people until the cows come home, and it's obvious when my verbal diarrhea starts putting people to sleep, but Graham gave me his undivided attention the entire time.

When I walked away, I felt...*appreciated*.

Now I wonder if he only stayed quiet so I would stop

rambling. It stung when he didn't reach out, and I concluded that it was due to one of two things:

1.   He dislikes me.

2.   He doesn't like my baking.

I have no idea which one is worse. Neurotic? Maybe a smidge. I'm an Enneagram four, what do you expect?

"Quinn," Jo says with a smirk. "I hear the wheels turning from here. Don't overthink it."

"Lemme think about it." My shoulders relax, and I hope the faux cheer in my voice signals her to change the subject.

We chat for a few more minutes, making plans to meet up over the weekend, and then I'm alone again.

Huffing out a big breath that blows my bangs off my forehead, I connect my phone to the speakers and let the voice of Harry Styles drown out the noise in my head.

I lose myself, singing along, until the last chorus is interrupted by a text notification.

The number is one I should have blocked years ago and I stare at the hateful message until the bitter smell of burning fills the air.

Shit, the muffins.

CHAPTER THREE

graham

"Curly, you've been circling that tree for five minutes. Go pee already."

He stares up at me with a look that says *Don't rush me, motherfucker.*

The park is empty this time of day, exactly how I like it. I've always been an early riser, but since getting a dog, my days now start with a morning walk. The air is cool against my skin, and I close my eyes for a second, listening to the constant chirping of birds in the tall trees.

There's a hint of smoke lingering in the air from a wood-burning stove, and the scent of damp leaves is strong as we stand at the base of a large oak. I can't help but take a deep inhale of crisp, fall air. You'll always get a whiff of salt wherever you are in Sutton Bay, but there's something revitalizing about the smell of autumn.

Curly isn't the friendliest of dogs, and I suppose I'm not the warmest of people; a perfect pair. I'm not rude, I just value peace and quiet, and for a small town, Sutton Bay's eleven hundred residents sure like to make themselves known.

When my dog finally does his business, we leave the park

and head onto Robin Road, the main street leading through town, which ends right at the heart of the bay. When we turn the corner at the bottom of the hill, I'm greeted with one of my favorite views. Seeing the bay blanketed in a thick veil of fog is wistful and hypnotizing with the way it snakes around the docked boats suspended above the still water.

Fishing boats have left for this morning's catch, and there's about a month left of good lobster catching before the season is over. As the head chef of Our Place, Booth will be down there later today to collect fresh stock for the restaurant.

My pocket buzzes when we reach my shiny black Jeep, but I ignore it until Curly is securely fastened into his harness in the front seat. Once I'm behind the wheel, I pull out my phone and find an incoming call from Patrick.

"Hey," I greet as I turn on the engine and connect my phone to the Bluetooth.

"No surprise you're up this early. Good walk?"

"Hmm."

A long sigh greets my ears. "Gray, full sentences, please."

Scratching Curly on his snout, I wait for Patrick to continue. After a moment's silence, I glance at the console screen to check that the call hasn't dropped. "Are you still there?"

"Yes. I was waiting for you to speak."

"Have fun with that. I'm going now."

"Ugh, fine, Johanna made me call you. You know I don't like getting involved in other people's business." I hear some scuffling and muffled voices in the background. Figuring it's my niece, I ignore it.

"But?"

"*But.* She spoke to Quinn, you know, the owner of Just Brew It?"

Know her? I haven't stopped thinking about her for the last...196 days.

I've hardly thought about anything else but Quinn Jackson

since that night at Shirley's seven months ago. The tiny, curvy sunshine of a woman has infiltrated my brain, with just a smile and a gentle touch to my arm.

All I think about is that first meeting with her, and how royally I fucked it up. Barely able to get any words out, gawking over her like some fumbling idiot, and chickening out at the chance to ask her out. Even if it was under the guise of a business meeting, I missed my opportunity for even five minutes of her time.

Sure, I have her number safely stored in my phone, but I don't have the slightest idea where to begin with a woman like her. The only other time I've spoken to her was when Patrick ran into the bakery looking for Jo after it was announced the restaurant would be sold. Other than that, I've been too nervous to talk to her. I see her almost every day when I purposefully walk Curly along Robin Road, hoping to catch a glimpse of her through the bakery window. She's spotted me a few times, and each time her dazzling smile blinds me.

"Yeah, I remember who she is." *And everything about her.*

"So, Jo mentioned to her a few months back about us working together, but she seems a bit apprehensive. She said something about getting her bookkeeping in order first. It's a good idea, working with her, Jo just thinks she needs a push in the right direction."

"And what direction is that?"

"Well, not what, but who. Jo thinks..." There's more noise from his end, and I definitely catch a few words from a female who is not my five-year-old niece.

"If *Jo* has so much to say, why don't you put her on?" Exasperation bleeds from my tone as I brake at a stop sign.

"What? No. Jo, isn't he—oh. Yeah, she's here, let me hand you to—"

"Hey, Gray." The chipper voice of Patrick's girlfriend echoes down the line. "Fancy meeting you here." The British accent she uses is a dead giveaway she's nervous.

"One: we're on the phone and your boyfriend called me. Two: What is it that's got you speaking like the Queen of England?"

She lets out a big sigh, and it makes me antsy that she's nervous when the topic of conversation is Quinn. Is she not well? Did something happen? Is she dating someone?

"Please, don't tell her this. Patrick's already gone over the gist of it, but basically, I think she's a little scared of asking you about partnering up with the restaurant and for your help looking over her books."

"Me?" I feel hollow all of a sudden. As if someone has carved me out, leaving only my heart to beat pathetically in my chest.

"Don't take it like that. She didn't say *you* explicitly. The few times we've spoken about it, she was so excited to collaborate. After she made a comment about her books being a mess, I thought maybe you could help her."

"Me?"

"Jeez. Yes, you, Graham. We're talking about you and Quinn. Graham and Quinn..."

I block out the rest of Jo's sentence, too busy liking the sound of our names interwoven in one breath.

"Gray, did you hear what I said?"

"I didn't," I answer honestly as I pull up outside my apartment.

"Christ on a stick, I thought you were the clever brother."

"Hey!" Patrick protests in the background.

"Yes, yes. You're the caring daddy figure, don't worry," she reassures him. "Graham, listen. Do me a favor, please. Go into the bakery this week, order whatever—it's on me—but try to convince Quinn to come around to the idea of working with the restaurant. Don't let her know I'm asking for this favor. And don't make it obvious."

"How am I meant to speak to her about working with the restaurant, without talking about working with the restaurant?"

"You'll work it out. Will you do this for me? Please?"

Heck. I already know I'm doing it, but the earnest tone from Jo makes me want to do it sooner. "Of course I'll do it."

She sighs in relief.

Am I really that much of an asshole, she thought I'd say no?

"It means a lot. Quinn was my first real friend when I moved back to town, and she helped me out a lot. I want to be able to repay her."

"I get it. What's family for, hey?" I fake an upbeat tone.

We say goodbye, and I guess that settles it. My 196 days of avoiding Quinn Jackson are over. Curly stares up at me without a thought between his big, round eyes.

"Any advice, bud?"

He tilts his head at my question, and I know I've lost it, but his unwavering stare is all the answer I need. People think Quinn is intimidated by me. In reality, I've been petrified to figure out why my heart jackhammered in my chest the moment I laid eyes on her.

"Yeah, we're fucked."

THE COOL EVENING AIR SENDS A CHILL UP MY SPINE AS IT HITS MY sweat-soaked back. I pull my T-shirt away from my body while my heart rate comes down from my run. My watch tells me I've run six miles through the trail, beating my personal best.

When my apartment comes into view, I slow my steps until I'm standing outside the modern brick building, so out of place in Sutton Bay. It's not huge, only holding four apartments and has been my home since last February. There was a bit of uproar when plans were approved for it to be built, the local residents citing it would pull away from the natural and historic beauty of the town. I wholly agreed, until I found myself in need of a place to stay and desperate not to move in with my mom or brothers.

The lock on the main door snicks when I hold my key fob against the buzzer, and then make my way up the flight of stairs. The scampering sound of little claws starts on the other side of the door the moment I push the key into the lock. I'm greeted with licks and scratches to my sweaty legs before I pick up Curly and playfully scratch his belly. "You'll never stop acting like I've been gone for an eternity, will you?"

I place him on the floor, and he scurries away to his bed to hump something inanimate. *At least one of us is getting some.* Most people make rash decisions post-breakup; mine was adopting a wiener dog. He's a little prick who only likes me, my niece, and his stuffed toys. Having him around makes me feel a little less lonely though.

Making my way into the kitchen, I down a bottle of cold water from the fridge before sifting through the pile of mail I dumped on the counter this morning. It's all standard junk or bills until I spot a crisp white envelope with my name and address written in neat, cursive writing.

I know that handwriting. But it's the stamp on the back with the sender's name and address that confirms what I already knew.

I'd heard the news in January, and thanked my lucky stars I didn't have social media so I could avoid the video of their "utterly adorable proposal." The knife she left behind is still firmly lodged in my back, and it looks like she was saving the killing blow. When my phone buzzes, I know it's my mom. She probably got the same envelope from the woman she thought would be her daughter-in-law one day.

Morbid curiosity gets the better of me. With surprisingly steady fingers, I tear open the envelope and pull out a gaudy invitation. Booth managed to intercept the save the date a couple of months ago. I'm pretty sure he ate the card to hide any evidence, but there's no avoiding this one.

Jenna & Ralph, together with their parents, are pleased to invite you to celebrate their marriage.

I rip the invitation in half, then again for good measure, before throwing it in the trash.

It's comforting to know my ex-girlfriend of twelve years still remembers me enough to invite me to her wedding, but forgot I existed when I caught her and *my cousin* fucking in our bed. Fuck, that wasn't even the worst part, which only proved our relationship had been over well before that.

Her parting words were the last nail in the coffin.

"You seriously can't sit there and tell me you didn't see this coming, Graham?" Jenna's shrill voice echoes through the apartment while I sit motionless on the edge of the sofa.

I should feel something as I watch my girlfriend of over a decade pack her things up. Most people would be furious that they just found their partner in bed with someone else. It should gut me. To see the woman, I've spent almost half my life with, in bed with another man.

Yet I feel nothing.

"You don't even have anything to say now," she whines. "This is the problem. You don't talk. And when you do, it's always the wrong thing. I'm over it. This"—she throws her hands out at me in aggravation—"you. It's not what I want. It hasn't been for years."

"Maybe you could have told me this before you started sleeping with my cousin."

She pauses her packing and looks visibly shocked that I've spoken. "Well, at least he doesn't mope around, writing in some diary like a teenage girl. I'm tired of staying in every night. Of you working all hours of the day or hanging out with your family. I'm not wasting any more of my time on someone like you."

Embarrassment heats my skin like it always does when she throws the fact I keep a journal in my face. She knows why I prefer to write everything down, and her dismissal over it is like tiny daggers being shoved into my sternum.

My hands hang between my open legs as she continues to throw her belongings into a bag in a hurry. She probably doesn't want to keep Ralph waiting, who is outside hiding in his truck.

Perhaps I'm broken. The only things going through my brain are how I'm going to explain this to my mom and what a pain it's going to be to find a new place to live. If I allow myself to think about it for much longer, maybe I can find some sense of regret or an apology for wasting so much of her time.

With her coat on and bag slung over her shoulder, she reaches for the door handle but pauses. Her bright blue eyes I once found so piercing only hold resentment for me now.

Her farewell words should hurt, yet they do nothing but leave me feeling numb as they settle among the hollowness and doubt that's been brewing for longer than I'd like to admit.

Hours after she leaves, I finally feel something.

It feels a lot like relief.

That sense of relief didn't disappear, but the words she left me with before she walked out of the door have stuck to me like thick tar. They still sit heavy on my chest, and to this day, I don't disagree with her.

She moved to Augusta after that. We haven't seen each other since the night she walked out, but that might change soon. It makes sense the wedding is being held in Sutton Bay; she grew up here.

What surprises me is that it's the weekend after Thanksgiving.

Less than two months away.

One thing I learned about falling in love with someone from your hometown is that, despite growing up together, it's very easy to grow apart.

My phone vibrates with another incoming call, the sound of it intensifying the headache pulsing in my temples. Only my brothers know the truth about what went down between Jenna and me. Mom had just lost her own mother, which brought up a load of memories about my dad's passing. It wasn't the right time. And almost two years later, it still isn't.

When is it ever the right time to tell your mother that your girlfriend cheated on you with your cousin?

She's not oblivious to the situation and has questioned me plenty about my feelings toward their relationship. It was easier to keep my response simple.

We'd been having issues for a long time. Ralph and Jenna had been friends since high school. I'm happy for them. That's been my go-to response since we broke up.

Texts ping through the device now, one after the other, likely from my brothers. Not many people would be contemplating going to their ex's wedding after it ended so catastrophically, but I'm a big enough person to know we have to keep the peace, if anything, for my mom's sake.

If I were a different man, I wouldn't be pulling the torn-up invitation out of the trash and taping it together. I'd be honest with my mom about why attending the wedding is the last thing I want to do.

I'm not that man, though, or the man Jenna wanted.

These days, I don't know what kind of man I am.

quinn

"Ow, FUCK A DUCK!"

Jumping up and down, I clutch my foot in both hands, cursing at random birds with each hop.

When the throbbing in my big toe fades, I point a finger at the shitty generator in front of me. "I really need you to not break right now. I'm PMS-ing and would like to boil water for my water bottle. Please." I give it another kick with my other foot and then the sound of some gear, battery, or whatever a generator is made of, coming back to life blesses my ears. "Oh my god! Thank you, thank you. You really are the little engine that could."

I walk down the length of my van and skip up the steps, scrambling toward my kettle and flipping the switch. This time it doesn't trip the small generator that powers my tiny orange home, and I can finally soothe the cramps that have been pulling at my lower belly all day.

This tin can has been my home for the last six years and has carried me across twelve different states. After I left San Diego, the money I had only got me a bus as far as Salem, Oregon, so that's where I set up camp for three years. I scraped and saved every penny I made, taking odd jobs in restaurants and cafés. To celebrate my twenty-first birthday—a gift from me to me—I bought Nelly, my VW van. She's been my confidant across every state border, and though she's a little rough around the edges, for the first time in my life, I had something to call my own.

The dark orange van is about thirty years old. She really struggled to make the trip from Colorado to Maine, but she's my home. The guy I bought her off just wanted rid of it, and sold it to me for a steal, leaving me with some spare money to renovate it a little. Over the years, I've refurbished the small dining table and bench and bought myself a new gas-top stove. It's not big enough for a bathroom, which is why I'm grateful Mr. Willis allows me to park on his land and gives me full, undisturbed access to the little guesthouse at the side of his farmhouse.

Sadly, the tiny kitchenette isn't great for baking, but I was fortunate enough to work with some generous people over the years who allowed me after-hours access to state-of-the-art kitchens and appliances. I'd sell whatever baked goods I made at local farmers' markets or made bespoke cakes for friends of friends, though for a long time, it remained a hobby until I saved up the money to start my own business. It was hard work, and it wasn't uncommon for me to put in over sixty hours a week. But it got me where I am today.

I can't help but shimmy my shoulders whenever I remind myself of that. *I did it.* No handouts, no loans, no shortcuts.

As I carefully pour the steaming liquid into my fuzzy water bottle, my triumphant mood fizzles out. I may own my van, but the bakery isn't 100 percent mine. Realizing my finances aren't as organized as I'd hoped felt like owning it officially was a pipedream. Whenever I think about asking for help, those intrusive and spiteful voices whisper words of disappointment and resentment down my ear.

I have to do this on my own.

Quinn Jackson, get your lazy, fat ass in that kitchen and start our supper.

It's funny how words left more of a sting than the slap across my face that usually followed that demand.

I will not allow myself to be dragged down misery lane!

Settling on the small bed tucked at the rear of the van, I swaddle myself in blankets, and groan when the heat soothes my cramps. The lumpy mattress needs replacing, but money isn't a blessing right now.

Fucking ovaries.

It's been a few days since Jo came into the bakery and I chickened out. She sensed my hesitation from miles away, and I hated that I made her think she was overstepping. It should have been simple for me to explain that now isn't the right time for us to work together. Instead, I allowed old insecurities to take the wheel.

If and when I get my books in order, then I can think about collaborating with the restaurant. After that, I pray I can convince a bank to lend me the money to buy the bakery. Mr. Willis, the elderly gentleman I rent the space from, has mentioned on a number of occasions he wants to move away from commercial properties, and when that time comes, I want to be the person he sells to.

If only I knew an accountant.

Maybe Graham has forgotten about my tipsy introduction.

"Stop being ridiculous," I scold myself when I switch on my laptop and pull up accounting articles, hoping they can educate me. "The guy probably doesn't even remember my name, let alone who I am."

"There you go, Mr. Willis. One blueberry scone and cappuccino." I place the coffee and plate in front of my stoic landlord, who sits at a table by the window, where the late afternoon sun pours into the bakery like a blanket of sunshine.

"Thanks, Quinn. Looks good. Please call me Martin, though."

He's a nice man, hard to read, and has been nothing but helpful since I started renting from him earlier in the year. At first I thought he was one of those nosy landlords, but I've come to learn he has a huge sweet tooth and enjoys the company, quickly becoming one of my regulars and one of the reasons I keep the blueberry scones well stocked. He's always alone, and from what I gather, he's a little bit of a recluse.

"Sure thing, Mr. Willis." I earn myself an eye roll as I walk to the table opposite him to clear it after the last customer. I'm giving it a final wipe over when a shadow appears from through the window, passing over me from the outside. Looking up, I find the man who's been occupying my mind a lot the last few days.

Graham.

Every day he walks past the bakery around this time with his dog, but whenever I wave, he's gone in a flash. If he were a cartoon character, a trail of smoke would follow his swift departure.

Straightening my back, I raise my hand, wiggling my fingers with a big smile, ready for him to dart out of sight. His posture goes rigid, but rather than tug on the leash and walk away, he surprises me by picking up the dog, tucking the cute little thing under his arm, and heading toward the front door.

The second the bell chimes, the pup goes berserk, yapping at every customer.

"Curly, not now. *Please*, not now." Graham looks at me sheepishly and mouths, *Sorry*. I'd normally smile, but I'm shocked to see him, almost like I manifested him with my thoughts.

"Did you want a table?" I ask, just as one of the plates starts to slip through my fingers.

"Let me help." Eyes downcast, he easily takes hold of two plates in his large hands while balancing the pup.

"Thank you." Brushing my free hand on my apron, I nod toward the dog. "What's your wiener called?"

Our eyes widen at the same time, because I absolutely hear how that sounds.

"What's your sausage called? Oh my god, that's worse. Your *dog*." I quickly turn away to set the dishes down next to the sink, and Graham hands over his stack too.

I'm too busy trying not to die from embarrassment when Graham murmurs, "Curly. He...he usually hates people."

"Curly? Well that's adorable." I reach over to tickle the dog's pink belly. He's got a shiny chocolate coat, with a tanned snout and paws. "You don't hate humans, you love belly rubs, don't you? He's not curly though, what made you pick that name?"

"It's dumb." He scratches the scruff along his jaw, which does a terrible job of hiding his crimson cheeks, and a curious part of me wants to reach out and see how warm his skin is. "It's ironic. He's not Curly. See? Dumb."

"It's definitely not." I chuckle. Standing this close, I smell his spicy aftershave. Was he always this tall? He must have at least a foot on me. "You boys having a nice walk?"

"Yeah, it's a good one. Are you, um, having a good day?" he asks as he puts the wriggling, whining dog down on the floor.

"A super day. It would be even better if you came in for a

coffee and maybe a pup cup for the furball. I've been waiting for you to show your face here."

His dark brows shoot to his hairline. "Me?"

"Yep." I'm already pulling out a chair for him and heading back toward the cash register. "C'mon, I'm not taking no for an answer."

The scuffing of boots and the clicking of claws on the tiled floor sounds behind me. I'm not going to question what has him coming in after months of me waving at him through the window. There's something about his mysterious disposition that has me wanting to peel him back, layer by layer. Like a handsome onion.

After a deep breath, Graham settles into the chair, with Curly sitting patiently at his feet. He looks out of place, sitting there awkwardly, pulling at the sleeves of his cable-knit sweater, but he also doesn't.

He really is unfairly handsome, and I'm certain he doesn't even know it.

Who knew glasses and wool were so sexy?

As if I said that out loud, Graham's gaze catches mine before it darts away, and he nervously fiddles with the laminated menu on the table. He offers a curt nod to Mr. Willis who is watching the whole interaction closely.

"What's your poison? You look like an Americano kinda guy."

"I actually don't drink caffeine, sorry..." He looks at the ground like he just broke the most devastating news in the world.

"You don't need to apologize for that. I cater to everyone's needs." I throw my hands up, gesturing toward the small space before moving behind the counter. "I've got decaf, herbal tea, fruit smoothies, soda, and water. Dealer's choice."

He peers over the rims of his glasses and scans the small chalkboard to my left. "Sparkling water would be good. And a, what did you call it, pup cup? One of those for Curly, please."

"Do you want a blueberry scone? Mr. Willis here loves them." I nod to the older gentleman, who holds up his half-eaten scone in confirmation.

"Umm, no, I'm good. Thanks, though. I wa—"

"A lemon bar? Or pastry?" Jeez, I don't know why I'm being so pushy, but I have this sudden urge for Graham to eat something of mine. *Something that I baked!*

"I don't really like..." He looks around the room before leaning in close. "I don't like sweet things."

I blanch dramatically, hand clutching at my metaphorical pearls. "Graham! Get out of this establishment immediately!"

His shocked expression quickly morphs into amusement when he catches on to my sarcasm, eliciting the teeniest chuckle, but no smile.

Throwing him a wink, I turn toward the small fridge and start on his order. "Make yourself comfortable," I call over my shoulder. "I'll bring Curly some water too."

A couple of minutes later, Curly is lapping from the bowl I set down in front of him and I slide the paper cup of whipped cream and bottle of sparkling water across the table to Graham, who nods his thanks.

With the small lavender latte I made for myself, I sit in the chair opposite him. He studies me for a beat, with a look I can't decipher, before his gaze drops again.

"You're sitting with me?" His voice is tight as his hands flex on top of the table.

"I hope that's okay. I've been on my feet all day and it's that time of the month. TMI, but I think it's important for men to understand female challenges. I'm cramping big time."

His frown makes it look like he's personally annoyed at my womb. "I could head to the drug store and get you some aspirin if you want? Or a heating pad?"

A laugh of disbelief bursts from me and a warm, fuzzy sensation blooms in my chest. "I'm fine, honestly. Thank you, though."

Maybe he doesn't dislike me after all, and I read him wrong. He takes a slow sip of his water as he takes in his surroundings. The bakery's decor is such a contrast to his beige sweater and dark brown corduroy pants. None of the furniture in the bakery matches, each item having been thrifted and given a face-lift. I bet he despises the pink wallpaper with rows of lemons and raspberries, and I'd put money down that he thinks the handmade pom-poms hanging from the ceiling are childish. But I like it. If people didn't know who owned the bakery, my flamboyant style would confirm it.

Now would be the perfect opportunity to talk to him, only unease swirls in my stomach over how he'll respond. My fingertips trace along the grain of the table until they go numb. I'm a new business, with not even a year under my belt, and no business plan or strategy. No credit to my name. I'm a laughingstock to the banks. This is a terri—

"Hey, Quinn?" Graham's deep voice interrupts my spiraling thoughts. He bends his head so there's no avoiding his piercing green eyes.

Looking up at him, I chew on my bottom lip. "Mm-hmm."

"You make really good sparkling water." His face is so serious when he talks, and my head whips up and down between the glass of bottled water and him.

"Graham, it's water, you don't hav—"

"Best I've ever had."

A loud, obnoxious laugh escapes my lips, and before I can slap a hand over my mouth, a snort rips free. I don't know how he did it, picking up on my nervousness and making me feel a little more at ease with his joke, but it worked. "You're teasing me, but I'll let it slide."

He sits back, shoulders more relaxed now. "I've been meaning to speak to you."

"You have?"

He nods. "That night at the bar. You mentioned about working with the restaurant. Is that still something you want to do?"

Oh no. He didn't forget about that shameful interaction.

"No, that doesn't sound like me. You must have had one of those weird shots Lenny was serving that night. Went straight to your head."

"I don't drink."

"Well, shoot." I laugh nervously and then sigh. "It doesn't matter, honestly. It was stupid of me to even bring it up."

He doesn't speak for a minute, his face blank as he picks at the label on his bottle. There's something calming about his presence and because of that, I can't lie to him.

My shoulders drop and I bite the bullet. "I did—*do* want to work with the restaurant, but my bookkeeping is a shit show. With the new owner and everything else going on, I don't want to waste anyone's time. Maybe next year." I shrug, pretending that confession hasn't chipped away at my already low hopes.

"I could look over your books. It is my job."

After Jo and I talked the other day, I looked up the firm Graham works for. He has a stellar portfolio, with shining recommendations from a plethora of clients. I rang them, hoping for an estimate, and ended the call almost in tears over the cost of hiring an accountant of his caliber.

The bakery does well enough, but any penny I make is either invested or saved for a potential down payment on a mortgage.

This conversation is going downhill fast. "I appreciate that, but I wouldn't be able to afford it."

"Oh, I wouldn't expect you to pay me," he offers, sitting up straighter.

That twinge of discomfort pulls deep in my chest. Accepting help isn't a bad thing, yet the sound of *her* raspy voice in my head tells me otherwise. "I can't let you do that."

His passive expression slips into something like surprise, but his furrowed brows are gone before I can blink. He pulls his wallet out and passes me a business card. *Fancy.* "Why don't you sleep on it? I think teaming up would be a great idea. I can help with the finances and when you're ready, we can talk about you working with the restaurant."

The rectangular card is balanced on my fingertips, and I spot his contact details on there. "You could call me, you have my number, right?" I'm not sure why the idea of him finally using my number excites me.

He opens his mouth and then clamps it shut, his eyes bouncing around in front of him as he looks for his response. "No. I, um, my sweater rubbed some of the numbers off after you left. If you text the one on the card, I'll save it in my phone."

"Oh. Okay, yeah, of course." It stings more knowing he didn't even save it in his phone. My chair scrapes across the floor as I stand abruptly. This embarrassing conversation needs to end. Graham rises with me and looks as uncomfortable as I feel, but I'm the only one to blame for this discomfort.

I'm a people pleaser down to my core and I desperately want everyone to like me. It's clear that Graham doesn't. He's only being polite.

"Thanks for the offer," I rush out just as Mrs. Stewart, one of the town's council members, walks in with her son. She's quite literally the worst customer to come in and will be complaining about something in approximately five minutes, but her arrival is my escape. I make a dash for her table, avoiding eye contact with Graham.

As he turns to leave, shoulders low, head down, I finally take a breath.

I curse the people in my past life who have left me incapable of accepting help and filling me with this obsessive need to prove my worth. He was nothing but nice and any chance I had of convincing him I'm not an impulsive, immature woman starting their own business on a whim has been blown out of the water.

As the door shuts behind him and he walks down the street, it feels like my dream of owning this place is a million steps away.

CHAPTER FIVE
graham

Broken hearts still yearn
They need love more than ever
To heal those old scars

I'M NOT SURE WHAT I FIND MORE IMPRESSIVE: BOOTH PICKING someone up while in a pair of extremely tight cycling shorts, or the fact the woman didn't even notice he's without a bike.

After exchanging numbers with her, he turns and saunters back over to where I'm sitting on the bench along the dock. I keep my eyes trained on his face. Seeing my little brother's junk highlighted in black spandex was not on today's bingo card.

"When was the last time you even rode your bike?" I ask as he sits down next to me and stretches his legs out to rest on the railing between the dock and the water.

"Springtime." He folds his hands behind his head and shuts his eyes, enjoying the early evening sun.

The trees across the bay have started to shift from deep greens to yellows and ambers, their bright colors reflecting in the calm waters. I usually rely on this very spot to settle myself after an overwhelming day at the office or when I need to feel close to my dad. This is where we'd meet up for lunch some afternoons, silently taking in the scenery around us or catching up.

This time it's done little to ease the guilt I've felt since leaving Quinn's bakery yesterday.

"Why are you wearing those god-awful shorts?"

Without opening his eyes, he gestures toward his crotch, and I scoff at his ridiculous yet oddly effective tactic at picking people up. Curly, who is lying at my feet, growls at him before going back to sleep.

"For a little wiener, he's a massive prick." He scowls at my dog and then waves the stranger's number in my face. "Don't hate on the shorts, either, they work."

I stare at the slip of paper in his hand.

Those ten digits send shame coursing through me, reminding me how I lied, and clearly embarrassed Quinn, when I told her I lost her number. As if I hadn't been drafting texts to her for months. It was one of the few times I spoke before thinking, not wanting to come across as overeager.

And instead, I upset her.

She couldn't get away from me quick enough and I knew I'd fucked up. Despite Jo's pleas about warming Quinn up to the idea of the two businesses working together, I sensed something more going on with her.

I catch Booth eyeing me curiously.

"What?" I ask, even though I know exactly what he's about to say.

"Has Mom spoken to you?"

With a huff, I turn to face the water and follow the small swells coming from a fishing boat as its bow bobs toward the mouth of the bay. I brace my elbows on my knees and myself for this conversation.

"I've told her I'm going to the wedding. She'd ask questions I don't want to answer if I didn't."

When he doesn't respond, I find him looking at his hands furiously. His teeth grind together before he spits his next words out. "This is ridiculous. I don't like speaking badly about women, but she's a piece of work. After everything she did, she has the audacity to invite you to their wedding."

"Let's remove her from the equation. He's our cousin." My fingers flex, hoping to ease the tension building in my muscles.

"No cousin of mine," he scoffs. "I'm going to invite that girl I met last summer. You know, the one who threw up after drinking one too many glasses of red wine? Maybe I can aim her toward Jenna during the speeches."

My head spins and my stomach churns. *A date.* Fuck, it will be mortifying turning up alone. There isn't a single ounce of me that wants Jenna back, but I can already picture the conceited look on her face when she receives my RSVP with just my name on it.

He must sense the shift in my mood. "We're not going. I'll find something better for Mom to do on that day."

"We have to go. Nancy is Dad's only sibling, it would break Mom's heart if we didn't go. No matter how much of a prick Ralph is." Aunt Nancy is the sweetest woman. I have a lot of memories in her house as a kid, and with Ralph, until he turned into an insufferable asshat.

Booth's strong hand pulls at my shoulder, forcing me to face him fully. "Be serious, Gray. You think I'd go? Patrick called me the minute he opened his invitation. Even our calm big bro was blowing steam down the phone. You're not really thinking of going, are you?"

I throw a hand through my hair. "Mom thinks we ended things amicably. She's still under the impression Jenna and I broke up months before we actually did and that her and

Ralph's relationship started long after that. You know what Mom's like, she'll refuse to go to the wedding if she knows the truth, and I don't want her cutting herself off from the only family left on Dad's side."

Booth's knowing look tells me he shares the same concern.

Mom never exactly warmed to Jenna, but she was always civil and kind to her. I explained that we broke up two months before the night Jenna walked out, which softened the blow when she found out Jenna had moved on with her nephew. She pried a little, but I shrugged off her questions and reassured her it was for the best.

Looking back, my mom would have been nothing but supportive. I just took the coward's way out and it's too late now to reveal what actually happened.

I blow out a breath and reveal my actual concern. "I'm over the affair, you know this. But...if I don't show, Jenna will think she won. I'm not sure what's worse, though, not going or going alone."

"She gave you a plus one, right?"

"Yes. But I have no one to take."

"So, get a girlfriend." He acts as if it's that simple. I mean, for him it probably is.

I fix him with a pointed stare. "Yeah, and who would that be, smart-ass?" Or better yet, who would even want to date me? I know who I'd like to take as my date...*No.* I shake that delusion away.

"That!" He shoves a finger in my face. "What was that look? Your eyes went all soft, like you actually have emotions."

"Fuck off," I grumble and slap his hand away, angry at myself for that momentary slip.

He jumps off the bench, and Curly barks at him as he raises his arms in the air in frustration. "Seriously? We tell each other everything."

"No. You"—I point at him—"tell me about all your sexcapades without my consent, and I try to block them out."

"You could share things with me. If you ever went out and spoke to women, I'd listen. Our mother, Johanna, and Lottie do not count."

With a swallow, I cast my eyes down and scratch Curly's smooth head. "I speak to women. Or woman."

At this rate, I'm just inviting Booth to meddle in my life. As much as it makes me itch seeing his eyes light up like a Christmas tree at my admission, I'd give anything to be half as confident as he is.

"Tell me, tell me," he pleads like a teenage girl talking about her school crush.

"Quinn." He nods slowly, the corners of his mouth turned up slightly as he waits for the rest of the story. "Jo asked me to speak to her about working with the restaurant." I downplay it, as if I haven't been imagining talking to her for months now. "We spoke yesterday, she's nice."

Understatement of the century, but this is all Booth is getting or he'll get too excited. Like when my dog gets the zoomies.

"Quinn's a great girl. Good choice. How did it go?" he asks.

The grimace on my face is all telling.

The bench creaks as he sits down again and bumps his shoulder with mine. "Oh god. What happened?"

Groaning, I scratch the back of my neck in discomfort. "I think I offended her. We met back in March, she gave me her number and...I kinda implied I'd lost it...but I haven't. It doesn't matter." I wave it off. "She doesn't want to work with me anyway. She needed some accounting advice but shot me down, so there's no reason for me to speak to her now." I scrub a hand down my face with a loud sigh, and Curly whines in unison.

"You're an idiot. It's offensive we share the same bone structure, and you don't even put it to good use. This is fixable, all we —" He gasps and squeezes my shoulder in a death grip. "Oh. I am a genius. Brains and beauty. Remember this day."

"I don't want to ask." Yet, I'm intrigued as I peel his hand off my shoulder and push him away.

"You like her, don't deny it. You need a date for the wedding but are inherently introverted. Ask her to be your date as a favor; you could do her bookkeeping or whatever it is in return." His hands are upturned waiting for my response.

"You've lost me."

"Fake date her. Go on a couple of dates around town so Jenna doesn't catch on it's fake. We both know she has her old high school cronies sniffing around. Do it all under the pretense that you need a date for the wedding, and in return, you'll look over her numbers, and then who knows, maybe her bedroom ceiling."

"That is ridiculous. But also..." My head falls in my hands, and I push my glasses back off my face. "Kinda smart. Jesus, I can't believe I'm considering it. I must be desperate."

"I think the fact you're considering it means you think she's more than nice." He smirks. It's not smug, though, more like he's happy for me. "There's no pressure, but maybe pushing yourself out of your comfort zone will do you some good." I turn to look at him. "Jenna does not get to dictate how you see yourself any longer. You're a good guy. And maybe as you get to know Quinn, she'll see that too."

"She has to say yes first. She'll probably agree out of pity. God, she's going to think I'm pathetic. *Fuck,* why am I even entertaining this?" My head falls back, and I stare up at the white fluffy clouds floating by.

"Just try it out. If you're not comfortable, it's not like you're actually dating, though, I think you're going to woo the pants off her." He pulls out his phone and taps away at the screen.

"Who are you texting?" I peer over his shoulder.

"Our dear little sister. I'm pretty sure she reads those kinky books about cowboys and fake dating. We need to do our research."

"My life is not a romance novel."

"No, because you need to experience romance for that to be possible. You two would look good together. If anything, you might gain some confidence again and if you show up to the wedding with Quinn on your arm, Jenna will realize what she lost."

"It's not about making her jealous or wanting her back," I protest loudly, gaining the attention of a couple passing by. "I'd rather a lobster take off my thumbs than be associated with her again."

"Christ, I know that. If you ever thought about getting back with her, I'd push you off one of the bluffs. It would show her that she no longer holds any power over you. I want to see you happy, Graham."

The longer I sit here, the salty air blowing away the veil I've been wearing since Jenna walked out of the door, the more I want to prove to her that I'm done living under her rule.

She probably thinks she still knows me well enough and expects me to decline the invitation with my tail between my legs. But the thing is, she doesn't know me anymore. When I look back, I don't think she ever did. Bringing a woman like Quinn—someone so unlike Jenna—with me will be the last thing she expects.

Maybe if I prove her wrong, I can finally stop overthinking everything I say and do. Stop seeing myself as lonely, pitiful Graham. Boring Graham. Unlovable Graham. *Gray.*

Is asking the girl I've been infatuated with for months to be my fake date the best idea? No. But she's the only woman I've managed to string whole sentences together with when we talk. She smiles at me freely and doesn't get annoyed when I stumble over my words or fall silent.

Pivoting toward my brother, I sit up straight and take a deep breath. "Call Florence. We need the names of those fake dating books."

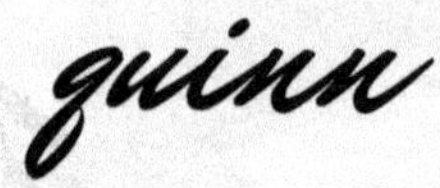

CHAPTER SIX

SHE FOUND ME.

It's taking her longer than usual, perhaps the years are slowing her down. She's never dared show her face in any of the towns I've settled in, but she has other ways of screwing with my life, no matter the miles between us.

Finding out where I work and spreading lies to my boss that resulted in me being fired, is a personal favorite of hers. I tried not to let it break me down, and if my boss believed her over me, I'd move to a new town. Easy. My end goal was never to work at a bakery; it was to own one.

She would never expect me to own *anything*, which is why she's resorting to other methods of ruining my life. It makes me seethe, but never enough to do something about it. I don't want a relationship with her, yet cutting her off and blocking her number is something I've never been brave enough to do.

Not only is Mr. Willis a great landlord and regular customer, but he lets me live on the far side of his land and charges me a fair rate for water and electricity. He called last night and calmly told me some woman sent him an email, informing him that I was an ex-tenant of hers and owed rent and property damage fees.

He saw right through her bullshit.

She doesn't know I haven't rented an apartment in years, not since I got the van, but Mr. Willis does. He blocked her email and didn't once question me.

Perhaps she'll finally leave me alone. It was no secret she despised me, yet the moment I was no longer under her roof, her interest in me increased tenfold.

My sneakers slap against the sidewalk with each angry step I take up Robin Road. I welcome the burn in my calves, but wish I'd worn some shorts under this dress, because the thigh rub is real on this oddly warm October morning. I'm so determined to get inside, I don't notice the wall until I go slamming into it.

A wall of man.

My head whips up when a strong hand holds me steady at the small of my back. Our fronts are squished together as something crinkles between us.

Graham Sadler really has a sexy librarian thing going on and I feel every hard plane of his body underneath his navy wool suit.

We stare at one another breathlessly, our chests rising and falling in tandem. Neither of us has spoken since I collided with him—or moved. I don't want to do the last one, but I'll happily break the silence.

"Graham. What are you doing here?"

He audibly swallows and I watch his Adam's apple bob with the movement. "I was waiting for you. I'm headed into the city and wanted to apologize before I left."

I'm so distracted by the deep timbre of his voice, like I've been dipped into a barrel of smooth whiskey, that it takes me a second to realize what he said.

"Apologize? For what?" I stare up at him in confusion.

The only reasonable explanation for me wanting to protest the loss of his touch is that my hormones are running haywire this week.

His hand slips from my waist as he steps back, and that's when I see the crumpled bouquet of flowers between us. "I think...I upset you the other day. I'm sorry. Sometimes, I say the wrong thing. I didn't mean to make it awkward."

I thought I had a really good poker face, but he saw right through the act. My heart aches that he thinks he did anything wrong. It was all me, getting irrationally upset over a phone number and my inability to accept help. "Graham, you didn't upset me. *I'm* sorry if I gave you that impression. It's totally a me issue, not you. No apology needed."

"Are you sure?"

"Positive." I hope the big grin I'm flashing is enough to convince him.

His eyes drop to the flowers in his hand and then he looks at me hopefully. "Can I still give you these? I'd really like you to have them."

"Those are for me?" I ask, mouth agape, heart in the soles of my Chucks.

"Yeah, um"—he runs a hand along the back of his neck— "the bright colors remind me of you."

"They're beautiful. Yellow is my favorite color," I whisper as my fingers trace along the soft petals. Yellow daisies, eucalyptus, and gypsophila. "No one has ever given me flowers before."

"Ever?" I ignore his dumbfounded expression and nod my head. "Well, that's unacceptable."

What in the world is going on? A laugh slips free, but when I look up again, it gets lost in my throat, because holy shit, Graham is smiling. It's faint, the corner of his lips turning upward a fraction, but it's all in his eyes. They shine so bright, like early morning sunshine on dewy grass.

Apparently my brain has melted, because it doesn't do

anything to filter my next words. "You're very handsome when you smile. I like it." I slap a hand over my mouth and my eyes bug out of my head.

Then it happens. He laughs. *A laugh.* It's a little shaky, but the deepness of it sends a shiver through my bones.

Graham isn't grumpy. I get why people would put him in that category, but he's just quiet and I suspect it takes him a little longer than most to open up. He probably doesn't laugh or smile freely the way I give mine out like candy. It's oddly endearing, and I suddenly want to do anything I can to see it again.

There's a moment of silence before he quietly says, "I like it when you smile too." Now it's his eyes that go wide. "We should get these in water," he mumbles and nods toward the front door of the bakery.

As I turn away from his hard, warm body, another girlish laugh bubbles in my throat. A smiling, chuckling Graham giving out flowers will do that to any female.

We shuffle into the bakery after I unlock the door, and I fumble around, switching on the coffee machine and the display fridge lights next to the counter. Graham standing awkwardly in the middle of my bakery is becoming a regular occurrence. How can I help him feel more comfortable?

I grab a ceramic pitcher I found at the thrift store and fill it with water before walking over to Graham, who is typing something out in a rush on his phone, before he pockets it. I hold my hand out for the flowers, but he doesn't budge.

"Are you taking back the flowers?" I ask.

"No. Do you know what you're doing?"

Pointing at the bouquet and then to the makeshift vase of water, I say, "Stems in water. Job done."

I swear to god, he rolls his eyes, before gingerly taking the pitcher from my hands and making his way to the small stain-less-steel table at the back of the kitchen. Once he has the bouquet unwrapped he glances down at me. "Do you have scissors?"

"I do…" I walk to the wall of utensils behind him and pluck down what he needs and place them in his open hand. Peeking around his shoulder, I watch as his long fingers peel away some of the leaves from the stems. "Why are you doing that?"

"You don't want the leaves to sit in the water, or they'll decompose and cause the flowers to die quicker."

"Huh. I really was about to ruin them. Now what are you doing?" I ask as he trims the bottom of the stems at an angle.

"If you cut them like this, it allows for better water intake."

"How do you know what to do?"

He pauses his nimble movements, and bends his head, his voice soft. "My dad used to do it for my mom and sister. After he passed, I didn't want them to go without having fresh flowers or have to do it themselves. It's stupid. My ex thought it was weird to get them flowers."

My hand darts to his arm and his eyes fall to where I'm creasing his well-pressed suit jacket. "Don't say that. It's not stupid. That's the sweetest thing I've ever heard. They're lucky to have you." I give his arm a final squeeze, before dropping my hand next to his on the table.

Note to self: find out who his ex is, and make sure she never finds the cold side of the pillow ever again.

It's the first time he's mentioned an ex, but it's not the first time he's shot himself down. I tilt my head to study him. He peers down at me, and even when the tip of his pinky brushes against mine, we don't break eye contact. This hushed moment with Graham is comforting and dangerous. His company feels warm, genuine, and calming, but it also stirs something unfamiliar.

"Thanks, Quinn." There's that hint of a smile again.

I'd happily stand here with Graham all morning, but I know he has somewhere to be, and I have to get set up for the day. The ten minutes I've spent with him have changed my mood drastically. With little effort, he scared away my fury and replaced it with a belly full of butterflies.

"You didn't need to apologize, but these flowers have really brightened my day. I'm sure you need to get on the road, and I've got a batch of blondies calling my name. Did you need anything else, or can I get you something? I have some fresh croissants—not sweet at all." The wink I give causes his lips to twitch.

He turns back to the flowers, blatantly ignoring my question, and from the thoughtful look on his face, I think he's searching for the right words to respond with. He shuffles the stems around before tucking his hands into the pockets of his slacks, shoulders hunching up with the movement. The telltale sign that he's uncomfortable stains the tips of his ears as his mouth opens and closes. "This might sound—I, um, don't know how to...it's fine."

"You can ask me anything," I encourage.

"No. Honestly. Forget I was here."

Unlikely, but I don't press him. "Okay then. Let me get you a take-out ba—"

"Will you be my girlfriend!?" he all but shouts, his face a similar shade to the jar of jam beside him.

Oh.

"So...is that a no to the croissant?

CHAPTER SEVEN

I've always loved numbers. Go figure, I'd become an accountant.

As a kid, probabilities fascinated me.

My chance of being attacked by a bear is 1:1.2 million.

A 1:15,300 chance that I'll be struck by lightning.

I'm wishing the odds of either of these happening were much higher right now so I wouldn't have to stand here after I shouted at Quinn. The humility of the whole encounter makes my skin crawl and I wonder if I walked out of here, moved towns—no, countries—and changed my identity, would I ever stop feeling this embarrassed?

I think I've broken her. That's bound to happen when a man you hardly know randomly asks you to be his girlfriend.

There was a script to follow; Booth helped me plan it. Tell her about my predicament with the wedding, ask her to go on a few platonic dates, and offer to balance her books free of charge and put in a good word with the new owner. Easy.

False. Because I'm hard-wired to say the wrong thing.

"Quinn?" I take a cautious step toward her.

She blinks a few times, eyes focused on the middle of my chest, before doubling over and releasing an almighty belly laugh. Tears stream down her face. When she finally straightens with a deep inhale to catch her breath, I fight the urge to hightail it out of here. Clearly the idea of going out with me is hilarious.

"I'm sorry." She wipes underneath her eyes. "I do this thing where I zone out sometimes and don't catch what a person says. I could have sworn you asked me to be your girlfriend."

Clearing my throat and trying not to let the resignation show, I undo my suit jacket, only to button it up again. "I did."

"Excuse me?"

"I said, I did. It wasn't supposed to come out like that. Fuck, I'm not good at...talking. It's good to know the idea of being with me is so ridiculous, though." I sound harsh and bitter, I know it, but this is a catastrophe.

Her face falls. "Oh my god, no. No! That's not what had me laughing. Okay, it was, but not the idea of it. You just kind of word vomited it and then I thought I misunderstood. The idea of being your girlfriend...well, I don't know what it would be like. I'm confused."

My head falls back, and I try to remember the odds of a meteor striking me.

"Can we sit down and do this, please?" I beg, eyes glued to the ceiling.

Her small hand closes around my wrist and pulls me toward the front of the bakery.

"Okay." Her voice is serious as she pushes me to sit at the same table we sat at the other day. "What is going on?"

She leans forward, arms stacked on top of each other, pushing her full tits up. I could really do without the distraction, especially as she sits there in a floral dress. It's fucking October, and yes, it's abnormally warm today, but I thought the season where Quinn tortures me in pretty dresses was over. It's one of the many reasons I found it so hard to avoid her over the summer. Today, she's in a pale lavender slip of a dress that falls to mid-thigh, and fucking fuck, those thighs.

Shaking away the thoughts of her killer curves, I cut to the chase. "Firstly, I want to say, I don't go around asking just anyone this, and I don't need an answer now. You can even pretend this conversation never happened when I'm finished." I pause, hoping she changes her mind, only to continue when she raises a brow. "I don't know if Jo or my brothers have mentioned it. I was in a relationship up until last January. We were together for twelve years. Almost made it to thirteen, if I hadn't caught her in bed with someone else."

A small gasp sounds from across the table, but I keep my eyes trained on the napkin holder. "It ended the moment I found them together. Looking back, it had been over for a while. You get comfortable in relationships and overlook things you shouldn't. Anyway...they're getting married. Next month."

I jump when Quinn's hand slaps down on the table, and when I look up, I see the sunshine woman is gone. Storm clouds might as well be rolling off her, she's so angry. "I'm all for girls supporting girls. She sounds like a real...you know what, give me her address. I'll speak to her."

She jumps up, and despite never having told anyone but my brothers this story, I find myself laughing at her chivalry. My fingers wrap around her arm, and I shouldn't love the way my hand engulfs her dainty wrist as I tug her back down. "Please don't go all white knight on me. My ego couldn't take it."

"I'm sorry, carry on." Her teeth are clenched so hard she's close to cracking a molar.

Angry Quinn is as cute as happy Quinn. If not, sexier.

"She sent out invitations and I knew I'd get one. My whole family would."

"What type of person invites their ex and his family to their wedding?"

If she was angry before, this is going to trigger something different entirely. "The type of person who is also marrying my cousin."

Quinn's nostrils flare, and I'm tempted to give her Jenna and Ralph's address just to see her roll through there like a little angry hurricane. "Long story short, I need to go. I'm over her—so over her—but Booth thinks this is a power play on her part."

She holds up a hand, stopping me. "Wait, why do you *need* to go?"

This is the part I was hoping to avoid, but I can't lie to her. "Ralph—my cousin and Jenna's fiancé—is from my dad's side. My mom is really close to his parents and only my brothers know about the affair. Saying that, I'm pretty certain my sister has her suspicions. Anyway, I know I should have been honest with my mom about it all, but she was going through a difficult period at the time, and then the moment passed. I also don't want to ruin what relationships she has with my dad's only living family. It's a lot. I know."

I study her face, waiting to see judgment or distaste. Only it never comes. Anger on my behalf paints her features, plus a little empathy.

"So you need a date?"

"I need a date," I echo. "I don't get, um, get out much and, well, you're one of the few women I know who I'm not related to."

Her next words shock me. "I'd love to be your date. I know you have to be nice to the bride on their day, but I'm a real klutz. Red wine may splash on her dress," she says with a wicked smile.

I offer her a weary one in return. "The thing is, Jenna is from Sutton Bay. She lives in Augusta now, but still has friends and family here..."

My sentence trails off, and I hope Quinn can piece together what I'm implying, so I don't have to repeat myself.

No such luck, because she sits there patiently, waiting for me to continue, and fuck, I'm going to have to ask her again.

"There's taking a random date and then there's taking my girlfriend."

Booth and I talked through this step in the process extensively. Jenna is a real stickler for rules, and I know for a fact she's not going to allow me to turn up with any random woman. Her friends know I'm not currently seeing anyone, and they'll report back to her the moment I put down Quinn's name on the RSVP.

Well, if she says yes.

She bobs her head, waiting for me to continue. When her head freezes mid-nod, I know she understands where I'm going with this.

"*Oh.*"

"You don't need to reply now, it's fine."

"I, um, wow. Okay, so you want to, what, fake date me? Make her friends and family believe we're together until...after the wedding?"

Groaning my face falls into my hands, elbows perched on the table to stop me from banging my head into it. "This is Booth's doing." My voice is muffled by my palms. Embarrassment is boiling me from the inside out.

"Can I think about it?" she murmurs, and my head shoots up. I must be seeing things, because does she look a little crestfallen?

"You're actually thinking about doing this?" My voice is laced with shock.

"You asked." She laughs. "I want to help, if anything, to show that b-i-t-c-h that she has no hold over you anymore."

"I'll be your official accountant, free of charge."

She waves me off. "You don't need to do that. I'm happy to

do it but give me a few days. It's not every day someone asks me to be their girlfriend, let alone a fake one. Would it be okay if I spoke to Jo? She's my only friend here and I'll make her swear not to tell anyone."

"Take all the time you need. I'm sure Booth has already told Patrick." I can't believe she's even contemplating this and without wanting anything in return. "If you decide it's too weird, there are no hard feelings."

"It's not weird, just a surprise. And here I thought a delivery of new cake stands was going to be the highlight of my day." She laughs before pursing her lips in thought. There's nothing in her tone or expression that makes me believe her relaxed persona is an act, and I can't decide if that's a good or a bad thing. "I'll have an answer for you by Monday."

"Monday." I nod, trying not to look too wishful.

If she agrees, I'll balance her books, file her taxes, and write up a business plan for her; no argument.

We both stand at the same time. This has gone better than I anticipated. Well, that is until I offer her a handshake in the form of a farewell.

Where is that meteor?

She stares at my outstretched arm in amusement before slipping her smooth palm over mine, putting me out of my misery when she jostles our joined hands.

"How very formal of you, sir." She smirks and I can't help but smile back. "I'll see you Monday."

"Right, yeah, have a good day." I walk backward, wanting to savor up every last drop of her. "Enjoy the flowers."

Her infectious smile stays on my mind the entire drive into the city and most of the day.

During my commute home, however, I think about how this would go if I were someone else. The happy mood I left with after walking out of the bakery slowly evaporates and is non-existent by the time I get back to my apartment.

Once the sun has set and I've frantically finished moving my schedule around for next week, making room for Quinn in the hopes she says yes, the sound of my laptop slamming shut is music to my ears. Opening the drawer of my desk, I pull out my worn leather journal. It's not even old, but I've flicked through the pages so many times, bending and folding the spine and edges, that it looks much more used than it is.

My dad was the one who taught me to journal. From a young age, he noticed how emotions would build up in me, making me feel overwhelmed or how I struggled to vocalize my feelings. I was thirteen when he bought me my first journal. It had my favorite baseball team's emblem on it, nothing like the boring brown one I own today. I've lost count of how many I've gone through now that I'm thirty-three. I'll never forget the intense relief I felt when I found somewhere to put the thoughts that were so difficult to navigate. Like someone finally threw me a buoy after years of treading rough waters.

Tonight, the words come easily, despite their reminders of an embarrassing day, and I feel ten times better when they've been scribbled down.

It's the perfect outlet for my emotions, and in the last few years of my and Jenna's relationship, I filled up dozens of them. We had been dating for a few years, when she found one of my old ones and recited some of the entries to me mockingly. Looking back, her spiteful words should have made me realize we were always going to end in disaster. No one should ever feel like they can't express themselves freely in a relationship, yet I'd found myself in a decade-long one.

I've always been quieter than most, that's just who I am. It takes me a while to feel comfortable around new people. Sometimes, words don't come as easy to me, but if you give me a moment, I'll get there.

My friends and family understand and accept those parts of me, and at first, I thought Jenna accepted that side of me too.

I just wish it didn't take me so long to realize how untrue that was.

She tried to change me. Mold me into something she wanted. And when she was done with me, she spat out a version of myself that I no longer recognized. Who doubts themself more. Overthinks everything they say.

I don't like this version, but as my eyes scan over tonight's entry, I'm not sure how to be anyone else.

In a world where I'm not awkward, I'd be taking her out for dinner.

I'd hold the door of my car open for her as the skirt of her dress blows in the wind.

I'd let her pick the music we listen to as we drive to the restaurant.

I wouldn't care when she picked food off my plate.

I'd eat dessert for her. Fuck, I'd eat her for dessert if I could.

In my ideal world, this would never be fake.

The feelings I have for her already scare me, and I know I'm asking for trouble proposing this idea.

But I am awkward. I'm not confident. I say the wrong thing the majority of the time. And the only way I could ever get someone like Quinn to be with someone like me is if it's fake. Quinn is so far out of my league. If she somehow manages to convince people she could be interested in me, she deserves a standing ovation.

Gray isn't a color you find in the rainbow and there's a reason for that.

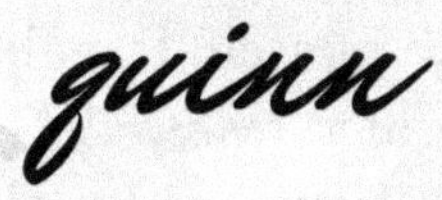

CHAPTER EIGHT

THE BAKERY CLOSED AN HOUR AGO, AND JOHANNA HAS BEEN sitting gawking at me for five minutes since I told her of Graham's proposal.

It's a good thing there were no customers around to hear her shocked reaction. *Shut your fucking mouth and shove it up your butt* is not exactly the best way to promote a serious business.

From the look on Jo's face, there are a million thoughts churning through her brain.

I've only thought about one thing since he dropped the bombshell on me yesterday. Which is a weird sense of dissatisfaction in finding out he wants to date me as a ruse.

I am in no way looking for a boyfriend, yet somehow, when he made it clear this was for mutually beneficial arrangements, it hurt. Without sounding cliché, he's very different from most guys I've dated in the past, and there's something more to him I haven't quite nailed down.

Sure, I have the opportunity to find out what that is, but this sudden pull I'm having toward him needs to be nipped in the bud, pronto, or I risk making a fool of myself.

Finally, Jo speaks. "This is very un-Graham-like."

"How so?" I take a sip of my sauvignon. It's a Saturday evening, so an impromptu wine night was on the cards. Especially after yesterday's turn of events.

"Well, for one this whole fake dating thing screams Booth, so I can't imagine Graham being the mastermind behind this plan. He likes to keep to himself. Even before Jenna came into the picture, he's been quiet, reserved. None of us would have him any other way, and I've always hated how people misinterpret his behavior for something it isn't."

The mention of his ex makes my blood boil. "Even her name makes me angry."

"Mm-hm," she hums around the rim of her glass. "I never liked her. Over the years, she somehow made him more introverted and unsure of himself. I have no idea how they lasted as long as they did."

"Were they ever happy?"

She sighs. "I wasn't here for the last five years of their relationship. Patrick tells me they basically coexisted. Graham is so many things; kind, attentive, faithful. She took advantage of those characteristics. I've never seen him so...detached. Not from his friends or family, but from himself."

My heart drops. His ex clearly did a number on him. I found it surprising he had to ask someone to be his fake date. He's fascinating, sweet, and extremely handsome. Any woman would be lucky to go out with him.

"Do you think he wants her back?"

"God, no," Jo gasps. "I one hundred percent believe him when he says it isn't about that. Pat and Booth hated her. Florence couldn't stand her. I'm not even sure Ted liked her. Claire was always friendly but that woman isn't stupid." She leans in, leveling me with a serious look. "Honestly, knowing Graham, he wouldn't ask just anybody."

A kernel of satisfaction glows in my chest at that. "I'm going to help him," I declare, squaring my shoulders like Jo is going to talk me down.

A knowing smirk plays on her lips. "I'm glad. I'm great and all, but you could do with another friend." She flicks her long hair over her shoulder. "No matter how fake it is, I think you'll be good together."

"Oh, lord. The meddling has already begun," I tease.

*S*CRATCH.

Scratch.

Scratch.

My eyes fly open, and I sit upright in a heartbeat.

Once the brain fog clears, I realize those noises are not from the depths of my deep sleep.

I'm grateful to be woken up from that specific dream—or nightmare. A recurring scene from the week I left home, as vivid and raw as the real thing. *Smashed glass. Cigarette smoke. The radio blasting. Blinding pain. Pitch black.*

"Ugh, not again. You critters are cute, but not at two in the morning," I grumble after squinting at the time on my phone screen. Dragging myself from the cocoon of blankets, I sleepily stumble toward the door. The other week, I was woken up in the middle of the night by similar noises and found a family of raccoons scratching at the back plates. I have no idea what they thought they'd find in the engine, but luckily I haven't seen them since I shooed them away.

By the scuffling noises outside, I'm guessing the furry little family is back. The closer I move to the rear of the van, though, the noises get louder: scratching, scraping, and squeaking. Wait, squeaking? Do raccoons squeak?

Throwing on my fluffy robe and fuzzy slippers, I unlock the door to investigate, using the flashlight on my phone to help light the way in the pitch black.

Once at the back of the van, I rest my head on the cool metal and listen. When the same squeaking meets my ears, I recoil backward in horror. "Ohhhhh no. No, no, no, no," I chant. Those are definitely not the sounds of raccoons. I turn the release lever, then raise the panel slowly.

"Don't scream. Don't scream. They're simply overgrown mice. They're more scared of me than I am of them." My self-reassurances don't help much when I take in chaos in front of me and a small plea escapes my lips. "Please don't eat my face."

The squeaking stops, and several beady eyes reflect back at me. Before I get a chance to shut the compartment, chaos ensues. They start to scurry and scatter among the grass, paper, and insulation nest they've built in my engine, and *nope.*

In my rush to get away, I lose my grip and my phone slips from my sweaty fingers. *Guess it belongs to the rats now.* I jump up and down, shaking out my arms and legs, as if the rodents have somehow managed to bury themselves in my pajamas.

The condensation of the grass soaks through my slippers and just when I thought it couldn't get any worse, the first few drops of rain fall against my face.

Sleeping outside is out of the question and there's no chance I'm staying in my van tonight.

My heart thunders in my chest as I stand in the middle of the field, with no idea what to do. All the lights are out in Mr. Willis's farmhouse, and I don't want to wake him up at this hour.

There is no way I am rooting around in my rodent-infested van for my phone, so that means there's no calling Jo or... anyone. Right now is the worst moment for the sad realization that Jo is my only friend. Even if I did have my phone, they're doing a ton of renovation work in their house at the moment, and they're stressed enough as it is with the restaurant. Plus, it's Patrick's night with Lottie.

I'm in a pickle.

I won't get a wink of sleep if I force myself to stay in the van, and I count my lucky stars I have the bakery to camp out in.

I've never moved so fast in my life as I dart around, packing up whatever clothes, underwear, and toiletries I can grab in two minutes. I'm a big animal lover, and I want to give the rats the benefit of the doubt. They've had a bad rap since the Black Plague, but I have to draw the line at them having zero boundaries.

My stomach drops when I realize there is no way in hell I can afford Graham's services now.

After swallowing my pride on his offer to help me, I called him last night and we settled on a very fair price for him to balance my books, despite him arguing it wasn't necessary. I shared with him what documents I had, and he promised to have a rough analysis ready for me on Monday. I haven't given him my answer yet, but he seemed adamant to help me out, regardless. Those rats have definitely done some damage under the hood. With the potential cost of a mechanic and a temporary place to live, I may as well kiss my savings goodbye.

With my bag and pillow in tow, and a saddened look over my shoulder at Nelly, I make the thirty-minute walk to the bakery. Hopefully I'll get another couple of hours of sleep before I have to open—then call the local mechanic and spend money I can't afford to lose.

Once at the bakery, soaked through to the bone, I try to get comfortable on the makeshift bed I've set up in the kitchen. Defeat weighs heavy on me and it's all I can do not to cry myself to sleep.

BANG. BANG. BANG.

The headache that's been brewing behind my eyes all night thumps without pause. I can hear the banging against the side of my skull as I burrow my face into my pillow. My alarm hasn't gone off yet, so I must have at least another hour of sleep left.

Pulling my robe up over my head, I shield my eyes from the early morning rays shining through the window and try my best to find sleep again.

The second I feel myself drifting off, a large crash comes from the front of the bakery. I'm jumping to my feet at the noise, but I fall back on my butt when my head smacks against the edge of the stainless-steel table.

"Ow! If you're the family of rats coming to finish the job, have at me!" I call out as I rub at the bump already swelling at my hairline. My fingers come away with a little blood, but nothing too worrying.

"Rats?! Fuck, Quinn, please tell me that's you." I recognize that deep voice. It never fails to weaken my knees anytime I hear it.

The stomping of feet lets me know someone is making their way to where I'm sprawled out on the floor, likely concussed.

Graham rounds the counter and stops short when he sees me, his shoulders relaxing the moment we lock eyes.

"Oh. Hey, you. We're not open yet," I greet him with a wince and a small wave.

The typically even-tempered man looks...*angry*? He's red faced, chest rising and falling, and hands shaking at his sides. "You're not open yet," he parrots, though his tone isn't upbeat like mine. He's definitely mad.

"Have I done something wrong?" I squeak and sit up right,

the blanket I've had wrapped around me falls to my waist. That's when I notice a wide-eyed Johanna and Patrick behind him. Jo is quick to slap her hands over Patrick's eyes, before dragging him behind the partition wall.

What in the world is going on?

"I thought you were hurt. All we could see were your feet sticking out from behind the wall. I've been bang—" His head snaps up to the ceiling and a groan that could shake the foundations of the building rolls from his throat. "Fucking hell, Quinn."

"Hey, we can't all look like Disney Princesses when we wake up in the morning." I pout and run my fingers over the tender spot on my head.

He brings his thumb and forefinger to massage his nose, pushing his glasses up from his face, but he still doesn't look at me, because clearly I look like a wretched monster.

"Quinn." I usually love it when he says my name, that one syllable sounding delightful in his voice, but right now it's said through gritted teeth.

"What, Graham? You barged into my bakery," I snap. "And now you come in here like a bear that's been woken up early from its hibernation."

"Jesus, woman! Your boob is hanging out!"

CHAPTER NINE

graham

I'VE LOST COUNT OF THE NUMBER OF TIMES I'VE PICTURED WHAT Quinn would look like first thing in the morning.

The real thing exceeds all expectations.

Flushed cheeks that look soft and pink like the petals of a rose. Caramel eyes shining bright in the early morning sun. Hair tousled perfectly, as if someone had been running their hands through it all night.

God, I wish it had been my hands.

A very deprived, filthy part of my mind had imagined what her soft curves and full breasts looked like too. Though, I hadn't expected to be flashed by her in the middle of the bakery.

My nerves and heart rate are still sky-high, even now that I know she's not hurt. Well, apart from the small cut on her forehead.

We were due to meet at seven thirty, where I would talk her

through my plan to look over her books and she would put me out of my misery and tell me that it was absurd for me to ask her to be my fake girlfriend. A simple Monday morning transaction.

I'd expected her to be here early, she told me she would be.

When my watch read 7:45, something felt off. Johanna and Patrick spotted me waiting outside and even Jo started to get a little antsy, stating this is very unlike Quinn. She called her cell but was met with her voicemail each time.

The moment I saw a pair of feet sticking out behind the counter through the window, I told Patrick to call Dex, who I knew would have no issue fixing the wooden door frame after I barreled through it. Dex is Patrick's best friend, who he's known since kindergarten. The guy has at least three inches on my six-foot-three frame, is covered head to toe in tattoos, and a very talented carpenter/joiner by trade.

I was lucky I didn't shatter the pane of glass when I shouldered my way into the bakery. When I was over the threshold, and a muffled *ow* echoed through the quiet space, my anxiety eased off, but I was still worked up from thinking the worst.

My eyes are still safely trained on the ceiling when I hear Quinn giggle. "Oops. Nipple safely away. You can look now, you big prude."

This woman. I've never met anyone who accepts everything in stride the way she does. Though, I don't meet a lot of women who would flash a boob and be so nonchalant about it either.

With a deep breath, I let my eyes wander back to where she's kneeling on the floor at my feet, legs twisted in a purple, knitted blanket. "I'm not a prude," I mutter, sounding exactly like a prude. "I—your"—I gesture toward her chest—"I didn't mean to look." *I didn't want to look away*, is what I'm really thinking.

"I'm just teasing. You're a gentleman, I respect that." She

wouldn't think I was a gentleman if she knew what I was imagining.

Her sitting at my feet, just like this, only with flushed cheeks and hair mussed for a completely different reason. Brown eyes looking up at me as she grips my thighs, taking me deeper with each shallow thrust of my hips.

Fuck, this is not good. I can't be thinking these things ever, let alone when I'm around her.

Needing to hide the stiffness pressing against my zipper, I crouch down in front of her, glancing over my shoulder to see Jo pulling down the chairs from the tables and Patrick walking around outside on the phone.

When I turn back, Quinn smiles up at me sweetly, and it does nothing to kill off my boner.

"I have two questions. One: Why are you sleeping here? Two: What happened?" I brush away her bangs to inspect her head. Luckily the cut isn't deep enough to need stitches or urgent care.

"To answer your first question, it's a long story. And for the second, I whacked it on the edge of the table. It's not that bad is it?" She flinches when she presses a finger to the injury. "Ouch."

That tiny noise of pain rattles me. "Do you have a first aid kit?"

"Under the sink, but I can do it. You must have somewhere to be?"

"I'm right where I need to be. We had a meeting. Remember?" I snatch her wrist before her hand can slap against her forehead. "Not the best idea. Now stay put and be good."

She smirks at my words and when I play them back in my head, I hear exactly how they sound.

Finding the small kit under the sink, I return to where she's waiting patiently for me and sit back on my haunches, our faces level again. Unlatching the plastic box, I find what I need: alcohol wipes, pain reliever, and Band-Aids. Most of them are bright blue, as you'd expect to find in an area used for food preparation, but when I spot a few with unicorns and stars on them, I decide she'll like one of those best.

"Can I?" I ask, holding up the wipe as I tear it open.

"Go ahead, Dr. Sadler."

As I shuffle forward, I push back her hair, careful not to brush against the tender spot. The smell of sugar and vanilla immediately fills my nose. From this close, I could get a sugar rush.

"I'm sorry if this stings."

I gently swipe the alcohol-soaked cotton over her head but jerk my hand away when she hisses loudly. "Joking, joking." She giggles, her hand wrapping around my wrist as the soft chime of her laughter tinkles around us. That addictive sound, paired with the sweet smell of her, is going to drive me insane.

Scratch that, I'm too far gone.

"You're trouble." I try to keep my eyes on the task at hand, not allowing them to drop to her bee-stung lips or look to where I feel her gaze burning into the side of my jaw. "Seriously though, Quinn, why were you sleeping here?"

She visibly shivers and I pause my movements, worried I've hurt her. "Rats. Lots and lots of rats."

"Rats in your apartment? House?" I realize I don't even know where she lives.

"My van."

"Your van?" My brows lift in surprise.

"Yeah, I live in a van. She's called Nelly. It's been renovated and is fully livable. Don't go cracking any hippy jokes," she warns with a stern look that does nothing to intimidate me. "It's cozy and has been my trusty steed for years. Anyway, raccoons have been visiting me a lot recently and I heard them scurrying around in the engine last night. Only it wasn't raccoons,

Graham. They were rats. *So* many rats. I swear one of them went for my throat. It was too late to wake up Mr. Willis and…I dropped my phone in their nest. So, I slept here."

"That's quite the ordeal. I think I know a guy who can help you out, let me call him."

"No," she protests. "You don't need to do that. I'm going to call a mechanic this morning. Now, finish patching me up, please, Doctor, I have a meeting to get to."

Feeling brave, I go along with the gag as I clean her wound, but immediately regret it. "Would you like a lollipop?"

Why is everything I say sounding like an innuendo today?

She snickers. "Oh my god, was that a joke?"

"Hmm." I blow across her forehead, making sure it's dry before I place the Band-Aid and hoping to all that is holy she doesn't notice my bright red face.

"How do I look?" She turns her head from left to right, showcasing the brightly colored bandage.

"Pretty as always." The words are out in the world before I can suck them back in. I try my best not to react to my slipup, but the heat clawing up my neck lets me know it's useless.

Quinn simply chuckles, pats me lightly on the cheek, and stands. She lowers her hand and helps me to my feet, though I do most of the work.

"Gimme ten minutes to freshen up. Would you mind switching on the coffee machine for me, please?" she asks as she steps toward the small restroom.

Nodding, I do as asked, quietly collecting my thoughts and preparing for all the possible things she could say to me. The more prep, the less stuttering.

"That was interesting."

I spin around at the unexpected voice and discover Johanna perched on a chair, legs crossed at the ankles, looking like some evil villain with the way the corner of her mouth is quirked up. I'd almost forgotten we had company and now I'm reminded that Quinn asked if she could speak to Jo about my fake dating proposal. From the curious look aimed in my direction, they've talked.

"Me helping someone out? I'm not that much of a dick, am I?" I ask, attempting to divert the conversation.

Her shoulders slump and she cocks her head. "You're far from that, Gray. It's good that Quinn has another friend to watch her back and you seem comfortable around her."

I try not to cringe at the nickname everyone uses for me, but most of all, I don't want Quinn to start using it.

"I'm also far from being friends with her," I murmur, scratching the back of my neck and eyes darting to the back of the kitchen, hoping Quinn makes an appearance soon. "Don't you have a restaurant to run?"

"Patrick left to open up, I'll head over soon. Dex will be over shortly to fix the door." She stands and walks over to me, a small smile on her lips. "Give yourself more credit. She talks very highly of you, but be warned, she's told me her plans to get you to eat something sugary. From experience, she's a really great person to have on your team." She rushes her next words out when we hear noise from the back. "That girl is as stubborn as a mule, so don't let her turn down your help. I think this arrangement is going to be good for you both."

I pause. "She hasn't agreed to it yet."

"She was never going to say no." She throws me a wink. "Anyway, customers to serve. Catch you later. Tell Quinn I said bye."

The sounds of footfalls come from behind me the moment Jo disappears through the door. Quinn is now in dark green overalls, an orange-and-white striped T-shirt, and a worn pair of Chucks. Her hair is tied back into two small buns at the back of her head. She beams up at me, because even after I damaged her front door and caused her to hurt herself, she still finds me worthy of that mesmerizing smile.

She pulls out a bottle of water and orange juice from the fridge, and like a lost little puppy, I follow her to the table in the middle of the room. This is the third time we've found ourselves at this table together.

"This is kinda like our table, isn't it?" she asks, as if she can read my mind.

It's insane how much I love the idea of this being *our* table. Another reason why asking her to be my fake girlfriend is the worst idea in the fucking world.

"I guess it is." Presenting the report I put together over the weekend from my satchel, I place it on the table between us and slide it toward her. "So, um, thanks for sending over all those documents. There were a few things missing, but we can work on that. For now, I was able to draft a financial performance report for the bakery. It could do with some work, but that's why I'm here—to help. I've made some initial suggestions; adjusting some price points on goods you sell, how you can better calculate inventory turnaround, and even some advice if you ever, I don't know, wanted to wholesale your goods or services..."

I let my words hang between us. Not wanting to push her but letting her know the option to work with the restaurant is still open. I'm candid, professional, and know what I'm talking about. If I were to be brutally honest, her books are a mess.

It's why I have a job.

"You said a lot of words and they went"—she slashes her hand over the top of her head and whistles—"right over my head. This is great, you clearly know your stuff. I really appreciate you putting in all this effort. The thing is..."

She flicks through the pages of the report, eyes downcast so I can't see her expression, but her voice has lost that bubbly ring to it. She sounds tired and defeated, like something's crushed her spirit. And I do not like this one bit.

She's had one hell of a night. With most people, I'd keep my opinions to myself, not wanting to stick my nose in their business, but I have this urge to do the complete opposite with her. To find out what's wrong, eradicate anyone or anything that upsets her, and protect her from the world.

That's why I don't hold back now. "Hey, what's up? You disappeared on me there."

A small sniffle breaks the silence, and when her eyes meet mine, they're filled with tears. I've never been a violent man, but suddenly the idea of rampaging through the streets of Sutton Bay in Quinn's honor sounds very appealing.

"I can't accept your help. It's just not going to work out. I don't even know why I'm crying, this is so stupid." Her voice wavers and she swipes at her eyes, before trying to hide her sadness behind a watery smile.

I scoot my chair closer and rest my hand on top of hers, dipping my head to meet her sad gaze.

"Nothing about your feelings is stupid. If...if you want the name of one of my colleagues, I can give you their number. I understand if it's weird working with me now."

"No, it's not you. I want to work with you. It's just I can't afford it—" Her voice breaks, and before her head collapses into her hands, I'm tugging her into me and muffling her gut-wrenching sobs with my chest.

"We don't need to talk about money now. I want to help, Quinn...as a friend." I test the word and it doesn't sound so bad. Being her friend is probably the most I'll ever get, so I better start accepting it.

"I can't let you do that," she whines into my cardigan.

I take hold of her shoulders, putting some space between us. "Why not?"

"Because I need another favor instead. A favor for a favor." She looks guilty at that confession, chewing on her lip, and I desperately want to pull it free from her teeth before she draws blood.

"I hate asking this, and I've tried to come up with so many other solutions. I'm not agreeing to this simply because I need your help, because I was always going to say yes...you know, being your faux lover."

My heart stops and I try to swallow the large lump in my throat. Holy shit, she's going to do it.

"Anything, I'll do anything." Despite my desperate tone, my expression remains calm. "I'll help the bakery and then some. You name it, it's yours."

Her mouth twists to the side. "You might regret this."

"Never. If you're even debating helping me out in such a ridiculous way, nothing you ask will be too big."

"Great. You won't mind if we become roommates then?"

I still.

Did I hear her correctly?

Before I can ask her to repeat herself, my mind is running away from me.

Simply imagining Quinn in my space has me charged up. It's bad enough I'm torturing myself by asking her to date me, let alone seeing her day and night. Would she walk around in the skimpy camisoles I found her in earlier? Would her sugary scent stay long after she leaves?

Is she going to take one look at my sad apartment and go running for the hills?

But what if she doesn't, a quiet voice says.

What if she likes what she sees and shares the same feelings?

What if she sees me for who I am and likes it?

CHAPTER TEN

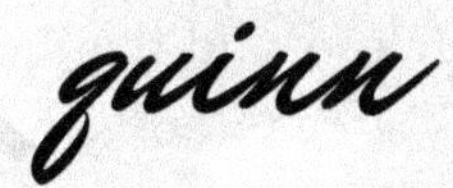

I'm a silence filler.

Holding my tongue has never been my strong suit. It's clear my inability to not say the first thing that pops into my head has shocked Graham as I take in his deer in the headlight expression.

I told a little white lie.

The idea of us being roommates only came to me seconds ago. When he said, *I'll do anything*, I saw a resolution to my current situation. I'm not one to ask for favors, preferring to do things on my own, so when I blurted out that question, it surprised me.

I haven't called the mechanic yet, but I know VW parts are hard to come by—and expensive—so it wouldn't surprise me if I'm without Nelly for a week or more.

Jo and Patrick's place was off the table because of their reno. Mr. Willis would be an option, if he didn't own three cats and I wasn't severely allergic. I'd grimly accepted I'd be throwing the majority of my savings at fixing my van and staying in a hotel while it was being repaired. There were no other options, and I couldn't sleep here long term.

Enter Graham.

Maybe I hit my head harder than I thought. Before I had a chance to reason with my brain, it had already taken over my vocal cords and I was asking him to be roomies.

A question he still hasn't responded to.

His mouth hangs open, glasses sliding down the bridge of his nose as he leans in close, and that's when I realize I'm still gripping onto his dark green cardigan like my life depends on it.

"Oops, sorry." I smooth down the knitted material against his chest. A very firm chest I might add. "Should we pretend I didn't ask that? Yes, let's do that. So, it's agreed, I'll be your fake girlfriend, and we won't muddy the waters with you being my accountant. No scratching your back, you'll scratch mine."

I stand abruptly, which is when I see Dex outside the window. He grew up with Jo and Patrick, but I'm not sure he ever stopped growing, because this man is a beast. Most people make me look short, but Dex towers over everyone. He's currently fixing the bent hinges to the front door, and I can only guess Patrick called him after I gave him a free peep show.

"Well...great talking with you. I'm already late opening up, so I better get a move on." I throw a thumb over my shoulder.

"You need somewhere to stay?" His deep voice halts my steps.

"No, silly. I have my van."

"The van full of rats?"

"I love rats." The lie sends a shiver down my spine, and he sees it.

"I think you're full of shit." He stands and levels me with a knowing look.

"That's not how a gentleman talks."

"Never claimed to be one." He slides his hands into his pockets but doesn't move toward me. "Now, tell me about your van. How bad is it?"

My shoulders drop, knowing it's pointless lying to him. "I don't know, bad? I have to call the mechanic, but it's an old model, and the last time it needed repairs, it took over a week. Seriously, it's not your problem to worry about, I'll find somewhere to stay."

I pull out today's cake selection from the fridge and lay them out. It's obvious I'm avoiding his gaze but when I finish arranging the slices of peanut butter sheet cake my eyes drift to where he's still standing.

"Where?" he asks.

"Huh?"

"Quinn, where are you going to stay? I already know Patrick and Jo's place isn't available." For such a shy man, he sure is asking a lot of questions today. The stern look and no-shit attitude he's giving off shouldn't be attractive, yet it is. Maybe it's because he seems so concerned about my well-being. It kind of reminds me of the Graham who shouted at his brother on my behalf several months ago. In this very spot too.

"A hotel."

"No," he gruffs out, arms crossing over his chest and stretching the knitted fabric across his broad shoulders.

"No?" I parrot back, trying to mirror the timbre of his tone and sounding like a squashed frog.

"Correct." He closes the distance between us until he towers over me. Not in an intimidating way, I don't think he's capable of that. Confidence ripples off him, not his usual look, but it suits him. "You sure you're okay with this fake dating business?"

Swallowing, I bob my head up and down.

"Then no hotel. If we're going to make this believable, there is no chance in hell I would let my girl stay in a hotel."

My girl. I shouldn't like the sound of that. *No, Quinn! Bad girl, this is fake.* He's just getting into character.

"O-okay."

He gives one firm nod, and I almost stop breathing when he reaches up and pulls away a few hairs that are stuck to the Band-Aid. His fingers linger above my eyebrow and those mossy-green eyes stare so intently into mine, I swear I can smell the earthy wood scent of the forest.

"Be ready at five. I'll pick you up."

"What are we doing?"

There was zero hesitation in my decision to help out Graham. The only reason I spoke with Jo was to understand him a little better. I'm probably not his usual type and he's right, if we want this to be believable, we have to do everything in our power to show the town—and his ex's friends—we're serious about each other.

Our eyes remain locked, an odd sensation bubbling between us, and for a brief second, I worry we're walking into dangerous territory with this agreement.

My moment of doubt disappears when Graham's next words might as well sign and seal this whole thing.

"We're getting your things and moving you in, honey."

"You have to go inside to pack a bag."

"Thank you, Captain Obvious." I turn to Graham and give him my best woe-is-me look, hoping he'll take pity on me. "Can't you do it?"

His face is impassive as he takes in my little orange home. Insecurity sweeps through me. In the light of day, there's no hiding the worn patches of paint, the Duct tape holding up the side mirror, or the missing VW badge on the front. I don't usually care what people think, yet his opinion—for whatever reason—matters to me. He's so put together and studious, I worry how we're going to fool anyone that we're dating.

He picked me up at five o'clock as planned and we spent the short ride over to Mr. Willis's land in silence. It wasn't awkward, I think we were both processing the fast-paced turn of events that have unraveled in the last week.

We still need to iron out the details of me being his girl-friend. I've never actually been anyone's girlfriend, deciding casual hookups were safer, considering I moved around so much. Some hand-holding. Dinner dates. Strolls in the park. Graham seems like a low-maintenance guy, how hard can it be?

Oh god. What if he wants us to kiss? Not that it's a bad thing...

I stare at his lips as the thought passes through my mind. They look soft, not too full, and he keeps his beard well-trimmed. Suddenly, I'm imagining the tickle of his facial hair against my skin. Those lips are moving now and shit, did he say something?

"Sorry, can you repeat that?" My eyes dart up to find him watching me closely with a slight smirk.

"I said, I think I'd feel more comfortable if you did it. I'll be on rodent watch." He places a hand on the small of my back and gently guides me toward the side door.

"Fine," I mutter. "I suppose asking you to pick out my underwear for the next week is too soon, huh?" I tease, making Graham's cheeks flash red. I'm pretty sure he'd go up in flames if I told him I didn't wear underwear a lot of the time. Thick girl habits. I usually settle on a pair of shorts under my dresses or go commando like today.

The golden hour light makes the orange exterior of the van pop and stand out against the green grass. This lighting does wonders on Graham, too, painting him in a warm glow. The cool breeze makes the longer strands on top of his head shift slightly, the color reminding me of the wheat fields I'd pass through when I lived in Kansas.

"We need a signal." I stand taller as we approach the sliding door, hoping the rats won't run up my legs if I look confident. *Can they smell fear?*

"A signal?"

"Yeah. If you see one, you need to warn me. Maybe you can *caw caw* like an eagle, and it will scare them off."

He shakes his head in amusement and gestures to the door, waiting for me to unlock it. "I don't think eagles caw, but I'll keep watch. You're safe."

Trusting him, I pull my keys from the tote bag slung over my shoulder and slide the door open once it's unlocked. We both lean forward, listening for any signs of the critters. We're met with silence, but I still don't budge. Graham gets the hint and steps in front of me, opening the door farther and climbing inside. The van shifts with his weight and I have to hold back my giggle when he faces me, his huge frame folded to fit into my small home.

His eyes roam over the space, taking in the bright blue comforter, multicolored tapestry rug that hides the awful green vinyl flooring, and the pocket-sized kitchen behind the front seats. I'm going to miss it.

"Hear anything?" I ask.

He stands still for a second, listening closely then shakes his head. "Nope." He steps back out and groans as he stretches. "This thing is impressive, but not really made for people above five feet."

"Hey! I'm five three."

"Shortcake." The glare I throw at him doesn't have the intended effect, but I like the playfulness that flashes in his gaze. "How did you even come across something like this?"

"Pure luck. I was in Oregon and had been saving up for a car. One evening I was walking back from work, and it was outside a house with a for sale sign. I did some haggling, and the guy either pitied me or he just really wanted to get rid of it. It was only a week later that I looked up the going price of this model and almost fell off my chair."

"Are you from Oregon?"

My hand freezes above the door handle.

It's a normal question between friends. Jo knows I've moved around a lot, I've told her about all the amazing places and states I've visited, just not the reason why I left San Diego. Questions like this always make me uneasy because I hate revealing too much about my life *before* I left.

"Umm, no, San Diego," I offer curtly and climb into the van.

My brusque response doesn't deter him. "Nice. Seems you've traded one corner of the country for another. Do you visit home often?"

Another simple question. I swallow the knot in my throat as discomfort churns in my stomach. Maybe it's because I'm tired from last night's events, because suddenly I'm back in that small trailer. The fresh air is replaced with stale cigarette smoke. Chirping of birds switched to drunken slurs. A light touch on my arm has me flinching and stumbling backward, only to be caught by a strong pair of arms.

"Hey, hey. You're as white as a sheet. Is it your head? Do you need to sit down?" Graham asks, worry etched into his face. I'm panting and my skin feels clammy, but I'm no longer drowning in the grim memory as I cling to his arm.

"I haven't eaten much today." The lie is easier than the miserable truth of my life.

It's clear he doesn't believe me, but he doesn't ask any more questions about my past, either, and I don't know why that makes me sad. Sharing stories about my travels is one of my favorite things to do. To tell people about the first time I saw the hot springs in Wyoming, or when I tried horseback riding in Montana.

Just not any stories from San Diego.

I hurriedly pack my small suitcase with enough clothes to last me a week, while Graham checks the engine compartment to see if my new tenants are still there. From the dire look on his face, they are. I hop down in front of him, slide the door shut, and lock up.

"Guessing this is yours." He holds out my phone between us and I take it from him with a quick thanks. "You might need to do something about the rats before the van goes to the shop."

"Ugh. Like what?"

"I can call pest control."

I gasp. "They won't kill them, will they?"

"Umm...do you want me to lie?"

"No, Graham!" I cry, slapping a hand over my heart at the idea. "We can't kill them, I think I saw babies."

"You don't even like them."

"I'm not a monster." I pout and fold my arms.

"Okay, okay. Humane methods only. I'll call a buddy over in Jacob's Bluff. The mechanic I go to also knows someone who does VW restorations."

Jacob's Bluff is one town over and just as beautiful and quaint as Sutton Bay. I trust Graham's contacts, but it feels out of character to let him take control of everything. What's surprising is how nice it feels to have someone helping me out for once.

We walk back to his Jeep, my suitcase tucked under his arm. I glance back at my van, the only home I've ever really known, with a sad ache in my chest. He must feel my mood shift because he bumps his shoulder with mine.

"We'll get it sorted, don't worry. Let's get you settled, and then how about some takeout for dinner?"

I swallow my sadness and try my best to siphon a genuine smile, hoping it hides the whorl of emotions threatening to shatter my façade. "Sounds good."

With a firm nod, he loads my things into the back of his car and we're on the road again.

Gone is the protective, stern man from this morning.

The moment we step over the threshold into his apartment, I can tell his nerves are getting the better of him. It's exactly how I felt when he was stuffed into my van earlier. Despite his timidness, he's taking the time to show me around his space. He points out which cabinets in the kitchen hold the glasses, plates, and pans. Then he shows me how to turn on the shower and reassures me it's fine if I want a bath while I'm here. Curly's little ears perk up when Graham reveals where he keeps the dog treats, and he hasn't stopped weaving in and out of my legs since I arrived.

As expected, his apartment is neat, clean, and simple; a lot like the man himself. It also looks like he's just moved in, not that he's lived here for over a year. Not because there are unpacked boxes but because there isn't any sign that he lives here. It's a bit like a showroom. No photos, pillows, plants. The only sign of life is the wooden desk and bookshelf in the corner, where I presume he works from home.

It's characterless, as if he doesn't want to put his own stamp on it.

"This is my room." He points to a closed door and then guides me to the one opposite. He slowly opens it, and we stand in the doorway of a decent-sized bedroom, furnished with a king-sized bed, side table, and small dresser tucked away in the corner of the room.

"And this is yours. Sorry it's a little plain." Graham scratches the back of his neck.

I might only be here for a short period of time, but we're about to spend a lot of time with one another.

I'm determined to get to know him as much as possible during this arrangement. My interest in him isn't out of pity, but I'd love to see him open up a little more and shed some of that uncertainty around what he says and does. From what I've seen, he's said all the right things, and his actions speak volumes about the type of person he is.

There's more to Graham Sadler than tentative words, endearing blushes, and numbers.

During my tour, I spotted the wedding invite pinned to the fridge and that small piece of card made me angry all over again.

Side mission: send a box of rotten fish heads to his ex.

We step into the room, and I wiggle my socked feet over the hardwood floor. "It's perfect. We clearly have very different tastes though. My bright outfits must give you a headache, along with my constant talking."

"I like it. The colors. And the talking," he rushes out, avoiding eye contact as he sets my suitcase at the foot of the bed. "I'll get you a key tomorrow. On Wednesdays I work in the city, so I'm usually up and out before six."

"Works for me. I'm usually at the bakery between five and six anyway. It's a good thing we're both early birds. Any house rules I should know about?"

"House rules?" He turns to look at me.

"Yeah, you know, like no feet up on the sofa or music after a certain time. Maybe you walk around naked. I'm cool with that, just warn a girl."

He chokes at that last bit. Swiping his glasses off his face, he rubs the spot between his eyes before placing them back on.

Poor guy. I should stop, but it's too much fun teasing him. I'm still trying to pull that handsome smile out of him again.

"No rules. No nakedness either."

"Killjoy." I jut my bottom lip out.

"Jesus, Quinn. Am I going to regret this?" He sighs, but there's humor in his tone. "Are you good with Thai?"

"I'm good with anything. Isn't that obvious?" I gesture down my body.

His brows furrow and his mouth opens slowly, unsure of how to respond to that. "It's fine. It's no secret I'm a curvy girl. I'm allowed to make jokes at my own expense."

Forehead still creased, he tucks his hands in his pockets and looks down at the floor. I feel a little guilty for making him uncomfortable with my comment, but I *am* a curvy girl. My stomach wobbles. My thighs touch. I have stretch marks on my boobs and hips.

I used to hate my figure. Anyone would after years of hurtful comments and people pinching my rolls, telling me that *fat* girls like me were "good for nothing, lazy bitches."

It didn't happen overnight, but I love my body. We all come in different shapes and sizes, and if someone is going to judge me for that, then they don't deserve a spot in my life.

"I'm gonna unpack and clean up for dinner. I'll be out soon." I step up to Graham, who's still looking down at the ground like it personally offended him. Wanting to pull him out of his thoughts, I push his glasses up his nose with the tip of my finger, finally getting his attention. "I really appreciate this. More than I can explain. I promise to be the best fake girlfriend you've ever had."

Before he has a chance to reply, I wrap my arms around his middle and squeeze tight. The soft wool of his cardigan tickles my nose at the same time his warm, spicy scent hits me. It's like that first whiff of hot cider in fall: orange, cloves, cinnamon, and something totally him.

For a second I think he's not going to hug me back, but when his strong arms envelop me, I melt into the embrace.

There's a thrumming between us; a feeling I've never felt before.

We pull away at the same time, smiling softly at each other, before I can pinpoint what this new sensation is.

I'm grateful for him and the friendship we've sparked under bizarre circumstances. We're quite the pair; different in so many ways. And I decide as he walks out of the room that I like that about us.

After I sort through my suitcase, I'm unbuckling the straps of my overalls when there's a knock on the door.

The second I open it Graham starts talking with his eyes glued to his feet. "It's your body and you're allowed to make whatever comments you want about it. But for what it's worth..." When he finally looks at me, there's no missing the reverence in his expression. "I think you're fucking perfect."

CHAPTER ELEVEN

graham

I'M GONNA NEED AN ENTIRE JOURNAL FOR TONIGHT'S ENTRY.

Despite being way out of my comfort zone, I'm not uncomfortable.

I'm just losing my mind.

This is not the plan Booth and I laid out. Things have escalated way out of my control. She's *living* with *me*. How am I supposed to control my thoughts, words, and actions around her? With just a smile she unknowingly has the ability to turn my life upside down. It's such a bad, bad idea letting her stay here when the crush I have doubles in size with each second I spend with her.

The next week is going to be the best type of torture.

I've never met someone who speaks so openly—with no filter or shame. It's refreshing. She's left me speechless on a number of occasions, and I'm guessing there are only more unfiltered observations to come.

I still can't believe she agreed to this whole thing, and sure, she's gaining something from it, too, but I suspect it wasn't easy for her to accept my help.

When she stepped into my apartment, I felt cracked open

like an oyster and left out on the shore for all the world to see. Only my family has visited, and it killed me not to know how it looked through her eyes.

I didn't have much time, but I tried my best to make her room look as inviting as possible, even if it is only for a week. She'd thanked me plenty on the ride over here, I just hadn't expected her to hug me. Twice in one day I've had Quinn in my arms. I just wish she hadn't made that comment about her body. I could tell it wasn't the first time, as if she thought someone was going to make it first.

So many responses had zoomed in and out of my brain. Not a single one seemed like the right thing to say in the moment, and I hated that I wasn't able to give her the words of reassurance I was so desperate for her to hear.

I stood outside the door to her room for a few minutes, frozen in place. Determined to not let our conversation end with her having any self-doubt or not knowing what I thought about her.

But for what it's worth, I think you're fucking perfect.

So fucking perfect.

I'd give anything to trace my lips along every dip and curve of her soft skin. To have those thick thighs wrapped around my waist. Or head. I could die happy, if I knew what those full breasts felt like in my hands. Everything about her has me infatuated. It's only made better that she's like my walking fantasy, with a beautiful body I want to sink my fingers and teeth into.

Fuck me.

I press down on the growing bulge in my pants, so I don't have a boner when I talk to my brother. I've already called the Thai restaurant in Jacob's Bluff to place our order, and now I'm waiting for Booth to answer my call. The longer the ringing echoes through my phone, the more antsy I get.

"What's up?" he finally answers.

"She's here," I hiss, cupping my hand around the phone so Quinn doesn't hear.

"Umm...who is?"

"Quinn."

"Where?"

"In my apartment." I swipe a hand across the room like he can see me as I march back and forth along the tiled floor. "She just moved in."

The howling laughter from down the line has me wincing. It takes him a few deep breaths to stop the wheezing until he's able to form a full sentence, and even then, he's still chuckling. "Christ, Gray. I said fake date her, not move her in, propose, and start a family. How did this happen?"

"She needed somewhere to stay for a while. Plus, I felt it was the least I could do considering she's helping me out." I ignore the pang of excitement I get when I hear him mention *propose* and *family* when talking about Quinn and me.

"Is she staying with you until the wedding?"

"No. Her van needs repairs. I think she'll be here for a week max."

"Hmm. Well, if this doesn't make it believable, I don't know what will. Are you going to bring her to Mom's on Thursday? It's the only evening Patrick, Johanna, and I can get time off from the restaurant for a while. Might be a good way to ease Mom into it."

"I'm telling her it's fake."

"Nooo. Don't do that," he groans.

"Why not?" I'm bound to wear a hole in the floor, I'm pacing so much.

"She's coming out of her obsessive phase with Pat and Jo finally being together and now she's sniffing around me. If you have a girlfriend, she'll get off my back for a while. Please."

"Or you could find yourself a girlfriend and bring her to dinner."

"Just do it. I'll walk Curly for a month."

My eyes roll so hard. "No, I like walking him. You can follow us around with a pooper scooper."

"Deal."

"Now what the fuck do I do? She's here and she's agreed to go along with this ridiculous plan, but what do I do next?"

"Hang on, let me get the texts up from Florence." The line is silent for a moment and Booth hums to himself as he searches through the advice from our little sister.

I've been avoiding texts from Florence all week since Booth told her about this plan. It's a good thing she's backpacking around Central America right now, or I would never hear the end of it from her. Her last chain of texts went a little something like this:

> Florence: If this works, do I get to officiate your wedding?
>
> Florence: On the flight to Costa Rica I read this cute small-town romance, and I couldn't stop laughing. This is your life now.
>
> Florence: It's a shame you have a two-bed apartment...people go wild for a one bed trope.
>
> Florence: She sounds like a cutie. Anyone is an upgrade from that reptile.

Safe to say Florence wasn't a fan of Jenna's either.

"Ah-ha." My brother breaks the silence. "So you need to set some boundaries. Like, will you kiss or hold hands in public? Apparently, one of you needs to tell the other that 'you have to promise not to fall in love with me,' but...I fear that's too late for you."

"Shut up or I'll remove the pooper scooper and you can pick up Curly's sh—oh, hey!" I shout in panic when I see Quinn standing at the edge of the kitchen. Turning away, I bend my head and whisper into the phone. "Forward me those texts. Goodbye."

After hanging up, I slam my phone down on the countertop and spin around to face her. She's in a pair of pink sweats, a white T-shirt tied at the waist, and yellow fuzzy socks. Her hair is split in two and braided back from her face. She looks fresh, cozy, and delicious.

"Sorry, I didn't mean to interrupt." She looks around the space with a slightly apprehensive expression. It's my responsibility to make her feel at home, but how the fuck do I do that? *Oh, here you go, Quinn, want to do a crossword with me until you die of boredom?* No. I didn't think this through. She's going to regret taking up my offer in less than twenty-four hours when she realizes I'm not only boring and dull but can't string a coherent sentence together to save my life.

"Umm. Did you get settled in your room okay?" I ask.

"Yes, thank you. It's a really nice place you've got here."

"Thanks."

We stand there, her rocking on the balls of her feet and me trying my best not to spontaneously combust. It's obvious neither of us are sure how to navigate these next steps. There's no manual for our situationship, but considering it's my idea, I need to be the one to take the lead.

The buzzer sounds and I excuse myself, running down the stairs to collect the food. When I return, I find Quinn balancing on her tiptoes, reaching for the bowls on the top shelf. The movement causes her T-shirt to ride up, revealing the tiniest sliver of skin that shouldn't make me hard as stone.

"Let me." I rush over and set down the bag of food on the counter.

She's trying her best, huffing and puffing, but her fingertips barely reach the middle shelf. Stepping up behind her, I pull two bowls down with ease, not really thinking about our positioning until the front of my pants brushes against the small of her back. When she drops down from her tiptoes and grazes against my now-hardening dick, the sensation stalls the breath in my throat.

She stills when my hand drops to her shoulder, pausing her movements but also desperate to pull back the braid and press my lips to her pulse point, just to test if it races as wildly as mine. I might be mistaken, but I swear she pushes her hips back, pressing into me, both of us hissing when she finds the evidence of what she does to me. Her breathing turns into short pants.

What I wouldn't do to feel them being exhaled against my skin.

There was an electric current running through me earlier when we hugged. Now, a high-voltage wire wraps itself around me, dangerously close to touching the pool of desire sitting between us. I know the second it makes contact, electricity will flash, scorch, and burn.

It would be incredible.

Only, I'd be left burned at the end. Reeling from the aftermath of knowing what it would be like to have her only temporarily.

My hand flexes before reluctantly pulling away to plate the food up and grab us both some drinks.

The confused and dazed look in her eyes as we settle on the sofa across from each other has nothing to do with what happened in the kitchen. It can't be.

We sit on opposite ends of the sofa, splitting pad Thai, green curry, mini shrimp lettuce wraps, and dumplings. I could have sat in the armchair and played it safe; not allowed myself to be overcome by her intoxicating scent.

I'm glad I was a risk taker tonight.

We eat in silence, sharing brief looks in between bites. I don't watch TV often, it's more decorative than anything, and I panicked whether I should have put it on as we eat, but she seems content without it.

I could ask her how her day went.

Maybe I should ask her what recipes she's thinking of trying out next.

Check with her about what foods she likes.

I spend so much time overthinking what to say to her, that by the time we've finished eating, the moment has passed. She looks exhausted and is probably sore after sleeping on the hard floor of the bakery last night. We need to discuss what to do about convincing people we're an item, but that can wait until tomorrow.

You'd think I was the guest in this apartment with my rigid posture; spine flush against the sofa, shoulders back, and feet firmly planted on the ground. Whereas Quinn sits cross-legged, with Curly snoring at her feet. "You've probably had a long day. Tomorrow, after work, we should talk about how this is going to go."

"Ah, yes. I almost forgot why I was here." She smirks.

"I've never done this before, have you?" I wince. "Fuck, that's a dumb question, of course you haven't."

It sucks that the probability of being hit by a meteor is 1:840,000,000.

"How about we start with who knows this isn't real?" she asks and strokes Curly's ears.

"Patrick, Johanna, and Booth. Oh, and my sister, Florence."

"Cool, so basically your entire family. Are you telling your mom?"

My eyes clamp shut with a groan. "I promised Booth I wouldn't. It's a long story, but if you're not okay with that, I understand. Speaking of my mom, she's having family dinner this Thursday..." I grimace, but she seems to fill in the blanks.

"I'd love to come for dinner. Tell her I'll bake a cake." Quinn visibly gets excited as she straightens in her seat with bright eyes. Curly growls at the disturbance but when he sees it's her, he nuzzles in closer.

Leaning over, I scratch the top of his head. "He's really taken to you." *Which makes two of us.*

"He's a cutie pie. Did you and Jenna get him together?" There's a bite to her tone when she says my ex's name.

"No, after we broke up. He was found abandoned in the county over; no tags or anyone looking for him. I was watching Lottie one Saturday, and after a brief conversation about puppies, we found ourselves driving to the shelter to adopt him."

She shakes her head, smiling. "That little girl is going to rule the world. I'm both scared and impressed with her ability to influence people."

Chuckling, I nod my head. "Yeah, she's a force to be reckoned with."

She opens her mouth to speak, but it's replaced with a yawn, telling me that the evening is coming to an end. I just have one thing to say first.

"I want to look over your books for free. A full analysis and report."

"Graham, no, I can't le—"

My hand drops to her ankle, stopping her. "You will let me do it. You probably don't realize it, but you helping me is so much more than showing Jenna I'm over her. You staying here isn't a favor I need you to repay, or anything to do with this arrangement. I'm happy to give you somewhere to stay for however long you need. You're Jo's friend, and she'll have my balls for this, but she told me how much you were there for her when she returned to town. She wants to help the only way she knows how. So for Jo, let me help you."

As much as I love seeing her determined streak, I really hope she doesn't fight me on this.

She fiddles with the hem of her T-shirt, chewing on her lip

before mumbling, "Only if you're sure. I don't want to pull you away from your other clients or business with the restaurant. Just the bare minimum. I guess the rest we can figure out along the way." Her hand drops to where mine is still enclosed around her ankle and there's a softness to her voice now. "I know this isn't what we had planned, but I appreciate you and I'm glad we can help each other out."

I'm so tempted to squeeze her hand, but instead, I offer her a smile. "Me too."

Breaking our connection, she stands, reaching toward the ceiling, and giving me her back. I divert my gaze when the movement stretches her pants across her delectable ass.

We collect the plates and load them in the dishwasher; such a simple task made less mundane where she's involved. I walk her to her room, immediately shaking my head at how ridiculous the notion is. She's not going to get lost from the kitchen to her bed.

"I'll let you get some sleep. I'm across the hall if you need me." The second she opens the door, Curly trots in like he owns the place. "Hey, no, come here." I snap my fingers, but the little shit ignores me and hops up onto the bed.

"Looks like I have a sleeping buddy tonight." She laughs as he snuggles into her pillow.

"Lucky him," I grumble under my breath.

I'm so distracted by my traitorous dog, that I don't have time to prepare for what comes next. Quinn shuffles closer, balances on the tips of her toes, and places the softest of kisses against the scruff on my jaw. Heat blooms from where her lips touched me, spreading quickly across my body like a forest fire.

"I'll look after your wiener," the little minx teases, mischief flaring in her eyes.

With a soft smile, she pads into the room and shuts the door behind her just as I whisper, "Goodnight, honey."

After that whisper of a kiss, I know sleep isn't going to find me anytime soon.

I settle behind my desk, pull out the worn journal, and let my thoughts spill out onto the pages, feeling the weight lift with each doubt and worry. Only, today there are a lot more happy and funny moments to document.

There's so much I wish I'd asked her. Either way, it was one of the best evenings I've had in a long time.

Just like I thought, I burn through almost seven pages in my journal, filling them with my thoughts about today's antics. I read them back, surprised at how cheerful the last few paragraphs are.

There's no going back now. I can be mad at Booth all I want, but I'm the one who invited her into my home. I'm a sadistic motherfucker, clearly.

I haven't got the first clue of how to date a woman like Quinn, let alone fake it. Would she want to go out to dinner at my family's restaurant? I think I'd really like to see her there, sitting across from me, wearing something pretty.

~~Maybe I should get her a stool to reach the top shelves in my kitchen?~~ I like helping her.

She's mentioned going out to see the leaves change a couple of times now, and I can't stop imagining what she'd look like with the fall colors as her backdrop.

I think she'd like that.
She really likes the flowers, so at least
I'm doing one thing right so far.

My lips twitch as I recall the sparkle in her eyes when I brought her that first bouquet. I'd wanted to melt right into those liquid-gold orbs.

But like a swift kick in the chest, bitter reality sets in.

This has an end date.

It would be stupid of me to get attached—more than I already have.

I slam my journal shut and lock it away in my desk, along with my stupid, naïve heart that keeps tempting me out of my comfort zone and into danger.

This desire I have with Quinn is high risk and unpredictable.

She might be tiny, but she sure as hell has the ability to bulldoze me to the ground, and I know I'd never recover from a wreck like that.

CHAPTER TWELVE

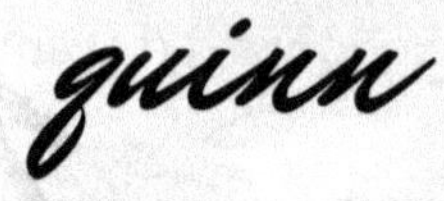

"One hazelnut latte and one decaf americano." I place the cups down on the table. "Can I get you guys anything else?"

The two customers shake their heads and politely thank me. When I'm satisfied they're happy, I sprint back behind the counter to fulfill the next order.

Torrential rain has been pelting against the windowpane all day, not letting up once, which brought in a ton of people needing shelter. Water rivulets run down the glass, and every time the door opens, the smell of rain and damp leaves follows in with a new customer. It's the perfect weather to soak in the tub, and I can't wait to use one of my new bath bombs after today's shift. My muscles and back are going to need it, and I plan on taking advantage of Graham's bathtub.

Today has been crazy. I've been running around nonstop since I flipped around the open/closed sign. It's great for business, I just wasn't prepared for it, considering it's a normal Tuesday afternoon, which proves how understaffed I am. The plan was to hire a part-time barista twelve months in, allowing me to concentrate on the baking and back-office stuff, but with the state of my finances right now, I don't see that happening anytime soon.

We survive and thrive, I remind myself as I pour hot water into the pot to let the chamomile leaves steep. Once that's done, I set two glasses of water next to the teapot, cup, and saucer, as well as a soy cappuccino on the tray, and head over to the waiting table.

I got weird vibes from these two when they walked in, and from the impatient looks they're throwing at me, the ten minutes I warned them about was too long.

"Here we go," I singsong as I set the tray down, hoping to ease the tension. "Sorry about the wait."

When the drinks are served, I smile at them both. "Can I get you anythi—"

"No ice?" the brunette butts in. She'd be pretty if she didn't have a permanent scowl on her face.

"Oh, no, sorry. The ice machine is on the fritz, I thought I told you when you placed your order. I can go an—"

"Are you sure this is soy?" the redhead snaps, my head pinging in her direction.

"Positive. I made it myself." My cheeks ache from the forced smile.

Kill them with kindness.

"It doesn't smell like it." She sniffs the foam that looks exactly like steamed soy milk and makes a disgusted face. "This smells like cow's milk. I'm going to need you to make another. I'm on a strict no dairy diet right now."

In through the nose, out through the mouth.

"Absolutely," I say through clenched teeth. Picking up the *soy* cappuccino without argument, it takes all my strength not to stomp away from them and throw the cup into the sink. Instead, I pour the *soy* cappuccino down the drain, prepare a double shot of espresso in the machine, and start frothing *soy* milk.

Again.

Customers like this are a rarity, but if you're going to work in the food and beverage industry, you better be prepared for them. Apparently "Karens" are worming their way into the younger generation, because these women don't look much older than my twenty-six years.

With the exact same drink as before, I return to their table with my patience hanging on by a thread.

"There we go. That wasn't so hard was it?" she says in a patronizing, nasally tone.

"No. How silly of me." I'm going to crack a tooth at this rate.

She opens her thin lips to make a comment, and from the viperous gleam in her eyes, it's not going to be a nice one. I'm saved by the bell when the door chimes to let me know another customer has walked in. I fix my face, making sure my smile is genuine, and turn around to greet them, but as I spin my heels, my eyes widen.

Graham is standing in the doorway, looking so deliciously handsome in a maroon cardigan, white button-down shirt, and navy slacks. His beard looks freshly trimmed today, giving me a great view of his strong jaw. So sharp it would be perfect in cutting the rye bread that's currently filling the bakery with that fresh baked bread smell.

It's been two days since I moved in with him, and we've hardly seen each other. He was called into the city yesterday, and our morning schedules have fallen so that when I'm ready to leave for work, he's out walking Curly. I usually don't leave the bakery until eight p.m—busy prepping for the following day and placing orders. We chat a little over dinner, but we're both so beat after our long days, we call it a night before ten.

There's a buzz of excitement seeing him now. I swear the corners of his lips start to pull up when spots me, but then his eyes narrow behind his glasses when he looks over my shoulder.

A high-pitched bark makes me jump. Curly is yapping away from where he's attached to the leash in Graham's hand. His other holds a bouquet of pale, yellow carnations.

The tiny dog lunges toward me, yanking Graham with him. At first, I thought he was aiming his dislike at me, but we've become quick friends, and it's clear now the difficult customers behind me are his target.

I drop to his level to distract him, tickling him under his chin and praising him in a baby voice. "Oh, you good boy. You have such a good sense of character, don't you? Yes, you do." Straightening, I look at Graham who is eyeing the two women suspiciously.

"What in the world is that?" I turn toward the owner of the voice. The question came from the redhead one, her eyebrows raised to her hairline as she glances between the dog and his owner with a snooty look.

"A dog," Graham responds dryly, though something is off with his demeanor right now. His shoulders are hunched and his eyes flit around the room cautiously. *Does he know them?*

"Clearly. But what are you doing with one? I didn't know you liked dogs. Seems a little too spontaneous for you." She looks at her friend and they laugh at a joke no one else heard.

Unease rolls off him. I can see him searching for a response, but they don't deserve one from him. They clearly know each other, and I have high suspicions they're the friends of Jenna's.

Spinning around, I look down at the table. "All good here?" They go to say something snarky, I'm sure of it, but I give them my back before they can respond and throw my final words over my shoulder. "Perfect. Enjoy your day."

With that, I grab Graham's hand, drag him past the register, with Curly hot on his heels. I love the little guy, but a kitchen is no place for a dog. We set him up with a bowl of water and tie him up just outside the back door.

"Well, they were delightful. Friends of she-who-shall-not-be-named, I presume?" I ask with my hands planted on my hips.

He nods. His eyes bounce between me and the tables around us, and he lowers his voice before speaking. "I've known them both since high school. Angela and Nina."

"Good to know Jenna keeps friends of the same breed." *That breed being little bitches.* "So those are the people we need to convince that we're in a relationship."

His Adam's apple bobs before he nods again. I don't blame him for looking nervous, because neither of us were prepared to do any convincing so soon.

Carpe diem and all that jazz.

"Okay, let's do this. Woo me."

"Now?" he sputters.

"Sure. What's your go-to move? How would you let people know that I'm yours?"

With a deep groan, he scrubs a hand across his mouth, and I just make out his muffled, "What have I gotten myself into?" He places the flowers on the table and pushes them toward me, my heart warming at the gesture.

Maybe I'm putting too much pressure on him and am getting carried away. The pleading look in his eyes confirms it. I give him my side profile, busying myself with the batch of cupcakes I've been trying to finish for the last hour. I only have half a dozen left to ice and I pick up the piping bag ready to get started. "Sorry, forget I said anything. We haven't even set any boundaries yet. How's your day been? It's been pretty cra—"

I'm cut off and gasp when something cold and sticky lands on my cheek. Blinking a few times, I look up to see Graham's hand hovering between us, fingers stained with royal blue buttercream frosting, and a look that's equal parts shock and amusement. His eyes are wide, but the smirk pulling at his lips says, *What are you going to do next?*

This side of him is new and undiscovered. And I love it.

"Excuse me. That was made with Madagascan vanilla. Do you know how expensive that is?"

"I'll get pods of vanilla shipped from the Indian Ocean just for you, honey."

Honey. There's that nickname again. The one that has my insides going all topsy-turvy.

I swipe two fingers across the same cupcake Graham destroyed and raise my hand toward him. "Two can play at that game."

With quick movements, I dive for his face, but he's quicker. My icing-smeared fingers are caught between his much larger hands, and he tugs me into him until our chests are crushed together.

That same rousing sensation I felt in his kitchen courses through me. It's stronger now, because this feels deliberate.

Slowly, so slowly he leans down, and brings his thumb to my cheek. With the gentlest of touches, he swipes the blue icing across my skin and over my lips. Intended or not, my entire body vibrates with delight, too stunned to lick the sweet mixture away.

Without breaking eye contact, he pops his thumb into his mouth and sucks it clean. I'm ready to melt into a puddle, but Graham isn't done yet. Far from it. "Sorry, missed a bit," he murmurs, his minty breath coasting across my face. "I'm going to kiss you now. Is that okay?"

Good. God. Who is this man?

I nod, and then his lips are on mine.

First kisses tend to be underwhelming and nervous from experience.

This is anything but.

I'm aware of every millisecond. It's brief, but he sure makes the most of it. When his tongue runs across my bottom lip, he hums in approval before pulling away.

I'm breathless as I watch him wipe at the corner of his mouth with his thumb.

I forget where we are, the aftereffects of the kiss having left me momentarily senseless, until the sound of cups on saucers and chatter starts to filter back in and we pull apart.

Graham kissed me.

Thankfully my voice doesn't shake like my knees when I finally speak.

"Well. What's the verdict?" He tilts his head in question. "Do you like sugary treats now?"

"Nah. I think there's something sweeter and more delicious waiting out there for me." His eyes are glued to my lips. Lips I very much want on mine again.

Apparently he's forgotten where we are, too, until his eyes scan the room. I follow his gaze and see they've landed on the now-vacant table where Jenna's friends were sitting, and it all makes sense.

It was all for them and I'm not even sure they saw it.

"Did they leave?" I spin around to face Graham, but he's already at the sink, trimming and arranging the bouquet of flowers he brought me. When he catches me watching him over his shoulder, his eyes snap back to his task, with a warm glow to his cheeks.

I internally kick myself for getting so lost in the moment that I forgot everything we do in public is for show. Any fuzzy, warm feelings I have toward him are foolish. That kiss was like nothing I've ever experienced, but he clearly had to ramp up the dial for effect.

Tingling lips and other body parts are natural. I mean, look at him.

Deciding to act like that interaction was an everyday occurrence, I pull out a large mason jar, fill it with water, and place it next to him.

I watch as he carefully arranges the carnations into the jar, knowing their yellow shade is going to look lovely up by the register.

"You remembered my favorite color?" I ask as my shoulder brushes his arm.

"I did. Are these flowers okay? I can get you others if you don't like them." He glances from me to the flowers with a concerned look on his face. How on earth would he think *any* flowers weren't okay?

"I'd accept weeds that you picked off the sidewalk. It's sweet, but really unnecessary."

He contemplates my words for a second as he places the remaining stems in the jar. "It always made my mom and sister happy. And I like seeing you smile." There's that delightful blush. "I've decided getting you flowers is a new clause in our agreement."

A laugh bubbles out of me. "Do I not get a say?"

"Nonnegotiable, sorry." From the quiver to his lips, he's holding in a smile.

"I see." I grin wildly. "Anything else you want drawn up in this mythical contract?"

With a look that makes me question if that kiss was fake, he shakes his head. "Laughing and smiling like that is my only ask."

The chime of bells reminds me I have a bakery to run and the whining from the back lets Graham know Curly is done waiting.

"Are you still okay for dinner at my mom's tomorrow? She's excited for you to come. Not that I'm trying to pressure you, it's just...she likes you. We all do, and you're always welcome."

I walk back toward the cash register, flashing a smile at the two new customers before facing him again. "I can't wait. Thank you for inviting me."

"Good. I'm glad." A small, satisfied grin slips free as his eyes track down the length of my body. I'm a mess of coffee grinds and spilled milk, yet something sparks in his gaze, making me flush. "I'll see you later."

With that, he makes his escape through the fire exit, leaving me standing in a puddle of overstimulated hormones and confused feelings.

I'm going to have to practice a lot of self-restraint not to get caught up in the unfamiliar, trancelike state he keeps leaving me in.

For a smart man, Graham Sadler is pretty clueless at how damn appealing he is.

CHAPTER THIRTEEN

graham

I KISSED HER.

No.

I kissed her and then licked her lips clean.

I've officially lost my mind.

I can never show my face in public again.

I'll have to move away.

What the fuck was I thinking, coming onto Quinn like that? We were supposed to set boundaries. To plan our dates meticulously, so the right people saw us at the right time.

Jenna's friends were quickly forgotten as soon as I swiped the icing across her face. It was like someone else had taken over my body, yet it was me. I was the one who played with her, kissed her, and made her smile.

It should bother me what Angela and Nina saw and what they're most likely reporting back to Jenna. It doesn't though. All that mattered was hearing her laugh and giving her a little break from what I know was a busy day.

That kiss though...

It left me feeling reincarnated.

My soul felt like it was starting afresh, in a new universe, with Quinn Jackson being at the center of it all.

Woo me, she had said. As if I had any idea how to woo an incredible woman like her. Yet, something overcame me. A need to show everyone she was mine. Our agreement was the last thing on my mind when I sealed my lips over hers.

I wanted to kiss her so there was no doubt in anyone's minds that we were together. Until she was breathless and craving me as much as I do her.

Only, I remembered who we were the moment the fog around us lifted.

I didn't miss the way she scanned the room, checking to see who had witnessed our intimate moment and like a bucket of cold water, realization of what it all meant washed over me. The only person I could be mad at, was myself. I'd willingly entered into this agreement despite my already budding crush on her. I should have known better than to allow myself to be swept up in *her*.

Which is why the second I had the flowers placed in the glass vase, I hightailed it out of there. Simply because I didn't want to submit her to the awkward aftermath. And I was a fucking coward.

Now, I'm minutes away from receiving a complaint from the tenant below as I stomp across the floor in a frenzy.

Did she look like she enjoyed the kiss? Sure, she nodded her consent, but it doesn't make it okay. Everything I've said and done plays on repeat in my head, and I analyze it for any clue that I've made her uncomfortable.

The sound of the front door opening halts my internal ramblings.

Quinn's back. Or perhaps a burglar has broken in to put me out of my misery.

"Hey, Graham, are you home?" Her voice carries through the apartment to where I'm hiding.

Does she sound...*happy*?

I nod my head, but she doesn't respond.

"Graham," she calls out. I'm about to nod my head again, when I remember she isn't Superwoman and can't see through walls. What is happening to me?

"Yeah," I croak out.

"Oh good, you're here." Her footsteps grow closer until they pause outside my door. "Can I come in?"

"Into my bedroom?" My eyes dart around the room in panic, but much like the rest of the apartment, there isn't much to see. That doesn't stop my heart rate from rising at the thought of us being in such close proximity again.

"If that's okay. Or maybe you could come out? I have something for you."

Probably a restraining order.

"S-sure. Come on in," I call out and stand in the center of the room.

The handle rattles and then turns slowly. The top of her head appears first, then her hazel eyes peek over the edge of the door. Without even seeing her mouth, the crinkled corners of her eyes tell me she's smiling. A good sign. When she spots me, she bounces into the room, vibrating with happiness, at what, I don't know.

Even when I'm freaking out, her delight is contagious. I want to bottle it up and save it for the miserable days.

She's always beautiful, but when she bubbles with excitement like this, it's impossible to look away.

Today's pop of color is the bright pink scrunchie holding her hair back in a low pony. She's still in the pair of light denim overalls from earlier, dusted in flour and splashes of coffee. Although Quinn could wear the dullest of outfits and still light up the room.

"Everything okay?" My voice wavers, because despite her

happy outward appearance, I'm still nervous about what she's going to say and if she will bring up this afternoon.

"I'm super. Sorry we didn't get to talk much at the bakery, it was a busy one today." It's then I notice her hands are behind her back, hiding something from my view, and her smile widens when she sees where my attention has landed. "Okay, don't be mad, but I got you a gift. Well, two gifts. One for you and one for Curly. I was scrolling mindlessly online, and I just knew you both needed these."

"What is it?" The guilty yet pleased look on her face has me worried for a completely different reason now.

She slowly reveals the gifts and it's near impossible to keep a straight face. In one hand is a teeny-tiny, knitted sweater; it's orange and decorated with pumpkins, vines, and leaves.

"Aren't they adorable?" she squeals.

Plural. Because in her other hand is a larger version of the sweater. "They're something all right." I point to the bigger one. "I take it that one is for me?"

Please say no.

"Yes! Oh my god, you guys are going to look so cute." She looks down at where my dog is prancing around her feet. I'm the one who rescued him, yet he worships the ground she walks on. Who can blame him though? "I thought you could wear it tomorrow for dinner?"

How can I deny her when she looks up at me with such hope and glee?

Gone is the worry about today's impromptu kiss. My main concern now is how to avoid my brothers, because they're going to have a field day when I rock up wearing this monstrosity of a sweater.

"I wanted to get you something to thank you for everything you've done for me. I'd usually bake a cake as a thank-you," she says with a sly wink.

Fuck my dislike for sugary snacks. I'd take tooth decay over this. I haven't even tried it on, but it's making me itch just looking at it.

"Well, here you go." She shoves them in my hands. "I'm gonna get washed up and start on dinner. Do you want to eat with me?"

"Oh, yeah, sure." She really isn't going to talk about the kiss, is she?

"Mr. Willis dropped off some squash after you left. I was thinking of making soup with it, if you like?"

"Sounds delicious."

With a clap of her hands and a megawatt smile that makes my heart double in size, she skips out of my bedroom.

And I'm left utterly confused.

"Okay." Quinn turns down the radio of my car. "What's our game plan?"

"Game plan?" My eyes bounce to hers, before moving back to the road. We're on our way to my mom's, and I wish I was half as calm as she is right now. She's in the passenger seat, and if I thought summer dresses were dangerous, the formfitting dress she's wearing will be my downfall.

Curves for days.

I almost choked on my tongue when I found her standing in my kitchen with a cake tin in her hands. Her hips, thighs, and ass are begging to have my hands molded to them. I want to watch my fingertips disappear into her soft skin, to leave my mark on it, to taste it.

But I can't.

So instead, I accept my fate: death by blue balls.

"We could wing it, like at the bakery yesterday..." She trails off, and I do my best not to react.

It's the first time she's acknowledged the kiss. Last night after she made a delicious batch of soup, neither of us brought it up, choosing to talk about other things instead. I didn't mind, but it was clear we were both avoiding the subject.

Apparently now is the time to discuss the boundaries we should have set from day one.

"I'm sorry about that." My fingers tighten around the steering wheel. "I shouldn't have put you on the spot like that. It was inappropriate."

"You're a really good kisser."

She gasps as my foot slams on the brake pedal with a little too much force as we near a stop sign, jolting us forward before being snapped back by our seat belts. Curly barks from Quinn's lap—or maybe it's in protest to the sweater she wrestled him into.

Did I hear her right?

"Shit, sorry," I groan and turn to find her laughing and brushing her bangs back into place.

"It's fine." She smiles and then glances through the passenger window. "Is this your mom's neighborhood? It's lovely."

"Quinn," I say, trying to catch her attention as she takes in the row of Victorian-style coastal homes. "At no point in this agreement are you required to kiss me."

"I don't mind." She shrugs. "Did you grow up in the same house your whole life?"

"Quinn."

She whips her head toward me, looking all innocent. "What's up?"

"No kissing. Hand-holding only." My body is turned to fully face her now with my arm hooked around the back of her headrest.

"I don't mind if you kiss me. I'll allow some light petting too."

"Jesus Christ." My head falls backward. "Why are you so relaxed about this all?"

"I dunno. I think one of us has to be." Her hand falls to the arm I have draped over the wheel, and when I find her gaze already locked on mine, there's no looking away. "I've said it once, I'll say it again. You're helping me out big time—with the bakery's books, letting me stay at your house this week, even being my friend. So if the opportunity arises and a bit of tonsil hockey is required, I'm down. You have my permission. Let's just hope those two wenches saw us yesterday."

The question is out of my mouth before I can stop them. "Why are you helping me?"

Her eyes are warm, but a sad smile pulls at her mouth. "When I was growing up, I didn't have a lot of people in my corner. No friends. Practically no family. I always promised myself that I would give back to the people in my life, to make up for the times I've been let down or hurt. It makes me think I'm putting good juju back into the universe. You're a good one, Graham, and you deserve an extra person in your corner."

Without another word, she pats me on the hand, and twists the volume dial to fill the car with music again. Speechless, my foot finds the gas pedal, and with Quinn singing next to me, I continue our journey to my childhood home. During the short ride, I decide anyone would be lucky to have someone like her in their corner, yet she chose *me*.

I had a very fortunate upbringing, with my parents being able to put all four kids through college and having a roof over our heads. It's the memories we made together that I'm most grateful for though.

We grew up with a small forest in our backyard, the scent of pine mingling with the salt air. The house is exactly as I remember it when I was younger. The white cladding wrapped around the exterior remains the same; a perfect backdrop for the pale pink, blue, and purple hydrangeas that will be back in bloom next summer.

"Wow," Quinn whispers beside me. "It must have been amazing growing up here." She gasps, and I follow her line of sight through the windshield. "Get out, you have a tire swing?" There's a forlorn expression on her face. I've tried a couple of times to inquire about her childhood, and from what she revealed minutes ago, I don't think we had the same experiences.

"You wanna go on it?" I turn off the engine and climb out.

She hurries to follow, with my dog trotting right behind her, and meets me at the hood with wide eyes. "Now?"

"Why not? C'mon." I unlatch the gate leading up the path and head toward the side of the house. The tall oak tree has been here since before the house was built, draping it in shadows and protecting it from the harsh easterly winds.

Quinn's footsteps crunch over the blanket of leaves covering the lawn; spots of orange and yellow sitting against the bright green blades. The sky is clear today, but the ground is waterlogged from the heavy rain we had yesterday.

"You'll have to trade those for boots soon." I nod to her muddy sneakers.

She looks down. "I can't imagine I'll be doing much walking, but I have a pair of old hiking boots. Even though the weather in California was nothing like this, I remember growing up wishing I had a pair of yellow rain boots. A girl in my class brought in a photo album from a family vacation for show-and-tell, and I remember being so jealous when I saw pictures of her in yellow rain boots." Her hand swats at the air, as if to shoo away the idea. "So dumb of me."

I want to ask what she brought in for show-and-tell but think better of it. Instead, I grab hold of the old tire and pat the worn, black rubber. "Right, hop up. Or do you need help, shortcake?"

"Rude." She sticks out her chest proudly, drawing my eyes downward. "You won't be able to pick me up anyway."

That has my eyes snapping to her face. "Wanna bet?"

I step forward, and before she can make a break for it, I scoop her up and deposit her on top of the tire. The weight of her means nothing to me; I'm just thankful for the excuse to feel her pressed up against me again.

She's still laughing when I grab hold of the rope and rock her gently back and forth. "You're just showing off your muscles." Booth must be rubbing off on me, because I flex said muscles when she wraps her hand around my bicep. "I felt that, you meathead."

"I have no idea what you're on about." I chuckle, and she laughs hysterically when I puff out my chest, the sound a melodic masterpiece I want to play on repeat.

She leans back, taking control of the swing, and her smile widens every time she flies by me. How easy it would be to brush my lips across that smile.

A few steps is all it would take.

Before I get carried away, my older brother's voice interrupts us.

"What the fuck is that hideous thing you're wearing? Wait a min—oh, this is brilliant. The dog is wearing a matching one."

My eyes shoot daggers at Patrick. "It's my new sweater that *Quinn* bought me," I reply, before mouthing, *Don't say a fucking thing.*

"Oh. It's, uh, nice?" he says, but shoves his fingers down his throat when Quinn isn't looking, earning him a slap across the back of the head. "If you two love birds are done out here, Mom is itching to see you both. Almost as itchy as that sweater." He whispers that last part with a barely contained laugh.

"If you don't stop, I'll tell Mom you've been researching rings," I hiss.

His eyes flare. "Don't you dare."

I wouldn't, but my threat does the trick.

We grab the cake from my car and follow Patrick into the house, wiping our shoes on the welcome mat before kicking them off. Lottie's happy squeal is heard through the house when Curly scampers into the den to greet everyone.

"I'm nervous," Quinn confesses quietly next to me.

"Why?" I help her out of her jacket and hang it up in the closet.

"What if she doesn't like me?" This version of Quinn is rare; white-knuckling the cake tin in her hands, chin tucked to her chest. It's similar to the side I saw when she wanted to ask for help but didn't know how to.

She's quelled my nervousness plenty of times in the few short days we've been living together. And that's what I want to do for her now.

My thumb and forefinger lightly pinch her chin to raise her gaze to meet mine. "That's impossible. She always gushes about you after a visit to the bakery. And not just about the cakes. But *you*."

"This is different. What if she sees right through our act then hates me for lying to her? I don't do well with people not liking me. It's a terrible character flaw."

"I can tell you with all the confidence in the world, my mother could never hate you." I drag the pad of my thumb over her skin, grazing her plump bottom lip. "You're very difficult not to like...believe me."

The honesty in my words sparks an ember in those golden irises, but just as she goes to speak, we're interrupted yet again.

"Did I hear 'Mother'?" the woman herself calls as she walks around the corner and my hand falls to my side.

Hair the same sandy shade as mine sits just below her jaw,

with streaks of gray framing her face. Icy blue eyes crinkle further when she spies the woman standing beside me. She's so eager to greet her, she practically barges past me on her path to wrap Quinn up in a hug.

"When Booth told me you were coming I just couldn't believe it." She throws an angry glare over her shoulder. "My middle son somehow failed to tell me he was dating; let alone that it's with the woman whose carrot cake I dream about."

"Thank you so much for having me." When Quinn is free from the embrace, a surprised expression lights up her face, and the warm welcome has clearly quashed her nerves. "Speaking of carrot cake..." She pulls back the lid of the cake tin.

My mom loops her arm through Quinn's. "You can come every week. Everyone else is through here."

Without a backward glance, Quinn is carted away toward the chatter of voices coming from the den.

Booth decides to emerge the second they disappear, a guilty look on his face. "I guess you can never stop fake dating her, or risk breaking our dear mother's heart."

Fucking Booth.

graham

She walks in and steals
Not just my words but my breath
I don't want them back

"QUINN, SWEETHEART, DO YOU TAKE CREAM OR SUGAR IN YOUR coffee?" my mom asks.

She's been buzzing with excitement since the moment we walked through the front door, peppering me with questions all evening. *How did you two meet? Where was your first date? How did you know she was the one?*

I managed to avoid two of the questions, but my own mother was close to punching me when I said we hadn't been on a date yet.

"Just creamer, please. Thanks, Claire." Quinn is next to me on the sofa, with Jo and Patrick on her other side.

It's a full house this evening. Jo's dad, George, is chatting to Dex and Booth in the corner; the latter having had nothing but a smug smile on his face all evening. Clearly, his plan is working, because all of our mother's usual matchmaking questions have been aimed at me.

"Uncle-Graham's-Girlfriend-Quinn, what are you dressing up as for Halloween?" my niece loudly asks from her spot on the rug where she's playing with a pile of LEGO.

"Her name is just Quinn." Patrick laughs.

"Ohhh. Sorry." She giggles. "Just-Quinn, what are you dressing up as for Halloween?"

This kid. Cute as a button and sometimes too smart for her own good.

"Well, *Just*-Lottie, I thought I was a little old for dressing up. What do you think I should be?"

Lottie taps a finger on her nose, contemplating her answer, before pointing it in the air triumphantly. "A lobster!"

"That's a good one. What are you being this year?" Quinn asks.

"I wanted to be Rapunzel." She aims a pout at her dad. "But Daddy said no."

"And we all know why that is." Johanna laughs, while my older brother groans and drops his head into his hands.

"That's what you get for canoodling with Johanna at your own daughter's party." Dex snickers before giving George an apologetic look.

Dex isn't wearing his hearing aid, but he has no issue lip reading the slew of insults Patrick mouths at him, causing him to chuckle.

"Uncle Gray." My niece directs her attention to me now. "Will Just-Quinn be nicer than the old one?"

"Lottie," Patrick warns, while the rest of the room grows quiet.

It's great to know my ex left a lasting impression on my niece—who was three when we broke up. I don't blame her; she's only asking what everyone else is thinking.

"What?" Lottie asks with a sassy shrug. "She never played

with me. Just-Quinn smells like sugar and dresses pretty. She can stay."

I think I stun everyone silent—me included—with my next words. "She's very pretty and I'd like it if Just-Quinn stays too."

Most people in the room would presume I'm saying this to keep up the façade. When really, I hardly thought that statement over before I blurted it out. Such an uncharacteristic moment for me, however it didn't feel unnatural.

Planned or not, it was the truth.

"From experience, once Lottie makes her mind up about coupling people together, there's no telling her otherwise," Jo whispers in my ear, looking between Quinn and me. She's not wrong. Out of all the meddling that went on between her and Patrick, Lottie was the chief instigator.

"I happen to love games. Especially LEGO." Lottie's eyes fly open at Quinn's words, and she starts bouncing on her knees.

"You wanna play LEGO? I'm making a fairy kingdom. Uncle Boo usually plays but he said his back hurts today and can't sit on the floor with me."

"It does hurt," Booth chimes in. "I'm getting old, you little toad."

Quinn doesn't need to be asked twice. She slides off the sofa and settles next to my niece with her legs tucked under her round ass. When I manage to drag my eyes away, they meet the delighted smile of my little brother, who just caught me ogling.

Even without her luscious figure tempting me at every turn, how can I not look at her when, in the last two hours, she's fit in with my family like she's been coming to these gatherings for years?

In our decade-long relationship, I didn't witness anything close with Jenna and my family as I've seen tonight. Jenna was quiet at dinners, getting lost in the jokes and laughter of my siblings. She was never made to feel left out but was either too distracted on her phone or chose to be aloof. The minute we were alone, she'd be moaning about one of Booth's jokes or how she felt my dad didn't like her. There was always something to gripe about. Eventually she stopped coming. And I gave up inviting her.

That wasn't long after my dad passed.

Yet when I mentioned earlier to Quinn that we didn't have to stay long after finishing dessert, she looked disappointed. Quinn wasn't just joining in with the laughter around the dinner table; she was the reason behind it with her animated storytelling about her travels across the country. Even promising to Lottie to show her the van when it's fixed.

Everyone is drawn to her.

The sensation building in my chest as I watch her play with my niece, has to stop. This is fake. Temporary. Wanting her isn't an option, because she's too good for me, so why even entertain the idea?

A nudge to my arm has me turning to find Jo looking at me curiously. "How's it going between the two of you?"

Even though my mom and George aren't in earshot, I keep my voice low. "It's fine. I think. It's just...I'm absolutely in over my head."

"How so?" Patrick peers around Johanna's shoulder.

"There's no way people are going to believe we're actually together." I sigh.

"Word on the street is that you two were caught in quite a heated moment at the bakery yesterday," Jo supplies with a playful smile. "Even Mrs. Stewart was overheard talking about it. It didn't come across as unbelievable to her."

That surprises me but I'm still not convinced. "She's so different from Jenna. Which isn't a bad thing. Far from it," I rush out. "She's so different from me too."

"As cliché as it is, opposites do attract," Patrick adds. "Now, let's say this wasn't fake, would you be doing anything different than you are now? Minus the roommates situation."

Would I?

Probably not—though, I can't see myself ever having found the courage to talk to her. I spent the better part of the summer drafting out multiple texts to her, only for me to delete each one. Mostly because I'd convinced myself any interactions with her would be awkward and tumble weed inducing.

But they're far from that. They're fun, genuine, purposeful.

"No. I wouldn't," I reply earnestly.

"Then keep doing what you're doing. I think you'll be surprised with the outcome." Jo squeezes my arm before changing the subject. "Question. Would Jenna mind if I wore a white, floor-length gown to the wedding?"

Shaking my head with laughter, I bump my shoulder with hers. "I didn't take you for the vengeful type."

"Pfft. She once told me she suspected my skin was breaking out because of all the cheese I ate. The fucking audacity."

"Uh-oh! JoJo swored," Lottie shouts, holding out an open palm. "One dollar, please."

With an eye roll, Jo pulls Patrick's wallet from his back pocket and drops a bill onto Lottie's hand. "Love, you need to start carrying your own dollars if you continue to curse in front of her. She's got bionic hearing."

"But you're my sugar dad—" Patrick clamps a hand over her mouth, pulls her into his side, and kisses the tip of her nose.

"Pat, did we put in the application for this year's Fall Fair?" Booth calls from across the room, thankfully halting the PDA going on beside me.

"Yeah, I dropped it off at the town hall last week." Patrick turns to Quinn. "Hey, you should apply, they're accepting applications for a few more days. The bakery would make a killing."

Excitement takes over her features and she opens her mouth, but then something snuffs it out, and her eyes dim. "Is it…umm…free?" she asks, tucking a strand of hair behind her ear.

"We wish," Booth replies. "It costs four hundred dollars for the table and then another two for the permits. More if you want to sell alcohol."

Quinn's bubbly and positive demeanor fizzles out, and I hate it. It's irrational for me to be mad at Booth, he's answering her question, but I really want to throw a cushion at his idiotic head for breaking her spirit.

Since that morning at the bakery when Quinn was crying in my arms, panicking over money and how she couldn't afford to fix her van—her home—and pay for a hotel, I'd guessed money was a little tight for her. It happens to the best of us, especially when you're first starting out as a business owner. It's obvious pride tends to stand in her way, and even now that she's agreed to let me help the bakery and live with me free of charge, I get the feeling she's itching to repay me.

Her earlier comment about not having people in her corner replays in my head.

I hate that she can't have this. I hate seeing her sad. I hate that I can't fix it.

She deserves all the things that bring her joy. The same type of joy she effortlessly brings others.

Theoretically, I'm not the guy to fix it. But I can sure as hell try.

And, like Jo said, maybe the outcome will surprise me.

"WOULD YOU RATHER HAVE LOBSTER CLAWS OR OCTOPUS tentacles for hands?"

"Easy. Tentacles. Next."

My roommate lets out an exasperated sigh. We've been playing this game for half an hour, each question more ridiculous than the last, but apparently my quick, logical answers aren't the way to do it.

Quinn arrived back at the apartment minutes after I finished work, ending her day much earlier than usual. My head was aching following hours of back-to-back meetings with difficult clients, so when she suggested we walk Curly together, I couldn't say yes quickly enough.

We're strolling along the boardwalk that spans the length of the bay, the old planks creaking with each step as we make the most of the nice weather this evening. A few clouds hang in the sky, each painted a pastel pink or purple to match the setting sun, our lungs filling with fresh, ocean air. The temperature is quickly dropping the closer we get to November, and we'll soon be trading flannels for thick, winter coats.

A small line of boats bob back into the bay, the shouts and cheers from the fishermen taking in today's haul ricochets off the row of colorful houses facing the water. Booth was down here first thing this morning when the first load of boats returned, ensuring the restaurant had the freshest catch on the menu. He took a class in how to filet fish a couple of years ago, allowing him to purchase it all dockside, rather than waiting for the fishermen to prep the fish elsewhere.

"Why not lobster claws?" Quinn asks with a poke to my bicep.

"It's highly inconvenient."

My hand hooks around her hip when a truck speeds past us, and I maneuver her until I'm between her and the street. She's too busy muttering away about sea creatures to even notice she's switched sides.

We stop so Curly can sniff a trash can, and while Quinn

stares out at the choppy waters, I take in her flushed cheeks and windswept hair.

I avert my gaze when she turns to look at me and asks, "And tentacles aren't?"

"Why won't you just let me be happy with my tentacles? If you want lobster claws, you have them. I've made my decision."

"Yesssss." She drags that one syllable out with an eye roll. "But you have to explain your answer."

"Show me the rule book that says that."

"Graham, there is no rule book." She blows out a frustrated breath—it's quite fun winding her up. "Dems the rules, pal."

Curly trots ahead again, tail wagging, and we follow the light pitter-patter of his paws. I look down at Quinn, arms swinging as she keeps a tight hold of his leash. She's a stubborn thing when she gets frustrated; her nose crinkles and a little dent creases between her brows.

I give it some thought before replying. "You can multitask with tentacles. Plus, claws make it hard to hold certain things."

"Like what? Actually, I guess it would be hard for you to put your glasses on or type on your keyb—*ohhhh*. You wouldn't be able to jerk off." Her free hand is thrown up in the air, as if to say *duh*.

I almost go flying into the frigid waters when I trip over my feet at her blunt observation. A cold bath is probably what I need when she talks like that. She does this a lot, says things with zero filter, and now I'm thinking about rubbing one out. With her in the room. God knows I've had enough cold showers since she moved in, especially when she skips around the apartment in those tiny shorts that mold to her ass like a second skin.

Imagining her in those shorts is not helping the situation between my legs.

She's not wrong—the idea of holding my dick between a

pincer and a claw does not sound appealing. I just didn't plan on telling her that was the main reason behind my decision.

"So, you'd choose lobster claws?" I gruff, trying my best not to let images of Quinn watching me intimately flood my brain.

"Oh, heck no. We'd be tentacle buddies."

"And your reasoning?"

"Same as you." Her shoulders jerk.

Fuck. Shit. Fuck. Now I'm imagining her, spread out, hands drifting down to the apex of her thighs. Moaning and writhing under the caress of her delicate fingers as I tower over her. Desperate to touch and taste.

"I looked over that report you gave me." Thankfully her words pull me out of my inappropriate thoughts. "There were a lot of things on there I wasn't clear about. Could we talk over it one day this week?"

"Yeah, sure. I can swing by the bakery—"

My sentence is cut off by the ringing of Quinn's phone. There are so many pockets to her jacket, it takes some patting down until she finally locates it before stabbing at the screen to accept the call.

"Hello?" We carry on walking as she talks on the phone, nodding along and saying *okay* to whomever she's speaking to. My hand hovers behind her, guiding her, and ready to catch her if she loses her footing. "Oh. Is it really that bad?" Her shoulders slump farther with each question and answer until all the spirit she had in her has vanished. "Right. I'll...I'll have to look into that and get back to you. Thanks for keeping me updated, Ricky. See ya."

Ricky. The owner of the garage I recommended. From the crushed look on her face, the news he's just delivered isn't good.

She ends the call but doesn't look up from her phone, even after it locks, her eyes stay glued to the black screen.

"Hey. What did he say?" I ask quietly.

A corner of my heart cracks and breaks off when she sniffles. Goddammit, people need to stop upsetting this woman because I'm going to get a savior complex. It guts me in ways I can't explain when her bright spark dims.

I bend at the knees and duck my head, bringing us to a standstill. She still refuses to meet my gaze, so with the tip of my pointer finger on her chin, I tilt her head up slowly.

"Honey, what have I got to do so I can see that beautiful smile again?"

The corner of her lips pull in, catching the tears streaking her rosy cheeks. "I don't know." Her voice is so weak and full of turmoil. "My van. *My home.* There's more damage to it than we thought. It's not even just the electrics the rats have chewed through—which costs thousands alone—the air filter is useless. The radiator is destroyed. The rats trashed it with all their nesting. It's not only unlivable right now, but unsafe." She worries her lips between her teeth, chin wobbling, and for whatever reason, those glassy, golden eyes look at me like she could...*No.* Like she does trust me.

Quinn looks at me like I hold all the answers in the universe—its stars, galaxies, and all undiscovered planets. And, fuck, do I want to be that person for her.

I don't just want to hold the stars in the sky for her; I want to create a million more, to see them twinkle in her eyes.

"Graham," she whimpers. "What do I do?"

From what I've picked up, that question isn't easy for her. I suspect she's spent a long time fending for herself, too scared to ask for help or perhaps not having the right people around her.

She's headstrong to a fault, and I sense there's more behind that.

The bakery is successful. I've seen the figures, but it's in its infancy. Any new business owner knows it's tough to make a profit within the first two years; you're funneling in your own money constantly, investing in new equipment, and that's before you even hire staff or expand.

For Quinn to be in a position where she has to find temporary housing and fix a rare Volkswagen van that doubles as her home, it's no wonder why panic and worry morph her features.

I'm not just playing with fire with my next proposal, I'm dancing in the flames barefoot.

It wouldn't change much. We'd still play along with this fake dating scheme. I'd still help out the bakery. And she would still live with me.

Just for a little longer than planned.

As she patiently waits for me to respond, all doe-eyed and pretty, I step closer to brush away a tear with my thumb before it can track down her cheek. "I think what *we* do is go and get the rest of your stuff from the van. Stay with me—for now. Until you can get it fixed and Ricky says it's safe to live in. It makes sense. You're already living there. Plus, Curly likes your belly scratches."

And I like you in my home.

I see her turning the idea over in her head; eyes darting between mine. I expect her to fight me on this, and I'm glad she doesn't, I just don't like what she says next. "It would stop anyone from questioning our relationship."

That reason hadn't even come to mind, simply because I was allowing myself to get excited about the idea of Quinn in my space. Her scent, smiles, and warm presence mine to cherish and hide away from the world, like they were made for me. But it would be a tragedy to civilization to keep her to myself.

I never knew the second deadly sin would be one of my biggest vices. Yet here I am; greedy for her.

"That too," I stubbornly agree.

"I need to pay rent though. It's almost winter. An extra person living with you is sure to increase the electricity and heating bill. I'll buy my own food. And walk Curly every day." Her voice rises with each suggestion.

"It's not necessary, Quinn. Trust me. I'm not strapped for cash. It means you can save the money needed to fix the van quicker, right? Don't argue with me on this one, please." I nod at Curly, who has fallen asleep on my shoe. "And I enjoy walking this guy. Maybe...we can do it together?"

"I'd like that." She smiles, and hope filters back in as her posture straightens and the tears stop. "I'll cook. Every night. No argument." That last part comes out all deep and surly, and I know she's mocking me by the cheeky grin on her face.

"What a hardship for me that will be."

She pulls her shoulders back, and I'm unsure what her next move is going to be. When her hand falls between us, I think we're about to shake on it—like my awkward gesture the other week.

That's not what happens.

Her fingers wrap around the collar of my sweater to tug me down a few inches. Balanced on the very tips of her toes, her lips find their way to the same spot she kissed the other day.

I'm a reasonable man, never one to make rash decisions or let my head float in the clouds. I know what my next steps will be. I strategically plan my life.

There was no planning for Quinn Jackson.

I don't prepare myself for how this is going to end.

The probability of me falling for her even more is inevitable.

And the chances of her feeling the same: 1,000,000:1.

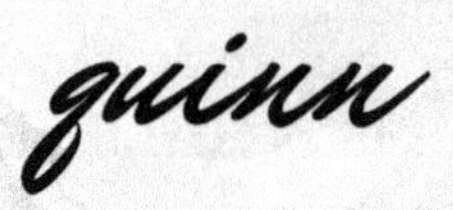

CHAPTER FIFTEEN

I'm really horny.

To the point where it's distracting and causing me to make stupid mistakes.

When Jo came in for her morning coffee, she almost sprayed it all over the cash register when she took her first sip and found I'd pumped ten times the normal amount of syrup in it.

I served Mrs. Stewart a pot of tea made with cold water. She was not happy, and for once, her can-I-speak-to-the-manager attitude was 100 percent justified. It's a good thing I'm the manager.

My trusty vibrator usually does the trick in sating me, but I've been too nervous to whip it out, conscious of the thin walls in Graham's apartment.

I haven't had sex in almost a year or touched another man since moving to Sutton Bay.

Well, apart from when Graham kissed me.

Which is irrelevant because it wasn't real.

So why did it feel so good?

"Because I'm a horny little tart," I mutter as I mess up yet another tulip in the latte foam.

"What was that, sweetheart?" Claire asks sweetly as she waits for her take-out coffee.

Perfect. Now Graham's mother thinks I'm a horn dog. I should probably tell her it's her son's fault anyway, because he is a walking, talking contradiction. Lethally silent. Death by his spicy scent, knitted sweaters, and sweet gestures.

I don't think that man knows what a snack he is, which is a crime.

Not only am I stuck under the same roof as Mr. Sexy Spectacles for the foreseeable future, but he's the reason I'm hornier than usual, and I can't do anything about it.

Despite my inner turmoil, it's easy to put on a happy face when you're around Claire. She's not much taller than me, but more petite compared to my voluptuous figure. The nervousness I had about dinner last week quickly disappeared when she embraced me like a mother is supposed to. The evening was some of the best fun I've had in a long time. My favorite part was seeing how relaxed Graham was around his family; joking with his brothers, helping his mom, and playing with Lottie.

At no point was I made to feel like an outsider. There was laughter, inside jokes, sentimental moments, and each second that I spent with his family, my smile and heart grew in size.

It was also a stark reminder that I have never experienced a dinner like it before. Have never known a mother's love or reminisced over family pictures that line the walls of a home. I'm not even sure there are baby pictures of me.

It was bittersweet, but I've been holding onto the sweet.

"Oh, just me mumbling away to myself," I say with a flick of my wrist and slide the latte over the counter. "What are your plans for today?"

"I video-called with my baby girl this morning. She landed

in Puerto Rico a couple of days ago and was going on a rain forest tour later this week. I told that little jet setter we have forests here she could stomp around in." Claire rolls her eyes, making light of the situation. It's clear she misses her youngest child. "You and Florence could probably spend hours swapping stories about your travels. Anyway, has my darling boy been treating you right?"

With an awkward laugh, I tap out the used coffee grinds into the trash and top up the beans in the grinder. "He's a gentleman. We, um, didn't plan on living together so soon, but it's working out. No lover's quarrels yet." I hate lying to her. "All your boys are wonderful, but Graham...he's really been the best surprise since moving to town."

My anxiety eases with that last part, because it's far from being a lie.

"I'm glad to hear it. They're all so different in their own ways, but Graham has always been a quiet soul, with a strong heart. Some people don't know how to appreciate it..." Her brow furrows as her words trail off, clearly wanting to say more. Graham said she doesn't know about Jenna cheating, but I don't think he gives his mom enough credit for how perceptive she is.

"Anyone would be stupid to not see what a catch he is. I'm sure when he finds the right gi—I mean, I'm so...he...um..." Shit on a stick, I'm blowing our cover. The backs of my thighs are sweating as I scramble to find the right response.

I have plenty of nice things to say about him. He's an amazing listener. He has a great butt. Pulls off a pair of glasses like it's nobody's business.

I'd really like to steam those glasses up.

Oh my god, not helpful. The panic is fueled by the fact I've been thinking dirty things about her son all day.

"Well, it's good to know he's leaving you speechless." With a tap on the counter, Claire winks at me and saunters over to say hi to a table of ladies in the corner.

I'm close to smashing my face into the bowl of cookie dough behind me, when the chime of the bell pulls my attention to the front door. Jo, Patrick, and Dex wave at me before spotting Claire. Patrick goes over to speak to her, while Jo and Dex head my way.

"Hey, guys. What's going on?" I ask.

"The peepers have started to accumulate," Dex groans.

"Ah, yes, the infamous leaf peepers. Wait! Does that mean the leaves have finally changed?" I've been dying to see Maine in the fall. I doubt the pictures Jo has shown me do the real thing any justice.

"That's why I'm here." Jo smiles widely. "I promised I'd take you to the best spot in the state to see the trees changing. Do you think you could close the bakery early on Wednesday?"

"Absolutely, I can. Does two work?"

"Perfect. I'll pick you up then."

Slapping my hands together, I bring the tips of my fingers under my chin, with an ear-to-ear grin on my face.

After placing an order of coffees to go, they say their good-byes. The rest of my shift goes by quickly, and before I know it, it's closing time and I'm on my way back to Graham's apartment.

All of my things have been packed up until the van is repaired. Whenever that is. I can't afford for Ricky to start work anytime soon, and it breaks my heart that Nelly is stowed away in a damp, cold garage without me. Apart from my suitcase of clothes, my kitchen, living, and bathroom pieces have remained in boxes in Graham's living room since we collected them a couple of days ago.

Only, when I step into the apartment, they're nowhere to be found. And neither is Graham, who is probably out for a run.

He must have moved the boxes into my bedroom while he was working from home today.

Not thinking much of it, I refill Curly's water bowl and get started on dinner. I lived up to my word and have been making dinner for the two of us; tonight we're having tacos. After pulling out all the ingredients from the fridge, I open a cabinet, but instead of plain white plates and bowls, I'm met with shiny pink ceramic. Picking one up, my eyes drag over the palm tree print painted across the plate.

Unless Graham's taste has dramatically changed, these are my plates.

Dashing to the next cabinet, I whip it open. Alongside his plain white mugs sit two cactus-shaped ones. In the silverware drawer, the utensils have been replaced with my rose gold ones. Every cupboard, every drawer in the kitchen is filled with my things.

I pivot on my heels, run into the living room, and come to a sliding stop. Pom-poms. Are. Everywhere.

My cushions are placed perfectly on either end of the sofa —he's even karate chopped them. My lavender-colored blanket is neatly folded over the back of it. Little trinkets I've collected over the years are randomly set on the small coffee table.

The thumping in my chest increases in tempo with each new find, but when I spot my brightly colored photo frames on his shelves, I struggle to breathe. He unpacked all my belongings and placed them around his home.

But why?

The sound of the front door opening echoes through the apartment. My fingers drift toward my mouth to stop the tremble of my lips.

"Oh, hey." The thud of his sneakers and heavy breathing nears closer. "How was your day?"

With my back still to him, I raise a shaky hand toward the sofa, and croak, "You unpacked my things?"

The pad of his feet gets louder as he steps up beside me. "Yeah...is that okay?"

"Why?" His arm brushes against mine, the heat of his skin searing through my long-sleeved T-shirt.

"Did I overstep? Fuck, I did, didn't I? I'm sorry, Quinn, I should have asked. I thought it would make this place feel a little homier for you. I know how upset you've been over your van. I'll put it back." He steps in front of me, reaching to collect the blanket. My hand clamps around his sweaty forearm, stopping him.

His head slowly turns, eyes dropping to where my fingers are wrapped around his arm before they travel higher until our gazes meet. With a tentative step toward him, I close the space between us, his spicy scent mixing with the fresh air and something mouthwateringly masculine.

"You keep doing all these nice things for me, and I don't know how to repay you." My voice is barely above a whisper.

He relaxes a little, but there's tension brewing in his muscles. A lot like the rubber band of my self-control that is ready to snap. "I don't need you to repay me. Seeing you smile makes me...it makes me feel good."

A bead of sweat runs down the length of his neck and over his Adam's apple as he swallows deeply, before it disappears beneath the collar of his athletic T-shirt. When I look back up, my thighs clench. Those usual mossy-green eyes might as well be void of color with how blown out his pupils are. They're not lacking in emotions, though; they burn with desire, want, and tested patience.

Things between Graham and I have started to blur since that kiss in the bakery and each day, he seems to shed a layer of nervousness and self-doubt.

Right now, I can see the war going on in his head.

He wants to kiss me as much as I want him to do it.

I wasn't lying earlier; Graham is very much a gentleman.

But I don't want that side of him in this moment. Which is why I reach up with both hands, grip his cheeks, and slam his mouth down to mine.

It's not a sweeping kiss like the one we shared the other day. This is fever inducing. Obliterating the lines between us. Not a drop of hesitancy as our tongues tangle together.

A deep, hungry moan vibrates from low in his throat, and his hands fall to my hips to tug me close until our bodies are flush. I lean into his strong chest, the pounding of his heart beating against my own as he bends at the waist. His hands haven't stopped roaming my body from the moment our lips touched, and from how they keep drifting back to my butt, squeezing and cupping each cheek, I know he's an ass man.

Good thing I have a lot of it.

I'm so swept up in it all, I don't realize he's spun us around until he's gripping the backs of my thighs and hoisting me up on the back of the sofa. This new angle allows Graham to stand between my open legs, our mouths now at the perfect height.

I'm breathless, yanking at the front of his sweat-soaked T-shirt to stay upright as he kisses the ever-loving shit out of me.

Gone is the gentleman.

A gasp escapes me when he thrusts his hips forward, and the very hard, thick length of him presses into me.

When Graham's lips leave mine, I mewl—*fucking* mewl. Another desperate sound purrs from my throat when he starts trailing hot kisses down my neck while grinding himself into me. My legs hitch over his hips, drawing him closer, and I really wish his shorts and my jeans weren't in the way.

"Oh god, Graham," I moan, when he sucks at the skin behind my ear, causing me to wiggle my hips in search of the friction I'm desperate and aching for.

"Fuck. You taste like a dream come true." He licks my pulse point. "How can you feel so fucking right in my arms?"

"I don't know," I breathe out. My hands drift down his sides, fumbling to find the hem of his T-shirt, eager to feel the heat of his skin against mine. "Please don't stop."

"Why would I stop when you feel like you were made for me? Nothing has ever felt more perfect," he pants against my skin. "Tell me, Quinn. What does this mean?"

What does this mean?

Living together has tested my willpower, and sure, we're attracted to each other. Or at least I'm attracted to him. This can't go further than those feelings or disrupt the plan we have laid out though. If we catch feelings and things go south, this whole agreement would have been for nothing.

I can't let him down.

"It's just p-practice," I stutter, the lie tasting bitter on my tongue.

He freezes, going rigid beneath my hands. His head is buried in my neck, so I can't see his face, but I hear and feel his heavy breathing.

"Graham?"

The sound of his name pulls him from whatever stupor he was in. He's no longer draped over me but standing at his full height. Lips swollen, cheeks so beautifully flushed, with a bested look that shatters me.

He scrubs a hand across his mouth, wincing when he clenches his eyes shut before letting out a heavy exhale.

"I'm so sorry, Quinn."

I shoot to my feet. "What, why?"

"That wasn't...I shouldn't have done that." He can't even look at me.

His chin is tucked in tight to his chest, hands shoved in the pockets of his shorts, and shoulders hunched up to his ears. I've seen Graham get embarrassed before, but it's usually in an endearing, bashful kind of way.

He looks utterly humiliated right now, and I want to scream at myself for causing this.

"*I* kissed you, Graham. It's me who should be apologizing. I don't want to take advantage of all you've done for me." I go to take a step forward but think better. "We agreed that was only for public."

"There wasn't anyone to watch the show," he grits out.

Then he's turning away and striding to the front door.

The slam that follows his hurried exit makes me jump from where my feet have been glued to the floor, the sound echoing in my ears long after his escape.

That kiss was unexpected, but his words, spoken with such conviction as his hot breath coasted across my skin, they were what shocked me the most. If I know one thing about Graham, it's that he doesn't say anything without meaning it.

And as I glance around the home he's tried to make me feel welcome in, I know that I've gone and fucked it all up.

graham

THE SWINGING DOOR WHACKS ME IN THE BACK AS I STAND IN THE doorway of the kitchen.

The heat in here is an intense contrast to the chilly October air. The smell of roasted garlic and melted butter fills my nostrils.

No one has noticed my arrival, too busy plating up dishes or shouting out orders. Booth is behind the pass, and even under the bandanna wrapped around his head, you can see his brow furrowed in concentration.

"C'mon, this dish is dying on the pass here. Where are those fries? Kyle, I need that haddock boat in the next two minutes." His calm, firm tone is heard easily above the noise of pans clattering and sizzling food.

He's not a dick like most chefs I've interacted with. Sure, he's authoritative and will put pressure on his team when they need it, but he's earned their respect. It's clear from the chorus of *Yes, Chef*s he receives.

I didn't even think to check how busy Our Place was before I stormed in here, and it's clear my brother doesn't have time for my crap right now. I'm half turned to retreat, when he calls out, "Hey, Gray. You good?" Reluctantly, I face him, just as one of the servers walks in to collect two plates of food. "For table seven, Macy. Apologize for the wait."

Moving farther into the kitchen, I scratch the back of my head. "It's no big deal, I should have called ahead first."

Booth's eyes narrow as he tracks the movement of my hand. "Simon, take over the pass, would you? We've got two entrées left to send out and then I need someone to start prepping some more burgers and scallops."

"Yes, Chef," Simon, Booth's sous, says as he switches places with him.

Before I can even protest, he's untying his apron and washing his hands. "Let's go to the office."

There's no point in arguing, and let's face it, I came here to speak to Booth; to vent and run away from the humiliation of what just happened in my apartment.

We walk in silence to the office, and the moment the door clicks shut, I'm pacing and pulling at my hair. "I can't do it."

With a slow nod, he takes a seat on the cracked leather sofa in the corner of the room. He's quiet for a minute until he casually replies, "Okay."

"Okay? That's it? You're not going to ask questions?" I snatch my glasses off my face, my vision blurring while I massage the bridge of my nose.

"And convince your stubborn ass? Unlikely. If you don't want to continue with it, then call it off, simple. I can deal with Mom's matchmaking antics." He tilts his head and drapes an arm over the top of the sofa.

His reaction surprises the hell out of me, and I stand rooted to the floor. I expected him to fight me on this.

"It was stupid of me to even propose this idea to her."

All he offers is a limp shrug and one word. "Okay."

It's obvious what he's doing now. He's forcing me to explain why, without even asking.

I swallow down the urge to hide my words. "I really like her."

A quiet Booth is something I'm usually begging for, but his silence pushes me closer to verbalizing my feelings.

"I kissed her. Again. Or...she kissed me. But I stopped it."

"Why'd you stop it?"

Dragging my feet over to where he's sitting, I drop next to him with a sigh. "She called it 'practice,' and it reminded me it's all fake. It's going to be fucking torture pretending we're in a relationship until the end of November. I keep coming on too strong and doing dumb shit."

"So you're going to kick her out and stop helping the bakery?" he asks.

I blanch. "No. That's not fair to her. It's not her fault I have this stupid crush. I'll leave it up to her, but after today, I wouldn't be surprised if she's already packed her bags and left."

"At any point has she said or acted uncomfortable around you?"

Has she? I don't even know if Quinn is capable of getting uncomfortable; she's confident in her own skin and with her words. It's one of the things I find so lovely about her. It's also what scares me, because it proves how different we are.

"No," I reply. "We hang out a lot. Walk the dog. Eat dinner together. Watch TV. But we also...talk. It's easy with her. And fun."

"Like an actual couple..."

I don't bother responding to his comment, but he continues anyway.

"Maybe you should speak to Quinn first. Mom hasn't shut up about her since dinner." He shoves a hand in my face when I go to argue with him. "Hush, you robot. You like her, and honestly, I caught her looking at you a few times the other night like she'd forgotten it was all an act. I know you're nervous to get back out there, and I fucking despise that Jenna turned you into someone who doubts themself. I'm not going to pressure you, and if you need to tell Mom, I get it. Let me just say one thing before you throw in the towel.

"If there was any chance of her feeling the same, would you fight it or run with it? You can go on exactly as you are, doing things together as friends, but if the opportunity arises where you feel something more could happen, why waste it? It could turn out that the reward is greater than the risk. And you, my brother, deserve a hell of a lot."

I look at him in confusion. Mostly because that's the most he's ever said without cracking a joke.

"Christ," he groans. "I thought you were the smart one. Patrick is the levelheaded brother. We know I'm the best look —*ooof.*"

"I get it," I snap, pulling my fist back from his stomach.

The little shit laughs. "Treat this as a test drive. Show Quinn what a great guy you are—what it would be like to be your girlfriend without the official label. At the end of it, she'll realize she wants the real deal. I'm tired of seeing you hide yourself away because of one woman. And hey, if you get a little smoochy-smoochy, you're both winning." He waggles his eyebrows.

"You're an idiot."

"But you love me." He claps me on the back.

Could I do this until the wedding? Pretend to date her, with the end goal to make it real? Is there even the tiniest possibility she could return the feelings I've had since I first met her?

I like the way she makes me feel—wanted, needed, and valued. The exact way I want her to feel with me.

When I unpacked her boxes, I did it to make her feel comfortable in her temporary home. The look on her gorgeous face when she found all her things scattered around my apartment was one I wish I'd taken a picture of so I could cherish it.

She deserves to feel cherished.

Booth doesn't need my reply to know I'm considering it.

We stand at the same time. "You ran out of there faster than a greased pig, didn't you?"

With another swift punch to his gut and a murmured, "Thanks," I leave the restaurant. I make one stop on the way home, and with an apology in hand, I walk back into the apartment, armed to handle whatever Quinn has to say.

Only, she isn't alone.

She and Jo are snuggled up on the sofa, the purple blanket I was so close to laying Quinn out on draped across their legs, both with a steaming cup in their hands. They're so engrossed in whatever they're looking at on Jo's phone that they don't hear me come in. Before they spot me, I bolt into Quinn's room, where I find Curly snoozing on her pillow, and I lay the bouquet of yellow tulips next to the snoring hound.

Maybe today's bouquet will be her favorite.

I decide not to intrude on their girl time just yet, wanting to give her some space, so I hop into the shower and rinse away the sweat from my run and, sadly, the scent of her from my skin. Once I've changed into a plain white T-shirt and gray sweats, I make my way into the living room.

Standing a few feet behind them, I listen as they gossip about all the different customers they've served this week, but pause when I clear my throat, and their heads snap toward me. "Hi."

"Hey, Gray," Jo greets. I hear her, but my eyes are on the woman beside her. The smile on her lips looks subdued, nothing like the excited and wanton one she was wearing earlier.

"Having a girls' night?" I told Quinn she could have whoever she wanted over, and I meant it.

"No, but we do need one soon." Jo turns to Quinn. "I came around to plan out our itinerary for next week."

With my back to them, I grab a water from the fridge. "What's next week?"

"I'm taking Quinn out to Acadia. You remember the year we found that hidden trail?"

The plastic bottle crinkles under my grip. My heart drops. "Yeah, I know the one." I know it, because it's where I wanted to take Quinn to see the changing leaves. I had the perfect day planned.

"When are you heading up there?" Sitting in the armchair across from them, I keep my face void of emotion, not wanting to show my irritation. It's not Jo's fault she's being a massive cockblock.

"Wednesday. Dex was driving through the park on the weekend, and he said the trees had all changed." She turns to Quinn again. "I can't wait to see your face when we get there."

Yeah, you and me both.

I remind myself that I like Jo, and my brother loves her.

"Anywho," Jo sings and stands from her seat. "I better get going, we're Lottie-free tonight and might head to Shirley's for a drink. Do you two want to join us?"

Quinn and I share a look. "We're good," I reply at the same time she says, "I'm gonna pass, have fun."

We both know there's a lot to talk about once we're alone.

I walk Jo to the door. To Quinn, it looks like I'm walking our friend out, when in reality, I'm going to politely ask her to *Back the fuck off.*

"You're sick on Wednesday," I hiss.

She has the audacity to laugh in my face.

"I need to take Quinn to the park."

"You need to?" she asks, crossing her arms and quirking a brow.

"I want to. Please, Jo. I'll do anything." Jesus, I reek of desperation.

Something in my pleading tone or pathetic face must speak

to Jo, because her features soften. "Fine, but I want iced coffees delivered to the restaurant every day until the end of the year."

"You and your freaking iced coffees," I grumble.

She peeks around the corner before stepping closer. "Why don't you just invite her? I don't mind faking the flu, but wouldn't you rather her know it was your idea, than be my stand-in?"

Yes! I want to shout, but then I risk putting everything on the line, and I don't think I can handle the hit of being rejected by Quinn. Especially after today. Slow and steady wins the race. At least, I sure fucking hope so, or it'll be the last time I ever listen to my little brother.

"If you're not comfortable bailing on her, I get it, and I won't ask you again," I whisper.

"I'll tell her first thing Wednesday that I can't make it. I just hope you know what you're doing." Without a backward glance, she disappears out of the apartment.

With careful steps back to where Quinn is sprawled out on the sofa, I approach her slowly, like she might pounce on me at any second. Though, if it's anything like her earlier attack, I wouldn't mind.

No. Listen to Booth's advice, no matter how ridiculous that sounds.

"Hey." My voice holds steady despite my heightened nerves. "Have you eaten?"

"I'm not too hungry," she replies with a jerk of her shoulders. "I hope it's okay that Jo was here?"

"Of course. You can have whoever you want over." Provided it's not anyone of the male variety. "My home is your home."

Her eyes warm at my comment before dropping, her fingers now tapping at the side of the mug nervously. "So...um, I guess we should talk."

I settle into the armchair, needing some distance between us for this conversation. "Ladies first."

With a deep breath, she straightens her spine, like she's trying to channel some confidence for what she's about to say. "I shouldn't have kissed you." *Ouch.* She must catch the twitch in my jaw. "Not like that. That kiss was...something else. But it blurs the lines in our agreement. I think moments like that"— she waves to the empty space behind her where we were tangled up in each other just an hour ago—"needs to be saved for the public eye. Well, maybe not with as much zest. We might give someone a heart attack." Her voice is uncharacteristically shy, a blush dusting the apples of her cheeks.

I'd much rather kiss her until we don't know what day it is, but I'll respect what she's saying. I'm also too busy preening like a fucking peacock as my brain clings to the words: *that kiss was something else.*

I can do this. Keep up the sham. Help each other out. Not make it weird. And hope with all that I am, that she can see this being more.

If I could shift the odds in my favor I would do it in a heartbeat.

For now, I'll have to bide my time and pray she likes me for me. Even thinking it sounds bizarre, but Booth is right. I have to stop allowing Jenna to control what I think about myself.

With my forearms resting on my knees, I nod my head as I stare at the upholstered rug now sitting in my living room. A bright addition to my home I didn't know I needed. "I agree. Let's keep things uncomplicated." I look up to find her already watching me. "When we kiss again, it'll be for good reason."

Her hazel eyes flare and I'm certain she hears the hidden meaning in my words.

Two hundred and thirteen days of knowing and wanting Quinn Jackson. I can wait a little longer.

I just hope I don't have to.

CHAPTER SEVENTEEN

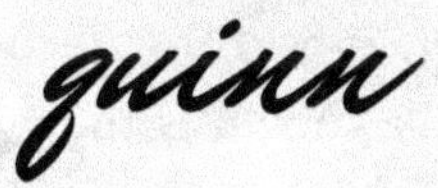

I'M A VERY SUNSHINY PERSON, I KNOW THAT.

With great power comes great responsibilities. Over the years, I've found people expect a lot from us overly positive characters; always smiling, seeing the bright side of things, *blah blah blah*. The biggest one of them all, though: don't show any other emotion.

People lose their shit when an innately happy person is sad or angry. They look to others when the ship is sinking.

So when Jo called me this morning—sounding like she's been smoking cigars her whole life—to tell me she couldn't make it this afternoon because of a sudden bout of tonsillitis, I was bummed. She couldn't see the disappointment swarm my features, though I worried she could hear my crestfallen tone. It couldn't be helped, plus, I could have sworn she told me her tonsils were removed when she was fourteen.

I've been looking forward to our outing, and it sucks we had to cancel last minute, but I've kept myself distracted by experimenting with some new flavors. Some people eat their feelings, well, I bake them. I go full Dr. Frankenstein with my recipes.

I've just finished frosting some peanut butter and bacon cupcakes, when my roomie walks in.

Graham is a naturally guarded guy; carefully selecting his words and silently absorbing his surroundings. I enjoy studying him as he takes it all in, wondering what it looks like from his perspective. Higher up, probably.

At first I was sure he'd find the decor of the bakery ridiculous, but when he was showing me a mind-boggling Excel formula yesterday, he told me a lot of people around town—including himself—find the bright wallpaper and decorations inviting.

His gaze passes over the room, scanning the two tables of customers, and when they land on me, something sparks in his eyes. I shudder—*shudder*—from his innocent glance, as his eyes scan over me slowly from head to toe. If a look could strip me bare, his would do it.

I freaked out a little after our kiss. Hating both the idea of being rejected and him being embarrassed. The sexual tension and rapidly growing feelings I have for him have to be pushed to the side. If it got messy, I wouldn't feel right living in his home and having him help me out, and I'm sure he wouldn't want me as his date at his ex's wedding.

My heart sank when he agreed we needed to keep things friendly, but I knew it was for the best. What shocked me, however, was his sudden boldness. At first I was sure I'd misheard him. *When we kiss again.* Not if. *When.* Nothing in his tone or expression gave anything away, but the air between us crackled when he looked me dead in the eyes and said that statement like a promise.

"Hey, you." I slide another tray of muffins into the oven, and slam the door shut with my hip as I greet him with a smile. "How was work?"

He ducks his head, hiding that subtle smile. "It was good. I'm actually all done for the day."

"Oh nice, what are you gonna do with your afternoon?"

Graham hesitates, his large frame shifting from left to right. I wait. He's not being rude, and I've started to catch on that if you rush him, he gets more flustered. While he gathers his thoughts, I happily stare at his handsome face.

He's always so put together. Beard neatly trimmed, hair styled back with just the right amount of product. I'd love to muss it up and see him look a little *less* put together.

"I thought maybe you'd like to go on a walk." His gaze meets mine now.

"A walk?"

"Yeah, you know"—he marches on the spot, arms swinging—"a way to move from point A to point B."

"All right, wise guy." I giggle and lightly shove him in the stomach as I round the counter, and suddenly remember what it's like to have my breasts crushed up against his firm body. I bet he looks glorious naked, and I know for a fact he is pack—

"So..." he drawls, dragging my thoughts out of the gutter. "Would you like to come with me? I heard Jo wasn't feeling well, and I know you were looking forward to it."

"Sorry, what?" My cheeks heat knowing I missed whatever he said because I was thinking about his...*you know.*

His deep chuckle warms them further. "To see the leaves change. I'd like to take you, if you'll let me."

Without hesitating, I stomp my feet and squeal in excitement. "I would love to!"

There's a different spark in his eyes now, and it stokes a small fire in my chest I'm certain isn't going to extinguish anytime soon.

"Ooh, ooh! Did you see those ones?" I tap Graham's arm incessantly, too busy pressing my nose up against the passenger window to see if he's looking.

We've been driving through Acadia National Park for thirty minutes. Every curve and bend gives us a new view, each one better than the last. Apparently we haven't gotten to the good spot yet, which I find hard to believe. It's as if the sunset has kissed all the leaves in the forest and blessed them with an ethereal glow.

"I'm seeing what you're seeing." Graham chuckles from behind the wheel.

After I closed the bakery, I met him at the apartment where we changed into our hiking gear. I had to hold back my whimper of appreciation when he walked out of his room in a pair of hiking pants that hugged his ass like their life depended on it. Graham has a bubble butt; one I couldn't stop checking out as he loaded up his Jeep. Tight, high, and with the perfect curve.

"You don't sound half as impressed as me." I poke him in his side, evoking a grunt. "Oh my god, are you ticklish?"

"No," he responds way too quickly, and rather than tease him, I lock that information away in my arsenal. "It's pretty spectacular, but remember, I've seen this view every fall for thirty-three years."

"I'd never get bored of it." I sigh as I take in the whimsical scenery. "How far are we walking today?"

"Not far; about three-quarters of a mile."

"Will I be okay in my sneakers?" I'd misplaced my hiking boots, probably snowed under all my clothes and knickknacks.

With a quick glance down at my white sneakers, he smirks. "Yeah, they'll do. Not many people know about this trail. Patrick, Johanna, Dex, and I came out here one year, just before winter hit. We were going to hike our usual," he says and points toward a sign that reads Honeybee Loop right as we pass it.

"But Dex wandered over to a fallen tree and we found what looked to be an old trail."

"What's it called?"

Graham flicks his turn signal and steers into a small parking lot, overshadowed by huge evergreen pines that stand out against the auburn colors of the elm, beech, and oak. He pulls into a spot and turns off the engine.

"That's the thing, it didn't have one. We contacted the local parks team, and they didn't have any record of it. I'm guessing it was created unofficially by someone. It became our new hiking spot, and to this day, the park still hasn't officially recognized it. So we took ownership and named it ourselves. Beaver Moon Trail."

"Beaver Moon?" I twist my body to face him.

"Yeah. It means the first full moon in November. There's a lot of folklore around it. Most people see it as a time for preparation or transition."

"I love that. I'll have to keep that in mind come November. There's so much history to this place." I peer up through the panoramic top of the Jeep, hypnotized as I watch the leaves pirouette toward us.

"Just wait," he says with a twinkle in his eyes.

Once we're out of the car, Graham pops the trunk to get his pack ready as I take in the scenery surrounding us. I throw my arms up in the air, head tipped back as the late afternoon sun warms my cheeks. All of a sudden my foot snags on something, and I careen forward, but luckily he's quick to catch me.

"Whoa, you okay?" Graham keeps a tight hold of my shoulders and we both look down to see my shoelace is undone. "Maybe your sneakers aren't a good idea. How about these?" He steps to the side, revealing his open trunk. It takes me a second to work out what he's referring to, but when I spot the bright yellow rain boots sitting front and center, I gasp.

"You didn't," I whisper, my voice clogging with emotion. I'm vaguely aware of his hand pressing between my shoulder blades, guiding me forward.

"I did," he murmurs. Patting the open trunk, he smiles down at me.

Now I'm blown away for a totally different reason.

This smile isn't like the muted, cautious one I've seen so many times. This one takes over his face, pushing his cheeks up to his bright eyes. Maybe it's a good thing Graham doesn't smile often. Or I'd find myself in a dumbstruck state twenty-four seven. Somehow he's even more handsome and I feel honored that I'm the one to see him like this right now.

He kneels in front of me and slips off my shoes when I sit. Carefully, he rolls my socks over my leggings and holds up the boots between us. "Ready to get these muddy, Maine style?"

A delighted laugh peels out of me and I wiggle my toes. "Ready as I'll ever be."

It's rare that I'm left speechless, yet here I am, stunned silent as I watch Graham slide the boots on. They're the perfect fit, but not more perfect than this moment. To most people it would seem silly to get so emotional over a pair of boots, but not to me—or the sad little ten-year-old who was desperate for any sort of affection growing up. I wonder if Graham even realizes the weight this seemingly small gesture carries.

When I stand and walk in a circle around him, he follows each step with that same devastatingly beautiful smile on his face. I want so badly to kiss it. To imprint his joy onto my lips.

"I can't begin to explain what this means to me. This world doesn't deserve people like you."

"It's not that big of a deal." As usual, he brushes it off, but I won't have that today.

"Well, sometimes being kind is difficult for people, so to me, when someone does something like this, it means a hell of a lot. I'm not used to nice things, so let me have this."

He goes to speak, probably wanting to downplay the act, but he thinks better of it. "Okay."

"Okay!" I shout with a lot more enthusiasm and clap my hands together, which causes a flock of birds to evacuate a nearby tree. "Oops."

Graham huffs, humor replacing the doubt on his face. With his hand on the small of my back, he clicks the fob to his Jeep over his shoulder and directs us toward the tree line. He helps me over the trunk of a fallen tree, and I find a boardwalk-covered trail.

"I thought you said it wasn't an official trail?"

"It isn't. The boardwalks are all Dex. Like I said, it's ours now, and when Dex gets a project in his head, there's no stopping him. He did run it past the park staff first and they were more than happy to accept the free labor."

"I'm gonna need to ask him to build me a house."

"He'd probably say yes."

There are patches of pale green moss along the boards, and the farther in we trek, the thicker the auburn foliage. Graham's touch hasn't left my back, probably because I'm too busy admiring the view around us to check where I'm walking, but I revel in the feel of his large hand splayed against my spine. Deeper and deeper we walk; every step more bewitching than the last. We're just about to veer left on the trail when Graham brings us to a halt.

"Why are we stopping?"

"I want it to be a surprise," he says shyly. There's something like excitement flickering across his features as he pulls out a maroon beanie and fits it over my head.

"Ugh, I don't suit hats."

He bops me on the nose. "You suit anything. But this helps with the grand reveal."

"What's the grand reveal?"

"I can't tell you that. It defeats the purpose of it being a surprise."

"Well, lead the way then, oh wise one." He tugs the hat down over my eyes and I hold out my hand to him. After a few beats, he doesn't take it, so I peel up the edge of the beanie to find him staring down at my open palm in indecision. "You're not going to hold my hand? What if I trip?"

His eyes dart up, and he clears his throat before weaving his fingers through mine. "I'll never let you fall, Quinn."

Rays of sunshine filter through the wool as Graham leads us down the path, the warmth of his skin is calming alongside the zing of excitement that builds with each step we take. The sudden gust of wind startles me at first, and I presume we've walked into an open space. The ground beneath my feet changes from creaking wood to something smooth. I take in a deep breath, and crisp air sends a zap of energy running through my veins.

Eventually we stop and the left side of my body tingles as Graham steps closer. With our hands still intertwined, he leans down, his breath tickling my ear as he whispers, "Are you ready?"

I squeeze his hand and nod eagerly. He peels the hat off my head, but I keep my eyes clamped shut.

"Open your eyes, honey."

Slowly, I open them. The low sun blinds me at first, but when my vision clears, I'm at a loss for words at what's revealed.

We're no longer surrounded by imposing trees; we're high above them, like we're floating. The view before me is endless. Infinite. Vast land stretches out in front us from where we're standing at a rounded cliff edge. We must be one hundred feet up, giving us the perfect 360-degree view of the treetops below. An abundance of colors greets me wherever I turn, and it would be silly for me to describe them simply as reds, oranges, yellows, and purples. No leaf or branch looks the same. The fierce winds sweep over the tops of the forest, creating a fiery tidal wave.

"Graham." I clutch his hand harder. "Have you ever seen anything like this?"

"Never." His deep voice ripples through the air.

I turn toward him and find him entranced, like he's as completely enraptured as I am. Only, he isn't looking at the view.

He's looking at me.

I expect him to glance away but he surprises me when he holds my gaze, steady and sure.

He swallows deeply. "I've never seen anything so beautiful in my life. In all my years of seeing this view, it's never looked like this."

Those feelings I'm trying my hardest to push down are attempting to break loose. How can we draw lines and set boundaries when he stares at me like I'm something special? And why would I want to? In the few weeks we've spent together, no one has ever treated me the way he does. He claims he's just being nice, shrugs it off as nothing, when in fact, it means everything.

I've never needed materialistic things or money. Having been raised in a household where words were spiteful and used to inflict pain, actions have always held the highest value.

And Graham makes me feel rich.

Neither of us look away; the view momentarily forgotten. Like we've been doing it for years, he tucks me underneath his arm, and I rest my head against his chest. "Thank you for the boots and for bringing me here."

"Do you like it?"

I sense him looking at me, but I've been held captive by the view again. "I love it. Can we stay forever?"

Chuckling, he nods against the top of my head. "Yeah, honey, forever. At least, until we run out of food." I want to protest when he pulls away, but it dies on my lips when I spot the small picnic laid out to our left. For such a "last minute" change of plans, he sure is prepared. We lower onto the dark red plaid blanket, sitting among containers of food and a thermos.

The gifts and surprises he keeps on treating me with are just the cherry on top, but even without them, this would be one of the best days of my life.

"Hey, Graham?"

"Yeah, Quinn?"

I settle on my knees in front of him, and he pauses what he's doing, hands hovering above the two plastic mugs he's setting out. "This day is one for the record books. It might just be one of my favorites."

His shoulders relax, like he was waiting for me to say something negative, and I hate that he's always anticipating the worst. He's clearly planned out this entire day—despite having a few hours to prepare for it—yet, he still thinks so low of himself.

"I'm glad I could be here for it," he replies and gets back to his task. When he unscrews the lid of the thermos, the smell of apple, cinnamon, cloves, and citrus blows with the wind.

"Oh boy, you've pulled out the big guns here. Changing leaves *and* apple cider, you spoil me."

We get comfortable, sharing sandwiches, a slice of apple pie, and hot cider as we look out at the horizon. It's a little chilly, but the late afternoon sun and spiced drinks warm us up. Once we finish eating, we prop ourselves back on our hands, side by side, and enjoy the view.

After a while, I have an itching to break the silence, if only to get to know Graham a little more. "You and your family came out here a lot?"

"Yeah; camping, hiking, fishing, you name it. Our dad loved the outdoors, and wanted to make sure we all knew how lucky we were to have this," he gestures in front of him, "on our doorstep. Dad was born and raised in Sutton Bay, and it's kind of hard to imagine myself living anywhere else."

"He sounds like a really great man."

"He was." Graham swallows but doesn't stop talking, and although his expression is tainted with sadness, there's no mistaking the love and adoration in his tone when he talks about his late father. "He was a really smart guy, always listened to us, and made sure we felt valued and loved. All of us kids are very different, but he seemed to know exactly what we needed. I was, um, a quiet kid, to say the least."

"There's nothing wrong with that. We don't all need to be the same."

"Hmm. It made making friends hard and I struggled a little with how to navigate and communicate my emotions, but Dad helped me." He pauses and contemplates what to say next. "What are your parents like?"

When he asked about where I was raised a couple of weeks ago, I shut down, hating that my years in San Diego were ever part of my timeline. Not all childhoods are happy, and it doesn't make me jealous of Graham—it makes me grateful for the life I have now.

My head falls back, and I follow the path of an airplane. "I don't know if you could call them parents. Or *parent*." He looks at me in question. "I didn't know my dad. I'm not really sure my mom knew him either. If he was one of the lowlifes she associated herself with, it's probably for the best that I didn't. You already know I grew up in San Diego, but I left the moment I could; the day I turned eighteen, actually."

He doesn't ask why. I think he wants to...or maybe I want to tell him? I haven't told many people this story, and I usually fill in the gap of my childhood with stories about my travels in my van. It feels safer, but something about Graham makes me feel protected, and I know he won't pass judgment on my history.

"My mom wasn't a nice woman. Probably still isn't, but I wouldn't know. We haven't spoken since I left. I'm not sure she ever wanted to have children, though, if she did, she made it very clear she pulled the short straw in having me. Regret was a common theme in our relationship." I give him a forced smile. "I don't share this for pity, by the way. I trust you and I want you to know. No secrets."

"I would never pity you, Quinn. I'm sorry you were dealt that hand of cards." He turns his torso to face me and shakes his head slowly. "I don't know how anyone could have regrets when you're involved. Maybe regret in not knowing you, but not regret in having you in their lives."

My hand inches closer to his, our fingers a hair's breadth apart, but I worry if I take his hand, the tears stinging behind my eyes will be set free. "I grew up dirt poor, sharing a one-bedroom trailer with a woman who despised me. Simple things like food, clean clothes, and running water weren't just a necessity, but a privilege. Kids were unkind because my clothes were dirty, and my shoes were two sizes too small. All of that would have been okay if I'd had a mother who loved and cared for me. As I got older, my mom found more ways to poison my mind with her insults. Comments about my weight, having no friends, calling me out on my failures. I could have survived the poverty, but I knew I wouldn't survive her. The plan was to finish high school, get my diploma, and leave town at the beginning of the summer. Plans fall through, though, and the day before my eighteenth birthday, her slaps turned to punches."

Graham sucks in a sharp breath, and his limbs go rigid at my admission, but he remains quiet.

"She'd slap me around now and again, but she preferred to use words. I'm not even sure she knew my birthday was coming up, thanks to the liquor. I'd forgotten to clean the dishes or something—whatever it was apparently warranted her fist to the side of my face." Graham laces our fingers together, the point of contact helping me find the courage to continue. My voice trembles as I retell the worst day of my life out loud for the first time in years. "She knocked me unconscious. I don't know how long I was out for, but she left me on the dirty kitchen floor and must have wasted half a bottle of gin pouring it over me. My ribs were bruised and there were scratches on my face when I woke up. After that, I knew I had to leave. I didn't want her to have any power over me anymore. So I left. The money I had been saving got me as far as Salem—where I stayed for a couple of years, before buying Nelly and hitting the open road."

His fingers run over my knuckles, silently comforting me.

Most people look at me differently when I share that side of my life. But without those pages to my story, I wouldn't be the woman I am today. And maybe I wouldn't be here, upon this rock, with Graham.

"Quinn," he says softly.

I turn my head, and despite my painful retelling, the smile I give him is genuine. "Mm-hm?"

Graham's presence is like a balm to my soul. Without speaking, he soothes and settles, though his next words warm me from the inside out, starting deep in my chest. "I can't begin to imagine how hard that would have been for you, and I'm so sorry you had to go through that. The fact you've come out the other side as this beautiful, incredible, vibrant woman, never letting those memories tear you down, is...I'm in awe of you, Quinn Jackson. I hope you know that."

"I do now." I squeeze his hand.

With a squeeze in return, he smiles. The golden hour paints him like the ember leaves below. Nice doesn't begin to cover what this day means to me. I never would have guessed that a simple arrangement like ours could bring us together like this.

As I rest my head on his shoulder, I like to imagine that even without it, our lives still would have crossed, and that we would have found ourselves on this path regardless.

And something tells me this is only the start of our journey together.

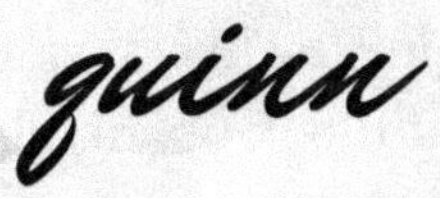

CHAPTER EIGHTEEN

THE NOISE OF LITTLE PAWS SKATING AROUND ON THE OTHER SIDE of the door is quickly becoming one of my favorite welcome home sounds.

Home. Huh. That's new.

My home is due to be ripped apart. *This is just temporary*, I remind myself. No matter how homey Graham's apartment feels.

"I hear you, buddy," Graham calls as he pulls out his keys.

A little rocket of shiny, brown fur zooms around our feet the moment we walk in.

"Oh, hello, sweet boy. Did you miss us? Yes, you did," I coo. As usual, Graham rolls his eyes at the baby talk I use for Curly. He doesn't know that I've caught him on a number of occasions speaking to him in the exact same way when sneaking him treats.

"I'm gonna jump in the shower. Did you want anything to eat?" he asks as he unties his boots.

"No, I'm good. I'm pretty beat, so I think I'll take a shower after you and go to bed."

"You go first then. I'm gonna check some emails."

After a long, steamy, everything shower, I'm dressed in my pajamas and walking back out into the kitchen to grab a glass of water. I've just turned the corner when a pair of strong hands catches me by the shoulders before I collide with a wall of muscle.

"Oops, sorry."

"We've got to stop meeting like this," Graham jokes.

I chuckle, and when I look up, his short hair appears more brown than blond from his shower.

My eyes are no longer on his hair though.

Ho-ly. Fuck.

Graham is shirtless.

Half nude.

Pecs. A lot of pecs. Well, just two, and there they are. At eye level.

I knew he wasn't scrawny, but I was unaware how built he is. Thick, defined muscles run across his arms, chest, ribs, and stomach. The hair decorating his chest and taut stomach matches the darker shade of his beard; and adds to his masculinity. A pair of athletic shorts hang low on his hips, and I follow the path of a water droplet until it disappears into the elastic band.

Would it be inappropriate to lick him?

Yes!

"Yes, what?" he asks.

Great. I just answered my internal ramblings aloud. Graham has hypnotized me with his body and that horniness dilemma from last week is now back in full force.

"Oh, nothing. Just thinking out loud." *About running my tongue over your abs.*

"Well, I'm gonna head to bed. Do you need anything?"

"No, wait, yes! To thank you," I hurry out and catch hold of his wrist before he steps away. "For today. It was...Graham, it really was amazing. Thank you for sharing it with me and for stepping in when Jo pretended to be sick."

"You're welcome. I'd be happy to ta—what?" His eyes widen.

"Which part are you confused about?" I tilt my head, a smirk playing on my lips. "The part about me being thankful, or you colluding with Jo?"

"I-I...I literally have no idea what you're talking about. Jo was so sick. The sickest. It was close for a second..." His head drops with a big sigh. "You're not buying any of this are you?"

"Nope. Nada. Nein." I shake my head.

"Fuck. Listen, I can explain."

I prop my fists on my hips with fake annoyance. "Oh, please do."

"It's going to sound childish." He blows out a breath. "When I heard Jo was taking you to see the leaves change, I got...jealous. I had a whole day planned."

Oh.

Well, I was not expecting that. I'm not really sure what I was expecting.

Shortly after Graham left the bakery, Jo walked by with Claire. Clearly, she had forgotten about the little white lie she told me that morning, because she waved at me through the window looking healthy as ever. After about five seconds, her waving slowed, eyes widened, before she gripped her throat with a pained look and scurried away.

It was then I suspected all the whispering I heard between her and Graham the other night had something to do with this afternoon's trip.

"Why would you be jealous about that?" I ask, genuinely confused at his confession. He's trying his best to keep eye contact, but I can tell this is making him uncomfortable, and that's the last thing I want after such an amazing day. "Actually, forget about it. It doesn't matter, either way, I had the best time, and I'm so happy I got to experience that with you. I'm gonna go to sleep. See you in the morning."

I give him a brief smile and turn to head to my bedroom, but his words stop me in my tracks.

"I wanted to see the prettiest person I've ever met, standing and experiencing one of the most outstanding views for the first time. Two beauties in one place. You said today was one for the record books. And I agree. But only because I got to witness you shining bright and beautiful."

His voice is strong, unwavering.

The beating of his heart is obvious against his naked chest as I face him, and I think mine is pounding twice as fast. "Graham," I breathe. "You can't say things like that. I thought we were keeping this strictly platonic. That's not how friends talk to each other."

"Fuck," he growls, fingers swiping through his hair. "I know, but how can I not say it after seeing that enchanting look on your face? I wanted to experience that with you. Today was one of the best days of my life too, but only because you were there with me. Then you told me everything about your mom and I felt like a piece of shit, because I'd tricked you into coming with me. I know I'm screwing everything up and we keep blurring the lines of this agreement. I just had to tell you that." His shoulders lose some tension, like he's been holding on to the weight of his lie all day.

It's a sweet lie. Really sweet.

My lack of response has him shifting on his feet as he scratches the back of his neck. "I don't say any of this to make you uncomfortable. I'm sorry. I didn't mean to ruin your day out with Jo. Let's add this to the list of things that never happened."

I'm not sure I'll ever forget today or what he just said.

He just told me I'm the prettiest person he's ever seen. While I don't really understand why he wouldn't just ask if he could take me to see the leaves, it doesn't overshadow what an amazing gesture it is. He bought me my very own pair of yellow rain boots because of a story about me in fifth grade. He only buys me yellow flowers because I told him it's my favorite color. He unpacked all my belongings to make me feel less sad about my van.

The reason Graham is so quiet, is because he's been listening intently this whole time and stowing away every detail I tell him.

He steps up to me, and for one second, I think—*no, I hope*—he's going to kiss me.

At a glacial pace, he bends down and brushes his lips across my cheek. Far, far away from where I want them to land. "Goodnight, Quinn," he murmurs and then walks to his bedroom.

A wave of disappointment sweeps through me. We keep doing this; setting rules, breaking them, resetting them, and then finding ourselves with our feet raised, ready to cross the line again.

And right now, I have no idea which side we're standing on.

CHAPTER NINETEEN

graham

Everything I do and say is wrong.

Today was as perfect as she was, but I had to go and ruin it by opening my mouth.

Her smiles and laughter are out of pity, they have to be.

My pen hovers above the page. Are they out of pity?

I think about today. How she stared down at me as I put on her rain boots. How she didn't let go of my hand. How her head rested on my shoulder.

The look on her face when I told her how I was feeling wasn't because she was embarrassed or getting ready to reject me. Sure, she was shocked—so was I at that sudden outburst.

For a second, I could have sworn her expression was laced with longing. Desire.

Yet I walked away from her, too nervous to question what it meant.

I stare at my open journal as it sits in front of me on my bed.

It's so easy for me to express how I'm feeling when my thoughts are hidden between pages.

Tonight, however, I want to be bold. For her. To know Quinn is a privilege and she should never doubt that.

Snatching up my pen, I messily scrawl a few lines at the bottom of the paper.

1)   I'm never listening to Booth again.
2)   She makes me feel brave.

The sound of my journal slapping closed jolts Curly from his sleep, and he watches me with curious eyes as I stride out of my room and across the hall.

CHAPTER TWENTY

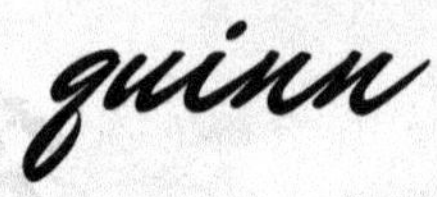

I LIKE HIM.

More than I should for a fake boyfriend. He makes it so easy, and without sounding vain, it's obvious he likes me too. We started this out as practically strangers and in such a short time we've become so much more. He has more self-control than I do, and I have to respect that and his wish to keep things neutral. Even if his words are in conflict with his actions.

As I settle into bed, I allow the memories from today to calm my racing heart and try to convince myself there isn't more going on between the two of us.

I'm just about to turn off my bedside light when there's a knock on the door. My hand hovers over the switch as I think about what to do. It's clearly Graham, but after our talk in the kitchen, I don't know what's left to say.

I climb out of bed, readjust my tank top, and walk to the door. When it swings open, Graham has his fist poised, ready to knock again. He looks...determined. To do what, who knows, but I keep the mood light.

"Hey, did you forget something?"

"Yes. This."

In the blink of an eye, he's over the threshold, in my space, and on me.

There's not an inch of space between us as he bends down, crashes his lips to mine, and makes me forget everything. He takes advantage of the gasp I make, and his tongue plunges into my mouth, demanding access. The taste of him a high I've been desperate to experience again.

Graham isn't just kissing me; he's owning, devouring, treasuring me.

He walks us farther into the room, the door left wide open, and all sense forgotten.

"Graham," I breathlessly whisper against his lips, but I don't tell him to stop as he palms my ass over my sleep shorts. "What are we doing?"

He pulls away, the tip of his nose brushing mine. "Not fighting this anymore. I can't do it, Quinn, I've tried. Needing you is like needing air." His hand tangles in my hair as he looks down at me intensely. "If you're not okay with this, tell me, and I'll go."

It doesn't really answer my question, or maybe I should have asked, *What does this mean for us afterward?*

The microscopic part of my brain that tells me to think this through, to slow it down, is overshadowed by the louder part of my brain. The part that has me whispering, "I've wanted this for a while."

He's crushing his lips to mine again before I've finished speaking. We step back, clinging to one another, and I expect him to push me onto the bed, but instead he hoists me into his arms, and I automatically wrap my legs around him. Had he not thrown me on the tire swing the other week, I would have argued I'm too heavy.

Our tongues continue their dizzying duel and at this angle, I'm able to grind my throbbing center against his hard length concealed by the thin material of his shorts. Still shirtless, I have the perfect opportunity to explore his warm skin; tracing the muscles on his shoulders and back.

I almost knock his glasses off his face when I run my hand across his neatly trimmed beard and up into his hair, gripping the strands tight to deepen the kiss. It could be minutes; it could be hours. Time doesn't mean anything when we're together like this.

Graham breaks the kiss, but my cries of protest are silenced when he nuzzles his face into my neck, his beard tickling and overstimulating my heated skin.

"Quinn, you're killing me with these little hip movements." That only makes me grind down harder.

"I need this. Need something," I whine.

"I'll give it to you. Whatever you need." With a deep breath, he tightens his grip on my ass, sure to leave bruises that I'll wear like a badge of honor. "Can I taste you? Before anything, please let me taste you."

A chill of excitement causes goose bumps to erupt over my body, my hardened nipples rubbing painfully against my tank top. Heat floods my veins, running straight to my core where I'm already soaking.

No one has ever done that before. He hasn't even touched me yet and I already know it's going to be an experience that triumphs all my others. Previous partners have either been uncoordinated or short and sweet.

"I want that."

That's all the permission he needs, because before I can take my next breath, my back is bouncing off the springs of the mattress as a version of Graham I've never seen before towers over me.

Hungry. Powerful. Assertive.

Those little pockets of confidence I keep seeing from him are nothing compared to the man looking down at me possessively. The rise and fall of his chest, the messy hair, and the way his eyes eat up every inch of my body has him looking rogue.

I very much like this version of Graham.

"You're talking out loud again." He chuckles deeply.

I huff a laugh. "I do that a lot around you. You have that effect."

"You have no idea the effects you have on me, though, do you?" he asks, strolling closer.

My eyes drop to the impressive bulge between his legs. "I have some idea."

"That's just one of many." He lowers his hand and palms his erection. "Are you sure about this, Quinn?"

My legs hang over the edge of the bed, feet swinging, hands propped up behind me as I watch him unabashedly. Nodding my head, I hope my response exudes confidence. "I'm sure."

He lets out a breath, like he was holding it in as he waited for my consent. "Then I'm gonna need you to get out of those shorts—the same ones that have been driving me crazy since you moved in."

A whoosh of air leaves me, because fuck, we're actually doing this. I scoot forward to plant my feet on the floor, then slowly shimmy out of my now-soaked shorts. When they drop to my ankles, I flick my foot toward him so they hit him square in the chest. His laughter dances around us, but when his eyes drop to between my legs, the humor leaves him with a gulp.

"Show me. Show me exactly what I've been trying my hardest not to think about." He sounds pained.

To ease the torment for the both of us, I widen my legs and lean back. With a sharp intake of breath, he takes me in; eyes darkening to hunter green as they roam over me. He steps between my open thighs, fists clenching and unclenching like he's finding it hard to keep his hands to himself. I really hope he doesn't. "So fucking pretty."

His eyes drift up to mine and I almost choke when he lowers to his haunches, inches away from my aching pussy.

Suddenly, my nerves start to get the better of me. "Umm, you don't have to…"

"I know I don't have to. I want to."

The old me would be self-conscious at how my thighs spread against the mattress, stretch marks and cellulite on full display, but with the way he groans in appreciation when his hands run over them, fingertips pressing into my skin, it's hard not to feel wanted. *Desired.* "Want it so badly." I watch in apt fascination as he bends and lays a kiss to my inner thigh, then does the same to the opposite side.

"O-okay," I say with a shaky breath.

He peers up at me, concern creasing his brow. "If you're not comfortable, we don't have to."

"It's not that. I want to, but…no one has ever, you know…"

"Ever?" he asks, and his concern morphs into something territorial when I shake my head. "I love being the one to experience firsts with you."

This man will be the death of me, but at least I'll be going out satisfied.

I take comfort in the slight tremble of his hands, because despite the confidence he's showing, he's just as nervous as I am.

"I want you to be the first."

"Then I don't want to waste another second to taste what I already know is going to be the sweetest fucking pussy."

"Oh my god," I breathe.

Our eyes widen at the same time. His filthy words have shocked the hell out of me. No one has ever spoken to me like that. He looks just as surprised at the outburst as me, but I'm more surprised that I…*like it.* A lot.

Maybe it's because I'm nothing but comfortable with

Graham, but the thrill of it sends a jolt of pleasure between my legs, where I feel my arousal growing.

"Fuck, sorry. That…I don't know where that came from," he groans and drops his forehead to my knee and sighs. "Did I make it weird?"

A nervous laugh slips free, and with a soft grip on his hair, I encourage him to look at me. "Far from it." I bit my lip to hide my grin. "There goes another first though."

"What's that?" he asks, eyes bouncing between mine.

"I think you helped me realize I *really* like dirty talk in the bedroom." My entire body flames at that confession. "Did you like saying it?"

The hand on my thigh flexes and a puff of air coasts across my pebbled skin. "I've never done it before. But yeah, I liked it. I like it even more knowing you do." He leans forward until his lips brush against the shell of my ear. "Would you like to hear about the filthy things I want to do to you?"

Despite the heat radiating from our bodies, I shiver from his touch and words. "I really do."

"And you'll tell me if I take it too far?"

Swallowing, I nod.

Pulling away, he removes his glasses and presses them into my hand. "Then hold these for me, honey. I don't want them to get messy while your beautiful thighs are spread out just for me."

I have died. Deceased.

This man is an enigma.

A mystery I want to solve, yet I equally love the surprises he keeps hitting me with. He said he's never talked like this before, either, which means Jenna never saw this side of him. Good. Because she's in no way deserving of the man in front of me. Or any version of him.

The jealous thoughts disappear the second I feel Graham's lips skim across my flesh.

All I can do is grip the bedsheets and watch as he works higher, widening my legs further to fit his broad shoulders in between them. His pace is torturous as he inches toward my waiting center. I want to scream in frustration for every second that passes.

Only I'm stunned silent when he licks a path up my leg until he meets the juncture between my thigh and pussy. As he inhales deeply, a starved, low moan escapes him.

"So. *Fucking.* Sweet."

"I thought you didn't like sweet things?" I say between short breaths.

Our gazes meet, and my god, the sight of him on his knees like this, eyes glassy with lust, is something I don't ever want to forget.

"I lied," he growls and then, he's there, finding my soaking entrance with the flat of his tongue, swirling it languidly.

My cry is quickly muffled by the hand I slap over my mouth, biting down on the skin to hide my moans. This new sensation has intense pleasure rolling through me with every swipe of his tongue. I'm not even mad this is the first time someone's gone down on me, because I'm certain no one could do it quite like he can.

With a strong grip on my calves, he plants my feet on the mattress and spreads me wider. My toes curl into the comforter, and I collapse, my back arching off the bed when he pushes his face into my pussy; slow strokes are now replaced with fervent laps of my clit. I tense and melt with each lick. The evidence of what he's doing to me pooling beneath me.

"Graham," I cry as the tip of his tongue strokes against the sensitive bud. "Oh god, that—that feels…Yeah, I like that."

He increases his efforts at my confirmation. Drawing sounds and sensations from me I didn't know existed.

His eyes haven't left my face once. My hands shoot to my

tender breasts, kneading and pulling at my nipples through the thin cotton of my tank, and he tracks every movement. One of his hands leaves my thigh and it inches toward the hem of my top to slowly reveal my stomach. I'm jolted from my pleasure for a second, so I grab his hand and pull it up to rest on my breast. Leaving my shirt in place. He doesn't seem to mind, happy to pinch and toy with my nipple in rhythm with his tongue.

It's been mere minutes, but I can already feel my orgasm building.

One of my hands falls to the top of his head, twisting and pulling at his sandy hair. I gasp in surprise when a thick finger enters me slowly. The fullness of it paired with his hot mouth has me biting down hard on my lip.

His tongue slows before stopping. "Don't hide those beautiful sounds from me. They're mine tonight. I want to hear you."

When I chirp my approval, he continues to work his finger into me. "Christ, you're so tight. You feel so good. I can't wait until it's my cock you're taking. Do you want that? Do you want my cock?"

I don't know if he sees my eager nodding, because I'm too busy staring up at the ceiling with wide eyes, chest heaving, and core clenching as he plays me like his favorite instrument.

There's caution to his dirty words, but my reply only spurs him on.

"I want it so much." His finger brushes a spot inside me that has me crying out, stars blinding my vision. "Yes, right there. There, more. More, Graham."

"Soak my face, honey. I want to taste you for days." The demanding words paired with his skillful mouth and fingers build, and build, and build until I'm no more.

My orgasm catapults through me, wave after wave of mind-bending pleasure, and he sees me through each ripple. He groans into each lick, as if he's enjoying this as much as I am.

My skin is on fire, my heart is racing, and my brain has no idea which way is up. Every fiber and cell in me has been renewed.

As my body becomes mine again, I push at his head, because he still hasn't stopped. "Oh, oh, no, too sensitive."

With one final kiss to my clit, he straightens, looking up the length of my body. There's no green left in his eyes, and a stuttered breath breaks free when I see his beard glistening from *me*.

My tank top is useless at this point, because one of my breasts has slipped free from where he was tugging at it. His eyes glow at that reveal of skin, even though he's already seen it —or was that my other boob?

Focus, Quinn!

"Are you okay?" he asks as he tenderly rubs at my jellied limbs.

"I think you've ruined me." I sigh, sitting upright and adjusting my top back in place. "Are you?"

He scrubs a hand down his face, but he doesn't do it quick enough to hide the small smile that peeks through his fingers. I mean, I'd be smug, too, if I made a woman come so hard she had an out-of-body experience.

"More than okay. It's just...I really didn't come knocking on your door with this being the end goal. Don't get me wrong, I'm glad it happened, but I kinda had a speech lined up." He slips his glasses on and combs his fingers through his hair, quickly shifting back into the composed version of himself.

"What was the speech about?"

"Beats me." He laughs. "I think I short-circuited when you answered the door in those shorts. You can't wear them around me, I'll lose my mind."

"So, you want me to walk around pantless?"

His hands fly to the backs of my knees, and he drags me toward him, until our noses are pressed together. "Do that, and we will never leave this apartment."

"That doesn't sound too bad." I press a quick kiss to his lips, only when I taste myself on him, does it deepen. There's enough space between our bodies for me to reach down and find his rock-hard cock. A throaty moan leaves him when I press the heel of my hand against it and the grip he has on me tightens.

"That's not necessary. I really do—" His words are cut off when my hand slips under the elastic of his shorts.

"I disagree." My fingers coast across the velvet skin, and I buzz with pride when I feel him twitch. "This feels like a problem. Don't be that guy who says, 'I didn't do it for you to return the favor.' Just let me."

"Honey, it's been a problem since the moment you walked into my life."

Without breaking eye contact I confess something. "I've only gone down on a guy once before."

"One too many if you ask me."

I flick him on the chest. "You're such a Neanderthal. I'm serious, I don't want to be...bad at it."

"Quinn." He shakes his head. "Where your mouth and my dick are involved, I highly doubt there will be anything bad about it."

"Will you tell me what you like?"

His eyes warm and he presses a kiss to my hairline before standing, my hand slipping free from his shorts. "Yes, honey, I'll tell you."

"Okay," I whisper. I wipe my sweaty palms over my thighs and slowly lower to my knees, eyes on Graham the entire time.

Before I hit the floor, he's leaning past me and sets a pillow on the floor, clearing his throat before he says, "For your knees. It's a hard floor."

Who the heck is this man?

As my fingers hook into his waistband and start to drag his shorts down, I get my answer.

He's a man with a very, very large penis.

CHAPTER TWENTY-ONE

graham

THE PROBABILITY OF ME DYING A HAPPY MAN RIGHT NOW? HIGHLY likely.

If the sight of Quinn on her knees at my feet is the last thing I see before I go, I'll greet the Grim Reaper like an old friend and ask him to show me the way.

She is a vixen who wields all power over me without even trying. My mind flashes back to minutes ago; her breathy moans, her thick thighs dropping open, her beautiful pussy glistening. I'm already desperate to have my mouth on her again.

I didn't come armed to her room with a plan, yet I can't be mad at the outcome. Right before I left her in the kitchen, I saw confusion shrouding her features. I don't know if I put it there or perhaps it was the weight of her confessions this afternoon, but I wanted it gone. I'd expected us to talk, for my words to eradicate any doubt she had, but my actions came out stronger. My mouth didn't stop working because I was nervous—quite the opposite. It was just too busy craving her taste to formulate sentences.

Surprise painted both our faces when the lewd words I'd been thinking escaped. I'd never had the urge or want to say anything to a woman like that before, let alone the confidence. Not even with Jenna.

I was sure my slipup was going to scare her off, yet when our eyes met, flames reflected back at me. Lust and need smoldering like a ring of fire around her pupils. Every dirty murmur had her thighs quaking and core clenching. Heat poured through me as she dripped onto my tongue like honey.

Everything about Quinn is sexy, but hearing her tell me what she likes and opening herself up to me, was the most erotic thing I'd ever witnessed. There are a lot of firsts tonight, and despite our earlier hesitancy, I can't imagine doing this with anyone else.

If there was one sight to top the one of Quinn spread out on her bed like the most delectable feast, it's her on her knees.

As her small hands grip onto the waistband of my shorts, my breathing stops. All blood flow rushes to my cock. It was a challenge to hide my filthy satisfaction that I'm the first man to ever taste her. From the slight tremble in her hands and earlier worry in her voice, I've got to keep my shit together. No matter how wild my heart is beating, or how badly I want to watch her lips stretch around me.

I remain quiet and let her take control, watching as she peels the material down my thighs. I didn't bother with briefs after my shower, so when my painfully hard cock is freed and slaps against my stomach, she gasps in surprise with wide eyes.

Fuuuuuck, I shouldn't love the way she stares at it like that.

She really needs to close her mouth, because my control is slipping.

After a beat of silence and Quinn staring between my legs, I speak. "You good?"

"Mm-hm. It's just that"—she points at my dick—"isn't going to fit."

That should not turn me on so much.

"We don't have to do this," I say, not wanting to pressure her.

I bend to pull up my shorts, only to pause when her molten eyes lock with mine. "I want to, Graham. Let me try. Just tell me if I do anything wrong."

The fortitude in her voice matches her expression. How can I ever deny her anything?

My knuckles brush down her flushed cheek. "Go as slow as you want. You call the shots here, but from where I'm standing, something so beautiful could never be wrong."

She chews on her plump bottom lip before her eyes flash with mischief. "Okay. Try not to kill me with the death trap between your legs though."

Before I can respond, she flicks out her tongue and drags it across the blunt tip. "Fucking Christ," I hiss. My hips jolt forward, hands falling to the earthy, glossy strands of her hair as I channel all willpower not to drive into her sweet mouth.

She swirls around the head and slowly—*oh so slowly*—wraps her lips around me. My knees nearly buckle when she looks up at me with a hooded stare, but the trust glowing in her eyes has the ability to shatter me.

"That's really good, keep doing that and take me deeper if you can." She hollows her cheeks, taking more of me, and heat builds at the base of my spine. "Wrap your hand around me. Tighter—*oh shit*, yeah, like that. So good. You're so good at this."

I'm in no rush, wanting to savor this moment for eternity as she takes me inch by inch. Without instruction, she twists and pumps in sync with her mouth. My hands fist her hair, pleasure coiling deep in me with each pass of her tongue.

Watching her confidence grow is addictive.

My limbs lose all control when her other hand moves to cup and massage my balls. "Harder. You can squeeze them harder. Fucking hell, you're perfect." I watch her in utter awe. Hips gyrating along with her movements; thighs rubbing together. She's still bare below the waist, which sends me spiraling quicker, and the idea that she's as turned on as I am has the pressure in me building faster. I'm close, but when I hit the back of her throat and she gags around me, I'm a goner.

"Are you okay?" She nods gently and continues to work me. "I bet you're soaking again, aren't you? Getting off with my cock down your throat."

Her moan vibrates over my cock, letting me know she enjoys my words as much as I like giving them to her. Fuck, if I don't want to whisper every filthy praise to her if that's her reaction.

My mind and body are fully entranced by this gorgeous woman on her knees, though, from the blinding pleasure she's pulling from me, I'm close to falling to my own.

When I attempt to pull away she shakes her head and increases her efforts until my whole body is lit up. "I'm close. So close." I loosen my grip on her hair and stroke through the soft strands. "I'm going to come down your throat," I warn.

She nods with hazy, caramel eyes set on me.

Not needing any further encouragement, my hips thrust in time with her mouth and hand. "You are a dream. I'm going to give you it all, honey, don't swallow it when I'm done."

My movements stutter, balls draw up, and I almost black out as my orgasm ricochets across every nerve ending. Unable to hold back any longer, I throw my head back and shout out a string of curse words as I come across her tongue.

Once down from my high, I slip from her mouth, and take a moment to collect myself. She stares up at me with tears clinging to her lashes and cheeks flushed the prettiest shade of pink.

She is *fucking* magnificent.

Bending down, I swipe my thumb across her swollen, wet lips. "Open your mouth and show me."

Without hesitation, she opens wide and sticks out her tongue to show where my cum pools and waits for my approval. This woman was made for me, I'm positive.

"Good girl. Now swallow." I watch her throat work and when she lets out a satisfied sigh, I drop to my knees and cradle her face. It takes all my strength not to kiss her viciously. "Are you okay? Was that too much?"

She shakes her head vigorously. "No, no. God, it was...who knew it could be like that? I felt like you were holding back. Was I okay?"

My willpower cracks and I pull her into me, sealing my mouth over hers in a powerful kiss. The taste of our combined pleasure is an aphrodisiac that stirs my arousal again.

"Quinn, are you kidding me? You were perfect. More than perfect." She might think she lacks experience, but she knew exactly how to wring me dry.

"You promise?" she asks carefully.

"I'd never lie to you." My lips drop to hers while my thumbs stroke her round cheeks. When I reluctantly pull away, I hold her gaze. "I'm serious, I've never been like that with anyone. I kinda surprised myself. But thank you."

"You're thanking me? For what?" Her brow wrinkles.

"For being you and sharing that with me."

Her smile lights up her face like the most beautiful sunrise.

I did that. There's no denying that smile belongs to me.

There's a lot more I want to say, but when my eyes fall to the clock on her bedside table, I see how late it is. With one final kiss to her forehead, I help her rise to her feet. "We're up early, we should get some sleep."

"Ugh, I feel like I could sleep forever. You're going to orgasm me into a coma, Graham Sadler."

Neither of us turns away as we slide our shorts on.

She leans up on her tiptoes and plants a light kiss to my lips, before dragging her feet back to her rumpled sheets. Disappointment weighs heavy in my stomach, because I want to curl up in those sheets with her, get lost in them, and say fuck it to our jobs. I'm already so lost in her, in so many ways that it scares me. The deeper I trek into my feelings, the harder it's going to be for me to find my way out.

I grab two glasses of water, only to return to her sleeping soundly. With a chaste kiss on her cheek, I leave the room.

Booth is going to slap me upside my head. There's no doubt we've complicated things now, the lines fully smudged into something unidentifiable. Internally, I'm freaking out.

What if we both have very different ideas of how this is going to end?

We both started off as a means to an end. Maybe having some fun along the way is a bonus for her. Why would this mean anything more?

Whereas for me, she feels like the end game. For so long, I've felt like a lonely traveler, even when I was with Jenna. Yet, with Quinn, I can see myself walking down a newly discovered path.

I just hope she sees herself walking next to me.

When I get back to my room, I score through my earlier entry with thick lines of black ink.

If I thought seeing Quinn out at Beaver

Moon Trail was incredible, seeing, tasting, and feeling her as she came around my hand and tongue was a fucking phenomenon.

Me. She trusted me with her beautiful body.

If this is too good to be true, at least I have this.

CHAPTER TWENTY-TWO

"Quinn," Johanna hisses. "Slow down."

I don't look back as I drag my friend down the hallway, through the kitchen, and into the pantry. When I'm sure the coast is clear, I shove her inside and corner her up against the tinned foods and spices Claire has stacked in here.

Tonight we're having a chilled-out dinner at the Sadler household. Though, I'm anything but chill.

"Isuckedmyfakeboyfriend'sdick."

Jo has a slice of pizza halfway in her mouth and almost chokes on her bite when I rush out those words in one long jumble. She slaps a hand to her chest, coughing and spluttering.

"Sorry. Did you say you sucked your fake boyfriend's dick?" she asks with watery eyes.

"Yes."

"Just so we're clear"—she tilts her head and smirks—"you mean Graham, right?"

"Shhh!" I flap my hands in front of her face. "Don't say his name, he might hear you. What should I do?"

"Firstly, I think you explain how you ended up with his penis in your mouth."

"Stop smiling like that." I stomp my foot like a toddler.

Tonight's dinner conveniently falls the day after Graham and I gave in to the feelings and tension between us. Claire didn't feel like cooking tonight and ordered in pizzas instead. Every time I looked up from my plate, I couldn't stop squirming in my seat when I found Graham's heated stare on me. I tried to play it cool, but I'm certain everyone around that table knew what we had done. *Hot Night of Oral* was stamped across my forehead.

I'd woken in the middle of the night, a little sad not to find him in bed next to me. Apart from sharing one of the hottest nights of my life with him, we hadn't talked about what it all meant. We had both slept in late and apart from a brief "Good morning" as we hurried to get ready for work, we didn't have the chance. But we would the second we get back to the apartment later. I'd be sure of it.

"Okay, let's just pause for a second. What led to...*you know*."

I throw my hands up in the air like it's obvious. "He gave me yellow rain boots."

She grimaces. "Is that a euphemism for something kinky?"

"No, you fruit loop. He *literally* got me boots after I told him some sob story from my childhood. Then he took me to the secret trail where he had a picnic set up for us. Oh, but it doesn't end there, he just had to throw in the best orgasm of my entire life. Ugh, Jo, he's just..."

"Just what?" She leans in closer, eagerness lighting up her face.

"He's amazing. And this is meant to be fake, but what the heck am I supposed to do when I like my 'fake' boyfriend?"

"I don't think I'm qualified to help you here. Booth and Lottie are usually the type to meddle in people's relationships."

She must catch the pleading look on my face. "Oh jeez, okay, well, have you guys spoken about it?"

"No."

"Of course not. Well, let's start there. You honestly think he doesn't feel the same? The poor guy looks at you like you hold his universe in your hands." She pins me with a pointed stare.

There's no denying the looks we share. One glimpse and the air between us suddenly becomes combustible. A single touch would be the naked flame that ignites it all.

"How am I sup—"

"I think Uncle Gray loves Just-Quinn. Like a lot. Like Daddy loves you, JoJo," a small voice chirps behind us. Completely oblivious to the fact this is a private conversation.

"Oh crap, I forgot she has sonic hearing," Jo whispers, before shooting Lottie a smile over my shoulder. "Hey, Lottie. Whatcha doing?"

"You said my name," she replies with a shrug and grabs a packet of Goldfish. "Uncle Gray asked where Quinn was. Found her." She points at me and smiles sweetly, but I know not to be tricked by her cuteness.

Lottie slips her hand into mine and starts tugging me out of the pantry. I turn to Jo with panicked eyes and mouth, *Help.*

She chuckles and wiggles her fingers at me. "Take it from me. Talk to one another."

Lottie is oddly strong for a five-year-old. She drags me back into the hallway just as Dex steps out of the den and nearly collides with us. He's quick despite his hulking frame and he throws Lottie up and over his shoulder like a sack of potatoes.

"Caught ya, you little raccoon," he growls and tickles her sides. "Have you been stealing snacks again?"

"No! No!" she squeals and tries to wiggle out of his hold. The crinkling coming from the inside of her pocket says otherwise.

"Hmm. Has she been misbehaving?" he asks me and

ignores Lottie crawling all over his shoulders and head like a baby koala. "Also, I forgot to ask during dinner, do you have a table at the Fall Fair? I'm building some new stands for Our Place. I can throw you some together too."

I make sure he can see my lips after Graham explained Dex is hard of hearing, after going deaf in one ear.

"Oh, no. I couldn't get a slot. Maybe next year," I lie, not wanting to reveal that I couldn't afford it.

"That sucks, but it means you get to experience your first time as an attendee. You'll enjoy it." He offers me a kind smile.

"I hadn't even thought about attending. I'm just going to work."

Just then, a hand glides across my lower back, and I turn to find Graham gazing down at me.

"We're going to the fair," he declares, and I'm too caught up in his sudden appearance to argue with him.

"Lottie, let's leave these two before they start k-i-s-s-i-n-g," Dex drawls and backs away with a wink.

She mouths the letters silently to herself before giggling. "Gross!"

Their laughter disappears around the corner, leaving us alone.

"Does everyone under this roof like to interfere in one another's lives?" I ask.

"Yeah, I think it's hereditary. Dex has just been hanging around us all for too long." He drops his hand as I turn to face him, and I immediately miss his touch. "You good?"

"Stuffed full of pizza, but I had a great time. Evenings here are always fun."

"It's pretty rare we're all available but we make time. Are you ready to head out?"

"Yep." My voice oozes confidence despite the giddy nerves I'm feeling at the idea of being properly alone with him again. Mostly because I want to jump his bones.

The car ride home buzzes with tension. The small space between us crackles and pops, but neither of us makes a move.

Twenty minutes later, we're walking up the stairs to the apartment, armed with leftover pizza, when my phone vibrates in my back pocket. I'm so worked up I forget to check the caller ID before answering. "Hello?"

"A bakery?!" a hoarse, haunting voice barks through the speaker. It's not the volume but the realization of who is behind it that has me flinching. "I see you're still a greedy bitch. Things never change."

My entire body seizes up, leaving my left leg suspended above the second-to-last step on the stairs.

I was never supposed to hear that voice again.

Her texts and calls have become less frequent and a naïve part of me thought she was finally done.

Graham notices my pause and turns to face me as he reaches the top. Whatever expression is written across my face has his falling, and he's by my side in an instance.

My lips part and I try to get my voice to work, but it's broken. She's sucked it up, along with all my joy.

"Are you there? How's fucking Maine? Just because you're halfway across the country, owning some fancy business doesn't make you better than me. You're still trash, Quinn. Fat trash. You'll fail at it like everything else."

He's close enough to hear her raspy voice now. Dread and mortification crash through me like a flash flood. I don't want him to believe her words. To see me as trash. I'm not. Not anymore.

No. I never was.

This is what she's always done. Laced my brain with a sense of worthlessness. Each word hollowing me out until all that's left is a husk of shame.

"Don't fucking ignore me. I know you're there. You owe me. Owe me for ruining my life."

Graham's nostrils flare and from the raw anger burning off him, he's heard every word.

"You're a worthless piece of shi—"

Before I even know what's happening the cell is ripped from my hands and Graham's deep voice fills the stairwell. "If this is who I think it is, you will never call this number again. You will never speak to her again. *You* are the unworthy one. You don't deserve to speak her name, let alone think about it. She is done with you, and I am done with this call."

I can hear the beginnings of a shriek before it's cut off when he stabs at the End Call button with his thumb forcefully.

In the space of sixty seconds, Graham has said to my mom what I haven't been able to say for twenty-six years.

We stand there motionless as the aftermath of what's just happened takes root. There are too many emotions whirring through me to sort them out and understand what I'm feeling, but he still simmers with rage.

With a gentle grip on my hand, he pulls me up the last two steps and then shifts me to stand in front of him so he can direct us toward the door of his apartment. I'm pressed against the wood when he crowds me with his huge frame while unlocking the door, and once the snick of the lock sounds, he's pushing it open and ushering me inside.

The sound of the door closing hasn't even reached my ears before he's spinning me around, pocketing my phone in his jeans, and cupping my cheeks with his hands. His eyes say so much. *I'm sorry. What can I do? How can I help?*

It's the soft kiss he brushes to my lips that soothes the archaic pain quaking in my chest. "You're brave." A kiss to my cheek. "You're selfless." The other cheek. "You're kind." My nose. "You're funny." He lingers longest on my forehead before pulling away. "You're exactly how you should be; and that is perfect."

My vision blurs, and I swipe at my tears, not wanting to lose sight of the man in front of me. "You heard her?"

"I heard lies. From the mouth of a woman who clearly has a lot of deeply embedded regret, that has nothing to do with you, no matter what she says. I find it hard to believe you came from her, and I hate you had to listen to her vile words. I'm so sorry."

His hands are still shaking as they caress my tear-soaked face, and I raise mine to cover them. "You have nothing to be sorry for."

"I'm sorry I couldn't stop her."

My heart stutters. He would take on that responsibility, because that's who he is.

I tighten my grip on his fingers as fresh tears pool in my eyes. "Why does she hate me?"

He shakes his head slowly, and before I can repeat my question, he scoops me up in his arms and pulls me to his chest; his warmth smothers the frost left behind by my mother. "It's not about you. It's about her. You were just caught in the crossfire, but you got out and now you're here."

With a steady gait, he walks us down the hallway. I think he's going to take me into my bedroom but when he turns into the bathroom, I look up at him in confusion. "What are we doing?"

"I'm going to run you a bath with those funky bath bombs you love, and you're gonna soak while I heat up some apple cider." He lowers me until my feet land on the fluffy bath mat —my pink and orange one he laid in here without question. I watch with bated breath as he pulls out my phone and holds it up to my face to unlock it—too emotionally drained to ask him what he's doing. "You want your sad or happy girl playlist?"

"I want to be happy." My voice cracks and his gaze lifts from my phone screen. His handsome face plastered with understanding.

"Happy girl playlist it is." He nods. "Why don't you go and grab your pajamas. I'll get everything set up in here for you."

A couple of minutes later, I trudge back into the bathroom with my flannel pajamas and freeze in the doorway. Calming lavender greets me. The room is lit up in a warm, orange glow. Several candles sit along the edge of the bath, their flames dancing with the soft melody of music. Graham is bent over the tub, the sleeves of his shirt rolled up as he stirs the bright pink water. Tears well in my eyes again, and I try to brush them away so he doesn't see, but he turns right at that moment. In the blink of an eye, he's in my space, his warm, wet hand wrapped around my waist.

"No more, Quinn. No more tears; unless they're happy. I can't stand to see anything but happiness on your beautiful face." He places a soft kiss on my forehead before leaving me to relax.

I'm not sure how much time passes, but the warm water and uplifting lyrics melt away the sadness. *You got out and now you're here.* As the water swirls around me, Graham's heartfelt words take me back to the day it all changed.

To the day I set myself free.

Most girls spend their eighteenth birthday showered with gifts. A new pair of shoes. Perfume. Jewelry.

I spend mine cleaning the scratches left on my face and packing up the few belongings I own.

The water has been cut off again, leaving the potent smell of gin to cling to my hair and skin.

I'll shower when I get there.

Where there is, I don't know.

It took five minutes for me to pack up my entire life into a small backpack, which I should find depressing, but it just means I'll be out of this godforsaken place quicker. I ignore the pang of discontent that I won't get to graduate from high school, because after last night I'm not sure I'd even make it to graduation.

My mother was already in an anger-fueled state last night, and as usual, it took the tiniest of inconveniences to have all that hatred directed at me. Only, things escalated well past the typical slap or hateful slur of words. When I woke in a puddle of gin with bruises and scratches all over my body, I knew I couldn't stay here anymore.

There's no sadness, regret, or anger as I stare down at my mom passed out on the sofa. I feel nothing as I look at her for the last time, clutching a bottle of vodka to her chest like a mother would a baby.

What will she do when she wakes to find me gone?

It might be my birthday, but she's getting the gift she's always wanted. Me out of her life.

I slip on my worn sneakers and steel my spine. With a few changes of clothes and $317 I've managed to save cleaning tables at the local diner, I carefully open the door to our trailer, cringing when the hinges creak. I don't dare look back to see if she wakes up or to take in the four squalid walls I grew up in.

I don't look back as I walk down the steps of the trailer.

I don't look back when I make my way down the gravel path leading to the main road.

I don't look back as I buy a one-way ticket to Salem.

I don't look back as the bus crosses the state border.

I don't look back once.

Telling people about my childhood has always been something I've avoided, worried that once they learned about it, they'd see me differently. It's also why I never stuck around the same place for too long. She'd never follow me; that was where she drew the line thankfully. But settling in one place for too long meant I had to set down roots and open up to people.

In the nine years since I left California, Sutton Bay was the first place that felt different. Finding a location to start my dreams and making a friend like Jo helped me decide that this little fishing town is where I want to stay.

But it's the man who brings me flowers every day who helps me see a future here.

A light tap on the door has me slipping down until the water hits my chin. "Come in."

The door creaks open and I snort a laugh when Graham peeks in with his eyes clamped closed. As if he didn't spread me out last night and devour me until I was boneless.

Cute, silly man.

"How's it going?" he asks.

"I feel like a new woman."

He creeps around the door frame, using his hands to fumble his way into the room.

"You can look, you know." I chuckle.

"I don't know if that's a good idea."

"Why not?" I skim my hands across the rose petals floating on the surface of the water.

"Tonight isn't the night." His jaw is set tight.

"For what?"

"For me to lose control and take you like I want to."

My heart skips and thighs clench from the sudden wave of pleasure.

Maybe he does want to lose a little control, because he cracks an eye open. When he sees me submerged in the tub, both eyes open to brazenly take me in. He tracks me from head to toe, and even in the dim light I see his pupils swallow the green of his irises.

I might be in a bath full of water, but I know for a fact I'm wet.

"Taking me like you want to is exactly what the doctor ordered. I need the distraction." I baulk the moment those last four words leave my mouth, and I don't miss the frown lining his face before he has a chance to hide it. "That's not what I me—"

"It's fine."

It's not fine, because it's not what I meant. Being with him would be a distraction, but that's not why I want it.

He lowers himself to the floor, his back to the side of the tub, and tactfully changes the subject. "It's been a long day, but I meant what I said back at my mom's. Robin Road is going to be deserted; everyone will be at the fair, so you might as well close for the day. I'm going to help Pat set up, but I'll meet you there."

"Like a date?"

"Umm, yeah. You know we haven't done much in the ways of hanging out in public."

Ouch. A date for appearances. Though, I can't act bitter until we talk, and I get these roiling feelings out in the open.

"Oh, of course," I say, hoping to mask the edge to my tone.

He nods his head, and though I can't see his face, the slump in his shoulders gives away his tiredness. I wanted to talk tonight, about what's going on between us, but after my mom's phone call, I'm drained of energy.

His arm rests along the edge of the tub, palm open in invitation, and I slip my wet hand into his. "Thank you for coming to my mom's tonight. She really likes you and I think it's stopped her worrying that I'm going to die alone."

He's joking, but I hear what he's not saying. *Even though it isn't real.* If now were the right time and I wasn't so burnt out, I'd tell him we can call it quits on the whole thing. Jenna can go to hell, but if he still wants to show his face at the wedding, I'll be by his side proudly. I'm so eager to rip this stupid label off and replace it with something else.

What we call it is up to us.

"Thank you for looking after me this evening. I'm sorry it ended how it did. She hasn't called in so long, and I wasn't paying attention when the call came through. It really took me by surprise."

"Please don't apologize for that. You never have to be sorry for being upset around me. Though I can't say it doesn't kill me to see you like that." He gives me a side glance. "You were made to shine only, just as you are now. The world isn't right when you're sad, honey. It's like an eclipse. And you're the sun."

I study his side profile, soaking up the warmth of his touch and words. "Sometimes it feels like I shine the brightest with you."

He shakes his head and scoffs lightly, dismissing himself as usual.

We sit there, hand in hand, not needing to talk to feel the others comfort. When the bath water starts to cool, I squeeze his hand, and he turns to look at me.

"Will you tell me a nice story from your childhood?"

He hesitates, thinking, before his rich voice pacifies all the remaining sadness. "My first memory of the Fall Fair is with my dad. He took Pat and me on the tractor ride. There are ten months between us, and the guy who runs it had a stupid height restriction. We were both an inch shy and would have had to wait an entire year before we could ride it again. Before we got measured, our dad stuck wads of newspaper in the heels of our sneakers, and we made the cut. Best day of my life. Well, for a six-year-old."

Laughing softly, my thumb strokes across his knuckles, and he relaxes into the touch. "Can we go on the tractor ride?"

"Hmm, you might be too short."

I splash the back of his head, and he flashes me that smile I know only few get to see.

Long after we say goodnight to each other, sleep is the last thing on my mind. Instead, I think how good Graham and I would be together.

And that I really, *really* like my fake boyfriend.

CHAPTER TWENTY-THREE

graham

"No. Not there. You can't have a savory pastry among the sweet ones." I swat Booth's hands away and take over.

It's not that big of a deal, but I only have a short while to make this small space look perfect for her.

"How did you even pull this off?" Dex asks as he assembles a small wooden shelf ready to showcase pies, muffins, and loaves of bread. The table is draped with a red-and-white checked tablecloth and decorated with wreaths and gourds.

"It was difficult. Quinn practically lives in the bakery, but Johanna repeated what I told her and said it wasn't worth opening. She left me a key for emergencies, and the minute Jo texted to say the coast was clear, we snuck in to snag some stock."

I'm worried I'm overstepping the safe boundaries of our relationship, but as I lay out the last of the whoopie pies, I'm confident she's going to love this.

I hope.

Shit.

"She's going to hate it," I groan and start to retreat from the table.

"Nope!" Booth shouts and grips hold of my elbow to drag

me back. "Quit doubting yourself. This is nice—*really* nice. If I were a chick and a guy did this for me, I'd be buying a one-way ticket to pound—"

"Booth Elias Sadler!" a voice calls, making us all jump. We turn to find my mom strolling our way with Lottie and Patrick in tow. "I raised you better than that." She points a warning finger at my little brother.

"Sorry, Mom," he says with a face like a scorned puppy.

"*Sorry, Mommy,*" Patrick mocks.

Booth whips his head toward him. "I didn't even call her Mommy. Get your ears checked, old man. Don't even ge—" His words are cut off, distracted by something, and a fascinated look sweeps over his features. We all follow his gaze and groan when he makes a beeline toward the woman standing in front of a table filled with art pieces.

The dark-haired woman doesn't notice him until he's standing right next to her, with a coy grin on his face as he points at some of the canvases.

"Does he ever take a day off?" Dex sighs.

"Never," Patrick and I say in unison as we watch Booth work his magic. Or try. Scratch that, *fail.* Because minutes later, he's stomping back over here, lips pressed in a thin line with his hands shoved in his pockets.

"Lady trouble?" I chuckle and hook an arm around his neck.

"Get off." He ducks out of my hold and straightens his jacket.

"What was that about?" Patrick asks with an amused face.

Our little brother throws his hands in the air. "She said my dimples weren't that impressive!"

"Aww, but they're cute." Dex goes to poke his cheek, but Booth slaps his hand away. "Don't sulk just because you found someone who is finally immune to you."

"Who is she anyway?" I query.

"Must be a tourist," Dex guesses.

"Well, I'm not going to lose any sleep over her." *He absolutely is.* "I have more important things to do. C'mon, Pat, we need to finish setting up our stall. Let's leave lover boy to it."

My brothers head over to Our Place's table, but not before Booth says, "At least you're working quicker than Pat. He'd still be single if it weren't for me." Which earns him a punch from Patrick.

I look at Dex, who shakes his head and sighs. "Your family makes me grateful I'm an only child."

"They make me wish I *was* an only child," I retort while looking over the table. "This looks great, man. I really appreciate your help in pulling this together so quickly."

"My pleasure. Quinn's a lucky girl."

"It's not like that." I avoid his suspicious gaze and rub my fingers under the edge of my beanie.

"M-kay, keep telling yourself that. You sound a lot like your older brother though and we see how that turned out." He juts his chin over my head, and I turn to find Patrick wrapping Johanna up in a hug as he rains her face with kisses until she's laughing hysterically.

He pats me on the back and joins the others, leaving me with my mom and Lottie, who have been chatting to the vendor next door.

"It looks amazing, sweetheart. Quinn will be over the moon. I'm so happy for you," my mom coos.

"She's going to be super-duper excited. Like this much." Lottie widens her arms as far as they'll go. "I can't wait for your wedding." The knot in my stomach tightens and I do my best not to imagine Quinn in a wedding dress, walking toward me like sunshine incarnate.

I have roughly ten minutes before she arrives. She's meeting me under the guise that we'll be walking around the fair, checking out what local businesses have to offer, and roaming around pumpkin patch.

We will later on. First, I want her to experience what it's like to be a business owner at one of Sutton Bay's annual fairs.

Sadness crept across her face when she said she couldn't afford the table. She works so hard, from the crack of dawn until early evening. There have been a few times when I've had to coax her out of the bakery, close up, and relax for the night. She's a one-woman show and is fantastic at it.

She deserves this day.

And after the vile things her mother—if we can call her that —said about her, she needs this.

Quinn is forever smiling, but I've seen small fissures in that gorgeous smile since that phone call.

I keep my nerves contained by fiddling around with the table and baked goods, checking if she has enough change in her makeshift register and that all the items are labeled correctly.

My phone vibrates in my pocket, and I pull it out to read her text.

> Quinn: Hey, handsome. Where are you?

> Graham: Opposite the chili-tasting stall. I'm the guy in glasses, wearing a green beanie.

> Quinn: Smart-ass.

> Quinn: Oh! I see you!

Here we go.

I pick up the bouquet of yellow roses and wait for her in front of the table.

That's when I see her. I love touching, hearing, and smelling her, but nothing beats seeing her shine radiantly like she is now as she smiles at me.

She breathes air into my lungs and steals it from me with just a look.

With a brisk wave and hello to my family, she skips over to me with an eagerness that makes me think she wants to see me first.

"Hey, you." She beams up at me with no clue of what's behind me, which sets my nerves on edge further.

"Hi, honey."

I want to drag her away, scared I've overdone it. It's too much. Too soon. I'm not even sure if she feels the same way.

"What are you doing over here? Oh! Graham, have you seen all these goodies? They look so goo—wait..."

Too late now.

She spins around and spots our friends and my family watching us and then pivots back around. Her eyes bounce around the table, taking in the homemade banner Lottie helped me make, with Just Brew It messily scrawled across the paper—I can't draw for shit and Lottie is bad at keeping in the lines. Her fingers run across the tablecloth as she quietly recites each item I've laid out.

Something thick forms in my throat as I watch her, keeping a safe distance away to allow her to take it all in. When she's done, she turns toward me. So many emotions wash over her face—shock, gratitude, disbelief, joy—it's hard to pinpoint one.

"You did this for me?" Her eyes shine bright.

I nod before silently handing over the bouquet.

She lowers her face and inhales the floral scent before placing it on the table.

When she takes a running jump into my arms, I'm ready to catch her.

Maybe I did do the right thing after all.

"I'm dreaming, right?" she gasps into my shoulder.

"If you were, would it be a good dream?" My hand runs in circles against her lower back.

Her arms tighten around my neck. "One I never want to wake up from as long as you're there."

Watching Quinn work is quickly becoming my favorite pastime.

The way she interacts with customers has the grumpiest of people leaving her table with a smile and a bag full of sugary treats they didn't even know they needed. She's a natural. It's no wonder people gravitate toward her.

I've been idly sitting on the sidelines for the last four hours, helping when things got busy. Every time someone bought something, she would turn and flash me a stunning smile. The table is barren now, and even though I offered to drive back to the bakery to grab some extra stock, she seemed happy to end the day.

And if she's happy, I'm on top of the fucking world.

My mom left about an hour ago, and I didn't miss the way she whispered in Quinn's ear as they hugged goodbye. She just can't help herself.

Our Place is stocked to serve customers until the end of the day, but a lot of the smaller businesses have started to pack up, likely wanting to make the most of the fall festivities.

It takes us half an hour to clean the stall, pack up my Jeep, and hand over her takings for the day to Booth to lock up securely. The entire time Quinn chats excitedly to me about each and every single customer she interacted with, not once blanching at my silence as I soak up her happiness.

I'm guiding her toward the pumpkin patch when she halts me. "Have I said thank you?"

"At least a hundred times, honey."

Her arms loop around my middle and she burrows her face into my sweater. "Not nearly enough then." She props her chin against my chest and stares up at me with golden eyes. "Seriously, Graham, what did I do to deserve this? I promise I'll pay you bac—"

It could be the way she fits so perfectly against me, or perhaps it's the smile that hasn't weakened since she spotted me hours ago. Or maybe it's just her. Yeah, that's probably it. Whatever it is, has me silencing her with a kiss.

The kiss is quick but enough to leave us panting.

Her eyes flick left and right, and I realize she's checking to see if I did it for show.

I didn't.

This has never been for show, despite how it came about. A thought that crosses my mind constantly.

I wouldn't be surprised if Jenna or her friends were here, but luckily the fair is popular enough to attract almost three thousand visitors, so I'm hoping we don't bump into them. Here's to praying the odds are on our side.

As Quinn slips her hand into mine, I don't want anything ruining this moment.

She's overcome a lot, and never complains about the challenges she's faced. She runs at them head-on, accepts the cards she's been dealt, and looks to shuffle a new hand. Starting a new business is tough, and a lot of the time, it ends in failure. Even businesses that have been around for twenty-plus years run into problems—Our Place is proof of that.

Today is her day though. And I'm the luckiest guy alive to witness her conquer it.

I revel in the feel of her hand in mine and ask, "What do you want to do?"

She draws a dozen sets of eyes our way with her squeal and

then reveals the long list of things she wants to get done before the fair closes.

We tick every item off as we amble around the fair for the rest of the afternoon. Everywhere you look screams small-town charm, with a punch in the face of pumpkin spice. In three hours, we help pick the winner of the scarecrow-making contest, decorate our own candy apples, go pumpkin bowling, taste chili, and hop on the tractor ride.

Now, we're standing in a pen surrounded by baby goats.

"Knock it off," I hiss and shake a black-and-white kid off the pant leg he keeps chewing on.

"Aww, he's just hungry. Here you go, cutie." Quinn holds out a handful of pellets and strokes its wiry coat. She looks up at the large man handing out feed to the horde of children petting the animals. "Dex, what made you get goats?"

"I hate mowing grass and I have about one hundred and fifty acres around my property. These guys do it for free and don't pump fumes into the atmosphere."

"Huh. Very smart."

A tug at my leg and an obnoxious bleat has me glaring down again. "Go to her. Not me."

"Ignore Vincent. He's a prick." Dex laughs with an eye roll.

"Vincent?" Quinn asks.

"Yeah. Vincent van Goat." He shrugs.

She cackles with laughter, falling backward in the hay, and the baby goats swarm her. The ridiculous name even has me smiling. I check the time on my watch and see we have an hour before the corn maze closes.

"Hey, you, ready to get lost in a maze?" Grabbing her hand, I pull her to stand, and help her brush the dirt from her coat and dress.

"So ready."

We say goodbye to Dex and head over to the last stop on our itinerary.

She's had the same dreamy look on her face all day and it morphs into a friendly smile when she spots Mr. Willis manning the entrance to the corn maze.

"Hey, Martin." I shake his hand and pass him ten bucks for our entry. He gives me a curt nod and greets Quinn with a warm smile. He's nothing like the surly man I grew up knowing, and he clearly has a soft spot for her.

"You two enjoy yourselves," he calls after us as we enter.

It's pretty chilly now, with a glint of golden sun peeking out over the horizon, giving us just enough light to navigate our way around. We're both wrapped up in coats and scarves, but despite the cold bite in the air, Quinn is dressed in a deep, red tartan dress, sans tights, and a pair of knee-high black boots. That creamy sliver of skin has been driving me crazy for hours. One look at her thighs has me wanting to bite up the length of them until I find that sweet haven between her legs again.

"Helloooo!" A hand waves in front of my face and I shake myself out of my thoughts to find her peering up at me. "Earth to Graham. Are you still with me?"

"Uhh, sorry, did you say something?" I widen my stance, hoping to ease the pressure of my hard-on pushing into my zipper.

"I asked which way. You were pretty deep in your thoughts there, care to share with the class?" she teases and pokes me in the ribs, causing me to jolt backward with a very unmasculine noise.

"Quinn, cut it," I warn, but my glare does nothing to deter the little minx, and she jabs me in the side again and cackles loudly at my discomfort.

"I love that you're ticklish. Listen to you giggle. Oh my god, where is my phone?" Tears shine in her eyes she's laughing so hard, and even when she fumbles around in her purse, she continues to chase me while shouting, "I've found your weakness!"

With swift movements, I grab hold of her wrists and trap her against one of the barrels marking the first turn in the path. "You're my weakness, but right now you're a pain in my ass." There's no point in trying to hide my hard cock as it rests against her stomach. "Shall we find out how ticklish you are?" I ask, bending down to skim my nose across her cheek. The playfulness seeps out of her until she's putty in my hands. So soft and pliant.

Her head shakes from left to right, but the smirk playing on her lips says otherwise.

"I'd run, Quinn." I step back, a fire licking low in my belly as I watch her chest rise and fall. "When I catch you, you won't be laughing."

Fucking hell, I think as the words leave my mouth. She and I both know this isn't some game. I've never been so bold as I am with her, and my behavior now is a stark contrast to my usual demeanor. Ever since that night in her bedroom, an unfamiliar, hungry urge has slowly been growing in me.

Flames light up her eyes, a twin to the fire building in me. The need for her that's coursing through me extinguishes any worries about who or where we are right now. I want in her tight heat again, to have her drip down my chin, and if I'm lucky and she'll let me, I'll bury my cock so deep into her she'll realize just how far from fake this actually is.

We both glance toward the empty entrance. Our eyes meet for a nanosecond before she's darting off in the opposite direction.

I catch the glint of mischief on her face as she rounds the corner and takes a hard left.

Locals know that the exit path of this maze hasn't changed in eight years, and she's headed right toward a dead end.

I've never been one to chase, but god, when I catch her, I'm never letting go.

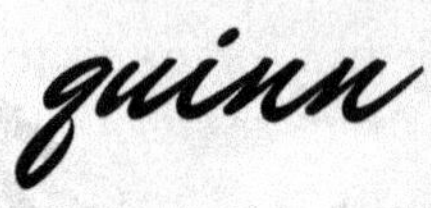

CHAPTER TWENTY-FOUR

My blood pulses through me like liquid fire as my heart pounds in my chest.

That's what Graham does to me.

Plus, we're playing a kinky game of cat and mouse in a maze.

I charge down the dusty path, breezing past the tall stems of corn, and gulping for air every time I check for him over my shoulder.

He is a walking, talking paradox, with no idea of the inferno he stokes within me. My teasing quickly turned into something that both scares and intrigues me. Never has it been like this with anyone. Every day is a surprise with him, and I love seeing his shyness fall away and his confidence shine bright in his own way.

Right now, however, there's nothing shy about him.

God, this is exhilarating.

The burn of his gaze sent a thrill through me. And it was clear he was as turned on as me when he pressed his hardness into my stomach, reminding me what it felt like to have him in my mouth. To be on my knees for him. The soft grunts of satisfaction he made when I took him deeper. The way he gripped my hair lovingly but looked down at me with a dark desire.

It's been over a week since the night in my room, and thanks to our crazy schedules, we haven't had the chance to talk. We need to, but there was nothing stopping the pent-up sexual frustration that's been brewing between us all day.

I whip my head around, and when I don't see him I make another sharp left.

Only to come to a dead end.

My heart thunders and I spin on my heels, ready to try the other route, but stop in my tracks when I find my exit blocked.

He fills the space despite the corn towering above us.

Leaves tickle my head as I stumble into the foliage. His steps are urgent as he strides forward. My swallow is audible as he consumes the space between us, until we're toe to toe. With his mouth level to my ear, he whispers, "Gotcha."

The vibrations of his chest beat against my breasts, pebbling my nipples, and making me want to rub up against him like a needy kitten.

He's not wrong; I'm not laughing.

I'm on fire.

My skin is tight and sensitive and only his touch will soothe the ache coursing through me. Jesus, apparently being chased in a corn maze does it for me, who would've guessed?

"You got me," I whisper breathlessly as my eyes track upward from his heaving chest, past his perfectly trimmed beard and strong nose, until I find his gaze. Even behind the frames of his glasses, I feel the heat in it. His eyes glow dark, like rippling reeds of grass blowing in the night sky. "What now?"

Hungry eyes burn into me, raking up and down my body, like he can't decide where to start. I want to be rid of this coat; of all my clothes. And preferably his. Although he's as affected as I am, he doesn't rush this. I like Graham's ability to slow down his racing thoughts, to rationally think things through. But fuck that. I want his thoughts as scrambled as mine.

The taste of spiced apple and all things Graham floods my senses when I drag his mouth down to mine, fingers gripping the collar of his coat until my knuckles turn white. There's zero hesitation now as his tongue plunges past my lips. Every kiss with him feels like it's our first but also like we've been doing this our whole lives.

The best oxymoron there was to ever exist.

My hands move to his head, ripping his beanie off while his palms roam down my body, underneath my coat, and slip beneath the hem of my dress to cup and squeeze me through my shorts.

He breaks the kiss and nuzzles into my neck. "This ass was made for my hands, I'm sure of it. I need to feel you again." His fingers inch inward to the cleft of my ass.

Never has a man's desperate tone turned me on so much. I pull him closer, until my chest is flattened to his toned stomach, and nod eagerly. It's all the permission he needs. With urgent movements, his hand moves to my front, and he rips my shorts down to my ankles to find me wet and bare.

"Where are your panties?" he mutters with a devilish look.

"I think you should be thankful there's one less layer for you to remo—*oh god.*" I claw at his shoulders when he strokes a thumb over my clit.

His hot breath ghosts over my collarbone. "I want you so bad, Quinn. I've never needed something so much in my life."

My response dies on my lips when he presses into me. My dress is bunched up around my waist and draped over his forearm, allowing the cool air to caress the overheated skin of my thighs.

I'm a shaking mess, such a contrast to his calm exterior. We both suck in a breath when he adds a second finger and thrusts deeper. "Drenched, honey. So wet and hot. I want nothing more than to sink into your tight pussy, but for now you'll have to make do with my fingers."

His crass words are still the best surprise, and it leaves me blushing all over.

With precise movements, he crooks his fingers, quick to find that tender spot in me that has my back arching into him. If it weren't for the firm grip he has on my waist, I'd be melting into a puddle from the delicious pleasure he's quickly mastering my body with.

"There, there, there," I chant, my eyes falling closed as he strokes deep inside of me.

Voices nearing closer should stop us, but he just works me harder. The heel of his hand finds my clit with each thrust of his fingers, and when he trails hot, open mouth kisses along my jaw, I clench around him.

"You're going to come. Now," he commands with a deep whisper. "All over my fingers, Quinn. I want to feel you; show me what it'll feel like when you finally grip my cock with this beautiful pussy."

"G-Graham," I pant and sputter.

I clutch the collar of his sweater, his face, his hair. I hold on for dear life as the coil deep in my stomach winds tighter and tighter.

When he breathes, "Now, honey," against my lips does that coil unravel at the speed of light. He's the only thing keeping me up as I fall apart in his arms, blissfully overcome by my orgasm until it gradually teeters off, leaving me draped over him like a sated blanket.

He slips his hand out from between my legs, and without breaking eye contact, draws his fingers into his mouth, humming as he sucks them clean. The sight alone is enough to bring on a second orgasm.

"Do you know what you taste like?" he asks.

Words, Quinn, find your words.

I shake my head.

I gasp as he dips the same hand back in between my legs and swipes across my sensitive flesh before raising two fingers to my lips. Without instruction, I wrap my lips around the digits and suck them into my mouth. The look he gives me as I slip my tongue over him could set the fields surrounding us ablaze. Nothing compared to the firestorm flaring between us though.

"You love tasting yourself, don't you? You're sucking on my fingers so greedily. Perfect girl."

He pulls his hand from my mouth and replaces it with his lips, searing me with a deep, sensuous kiss.

"Let's go home," he says with his forehead pressed to mine.

We're in such a hurry to get to the apartment, we almost leave my shorts and his hat on the dusty path.

After the fastest car ride ever, we race up the stairs, both breathless from the exertion but also for what's to come.

Curly scurries around our feet, and while the dog is cute and all, he's in the way. Graham locks him in his room with water and a generous helping of kibble.

When he returns to the living room, I'm about ready to burst out of my skin in anticipation. There's a constant buzz running through me when he's near, but it's been damn near impossible to control since he chased me into the maze. It threatens to take over my limbs; to tear the clothes from both our backs and finally let ourselves give in to the craving.

Maybe it scares him as much as it scares me, which is why we've been tiptoeing around this force field rippling between us for weeks. He's constantly on my mind. I look forward to seeing him after work. I think about ways I can pull that tentative, handsome smile from his lips. I get excited when I hear the jangling of keys when he's been working in the city.

He's invaded my mind, set up camp, and is making himself at home.

From the serious, hungry gaze he sets on me, he's thinking the same as me.

Let this happen.

With every step he takes closer, I take one step back, until my butt hits the edge of his desk tucked away in the corner of the room.

"This isn't a game, Quinn." His voice has dropped a couple of octaves and the deepness of it sends goose bumps across my skin. "I've already chased you tonight, and I know you need this as much as I do. I felt it when you came around my fingers." He emphasizes his point by squeezing the bulge in the front of his jeans.

"I'm scared," I admit but continue talking when his face softens. "Like a good scared, mostly. I've never felt like this before and I don't want to mess anything up."

In three long strides, our bodies are molded together, with his hands framing my face.

"I'm petrified. You have no idea the power you hold over me, but I can't ignore it or pretend anymore." He blows out a long breath and drops his head before raising it again. "Tell me I'm not alone here."

"You're not." My hands slide up his chest to encircle his neck. "There hasn't been a moment of loneliness since you walked into the bakery. I like you a lot."

A gentle brush of his lips on mine has all remaining nerves evaporating and my eyes shutter closed in relief.

"Look at me, honey." I do as he says and take in his handsome face—sincerity and passion written across it. "I like you more than a lot."

Warmth blooms in my chest, spreading outward until every surface of my body heats under his touch. "Graham, please kiss me."

"I was hoping you'd say that."

His lips meet mine in a bruising kiss and we grapple with each other's coats and scarves. My fingers find the hem of his sweater just as he lowers to a knee to take off my boots, allowing me to slip it off and over his head with ease.

When he rises, his hands slip behind me, fumbling to find the zipper of my dress and my stomach drops. I only have my bra on under here after not putting my shorts back on. If he takes it off, I have nothing to hide behind. I'm not ashamed of my body—but that old sense of dread trickles in.

He must sense my resolve, because he pauses. "Do you want to stop?"

"No, no. It's just..."

His eyebrows pull inward, and he strokes down my arms. "Will you tell me? I want you to be comfortable, and if you're worried about something, I'd like to know. I want this to be good for you."

The first time I had sex, I hid behind an oversized T-shirt, dimmed the lights, and asked them to take me from behind. My stomach was always a target area for my mom, she'd pinch and squeeze while throwing horrid names at me. Last week I made the mistake of searching social media for Graham's ex, and when I saw pictures of her tall, slim frame, I immediately closed down the app. I have no wish to look like her; my only wish is Graham likes *all* of me.

He isn't my mother. He's kind, thoughtful, caring.

With a deep swallow, I say, "I'm not thin or athletic. There's a lot of extra cushion around here"—I gesture toward my stomach—"and I don't want you to be disappointed. I love my body, and it took a long time for me to accept it."

I expect my confession to silence Graham. So when he plants his hands on either side of my hips, and speaks with such tenacity, I'm the one who's left speechless.

"Disappointed?" He shakes his head. "What about the way that I kiss you, crave you, *need* you, makes you think I'd be disappointed? I'm not a shallow man, Quinn, and it's your joy, passion, and outlook on life that has me crazy for you. But know this"—he leans in closer until our lips are a whisper away, and I feel his hard cock against my thigh—"your body makes me delirious. I want nothing more than to follow the path of each and every one of your curves with my lips and tongue. I'm glad you love your body; now let me love it too."

Valued, cherished, desired. That's how he makes me feel. I need him to know I want that, so I give him my consent by whispering, "Yes," just before I seal my lips over his.

He groans into my mouth, knowing exactly where this is headed.

My hands reach for the fly of his jeans, and he returns to my zipper. We work in tandem in between hot kisses until I'm standing there in nothing but my pale-yellow bra, and him in a tight pair of black briefs.

His hands land on my shoulders and he takes a step backward, eyes dragging a fiery path across my body as he drinks me in. He shakes his head in awe, his voice gravelly when he follows the swells of my breasts. "I'm going to fuck those one day."

Good god. Confident, filthy Graham is going to put me in the hospital.

"And today?"

"Today I'm going to fuck your pretty pussy. Lose the bra," he orders as he hooks his thumbs into the waistband of his briefs, and they drop to the floor. My mouth waters at the view in front of me. He's thick in his shoulders and thighs, but his abdomen is cut with lean muscles. A broad chest that tapers down to a trim waist. A dark blond trail of hair leads to his painfully hard cock, already leaking from the tip.

He really does want me as badly as I want him.

I don't need to be told twice. I reach behind to unclasp my bra, letting my breasts spring free, and dropping it on the sea of clothes at our feet.

"You're simply spectacular, honey. Thank you for trusting me with your body," he says quietly as his lips brush across my temple and his palms glide down my sides. We trace each other's bodies with gentle, exploratory touches and kisses. Though, our movements soon turn frantic. With a firm grip on my thighs, he hoists me up and sets me on top of the cool, dark surface of the desk. "Do not move."

I watch his wonderfully biteable ass disappear, and I savor the sight of him as he runs back to me with a foil packet in hand. I'm glad one of us is thinking, because I would have let him fuck me raw.

With deft movements, he tears at the packet with his teeth and sheaths himself.

My heart beats so loudly I hear it in my ears. I'm still wet from the maze, and when Graham taps the inside of my thighs, silently asking me to widen them, there's no hiding my arousal.

But he wants more. "Feet up on the desk."

Lust and need have me following his directions mindlessly and I bare myself to him with both feet planted on the wooden surface. My stretch marks are visible and stomach rolls are more obvious in this position, but I can't find a modicum of care when his hungry gaze falls to where I'm aching for him. Dripping onto his desk.

I whimper when he swipes two fingers through my wet folds and his cock twitches between us.

"Graham," I plead. "No more teasing or waiting. I need you."

With a wanton gaze that matches my own and chest heaving with short breaths, he steps between my spread legs and fists himself. "No more waiting."

He brings the tip to my pussy, circling the entrance and coating himself in me before pushing in. A sharp intake of breath escapes me, and deep hums of satisfaction rumble in his chest as he stretches me slowly.

He strokes and pets my face, kissing my fevered skin with every inch. He's big but the bite of pain is quickly replaced with pleasure when he whispers, "I could watch you take my cock forever. You're so fucking sexy." In dual awe, we watch as he disappears inside me, our panting breaths mingling between us. "God, look at you. So good at taking all of me."

When he bottoms out and his balls press against my ass, we attack each other with ferocious, needy kisses. He doesn't retreat at first, just rests inside of me as we lose ourselves in a battle of tongues, lips, and teeth.

"More, Graham. I need more," I moan into his mouth.

"What is it you need? Whatever it is, I'll give it to you."

"Harder. I want it hard," I beg breathlessly. "Can you...Can you talk dirty to me again?"

He raises his head, eyes darting between mine. I've surprised myself, but I want him to know I'm comfortable with the way he spoke in my bedroom that night. His filthy words make me woozy with lust and it's only made hotter by the fact it's new for us both.

"I wish I could give you everything in the world." With a deep breath, he cups the backs of my knees and pushes them to my chest. "Tonight, I'll give you hard and dirty."

I'm nodding my head frantically, pawing at his sides to pull him closer. "Yes. That. I want that. I trust you. Please, Graham. I need it."

He must hear the desperation in my voice, because with a firm press of his lips to my neck, he lets go.

"Hold on." That's all the warning I get as he snaps his hips forward and slams into me, jolting me backward.

"Oh my god," I cry out and scratch at his shoulders and chest to anchor myself. "Fuck, fuck, fuck. You're so deep. So good."

"I know. I know, baby. Never. Never has it felt this good," he murmurs into my neck and runs his tongue over the sensitive skin below my ear.

It's all consuming. *He's* all consuming.

Sweet, careful Graham is beautiful. But this version, which isn't afraid to take what he wants and handles me with robust care, is the version I need right now. He can whisper sweet nothings down my ear later.

Our hips meet with each punishing thrust, the slap of our skin reverberating around the apartment and echoing with our raspy moans and short gasps. My head falls between my shoulders as I grip the edge of the desk with one hand and his shoulder with the other. I know he's a giver, but I love that he's taking what he needs from my body. Seizing everything he desires but giving me so much more in return.

He bites a path across my chest, teeth scraping and marking the swells. My cries of pleasure turn to whimpers when he laves his tongue across each mark. Sucking and nipping at my nipple, while pinching the other before switching sides.

"You like that?" he breathes against my skin and repeats it.

"I really like it. God, Graham, I'm so fucking close already." I'm a garbled mess when his hand drops between us and he taps my swollen clit.

"I know you are. Can feel it with the way you're clamping down on my cock. This beautiful fucking body was made to bring me pleasure. I want to feel yours as you come around me," he grits out and works my clit faster. "Come with me, baby. I want you there right with me."

I'm sprinting toward my orgasm in record time. His movements become frenzied, kisses turn sloppy, and gaze darkens.

"Ah, so close. So close. I need you there, honey. Let me hear you. Feel you." The deepness of his voice, the feel of him, and what this all means take me to where he wants me.

And we fall so devastatingly beautiful together.

We're intertwined in euphoria as a powerful orgasm slams into me and he pulses inside of me. Despite feeling like I'm floating away into space, we ground each other as our tongues stroke and tangle, until the pleasure ebbs away, leaving us breathless and spent.

Minutes later, we're still kissing and caressing one another. Almost like we're too afraid to pull away and for this to end.

It's him who breaks the connection, but his glazed eyes let me know he felt it too.

His thumb strokes down the column of my throat. "Are you okay?"

"I'm...Wow. You're a dangerous man, Graham Sadler." I sigh.

"How so?" he asks, followed by a low groan as he pulls out, removes the condom, and throws it in the trash under the desk.

"You're sweet, mindful, and considerate; yet you fuck a girl like that. Ten out of ten. Bravo."

I feel the smirk on his lips as he kisses me stupid and palms my ass. "It wasn't too much?"

"Nope. But just to be safe, I think we should do it again."

With a squeak, he hauls me into his arms and carries me down the hallway. We bypass my room, and his steps don't falter as he walks us into his and lays me down on the bed to test the theory all night long.

CHAPTER TWENTY-FIVE
graham

TWO HUNDRED AND TWENTY-SEVEN DAYS I'VE BEEN CHARMED BY the woman sitting across from me.

But in the last twenty-four hours we've had a spell cast over us. Both overcome with a voracious need that can't quite be satisfied and kept us up until the break of dawn.

There wasn't an inch of skin we left untouched; exploring with our hands, lips, and tongues.

This morning, I was convinced it was all a dream and that my mind was playing tricks on me. That was until I found her curled up into my side, with an arm slung over my waist, hair splayed out across my chest, and snoring softly.

I was half tempted to hold her captive in my bed, but today was Sunday, the busiest day of the week at the bakery. I walked her to work with Curly in tow and without overthinking it, kissed her goodbye until she was grinning maniacally and blushing beautifully. Reminding me of the rosy hue of her skin as I lost myself in her last night. Over and over.

If it was a dream, sleep would quickly become my next favorite thing. Right after her.

The day dragged, however, the second she stepped foot in the apartment, I asked her if she wanted to join me for dinner. Which is where we find ourselves now.

I've been so busy admiring her in the dim lighting of Our Place, that my dinner has gone cold. Seeing her in my family's restaurant, a place where I grew up and made so many memories, is something special. I watch as she swipes up the last drops of broth from her steamed clams with a chunk of sourdough. Her tongue peeks out, fingers lingering on the pillowy lips I can't wait to kiss again.

She makes a show of licking her fingers clean, eyes on me the entire time. If I hadn't been hard for most of the evening, this would do the trick.

"How's the bread?"

She pops the last of it in her mouth and chews slowly. "It's good. I mean, not to blow my own horn, but I do it better."

"I agree. It just happens I know the guy in charge of ordering in the stock. Maybe I'll put a good word in for you."

Her eyes narrow. "I'm not ready for that. We have a plan; you wrote it."

She's referring to the three-month business plan I drafted. All her books are in order now and she has an easy, clear recording system so she doesn't get herself in the same mess I found her accounts in. I did some forecasting for her, too, which illustrated a healthy incline over the next year. She was shocked to find her financial position was in a much better place than she originally suspected.

Yet, she's still wary of taking these next steps.

"It's not like we're some big chain ready to screw you over. You can start out small, but I know there are plenty of businesses that would love to work with you. Even Ricky mentioned buying some of your muffins to stock in his waiting room the other day."

"You spoke to Ricky?" She tilts her head.

Shit.

"Um, yeah. He couldn't get through to your cell, but there weren't any updates, he was just checking in. He's ready to start work when you give him the go-ahead."

"Oh, okay."

I lean forward, catching her gaze. "Will you tell me what's holding you back from working with the restaurant? If I can help, I want to."

For a second, I think she's going to brush me off. I'm relieved when her shoulders lose a little tension, and she says, "It feels like cheating, you know? I haven't earned it. I'm only getting this opportunity because of who I know—you, Booth, Patrick, Johanna."

Her answer leaves me more confused. "It's cliché, but in business, it's about who you know. Networking is a big part of success; it's not cheating if it helps you get where you want to be."

She fiddles with the linen napkin on her lap. Discomfort twists her features, and she falls silent. I've learned that when she closes up like this, her mother is usually involved. Just thinking about that woman has white-hot rage simmering in me, but I need to stay calm. Quinn isn't trying to avoid the question, but she needs assurances before fully opening up. Especially when it comes to her past.

My hand stretches out across the table, and she takes it without question. "I know it's hard. Every step of your journey to get here, you've done alone. You should be proud of that; I know I am. Don't let pride get in the way of what you've built. You think my dad and George didn't use their connections to help them out?" I gesture toward the brick and whitewash walls of the restaurant, covered in old fishing gear and photographs of the town. It hasn't changed much since I was a kid, something my siblings and I treasure.

"Lenny and Martin Willis played a big part in helping them get this place open," I continue. "From putting them in contact with local brewers and offering fair deals on produce. That's what business is about. And what this town is about. Giving back to the people who live here."

I watch her digest my words.

"What if I fail?" she whispers. "That's what my mo—what *she* always said. She never followed me, but she'd leave me texts and voice mails, reminding me that all she saw was a failure. Anytime a teacher sent me home with a new pair of shoes or food, she accused me of cheating my way through life and taking the easy way out. It never made sense when I was a child. It doesn't excuse what she said or did, but a part of me wonders if she acted that way because she couldn't afford those things. I don't believe her words anymore...but sometimes they still haunt me."

My heart cracks as her voice falters and tears pool in her eyes. For all the joy and beauty she brings into the world, Quinn has scars like the rest of us. I'm greedy for her happiness, but I don't take her vulnerability for granted.

It's in these moments that I know my words mean the most to her. "We *all* fail. We're human." I bring her hand to my mouth and lay a kiss to the center of her palm, then let it rest against my cheek as I speak. "My dad would say, 'Let the failures of today build the foundations of tomorrow.' I can't see it happening, but if you fumble or trip, I'll be there every step of the way to help you get back up."

A shaky breath leaves her, and the tightening in my chest eases up when a small smile follows. "Okay. I'll speak to Booth. Just let me do it when I'm ready." Her hand coasts up my jaw. "Thank you for everything you've done for me."

"It's my pleasure." I place another kiss to the inside of her wrist before pulling away as the server comes over to clear our plates.

"Speaking of Mr. Willis. Have you heard he's thinking about selling a bunch of his properties?"

Shaking my head, I reply, "No, I haven't. Why do you ask?"

"I'm really close to getting a deposit together and I dunno" —she shrugs—"maybe the banks will take a chance on me. Do you think it's a long shot if I spoke to him about buying the bottom floor off him when the time comes?"

Pride surges in my chest. She's gone from doubting her credibility as a business owner to sharing this. "I think that's smart. He trusts you. Get in there first before anyone else does."

There's a twinkle in her eyes, and she goes to open her mouth, when she's interrupted by a voice I've unfortunately become very acquainted with over the years.

"Graham?"

Quinn has never met the woman standing in front of us, but from the way she straightens in her seat and narrows her eyes, she knows exactly who this is.

My throat grows tight, and a weight drops in my stomach so heavy, it could have me plummeting through the old parquet floor beneath our feet.

"Jenna." I keep my voice neutral and gaze steady.

Her eyes flit between the two of us before finally settling on me. "Sorry to interrupt this—" She waves her hand at our table. "Ralph and I wanted to come over and say hi before we left."

My fingers tense at her flippant tone.

I glance over at where my cousin is standing a fair distance away, looking like he'd rather gouge his own eyes out than speak to us.

"Have a good night," I say tersely.

A laugh I once found alluring but now sounds like nails on

a chalkboard, drowns out the last of my sentence. I chance a look at Quinn, worried this is making her uncomfortable but find her angry gaze trained solely on Jenna. "Don't be like that, Gray."

Gray. Everyone calls me Gray. Have done so for as long as I can remember. From her mouth, it sounds pitiful and holds a totally different meaning. Her parting words to me before she moved out tainted that name forever, yet I still can't bring myself to ask people to stop using it.

I remain silent, hoping it draws this conversation to a close, but no such luck.

"We haven't received your RSVP."

I'd laugh if my vocabulary wasn't slowly drying up. The RSVP was meant to be returned weeks ago. It's why Quinn agreed to our little scheme, but it seems there's been other things on my mind.

"The deadline was last week," Jenna continues. "We understand if you don't want to come, considering—"

"Considering what?"

Our heads turn toward Quinn, who looks ready to sharpen her pitchfork.

Jenna's blindsided by the interruption but schools her features quickly. "I'll be a second and then you can continue your business meeting." She barely casts Quinn a glance and dismisses her with a flick of her wrist, instantly making my blood boil.

"The only business I have is ordering dessert and then taking my boyfriend home. I think your brother is waiting for you." Quinn looks at Ralph, and I have to hold my breath to stop myself from snorting.

She's getting three orgasms tonight.

"B-boyfriend?"

"Yup." The little vixen reaches across the table and takes my hand in hers.

"Wait, no, that's my fiancé." Jenna's face is crimson now.

"Oh, my bad. You have that sibling bond thing going on."

That dread at hearing Jenna's voice has quickly morphed into pride at watching Quinn put her in her place.

"Is this new?" Jenna asks, her attention on me again.

"I'm not sure what business it is of yours." I've known Jenna for half my life—we were together for over a decade—and I've never sounded more confident when speaking to her than I do now. But it's short lived.

"I never expected you to act so pathetic. I've been home a week and no one has mentioned you're seeing anyone. If this is some ploy at making me jealous, you're—"

"I think you should go," Quinn cuts in.

The pride I felt moments earlier has quickly dimmed and humiliation takes a hold of me. This is the woman I was happy to spend the rest of my life with, complacent in my feelings and ignoring how toxic and manipulative she was.

It shouldn't be Quinn stopping this conversation; it should be me.

I'm suddenly reminded why this thing between Quinn and me started off as fake, and why it'll never work in real life.

My meek, muted exterior is exactly the reason my and Jenna's relationship broke down in the first place. I was never outspoken enough. Fun enough. Manly enough for her. And now those truths are out in the open for Quinn to look over and second guess everything about me.

"The end of the week. I need your answer by then," Jenna says through gritted teeth and then plasters on a forced smile. She turns away before we can respond and stomps out of the restaurant with Ralph on her tail.

It's then I spot Jo and Patrick behind the bar, both seething and muttering between themselves after witnessing that shameful interaction. I can't look at the woman across from me.

Too afraid to see the disappointment and secondhand embarrassment written across her face.

I hear her sigh over the table but keep my eyes trained on the row of liquor bottles along the bar.

"I have to ask. How did that last for as long as it did?"

This isn't a topic I want to dive into tonight. Or at all. The one and only interaction Quinn was supposed to have with Jenna was a quick "congratulations" at the wedding. Yet now, I can't even get my words out and stand my ground after seeing Jenna for the first time since we broke up.

When I brave a look at her, she meets my gaze with an apologetic look. My hands twitch to rub the back of my neck. If it were anyone else, I'd be avoiding eye contact, but I don't think I'll ever be able to look away from her. I do avoid answering the question, however.

"Do you want dessert here or to go?"

Her eyes fall to the table, hiding her dejected expression.

I hate this. Hate what Jenna has turned me into. I've always been quieter than most. It took most of my teenage years to feel like I belonged in my own skin. Until Jenna. My ex wrapped her claws around the parts of me that took so long to accept and easily obliterated the years of progress I made. She belittled me. Dismissed me. And left me as a man who hardly recognized himself.

Then came Quinn.

The last thing I want is for her to see me as the man Jenna discarded.

CHAPTER TWENTY-SIX

graham

WHEN WE GOT BACK FROM THE RESTAURANT LAST NIGHT, WE stood there in the hallway dividing our rooms. My arms ached to hold her as I had the night before. And from the torn look in her eyes, she wanted that too. But she also had questions she knew I didn't want to answer.

Instead, we said goodnight and slept in separate beds.

The pillow she used still smelled of her.

I hated every second of it.

Somehow, I managed a few hours of sleep. Now dressed, I sluggishly drag myself into the living room to find Quinn pulling on her coat, ready to leave for the bakery.

"Hey, you." Her voice is upbeat, and her smile meets her eyes, which chips away at the worry clinging to me from last night.

"Morning," I croak and cough into my fist. "Did you, um, want something to eat before you leave?" I stand there awkwardly as I fight the need to wrap her in a hug.

She shakes her head as she zips up her coat. "Nah, I have some leftover pastries I doubt will sell today. Unless I can finally entice you to try one..."

The laugh that bursts out of me when she waggles her eyebrows at me surprises us both and dissolves any last doubts. I internally curse myself for thinking Quinn would allow last night to monopolize what's been happening between us.

When Jenna accused us of fabricating our relationship to make her jealous, I should have jumped in and corrected her. This was never about making anyone jealous, let alone her.

Quinn had no qualms in opening up to me about her mom. She trusted me, and in return I closed myself off. I trust her, no question. I just don't want her to look at me in a different light. I'd give anything to know what she's thinking. And would also give anything to not know the truth, from fear she sees me just as Jenna did.

"I'm sorry about dinner," I say, my voice still groggy with sleep, and walk over to her.

Her brow crinkles as she slips on her Chucks. "You have nothing to be sorry about. Graham, she's awful, and I just can't understand how you could be with someone like that. I just wish you—"

The sound of my ringtone has her pausing, and I look down at my smartwatch to find an incoming call from Patrick. She peers down at my wrist and squeezes my arm. "It's fine, go ahead and answer it. Let's talk later though."

I nod slowly, thankful I'll have time to prepare for our conversation.

"Okay. Talk, yeah. We can do that." Pulling out my cell, I tap Accept. "Hey, what's up?"

My brother lets out a deep breath that sends a chill down my spine as a morbid sense of déjà vu hits me. "I hate it when people say this, but please don't panic..."

I panicked.

What else do you do when you hear that your mom is in the hospital?

If my mind was working in overdrive from last night, it's gone completely off the rails now.

As soon as I hung up the phone, I was throwing on my coat and flying down the stairs. Quinn didn't hesitate as she followed me into my car, and I was too rattled to remind her she had a bakery to open. We met my brothers at the hospital in record time, and Patrick managed to get in contact with Florence to let her know.

Now, the sickening fear from Patrick's phone call has died down, but I'm still on edge.

"Would you all stop fussing over me. I'm fine," my mom chides and shoos us away from her hospital bed.

"Not happening. We've all aged twenty years. We need to wrap you up in Bubble Wrap, you nuisance," Booth teases, but I can see he is weighed down with worry like Patrick and me.

She's not fine, but it's not as bad as my intrusive thoughts led me to believe. She was taking out the trash when she slipped on a pile of rotten leaves on her driveway, leaving her with a broken tibia, sprained wrist, and a nasty cut on her chin. According to the doctor, it was a clean break, and by the time we made it to the hospital, she was already getting her leg casted while cheerfully chatting away to the orthopedic nurse.

Our mother is formidable. But so was Dad. Our worry and panic aren't misplaced, and she knows that. The fact that she fell and injured herself while alone—so similar to how we lost dad—has us all reliving our darkest memories.

"Hey, Claire," Quinn says softly as she returns from the cafeteria. "All they had was diet, is that okay?"

"Oh yes, that's perfect, sweetheart. Thank you." She takes the can of soda from Quinn, but my little brother promptly snatches it out of her hand and pops the cap before handing it over. "Booth, I'm not broken."

"Get used to it, Mom. Because I'm moving in with you."

"You are not!" she shouts.

"I am," Booth counters.

"I do not need you babysitting me," my mom gripes.

They bicker for several minutes, but ultimately, she agrees to Booth living with her for the next two weeks, and despite her annoyance, Mom gets her precious baby boy back under her roof. She would never admit it, but she's been suffering from extreme empty nest syndrome since Florence moved out.

I've hardly said a word since getting here. The longer we sit in this hospital room, the more my skin feels like it's being stretched. I talked with the doctor when we first arrived, taking mental notes of her recovery, physio appointments, medication, and what to avoid as she heals.

Luckily, Mom is discharged a short while later and Quinn and I are sitting in my car, waving goodbye to my family as they leave the hospital parking lot.

I'm grateful to be out of there, but I'm so mentally drained that silence seems like the best option right now.

Despite my mom being in good spirits and the doctor giving her the all clear, I can't shake off the grief that's slowly been trickling in.

The call was too similar to the one Patrick made the day we lost Dad.

"Graham?" Quinn's soft voice cuts through the quiet like a breath of fresh air, but the fog overhead starts to close in again.

With all the effort I have left, I shift to face her. If I wasn't already struggling to speak, her beauty would leave me speechless.

"Do you want to talk about it?"

All I can do is shake my head.

"What do you want to do?"

My head tilts a fraction, enough to tell her I don't know.

"That must have been scary." She sighs. "When I'm in need of a distraction I like to do something that stops me from thinking. Usually I bake something for myself or do one of those adult coloring books. What would distract you right now?"

You, I want to say. She's the perfect distraction from the agonizing memories surfacing from seeing my mom injured. But that's not fair to her. I want so badly to explain how I'm feeling and to apologize properly for last night. Nothing sounds right as I recite it over in my head and the silence being dragged out becomes painful.

Not wanting to sit here for much longer, I go to start the engine when Quinn shuffles to her knees and jerks her head toward the backseat. "Move your seat back."

I don't question her and do as she says.

With enough space between the wheel and me, she hitches a leg over the console and settles herself on my thighs. Before my next breath, she wraps her arms around my neck and presses her face against my shoulder, relaxing into my rigid body.

"What are you doing, honey?" Despite my confusion, I tug her closer and breathe in the scent of brown sugar and vanilla.

"I'm distracting you with a hug. We don't need to talk. I just wanted to let you know I'm here for you."

She's doing more than distracting me as she molds herself to me. The calmness and sweet scent have the stress unraveling from me like a ball of string.

The sadness, grief, and worry gradually ebb the longer she stays in my arms. She has that power; to bring a shimmering light into the darkest of places. Jenna would get angry when I got like this, yet with Quinn, she joins me in the silence and brings the sunlight with her.

After my dad passed, Jenna placed a time limit on my grief, telling me to stop moping around and spending so much time with my family. *You have a girlfriend too. It can't all be about them,* is what she said to me four months after his death. Which had me pulling away further.

We sit here, wrapped around each other for what feels like hours. It allows me to piece together my emotions and put them into words. "You know how my dad died?"

She strokes down my arm and nods.

I'm glad I don't have to explain that side of the story. About how my family and I experienced a devastating loss none of us were prepared for. How he fell from a ladder in the restaurant and broke his neck. How Patrick was the one to find him. How we never got to say goodbye. How I lost one of the few people who understood me.

"It was a normal day. He headed to work and none of us knew that would be the last time we saw him. We were really close—my dad and me. I love my mom, but she's more outspoken and extroverted like Booth and Florence. Patrick and I are a lot like our dad. I've always been quieter than most people, and being the awkward, shy kid made school difficult. From a young age my dad understood my struggles with communicating how I felt. He sat me down after a particularly rough day with some bullies, but I was so embarrassed I couldn't even talk to him. He dropped a pad of paper and a pen in front of me and told me to write down what I was feeling."

"Like a journal?" She raises her head, eyes glossy.

"Yeah, exactly like that. It worked. And has for the last twenty years."

Confessing that to Quinn feels like I'm shedding a piece of

long-standing armor. Jenna never understood my need to write down my thoughts, even once telling me to *Man up*.

She drags her fingers down my jaw, combing through my beard. "I like that. Words hold a lot of power, especially when they're written down. Books, letters, poetry."

I hum in agreement. "When he died, I found it harder than usual to express myself, plus, I just wanted to be with my family more than ever. I think today reminded me—and my brothers—that we only have our mom left." My eyes lower, tracking the gentle rise and fall of her chest. "I wasn't prepared to see Jenna last night either. The last twenty-four hours brought up a lot of old feelings. I'm sorry for freezing up on you last night and today."

She studies me with a furrowed brow. "Why do you do that?"

"Do what?"

"Apologize or make it seem like you're not allowed to feel a certain way. They're your feelings, Graham. No one should fault you or hold that against you." The hand that's been resting on my cheek curves around my nape. "*She* did, didn't she?"

Quinn's body tenses, and I'm not sure what it is about my expression that answers her question. I wait for the mortification to strike, but it never comes. In its place, solace winds around my heart, settling me.

"I hate her for making you think you handled your feelings wrong. There hasn't been a single moment where I've wanted you any other way. I hear you talking confidently to clients over the phone. The way you tease and play with Lottie. The banter and quips you have with your brothers. The attentiveness and time you show your mom. Every act of kindness you've given me confirms you're an amazing man." She shakes her head softly, as if to say she can't believe I don't see it. But through her eyes, maybe I'm starting to. "And do you know what?"

"What?"
"Her loss is my gain."

CHAPTER TWENTY-SEVEN

GRAHAM'S HANDS COAST UP AND DOWN MY SPINE, PULLING ME closer until it's impossible to ignore the hardness beneath me. He's trying to distract me; clearly feeling much better after our talk. But I'm not done. This isn't how I saw this conversation playing out while sitting in his Jeep, but it feels cathartic for the both of us.

I had a suspicion Jenna had a role to play in his self-doubt, but for now I keep that anger at bay.

I'm so incredibly proud of him, for sharing that story about his dad, and his bravery encourages my own.

I didn't have any family growing up. No siblings or cousins to play with. Eventually, I learned to appreciate my own company; especially on evenings when my mother would get herself blackout drunk.

Teachers were kind; giving me clothes from the lost-and-found when I came to school without a jacket or sneaking me snacks when my lunchbox was empty.

Trusting people has never been an issue. It's what they'll do with that trust I've always been weary of. I once trusted my mom to love me unconditionally.

Graham's issue isn't about trust either. It's about being accepted for who he is, after so many people—his ex being the primary issue—made him feel like he doesn't belong.

Jenna's loss is *very* much my gain. She is in no way deserving of the man before me. Just like my mom doesn't deserve anymore of my energy.

Which is why I pull out my phone and do something I should have done the day I walked out of that trailer.

With me still balanced on Graham's lap, I open my phone's contact book and turn the screen for him to see. Under the contact: DO NOT ANSWER, I tap Block Caller.

His head lifts when I lock the device and throw it on the passenger seat. "Your mom?"

A deep sigh escapes me and with it I feel lighter. "It was long overdue. It gave her leverage over me. Now she has nothing. I know you can't run from Jenna with her marrying your cousin, but there are other ways you can let yourself be free of her."

"How's that?"

"The wedding. You have two options. We go, spread rumors about Ralph having some contagious rash, eat way too much food, and dance the night away with your family. Or...we snuggle up on the sofa with Curly while you complete your crossword and pretend I'm not crying over that baby turtle documentary."

He brushes my hair over my shoulder and rests his palm against my pulse point. "The scene when they all ran to the water got me a little choked up too."

My heart sings when that awfully handsome smile blooms on his face. The one he doesn't try to hide around me. The feel of it is as good as it looks, if not better when I graze my lips over his. I love the way his cheeks heat under my palms as we deepen the kiss, but when his hands move lower to the waistband of my jeans, I retreat.

"What do you want to do?" I give him a look, telling him he can't avoid this question; not like last night.

"Apart from keeping the peace between my family," Graham says. "There's only one other reason I'd want to go to that wedding."

"Which is?"

His hands flex against my hips, and then he lays a gentle kiss to the side of my neck. There's a mix of nerves and eagerness coming off him. When Graham takes his time like this, carefully choosing his words, I always anticipate something meaningful and genuine. This time is no different.

"I want to see you wearing something pretty. Dance with you in my arms. Be the one you leave with at the end of the night. I won't care who sees us together, because it won't be for show. It'll be for us. And just so we're clear"—he lowers his head, mouth grazing the shell of my ear—"there won't be anything fake about it."

If my heart was singing before, an orchestra has taken center stage in my chest now.

"Nothing at all?" I whisper.

He shakes his head, both our faces erupting into smiles so bright they could break through clouds hanging in the sky.

"Let me take you home and show you how not fake this is. How from the day I met you I wanted to make you mine."

His.

As much as I want him to show me here, we don't have much space to work with, and I want all of him. I'm off his lap and back in the passenger's seat in the blink of an eye, eliciting a chuckle from him as he starts the engine.

It's a good thing the hospital is a short drive to his apartment, because the moment we walk through the door, we're a tangle of limbs as we fall to the sofa, and he tugs me into his lap.

I'm eager to continue what we were doing in his car, but he's the one to break our kiss now. "When I asked you to be my girlfriend, it was never about making Jenna jealous or getting over her. That's what I should have said to you last night at the restaurant. It was Booth's idea to fake a date, and it sounded smart at the time. I mostly agreed to it for selfish reasons."

My fingers glide along his strong jaw and trace over the bridge of his nose. "What selfish reasons?"

"It gave me an excuse to talk to you."

The tempo of my heart increases in rhythm with his. "You talked to me before. At the bar."

"You think that was talking? Quinn, I said about ten words to you—half of which I stumbled over."

"That was our meet-cute." I frown. "But after that night, I didn't even think you liked me. You never texted or saved my number."

His head thumps against my shoulder, and he grumbles, "Honey, I saved your number in my phone the second you walked away. Didn't want to scrub my arm for a week. I didn't have the first idea about how to talk to someone like you. I'd do it over again if I could. I wouldn't have let you walk away, and I would have insisted I drove you home that night."

"Well, I wouldn't have it any other way. I remember thinking back to that evening and feeling valued and listened to. You were sweet. After a few months of you walking past the bakery and not coming in, I just assumed you were being polite."

"God, I'm the biggest fucking idiot. I'm sorry if you doubted my feelings for a second. I didn't think I ever stood a chance with you."

"Why would you think that?" My hands run down his biceps, enjoying the soft feel of his sweater against my fingertips.

"We're so different. You're you and I'm...*me*."

"Why would I want you to be anyone else?" I shuffle closer

until there isn't a sliver of space between us. "I like your quiet thinking, because it calms my chaotic thoughts. You never hesitate to help the people around you. You love your family fiercely. Your serious face is so handsome, but those smiles you save are my favorite. You don't judge; you listen. Your actions speak volumes, and they tell me you're one of the greatest men I've ever met."

There's a glow in his mossy-green eyes, a light I've never seen before. A lot like hope.

Whatever it is, it disappears when his lips crash into mine and he wraps me up in his arms.

Kissing Graham is a sip of warm apple cider. It's like sinking into a bubble bath after a long day. The warm rays of sunshine when they first hit your face.

It's exactly like coming home.

"No more." He sighs into my mouth before running his tongue along my bottom lip.

"No more what?" I tug his sweater out of his waistband, and he sucks in a breath when I skim my fingers along that line of hair leading south.

"Being something that we're not. *This* is real. It's never been fake for me, Quinn. Not a single moment."

Careful of his glasses, I pull his sweater over his head. "Can you do something for me?"

"Anything for you."

He slowly unbuttons my shirt and groans when he reveals the black balconette bra underneath. I agree, because my tits look fantastic in it.

I almost lose my train of thought when he sucks and licks the tops of my breasts, the tip of his tongue toying with the lace edges. "Fuck me like I'm yours."

A gasp slips from my throat when he bares his teeth and bites down on my peaked nipple through the sheer material.

"Haven't you realized yet? You are mine." He kisses a path

up between my cleavage before stopping at the base of my throat. "You're also going to be my undoing and I can't wait to fall apart with you. Now, lose everything. I want you writhing on my lap. Need to see every inch of your glorious body when I fuck you."

If getting naked was an Olympic sport, I'd win gold. Graham would place third, because he kept getting distracted every time I removed an item of clothing. I return to his lap where there isn't a stitch of clothing between us. Gone is the fear that he doesn't like what he sees, because he looks at me like I'm going to be his first meal after months of starvation. Heat floods between my thighs when he fists his hard cock as he looks me over.

"You're soaked for me already. I can feel it," he groans. "I really want another taste, but I need to be in you. *Now*." He pushes me back slightly to run his knuckles across my wet center, pulling a throaty moan from me when he brushes against my aching clit. I choke on a gasp at his next move though.

Graham spits into his palm and grips his length, coating himself, all the while keeping his eyes locked with mine. I'm already rising to my knees, craving the feel of him. I want to be the last woman to ever see this side of him again.

"Hurry," I whimper as I hover above him, but just as I'm about to lower myself, he squeezes my waist.

"Condom. Let me get one." He goes to move but my words stop him.

"You're the first person I've been with in over a year, and I've been tested. I'm on the pill too."

His breathing increases as he lets what I said sink in. "I'm the same. Well, minus the pill." We laugh but it dies when my knees begin to wobble. "Only if you're sure though?"

"I don't want anything between us."

Whatever else we had to say gets lost in a chorus of moans

and gasps as I slowly lower myself. His hand strokes my thigh while he grips the base of his cock with his other. I forgot how big he was, and it takes a minute for me to work my way down his length until my ass rests against his thighs, hitting me so deep my toes curl.

His head falls back when I rotate my hips, trying to ease the intense pressure building in me. The taut muscles in his neck are so tempting and I lean forward to run my tongue over them.

"This. You. Incredible." Full sentences are a thing of the past.

He raises his head and kisses me with fervor as he slowly starts to rock us together, thrusting up each time our hips kiss.

"Don't hold back, Graham," I plead, gasping as he increases the rhythm.

From the darkened look on his face to the punishing grip he has on me, he's ready to give me it all. With assured movements, he takes hold of my wrists, pushes them behind my back, and locks them together with one hand.

He looks at me, waiting for my consent.

"I trust you," I breathe.

"Your trust means everything to me." With his free hand, he slides it under me to cup my bottom, coaxing me to rise off him until just the tip remains. He has me hover there for what feels like an eternity as his mouth explores my neck, chest, and breasts. It's the sweetest form of torture, but without warning he tugs on my wrists, impaling me.

"Oh god," I cry out as he buries himself deep.

"Like that. Keep riding me like that." His voice drips with lust, and I know like me, he's barely hanging on.

I repeat the movement, rising off his lap, and then he drives me down again. Over and over we do that. It's intense and mind-bending. The angle and strong hold he has on my hands straddles a delicious line between pain and pleasure.

"Dirty girl. I can feel you dripping down me." He's not cocky or overly confident. He exudes power, and despite his words, I feel precious in his arms.

When his hold loosens on my wrists, I grasp his face to kiss him, and his hands fall to my ass cheeks in a bruising grip. Up and down he works me, thrusting his hips to meet me in a delicious reunion. One hands dips between my spread legs as I draw closer to my orgasm and my movements become weighted with the need to find release. When the tip of his finger glides over my skin and traces my asshole, I freeze.

"Is this okay?"

It's new and surprising. Surprising because of the jolts of pleasure it sends right to my core. I nod and continue to ride him, the anticipation of it driving me wild with need. "I want to try it."

He moves to where we're joined, coats his finger in my arousal, moves back to the puckered entrance, and slowly presses in. The sensation of being filled so deliciously like this has me nearing the edge of ecstasy. My hips undulate, chasing my pleasure and driving his finger deeper.

"Oh fuck. Quinn, I can feel you squeezing around me. Don't stop, honey. You're doing so good taking my finger and cock. Do you like it?"

"God, I love it. I'm gonna come. I'm gonna co—" My words are cut off with my raspy cries as my muscles spasm. I curl into Graham as he takes over, pistoning up into me as he pants against my neck.

"You feel that? This. Is. Real." He punctuates each word with a thrust. On the final one, he stiffens, his body pulling tight as he comes deep inside of me. Shouting my name and praising me the entire time. The act of it is so raw and erotic, I never want it to end.

We collapse into each other. Our sweat-soaked chests beat

rampantly as he hooks his arms around me and falls against the sofa with a content sigh.

"That was…" *How do I even describe it?*

He weaves his fingers into my hair and gently raises my head, a look of pure wonderment warming his handsome face. "That was us."

It's in this moment, I realize being with Graham isn't like coming home.

It is home. *He* is home.

When that dart landed on this small corner of the country, I'd hoped to make friends, find a place to put down roots, and grow my business. Never in my wildest dreams did I think I would find a person like Graham Sadler.

As this sweet man carries me to the bathroom, cleans me up, and cradles me tightly until we fall asleep in each other's arms, it's clear I didn't just find those things in Sutton Bay.

I found my person.

CHAPTER TWENTY-EIGHT

graham

I'VE HAD A GOOD LIFE.

Yes, I've experienced heartbreak and loss, but overall, I've been happy. I have a supportive family, a job I enjoy, and a roof over my head. I always thought this was it, this is as good as it's going to get. I'd made peace with it.

As I study the slope of Quinn's nose, the way her dark lashes brush against her round cheeks, and how the early morning sun picks up the different tones in her hair, I decide being wrong feels pretty fucking good.

She makes me better; makes everything better.

Never did I think I would be deserving of her bright light, warm smiles, soft kisses, and sweet noises. I'm still not sure I am, but who am I to question how things turn out?

She stirs and stretches her arms upward like a cat, arching her ass into my lap and rubbing against my stiff cock. Breathing in her sweetness, I bury my face into her neck, and a possessive surge shoots through me when my own scent lingers on her skin. It makes me want to waltz her around town so everyone knows she's mine.

The second we agreed this wasn't fake, it felt like a wrecking ball tore through our agreement, and I wanted to roar with satisfaction in the rubble.

This is real.

"Is that a tentacle in your pants or are you happy to see me?" Her voice is heavy with sleep, but there's no hiding the mischief in her tone.

Laughing into her neck, I tickle her sides until she squeals.

"Better a tentacle than a claw."

She rolls to face me, cheeks rosy and hair disheveled. Not wanting to forget what it feels like to have her in my arms and in my bed, I stare at her as if we have all the time in the world.

"What are your plans today?" she asks with a yawn. It's almost six a.m. She's usually at the bakery by now but confessed last night that she wanted to open later today. I texted my boss once we got to the hospital, asking to take a vacation day. Usually, I'd feel guilty about taking the day off or keeping Quinn in bed, but when her calf slides up the inside of my thigh, I find it impossible to find any probable cause to leave this room.

"I'm going to check on my mom. Are you still meeting up with Johanna at Shirley's tonight?"

"Yeah, it'll be good to catch up. Be sure to have that David Attenborough documentary and a blanket ready for when I get home. It sure is getting cold, so I expect cuddles every night. When do you think it'll snow? Oh! I should buy some snow boots."

I love her endless babble. This girl could hold a conversation with herself and not get bored. Her cheery voice is like music to my ears, but it's the word *home* she uses so casually that rings like bells and vibrates in my chest.

Is this home to her? With me?

When the van is fixed, she'll want to leave, I understand that. I don't want to take away the independence she's built for herself, but having her here, with all her brightly colored blankets, pom-poms, and candles has finally made this cold space feel like a home for me too.

"Let me text my brothers. Maybe I'll tag along." Her surprise quickly shifts into delight.

"I'd really like that. We don't have to stay long. I'm really obsessed with those sea turtles."

The usual discomfort and annoyance I feel about meeting up at the bar is nowhere to be seen. Weirdly, I want to join them tonight and it's not because I'm being guilted into coming or someone is trying to force me into a mold I don't belong in.

Among the many things missing between Jenna and me was compromise.

Quinn shuffles to the edge of the bed, but before she can unravel herself from the comforter, I'm dragging her across the mattress and into my chest. "Ten more minutes."

With one arm wrapped around her bare shoulders, I reach over and unlock my phone to drop a text in the group chat I have with my brothers and Dex.

> **Graham:** Are you all meeting up with the girls at Shirley's tonight?

> **Patrick:** Was planning on it. Why?

> **Graham:** I'll drive. Let me know what time.

> **Patrick:** You want to come?

> **Booth:** Willingly?

Booth: I think we have a certain little lady to thank for this. And me. Because I am clearly a top matchmaker. First Pat, now you. Dex, watch out, buddy.

Dex: Yeah, not happening.

Patrick: You had no part to play in my relationship.

Booth: Lies. You would still be crying into your puzzles without my help.

Graham: Your advice was horse shit. Concentrate on your own love life.

The phone slips from my fingers when Quinn's lips trail down my body until she disappears beneath the comforter, where her hot mouth finds my hard cock.

Yeah, we're not leaving the bed today.

"I'M REALLY HAPPY FOR YOU, BUT IT'S GOING TO TAKE ME A WHILE to get used to you smiling so much. It's kinda creepy." Patrick observes me over the rim of his glass.

"I'm not smiling."

I am. So fucking wide as I watch Quinn dance around the middle of the bar with Johanna. She's a lightweight and a very handsy drunk. Twice now I've had to stop her from groping me under the table. I'd love nothing more, but I'm sober and my brothers definitely saw her sly hand reach for me.

"I'll tell you who isn't smiling." Dex nods to the other side of the room. We find a slightly irate Booth storming toward us.

"Who pissed in your Cheerios?" I ask, sliding his gin and tonic over to him.

"It's nothing. Who wants a game?" He gestures toward the pool table.

Three sets of brows rise, waiting for him to reveal what's got him so worked up.

"The fucking audacity of our new *owner*. It's nine o'clock on a Monday night and they're sending me emails, telling me what to do with *my* staff." He downs half his drink before slumping onto a stool. "I'm grateful we didn't lose the restaurant, but I'm quickly losing my patience with all this faceless nonsense. *Who are they?*"

"Beats me," Patrick says. "I honestly thought that they would have showed up by now. It's almost been six months since they bought us." He knocks into Booth's shoulder. "Don't let it get to you."

"Why's everyone frowning?" Quinn asks breathlessly as she skips up to the high-top table. She leans into my side, and I snake my arm around her waist. Everyone's been eyeing us all evening; not in suspicion, but with a gleam of satisfaction.

"Just our mysterious owner getting Booth's panties in a twist," Dex teases.

"Fuck off. Let's move on," my brother grumbles. "Mom's gonna need some help this Thanksgiving with her leg in the cast. I can handle the turkey and most of the other dishes." He glances at the woman tucked into me. "Quinn, any chance you want to team up and help make this year's dinner?"

"I would love to!" she squeals. "Anything to distract me from that day. My birthday always sucks. I hate when it falls on Thanksgiving."

Everyone freezes.

"Your birthday?" I croak.

"Umm, yeah. What's the big deal? Why are you all looking at me like that? I don't celebrate it."

I am the worst...*boyfriend?* Who knows what I am, but I suck at whatever it is because I didn't know her birthday was coming up. I understand why she wouldn't celebrate it, but that doesn't mean I don't want to get her a gift or make her feel special.

"If our mom finds out, she's going to want to celebrate and bake you a cake. We'll keep it under wraps if that's what you want though," Patrick says softly, sensing a shift in the mood around the table.

Quinn rests her head on my shoulder and sighs. The sadness in that little breath is like a sledgehammer to the chest. "I'm not against it, I've just never had people to celebrate with. I've never even had a birthday cake. Oh god"—she slaps her hands over her eyes—"I'm being a real Debbie Downer. Sorry, guys. I'll shut up. But to answer your question, Booth, I'd love to help with dinner. I'll be your sous."

The conversation moves on, we play a round of pool, and have a fun evening. But the idea of Quinn having another birthday that no one celebrates sits like a lead weight in my stomach.

We're all ready to head out, waiting for the girls to return from the restroom when Patrick slaps me on the shoulder.

"I'm really happy for you, Gray. Not the most conventional start, but I can already tell she's good for you. You're good for her too."

"She's probably too good for me. But so is Johanna for you," I joke, ignoring the nickname.

"I totally am!" Johanna hiccups as she squeezes her arms around Quinn. "I am so happy you're my friend. Ugh, you're so cute. Patrick, let's adopt her."

"Okayyyy then. Water and bed for you." He manages to wrangle her away and convinces her a baby versus a twenty-six-year-old woman might be more fun. From the spark in Jo's eyes, she looks ready to make a baby tonight.

We say goodbye and I give Dex and Booth a ride home. By

the time we reach the apartment, Quinn is fast asleep with her head resting against the passenger window. I brush an errant strand of hair away from her face and she smiles softly at the touch.

Before I wake her, I drop my brother a text.

> Graham: Do you know how to make a cake?

Booth: I'm a chef. That's insulting.

> Graham: ???

Booth: I recall you not wanting my help anymore.

> Graham: It's for Quinn.

Booth: Fine! You'll have to come over to Mom's on Wednesday after work. I'm working all week.

Booth: You really like her?

I look at Quinn. The quiet has been my comfort for so long, but since she's come into my life it's been full of vibrant noise and flashes of color. Turns out, I don't miss the silence like I thought I would.

> Graham: I think I love her.

Booth: About goddamn time.

She's still a handsy little thing as I coax her into brushing her teeth and washing her face, but the minute her head hits the downy pillow, she's out like a light.

My entire body aches to slide in behind her, so I keep tonight's entry brief.

This is love.

Nothing before her matters.

From the moment I met her, I've been scared. Slowly, she's shown me there's nothing to fear.

When Jenna left me, I was sure I'd never find love again. The thing is, that was never love.

Love comes in the form of Quinn Jackson.

And I am ready to spend every day showing her how much I love her.

quinn

My nose twitches.

Something sweet and floral tickles my nostrils.

The birds are chirping happily outside.

The bed dips, and something spicy joins the floral scent.

Graham.

I crack an eye open to find him looking down at me with fondness. Streaks of sunshine sneak in through the curtains.

"Hi, honey." His smile has quickly become my favorite thing to wake up to, and today is no different.

"Hey, you. What time is it?" I stifle a yawn and stretch out my stiff arms.

"Don't worry about that." He lies down next to me, reaches behind his back with a rustling to reveal the biggest bouquet of flowers and lays them down between us. All different shapes and shades of yellow. Tulips, roses, daisies, dahlias. Unlike the previous arrangements, this one is wrapped up in brown Kraft paper and tied with string.

"Graham. They're incredible. Did you make this?"

"Nah. This is all my mom. I did help pick them out." He huffs a laugh, but there's a hint of pride in his smile.

"This one is my favorite so far. You don't have to buy me flowers so often though." Turning over, I fluff my pillows and settle against the headboard. Last night we slept in his room. We've been alternating between his and mine, and it's been the best two weeks of bed hopping. Almost every night I'm left satiated from Graham's hands, mouth, or cock. We're both insatiable and I hope it never fades.

Since I've been sleeping in here, there are a few new additions to his room: a sandalwood candle sits on the dresser along with a ceramic watch holder I found at the thrift store. He brought in my lavender-colored blanket last night after I complained it was too cold, but he quickly warmed me up.

"I don't have to. I want to." There's a dash of nervousness in his tone. He leans over the flowers, careful not to crush them as he lays gentle kisses across my brow, nose, and cheeks. "Happy birthday, honey."

I smile despite the dull ache of memories that try to force their way out. Deep from where I try to hide them away on this day.

Twenty-seven.

Nine years since I left the one place that should have kept me safe, yet the moment I lost sight of our trailer it was the safest I'd ever felt.

"I know you didn't want a fuss…"

"It wasn't that. Birthdays were never a thing for me, so I preferred to celebrate today as the day I set myself free." I stroke a hand down his bare chest. "I love the flowers. And without making this depressing, you're the first person in a long time to wish me a happy birthday."

The deep breath he lets out is filled with sadness, but he doesn't dwell on it.

"So you want a fuss?" He quirks a dark brow.

"I want to spend the morning in bed with you before we

head over to your mom's. That sounds like my perfect birthday."

"Can I give you your gift?"

My eyes widen and I glance down at the bouquet. "You already have."

"I'm going to bring you flowers every day, even though our contract is null and void." He winks, and then reaches under the bed to retrieve a small gift wrapped in blue paper with green polka dots, and places it on my lap. "It's nothing big or fancy."

Giddy excitement quickly replaces my morose mood. I peel back the gift wrap to reveal a small rectangular, wooden box. Intricate floral designs decorate the top and a bronze latch keeps the lid in place. Right in the middle, in beautiful cursive writing is my name. It's simple and delicate, clearly made with a lot of care and craftsmanship.

Inspecting it, I turn it over, and the sound of something sliding around inside has me glancing at Graham, who simply shrugs.

With a quick flick of the latch, I open the lid to reveal a small silver locket, engraved with three simple stems of what look to be tulips.

"Oh, Graham, it's beautiful. I love it. And the box."

"Really?" he asks hopefully.

"Of course. Where did you find it?"

"Dex made the jewelry box, and the necklace is from a small jeweler across from my office in the city. I had them engrave the flowers."

He's not even finished his sentence before I'm dragging him down to me and raining his face with quick pecks until our lips lock in a deep kiss. He laughs when I grip him harder as he tries to pull away.

"Let me put it in on you." He maneuvers me until I'm sitting between his open legs, front to back.

With my hair swept over my shoulder, I wait, but he doesn't move. I twist to find him staring at my naked body and watch as he leans forward to kiss up the length of my spine. My limbs melt into his embrace with each tender press of his lips.

"My beautiful Quinn," he whispers, leaving a trail of kisses until he reaches my nape. "Brave and beautiful. You deserve to be celebrated every day, but today of all days, you deserve to know what joy and happiness you bring into lives of the people around you."

Happy tears well in my eyes at his heartfelt words and then he's looping the silver locket around my neck and securing it in place. It takes him a few minutes because of his big hands, and I tease him every second. My mood shifts when it rests between the hollow of my breasts.

Gratitude. So much gratitude for the man who encompasses me in his arms as I fall into him. For everything he's done for me, but most of all, for being who I never knew I needed.

I turn to kiss the underside of his jaw. "Thank you. Already I have the perfect morning to replace the old memories."

When he leaves to place the flowers in water—because obviously I'm not allowed to do it—and to fetch us breakfast, my fingers trace along the cool metal. I fiddle with the tiny latch on the side of the locket and when it springs open, I'm left slightly disappointed that he didn't put a picture in there.

It's a stupid thought, one I quickly shake away. I'd just hoped that I'd find him in there to rest against the heart he's very quickly taking ownership of.

ALL THE SCENTS AND AROMAS FLOATING AROUND CLAIRE'S kitchen are making my mouth water.

My nose is having a mini orgasm.

Not nearly as good as the two real ones Graham gave me this morning after we finished breakfast. One while I sat on his face and the second when we showered together.

Happy birthday to me.

I haven't seen Booth in action before, only tasted what he's concocted when visiting Our Place. Without a shadow of a doubt he's a talented, skillful chef. I've worked alongside plenty of head chefs, and they always have pent-up anger or an air of arrogance to them. Not Booth. He commands the kitchen with grace and respect. And cooks up a hell of a storm without even breaking a sweat.

I'm in charge of the pies, cranberry sauce, sweet potato casserole, and creamed corn; he oversees the turkey, stuffing, and gravy. Everything else we've split. The pumpkin pie I made at the bakery yesterday is chilling in the fridge and the crust baking in the oven should be done in ten minutes before I fill it with a maple pecan filling. We make quite the team, blasting Taylor Swift and Ed Sheeran as we work in tandem. Baking is obviously my forte but it's fun cooking with him.

Poor Claire is still in a thigh-high cast and her wrist is still a little tender. Booth, being the overprotective youngest son, forbids her from lifting a finger, which she's finding difficult.

We both let out an exhausted sigh when we finish cleaning the work surfaces and the remaining dishes are in the oven or simmering over the stove.

"If I wasn't so obsessed with buying your banana bread every week, I'd try and convince you to come work for me." Booth unties his apron and holds his hand out for mine.

"Working in big kitchens isn't my thing." My mind wanders back to Graham's speech at Our Place before Jenna interrupted us. He hasn't brought it up since, but his words have stuck with me. *Getting help isn't cheating, it's a stepping-stone.* If I continue allowing my stubborn pride to get in the way, the bakery won't progress to where I want it to. "But, if you're ever in need of bread or muffins for the restaurant, let me know."

There. I said it. That wasn't as scary as I thought it would be.

"Wait, seriously?" Booth pulls us to stop on our way to the living room. "Our supplier is one my dad used for years, but recently the bread gets delivered to us half stale or with part of the order missing."

My mouth drops open, because this I was not expecting.

"If you're serious, I'd love to sit down with you. Usually I'd get Graham involved when working with a new vendor, but he knows you and, you know...conflict of interest." He smirks. "Before we both get too busy this winter, let's set up a meeting."

"Do you not need to speak to the new owner?" I think back to Jo's comment last month.

"Nah. They may think they own the restaurant, but considering they haven't stepped foot in there, I don't think they'll notice a change of vendor."

"Okay." I bite back a grin, trying and failing to play it cool. "That sounds good."

"Great. Now, beer? We've earned one."

We head into the living room and my eyes are immediately drawn to the man dressed in a deep maroon sweater and corduroy pants. The Sadlers get dressed up for Thanksgiving, so I threw on my nicest knitted dress and the knee-high boots Graham goes crazy for.

I saunter over to where he sits on the love seat in the corner. He raises his arm, and I revel in the way I fit so perfectly into his side as he presses his face into my hair and inhales.

"You smell delicious."

"I smell like garlic and sweat." I laugh as he grabs my legs and drapes them over his thighs.

"You two are disgustingly cute," Booth remarks with a sigh before taking a pull from his beer.

"Be nice to your brother." Claire slaps him in the chest and looks at us with heart eyes. "It means so much that you're helping with the dinner, today of all days."

"It's my pleasure." I mean it. I thought it would be a good distraction for what is usually a very polarizing day. Turns out, all I needed was the man next to me.

If this is the first and last birthday I ever celebrate, I'd still be the luckiest girl alive.

"The table looks amazing," I tell her.

When we arrived, Jo was helping Claire set up. Crocheted pumpkins, dried leaves, branches, and tiny wooden turkeys decorate the long dining table.

"Thank you, sweetheart. Florence usually helps me. This is the first year she won't be here to celebrate."

"That reminds me. We need an extra place setting. I've invited a friend," Booth adds casually as he types away on his phone.

"A lady friend?" Claire asks excitedly and squeezes Booth's bicep in a death grip. Poor woman is desperate to see her kids married off and popping out more grandkids.

"Fuck, Ma. I can't feel my arm." He removes himself from her grasp. "And no, not a *lady friend*. Just a guy from work who couldn't be with his family this year. Hope that's okay."

"Of course, it is. The more the merrier."

Just then, Patrick, Jo, and Lottie join us with Johanna's dad, George. It makes me all warm and fuzzy inside as we sit together in the living room waiting for the food, laughter and love filling the room. When I turn to look at the man next to me, that warm, fuzzy feeling ignites into an inferno.

I take him in as he chats away with everyone. It's here that he has all his walls down, fully relaxed, with no doubt to be seen. It makes me sad to know he struggled as a child and during his relationship with Jenna, but knowing he had family and friends like this through it all, brings me comfort.

"It's going to be a busy few days," Claire says. "It'll be nice to see some of the family on Sunday."

The room grows quiet and Graham's jaw ticks. We've avoided talking about the wedding that's happening in three days. Ignorance has certainly been bliss.

"It'll be good to see Aunt Nancy and Uncle Eric," Patrick replies, but I don't miss the tension in his shoulders.

"It will." Claire's eyes grow sad as she takes in the wall decorated with family photos. "Your dad loved weddings. Couldn't get him off the dance floor."

As much as I hate the idea of being in the same room as Graham's ex again, I respect his wish to keep his mom out of the drama surrounding his past relationship. But I have a feeling if Claire knew the truth, she wouldn't be going to the wedding.

Jo plops down onto the floor next to me just as Graham excuses himself from the room. I fight the urge to follow and check on him, wanting to give him his space.

"You've got that look." Jo nudges my knee with her shoulder.

"What look?"

"Like you've fallen in deep with a Sadler brother."

She's absolutely right, so why deny it? Plus, the huge grin on my face is a dead giveaway.

"So deep it's scary, but it feels so right with him. Sometimes I wonder if I'm dreaming."

Before she can respond, the lights dim, and Jo's eyes widen. She curls her lips around her teeth and shakes her head. "If you look behind you, you'll see that you're wide awake."

I whip around to find Graham in the doorway with a warm glow highlighting the contours of his face. I'm so distracted by him that I almost miss the large—slightly lopsided—yellow cake in his hands, with what looks like a hundred candles haphazardly sticking out of it.

With careful steps, and Lottie walking alongside him with the cheesiest smile on her face, a chorus of voices starts singing. Singing to me. The love hits me from all angles, but my eyes don't leave his as he makes his way over and crouches in front of me.

"Gots to make a wish, Aunty Quinn," Lottie whispers excitedly, and my heart threatens to burst at the seams at that name.

The candlelight makes the green of his eyes appear rapturous. "Happy birthday, honey."

With a shaky voice, I close my hand around his wrist as I say, "You keep giving me all these firsts."

His smile takes over his entire face. "What a lucky guy I am. Now blow out your candles, this thing weighs a ton."

After the candles are extinguished, I make a wish even though it's already come true.

He's looking right at me.

"Do you like your cake?" Lottie's question reminds me we're not the only two people in the room.

"I love it so much." I wipe under my eyes. "You did a great job."

"I didn't make it, silly. Uncle Gray did. It took him four tries." She giggles and lays her head on her uncle's shoulder. "He said it had to be perfect for you."

I smirk as Graham's cheeks flame. "Lottie, you're the worst wingwoman."

"Like chicken wings?" she asks in confusion.

The room breaks into laughter, and someone flicks on the lights right as the doorbell rings.

Booth shoots up from his seat and runs out of the room shouting, "I've got it!"

I stand with Graham, who carries the cake over to the side table. "You really made it?"

"Yeah." He chuckles and rolls up his sleeves to show me a fresh burn mark. "Got the scars to prove it."

"Ouch!" I grab his arm and gently kiss the red welt on his skin. "What did I do to deserve you?"

"It's just a cake," he mumbles, but I don't let him downplay this and keep a firm grip on his arm.

"It's so much more than that. You have no idea what it means to me. You've made the lonely little girl inside me feel very special today."

"All of your days should be special." His brow stays wrinkled, but before I can say anymore, a high-pitched voice has us all jumping.

"The prodigal child has returned!"

Claire screams and points at a tall, slim woman, with a white-blonde bob and septum piercing. She's stunning and the green eyes she reveals when she flips up her sunglasses tell me exactly who she is.

"Aunty Flo!" Lottie squeals and sprints into her aunt's waiting arms.

"We've talked about that name, Lottie." Florence laughs and scoops the little girl up.

Everyone follows to hug and greet her.

I stay behind, not wanting to intrude on the family reunion. There's no jealousy as I take in the loud, loving family, and I'm happy to watch until Florence locks eyes with me and spreads her arms wide with a toothy grin.

"And you must be the woman who showed Graham Cracker not all women are awful wenches." In the blink of an eye, I'm locked in her embrace until I'm gasping for air. "But know if you hurt him, I'll make your life hell," she whispers menacingly.

I like her.

"Flo," Graham warns and peels her arms from around me. "You're ruining the stereotype of protective older brother."

"Times are changing. Quinn, you'll sit next to me. I can't wait to tell you all the embarrassing stories about my big brother."

Booth and I shuffle back into the kitchen to plate everything up and for the next couple of hours, we all sit around the table, eating until our stomachs hurt, playing games, and giving thanks.

It's so easy. All of it. Most of all, it's easy with him.

Easy to open up to him, spend time with him, be around his family, and be a part of his life.

And to love him.

My heart stutters at that. Every rational thought tells me it's too early to have these feelings, but when he throws an arm around my shoulder and kisses my cheek like it's the most natural thing in the world, they disappear.

I've never loved anyone, let alone had someone tell me they love me.

He's given me so much. My first bouquet of flowers. My first pair of rain boots. My first birthday cake.

My first love.

CHAPTER THIRTY

graham

Patience was no chore
When I had her in the end
She was worth the wait

TODAY IS NO DIFFERENT FROM THE THANKSGIVING DINNERS I grew up with, but we all feel the absence of my dad on days like this. The surprise return of Florence has helped ease the pain, however. My family means everything to me; always has and always will. The people around this table have been a constant in my life, but I've been walking around blind.

Until her.

She waltzed into my life and, in the blink of an eye, showed me what it was to be alive. I must have done something good in a past life to have her sitting next to me, her hand resting on my thigh, and a smile on her face that somehow, I put there.

I can't lose her.

Since the moment this stopped being fake, I haven't allowed myself to question this. The temptation to ask *Why me?* still lingers in the corner of my mind. It's hard to believe that someone as incredible as her could be happy with someone like me, but I've convinced myself there are no risks to weigh or probabilities to determine the outcome of our relationship.

Actually, there is one probability.

I'm certain I love her.

"Little Sadler," Dex calls across the table. "How long are you in town for?"

Florence is sharing a large portion of pumpkin pie with Lottie, who is perched on her knee. The fork freezes halfway to her mouth, and she appears thrown by the question. "Umm, about that. I wanted to come home to help Mom out since the accident and all my friends have continued on to Mexico before heading home for the holidays. It seems like a good time to take a break from the hostel lifestyle. Plus, my savings didn't last as long as I expected."

"Oh, sweetheart, why didn't you call?" my mom asks.

She shrugs and keeps her eyes trained on her plate. "It's fine. Things just didn't go according to plan..." There's an avoidance in her tone, but before I can question her, Patrick taps a fork against his glass and stands.

"Before some of you get too drunk or pass out on the sofa in a food coma, I just wanted to say a little something. You know, in the spirit of being thankful and all that jazz. This past year has been a tough one." His hand rests on the back of Johanna's neck as she looks up at him lovingly. "I know things are still uncertain with the new owner, but I, for one, am very thankful for each and every one of you sitting at this table. To old friends"—he looks around, down at Jo, and then turns to Quinn—"and new ones."

We all raise a glass in cheers, then eat until there's nothing left.

An hour later, Quinn and I are cozied up on the swinging bench in my mom's yard, wrapped up in a blanket as the others crowd around the small fire pit to roast marshmallows. She's slotted between my legs, her back to my front.

"Another day for the record books." She weaves her fingers through mine. "Thank you for today. For helping me forget what this day reminds me of. I didn't know it could be like this."

"What could?"

"Having a family that loves you unconditionally."

My eyes close at her words. How anyone could not love Quinn is unfathomable. "It's hard to believe you haven't been coming to family dinners for years. You fit in here." *You fit in with me.*

She turns in my hold and looks up at me with her chin balanced on my chest. "Today, I'm thankful for you."

"And I'm thankful for you; today and every day." The tip of my finger traces over the apple of her cheek, rosy from the bitter November air. "Why don't you go and join everyone around the fire? I'll grab you another glass of cider."

Before she can respond, Booth shouts my name. "Your phone won't stop buzzing over here."

We walk toward my family, and I take my phone from his outstretched hand, finding Martin Willis's name flashing on the screen. "Martin," I greet. "Everything okay?"

"Thank god." He sighs tiredly. "I've been trying to call Quinn for the last half hour. Are you with her?"

"She's right here. What's up?" Quinn looks up at me with concern. I shake my head and mouth, *Mr. Willis* to reassure her.

"Sorry to do this today. There was a woman banging on the bakery door and screaming Quinn's name." My blood chills. "The tenant upstairs called me, but by the time I got here, things escalated. We had no choice but to call the cops."

"What did she do?" I ask through clenched teeth.

"Threw a couple of bricks through the window."

"Fuck." I wince.

I can't look at Quinn. Can't bear to see her face when I tell her what's happened. Today was supposed to be different. A distraction, like the one she gave me when my mom was in the hospital. She got away from the hatred, poison, and heartbreak. Built her life from the ground up. She doesn't deserve this.

"Do you know who she is?" he asks.

"Yeah. I think I do."

quinn

TARNISHED.

The universe never lets me have anything nice.

A day filled with so much happiness, laughter, and joy is now spoiled. It's ironic that the day I was born—despite telling me my whole life that it was the worst day of hers—is the day she can't seem to leave me alone. She's sadistic. Always wanting to be reminded of what causes her such hatred.

My feelings toward my mother varied throughout my life. In the beginning, I craved her affection. One time she gave me some of her half-eaten burger from the local diner and I remember thinking that's what maternal love was. As I grew older and saw other moms interact with their daughters, I felt envy and rage. Why couldn't I have a mother who took me to the mall or braided my hair? Why have me if I was such a burden?

The last couple of years under her roof, I pitied her. She didn't hold back in telling me her own upbringing was awful, so it only seemed fair I received the same treatment. Alcohol fueled her bitterness. Random drug use made her lazy.

Most of our lives, it was just the two of us. On occasion,

she'd bring some lowlife home or let her drug dealer sleep on the sofa I called a bed, forcing me to sleep on the floor or on some occasions, the porch.

I suspect she found the address of the bakery online or through my socials, considering I never changed my name when I left California. How she ended up in Maine is beyond me. We barely had enough money to keep the electricity on, let alone a cross-country ticket. From what Graham has told me, she was screaming on Robin Road, presuming I lived above the bakery. My birthday gift from her was a couple of bricks through the window, damaging several tables and the display fridge.

While I understand everything Mr. Willis, Graham, and the sheriff are telling me right now, I'm numb.

Why can't she just leave me alone? I gave her what she wanted. Distance. Me gone.

When asked if I want to press charges, I look at Graham, hoping he has the answer.

"There's no rush. Sleep on it. I want to get you home. Martin and Dex will get this sorted." He guides me away from my damaged bakery. Glass and carnage taint the sacred space I call my own. The insurance should cover the repairs, but it could take months to handle. Time I can't afford to not have a working fridge and boarded up windows.

He practically carries me to the Jeep, swaddled in his coat, and gets us back to the apartment in record time.

His words play on repeat in my head the entire journey. *I want to get you home.*

Home. Where is home? I'd tried so many times to make a place my home, and I thought I'd found it in Sutton Bay, but she's left her mark here too.

When we step into the apartment, Graham goes into full caretaker mode. Bubble bath. Warm tea. Fresh bedding.

Now, with his hand on my lower back, he guides me into my room. Before he can step away, I tug on his wrist.

"Stay with me." My lip quivers uncontrollably and my heart clenches in fear that he'll refuse me.

"Always." His instant response is said with such surety and is a tiny drop of relief in the ocean of emotions.

We settle on the mattress, and he pulls the comforter up and over our heads, burying us away from the rest of the world. Fingers caress along my cheeks, nose, and lips in soothing motions. I bathe myself in his strong, quiet aura.

I'm grateful when sleep finds me, and I dream of how the day should have ended.

IN THE NINE YEARS SINCE I LAST SAW MY MOTHER, SHE'S AGED well beyond her years. She was eighteen when she fell pregnant, and like me, she never got to finish high school. Her skin is now sallow from the alcohol, and her cheeks hollow from the drugs. When she looks around the near-empty parking lot, her eyes are vacant and glassy, but I know she's looking for me.

The afternoon sun glares against the windshield of Graham's car, sheltering us.

From a distance, we watch as the deputy drops his hand to the top of my mother's head before she ducks into the patrol car. The last glimpse of her I see is the hair color we share.

I pressed charges.

At first, I didn't want to, worried it would require me to attend a hearing. I was reassured that my statement and security camera footage should be enough, and Mr. Willis—as the owner of the building—offered to attend any court hearings on my behalf.

My charges aren't the only ones though. She stole a car and someone's purse from a diner when her money took her as far as Indiana.

Why did she want to see me? I'll never know.

And I can live with that.

I refuse to give her the satisfaction of seeing me, let alone any more of my time or energy.

The patrol car rolls away until it disappears from view.

"What would you say to her?" The heat of Graham's gaze warms the side of my face.

He's never usually one to break the silence.

It takes me a few minutes, but when I speak, my voice is clear and sure as I watch snowflakes dance around in the air. "I'd tell her I'm sorry. Sorry that her life was so awful before I came into it and that when I arrived, I didn't make it easier for her. But I'd also tell her I'm not sorry for being me. For existing. She tried to break me, with every slap and spiteful word, yet here I am. Thankful for the body she cruelly poked and pinched. Grateful for the places I've visited." I suck in a breath. "Had I stayed...I don't like to think what would have happened.

"I've spent the last nine years growing as a person. Learning to love myself and to show others we aren't defined by those around us. It's about what's in here"—I tap my chest—"that matters. What we think about ourselves is the only opinion that counts. When you know yourself, you learn to know the type of people you deserve to be around. And we should never settle."

When I turn to face him, his brow is creased deep in thought. I'm not sure what answer he was expecting; honestly, I didn't know I was going to say all that until I opened my mouth.

There's always peace in his silence, but his next words bring an entirely different sense of calm. "I'm proud of you. To overcome what you have and still see the good in the world is astounding. I'm not sure many people could. You're an inspiration. To me especially. I wish I could have stopped her last night."

I lean over the console and shake my head. "That's not your responsibility. All I needed was you by my side and you were." Desperate to be done with this conversation, I change the topic. With the tip of my pointer, I drag his gaze to meet mine. "I didn't tell you."

The tight hold Graham has on the steering wheel loosens. "Tell me what?"

"Booth and I are going to set up a meeting soon."

I bite my lip as understanding dawns and his eyes widen, before a smile full of pride stretches across his face.

"Fuck, honey, I didn't think I could be prouder." He grips my cheeks with both hands and smothers my gasp with a kiss. "Booth would be an idiot not to work with you. You built that all by yourself. He's seen what a hard worker you are and the quality of your work."

"She would have seen it differently. But I don't need her."

He rests his forehead against mine and kisses the tip of my nose. "What do you need?"

"I'd really like to pick up that leftover pecan pie from your mom's, get back in my pajamas, and continue watching our documentary."

"Then that's what we'll do."

TRYING ON CLOTHES IN AN OVERHEATED CHANGING ROOM WHILE already sweaty is most women's worst nightmare.

Johanna and I ran around the mall for an hour until we both picked out an outfit for the wedding.

At first, I couldn't understand why Graham would go, but now that I do, I want nothing more than to be next to him and support him through it.

According to Jo, Ralph's parents are delightful. Graham's aunt is his dad's only sibling and is still very close to his mom. Maybe one day he'll tell Claire the truth, but I, more than anyone, understand why avoidance feels like the best remedy sometimes.

Ever the pacifist, he did suggest we didn't have to go after the carnage with my mom. I'd love to lounge around on the sofa all day with him. He might say it was Booth's idea, but he would have never agreed to it in the first place had there not been a small part of his mind that told him he needed to attend the wedding for closure.

Just like blocking my mom's number and pressing charges was my goodbye to a toxic relationship, this is his.

It was only after my mom's surprise visit that it was clear I had a lot of unresolved baggage from my abusive childhood.

Although the idea of bringing up the past with a stranger makes me sick with nerves, I had never felt braver than after asking Johanna for advice on finding a therapist.

From what she's told me, finding someone to talk to was one of the best decisions she's ever made, and she's sure she wouldn't have returned to town had she not taken that step in her recovery.

I plan on telling Graham after the wedding, hoping that he can help me with my search.

Now that we both have dresses for the event and treated ourselves to a manicure, we're having a late lunch in the city before driving back.

"God, I hope there's barrels of wine at the wedding tomorrow. I'm going to need it to survive the day," Jo says as she slides her card into the checkbook and hands it to the server.

"I hate that she had him first," I blurt out.

She doesn't flinch at my outburst, just nods in agreement. "I think most of us are angry that she had him at all. I wasn't here for it, but after Ted passed away, it got worse. If it's any consolation, Patrick told me that you would have never known they were a couple in the last year of their relationship. I'll never know why he stayed. I'd warn Ralph, if he wasn't such a weasel."

My lips curl. "I'm glad you'll be there tomorrow. We can split that barrel of wine."

"Cheers to that." She raises her glass of water in my direction before asking, "Have you had any thoughts about what you'll do once the van is fixed?"

Graham and I have been so busy floating in this blissful phase of our new relationship that I haven't given the van any thought.

"After everything that's happened in the last couple of days, there hasn't been time. I miss Nelly. That little tin can has been my home for so long, but..."

"But home feels like somewhere else now?" Jo finishes for me, hitting the nail on the head.

"Exactly." My finger traces the edge of my glass. "It hasn't even been two months. And we've only been official for two weeks, we're not ready to live with each other. Right? God, listen to me, he hasn't even asked me to move in."

She laughs. "You think Graham—the man who's been obsessed with you since day one—is going to ask you to leave?"

"He's very logical."

"Mostly. With you, though, logic is thrown out the window."

I shake my head. We haven't shied away from our feelings since we finally admitted to them. But there are still moments I see him hesitate or question his actions. He's allowed himself to open up more compared to the man I met back in March. The confidence I've seen gradually flourish in Graham is obvious. But now and again it feels like he's waiting for the other shoe to drop.

"Was he like this with Jenna in the beginning?"

"God no." Jo grimaces. The server returns her card, but this conversation isn't ready to end just yet. "They were in the same class in high school and connected at college. Graham's quiet by nature and he kept to a small group of people right up until senior year. I don't think Jenna knew he existed until their paths crossed outside of Sutton Bay. I remember we came home for spring break, and she was there at the dinner table being introduced as his girlfriend.

"She was a nasty girl in high school, but we all gave her the benefit of the doubt. It didn't last long though. Even those small interactions we had during breaks from school were enough to tell me she wasn't right for him. He tried his best to be the person she wanted him to be. I'm glad he stopped trying though. It's just shitty it took her falling into bed with his cousin to realize she never tried with him."

Worry churns in my stomach. "Do you think he's trying to be something he's not with me?"

Her brows furrow. "No way." She leans in and squeezes my hand. "He is different. But it's like we have the old Graham again. Before his dad died and Jenna betrayed his trust. And I think we have you to thank for that."

She returns my smile, making me feel a little better.

I know firsthand how old scars can be reopened when the ghosts from our past return.

After tomorrow, we can finally put this all behind us.

CHAPTER THIRTY-TWO

graham

All good things must end
Savor each one while you can
Until the last hour

"THIS FEELS LIKE SENIOR PROM ALL OVER AGAIN," PATRICK groans.

"Why, because you don't have a date?" Dex earns himself an elbow to the ribs from Patrick.

"No. Because we're waiting for Johanna."

"Never rush a woman," my mom chimes in.

"Oh, believe me, I know. Lottie might as well be sixteen with her attitude recently. I love her, but I'm glad she's with her mom tonight. I need a stiff drink."

"Pat, don't you dare speak about my darling niece like that." Florence throws him a warning glare.

We're waiting at the steps of the venue, freezing our asses off as we wait for Quinn and Johanna to arrive.

While my family bickers beside me, I'm ready to crawl out

of my skin. Regret at thinking this was a good idea has been festering since I woke up. It's unlikely I'll even have to interact with Jenna or Ralph, I just hate the idea of having Quinn in her vicinity.

Tires rolling on gravel pull my attention to the long road leading up to the small orchard where the ceremony is being hosted. It started snowing on Thanksgiving evening and hasn't stopped for the last two days. The ground is draped in white and thickens before our eyes as large snowflakes float down from the sky.

The cab pulls up in front of us and Johanna is the first to step out. She looks lovely in a deep blue, knee-length dress and tweed coat. Patrick is quick to approach her and escort her up the steps.

When a delicate ankle laced in gold leather peeks out from the car my heart rate rises. Then Quinn reveals herself, and I stop breathing altogether. She's ethereal, draped in a shimmering yellow dress that shifts against her curves like liquid gold. A divine beauty poets would struggle to describe. Half her hair is tied up while the other half runs over her shoulders in a mess of chocolate and honey curls.

"Quinn," I breathe.

My hand falls to my chest, as if to keep my heart from falling out.

My Quinn.

I'm at the bottom of the stairs before my brain even registers I've walked toward her.

"Hey, you." There's a sweet shyness in her voice.

"Are you real?" My eyes skim up and down the length of her body, cataloging each detail.

"You don't look too bad yourself." She adjusts the lapels of my suit jacket and then grips the edges to pull me closer. "It's not fair that you look this handsome."

"It's not fair I have to share you with all these people tonight." I take hold of the thick coat she has folded over her arm and wrap it around her shoulders. "That's better. You're for my eyes only."

"Ohh, possessive." She giggles and then loops her arm through mine. "C'mon. Let's get this over with."

THE CEREMONY WENT ON WITHOUT A HITCH AND I FELT NOTHING as I watched the woman I thought I'd spend the rest of my life with share vows with another man.

When Ralph and Jenna were officially announced husband and wife the only thing that crossed my mind was that I hope I get to stand at the end of an altar with Quinn one day. If she wanted to elope or have the grandest wedding of the century, I'd give it to her.

The day has dragged, but it hasn't been awful, not with Quinn by my side.

We're now sitting around our table as we watch Patrick and Johanna sway among the other couples. Despite Booth's grumblings, he's slowly leading Mom across the dance floor, careful of her leg. Even Florence convinces Dex to join her and they laugh loudly as they tread on each other's toes.

My siblings would be shocked to the core at my next question, but I don't want her to miss out. "Dance with me, honey?"

Surprise paints her face, and she glances out to the black-and-white checked dance floor before turning back to me.

"Not here," she whispers.

I don't get the chance to ask her what she means before

she's dragging me to my feet, grabbing our coats, and guiding us through the crowd until we're out in the chilly night air.

"Here."

The thrum of the music is loud enough to reach us and the light from the party reveals the paved courtyard beneath our feet.

I hold my hand out, desperate to have her in my arms. I'm tugging her into me the second our fingers make contact and seal our fronts together.

"I would have danced with you in there," I tell her as I rest my chin on the top of her head.

"I know. But I think we've shown our faces enough for tonight. I want you to myself."

Her cheek lies above my heart.

Does she feel it? Feel how each beat is for her. The organ might as well have been useless before she came along.

The deep blue sky is adorned in twinkling lights and the moon shines on us like a spotlight; perfectly round from where it hangs in the sky.

November's first full moon.

The Beaver Moon.

It feels appropriate. Like folklore said, it's a time for preparation and transition.

I wasn't ready for her, but maybe all my life I've been preparing for the woman in my arms. And as she hums against my chest while we sway to the sounds of an acoustic guitar, it's clear we've shifted into something so beautiful and unforgettable, it would be a shame not to put it into words.

If there's going to be one time in my life that I'm impulsive, fearless, and say exactly what's on my mind, it's now. I'll happily stumble over all other words. Not these three though. I want her to hear them strong and clear. Leaving no doubt about how I feel.

"I love you."

There isn't an ounce of nervousness or hesitancy. Why would there be when those three little words were only meant for her?

Her breath hitches and heart beats against mine like a steady drum. Slowly she looks up at me. Soft fingers trace my lips, as if she's searching for the words again.

"There you go, giving me another first. I can't imagine any other person, in any other life, sharing those words with me but you." Tears pool in the corners of her eyes. She looks so damn beautiful as the moon reflects off those caramel irises. "I love you so much, Graham."

I can feel the truth in her words, and I can taste it when our lips meet underneath the tapestry of stars. This moment is one of many, and right now, it's ours.

Everything I know is rewritten with the knowledge that Quinn loves me and I love her.

"We're leaving," I declare. "I can't stand to be here for another second when all I want to do is worship your body. To sink into you and tell you I love you over and over again."

"Then what are we waiting for? Let's g—"

My lips devour hers before she can finish her sentence. She stumbles back from the force of it, but I keep a tight hold of her as I walk us to a darkened corner beside the barn. My hand rests against the wood, softening the impact when I push her up against it. The temperature has dropped to near freezing, yet we feel nothing but fire and yearning as we frantically kiss, suck, and bite.

Driving back to the apartment sounds excruciating. I want to fuck her here until the stars above us aren't the only ones she sees.

As badly as I want that, she deserves better.

"Quinn," I grit out as I pull away. "Honey, stop trying to take off my belt."

She fumbles with the buckle, her voice breathless. "Why? Do you want to do it?"

It's then I notice her feet are blue from the cold. We're wrapped up in thick coats but they're useless against New England winters.

"You can do it when we get home. I promise," I add when she pouts. "Why don't you say goodbye to everyone, I'll meet you at the car."

"Are you not coming?" she asks as we walk back to the large barn doors.

"I'm not hugging my mother goodbye with the world's most painful boner."

The little minx giggles and with one chaste kiss to my lips, she dashes into the crowd to say farewell to my family. My heart grows in size as I watch her hug each one.

After a quick trip to the restroom, I wander down the narrow hallway leading to the back entrance. A few tipsy guests have ventured into the parking lot to smoke or gossip. I'm looking around for Quinn when I hear her first. Walking toward the sound, my anxiety rises when anger and frustration lace her tone as she stands face-to-face with the bride.

"Jenna, go and enjoy your day. What happens between Graham and me is none of your concern. It hasn't been for a long time."

Disdain drips from Jenna's voice and from her slurred words, she's drunk. "He was my concern for twelve years. I know him better than anyone."

"Do you? Or did you take advantage of his kindness and trust, only to twist it against him?" Quinn's arms vibrate at her sides.

Jenna just *tsks* and rolls her eyes. "He's boring and useless. I'm doing you a favor. Girl to girl, you think you're happy now, but you'll soon work out why everyone calls him *Gray*. I'd cut him loose now if I were you. He's not worth it. I tried to change him for the better and all he did was bury his head in that stupid little jour—"

"Be. Quiet." Quinn's voice is hushed, but ripples with warning. She steps forward, and despite their height difference, Jenna is right to be unnerved. "Go back inside before I say or do something I'll regret."

Heat floods Jenna's cheeks and she saves herself just as her heel falls in a crack in the patio stones. She doesn't respond, just stares Quinn down for a beat before stomping away.

Buzzing sounds in my ears and panic swarms me as I watch the tension leave Quinn's muscles. I'm hidden behind a row of bushes, but when I step out from my hiding place, the scuffing off my shoes catches her attention.

Her hand flies to her mouth when she sees me. "How long have you been standing there?"

I should be thankful she stood up for me. I want to trust she doesn't believe the things she's heard, but I thought the same about Jenna. Thought we were *it* once upon a time.

She loves me.

So did Jenna.

I'm not Gray.

Yes, you are.

In one, five, ten years down the line, will she change her mind about me?

What if she quickly realizes I'm not the man she thought I was?

Maybe the Beaver Moon wasn't about us preparing and transitioning into the next step in our relationship. It was about preparing myself for the loss of her and transitioning back to how it was before.

Before sunlight broke through the gray skies.

"Are you ready to leave?" I ask, ignoring her question. I'm not sure how to even speak to her about this with so many doubts and worries spiraling in my head. This is my biggest fear. That Quinn will see how different we are, and I'll be discarded, unwanted by another woman I trusted.

I want so badly to get out of my head. To trust the words we shared minutes ago. To give her the words I'm struggling to find.

But I can't.

CHAPTER THIRTY-THREE

quinn

Why can't the people from our past let us be happy?

Just when I thought the storm following my mother's visit had passed, Jenna comes rolling in. Ready to cause destruction. Disrupting the peace.

Tremors still pulse in my hands following my encounter with the bride. She's like a weed. You think you've eradicated the issue, yet they keep growing back.

I couldn't stand there and let her talk about Graham that way. Anger rose in me with each poisonous lie she spat. Had I said what I was really thinking, everything in me would have boiled over like a volcanic eruption. As much as I dislike her, I wasn't about to turn into the angry girlfriend of the bride's ex.

She can try, but she won't ruin us.

Scraping from behind the bushes has me spinning on my heels toward the noise. When my eyes adjust to the darkness, my stomach drops and I clasp a hand over my mouth when Graham steps out.

His face is void of emotion.

Please don't let him have heard the horrible things she said.

"How long have you been standing there?" I whisper.

His eyes fall to his feet, confirming he witnessed it all. My heart thunders in my chest, so different to the happy beat it thumped to minutes ago when he told me he loved me. I wait for him to respond, plead at him with my eyes to speak to me. When he finally talks, my eyes fall shut.

"Are you ready to leave?"

Not wanting to drag this night out any longer than necessary, I start walking toward his car with him following closely behind.

Only few would spot the unease in his muscles, the way his hand finds the back of his neck, or how his eyes dart to the side. He's panicking. Quietly. And I don't know what to do.

Something lingers in the air between us during the journey home. It's nothing like the serene and quiet moments I'm used to. This silence isn't him taking the time to find the right words. It's avoidance.

I don't push him to talk and give him the space I know he needs, but after neither of us speaks for what feels like hours as we get ready for bed, I'm ready to combust.

When I return from the bathroom and find Graham sitting on the edge of my bed, some of my anxiety subsides when he opens his arms for me. I catapult myself into him and bury my face into his neck. His body is rigid, but I convince myself it's from all the socializing and being around *her*.

"Can you tell me what you're thinking?" I murmur into his skin.

He cups the back of my head and kisses along my jaw. "I'm thinking I want to make love to you. Can I?"

It's something, I think, and it's clear he craves the comfort of touch right now.

"I'd love nothing more."

The pajamas I put on are useless. He peels them from my body in no time. The same goes for his briefs. We settle on top of the comforter and when the blunt head of his cock settles between my thighs, he doesn't push forward like I'm aching for him to do. He lies there, cocooning me in his warmth, while breathing deeply against my pulse point.

"Look at me, Graham."

My heart cracks when he does. There's no doubt he wants me, and I'm right here, underneath him. So why does he look at me like I might disappear in his next breath?

"I love you," I whisper.

"God, Quinn. I love you so much," he says on a sigh and finally sinks into me. "You have no idea."

I gasp as he fills me, and my hands fall to his ass, encouraging him to move deeper. "Show me how much. Please."

With an agonizing slowness, he enters me until he's fully seated. Every time with him is incredible; whether it's sweet and sensual or fast and greedy. Tonight he's making love to me so gently, it makes my chest ache.

I love you. I love you. I love you.

He whispers against my lips with each roll of his hips.

I love you. I love you. I love you.

I moan into his mouth as I cling to him with each thrust.

We say those words to each other over and over long after he finishes inside me. It's only when our eyes fall closed that we stop.

I can't fall asleep, and with his head resting on my chest, I'm not sure if it finds him either.

Tonight we shared something sacred. There's no doubt he meant what he said.

So why does it feel like he's pulling away?

A THUMPING SOUND BESIDE MY HEAD IS THE FIRST THING TO greet me when I wake up. The empty space beside me is the second when I peel my eyes open. Curly's tail whips against the pillow as the dog whines at me. The time on my phone tells me it's still pretty early but Graham usually goes for a run on Sunday mornings.

I'm hoping he just needed a good night's sleep and some fresh air to clear his head.

"Morning, little guy." I stroke a hand down his shiny coat. "Where's your daddy? Where's Graham?"

As if he heard his name, the man himself walks into the bedroom just as my phone rings.

Rolling back over, I accept the call. "Hello?"

"Hey, Quinn. It's Ricky from the garage."

"Oh, hi, Ricky." I clear my throat. My eyes haven't left Graham's but at the sound of the mechanic's name, his body pulls taut, and he goes to speak before snapping his mouth shut.

"I hope you guys had a good Thanksgiving. Good news! The van is ready to be picked up."

I rub at my eyes, but maybe I should clean out my ears. "Sorry, *ready?* Can you not keep it at the shop anymore? I'll have the money together soon, but if you need me to pay for storage—"

"What? No. Did Graham not tell you?"

Confusion has me sitting up. "No, he didn't. What's happening?" I take in Graham's torn expression and barely hear Ricky's reply.

"Your man paid for everything. And then some. Sorry, I thought you knew. I hope I didn't ruin some big surprise. Anyway, I'll be here until five today if you want to swing by and get her. Call me if there are any issues."

"Okay, will do." My voice is robotic and when the call ends, my hand falls to the plush bedding. "You didn't?"

This goes way beyond baking me a cake or buying me flowers. The cost of fixing the van was already pushing four thousand dollars. I don't want to imagine what this *then some* means.

"He was supposed to call *me*." He's annoyed and avoiding the real question here. With rigid shoulders and clenched fists, he stares at the ground.

I rise from the bed, still naked, but wrap myself in my robe before taking a timid step toward him. "Do-do you want me to leave?"

His head shoots up, eyes wide. "Of course not." My body relaxes, but he's still unsure as he shifts in place and rubs at the back of his neck. "It was going to be a gift for Christmas."

"This is too much. I can't accept this. Not after everything you've done for me. You don't have to keep doing these things for me." I take another step.

"I do."

"Why?"

His fingers drag through his hair, almost knocking his glasses off. The need to know what's going on in that head of his becomes too much. "Graham, please look at me." When he finally does, the crushed expression on his face stops me in my tracks. "Tell me what you're thinking. Don't sit with your thoughts when I'm here to listen."

He hasn't struggled with words in front of me for so long. Even then it was because of nerves. This is something completely different. The defeated, broken tone of his voice is enough to send me crashing to my knees. "Since we met, I've never understood how a relationship between us could work— let alone a fake one. I thought that maybe if I fixed your van or bought you gifts you wouldn't see what she did. Then after I heard you speaking with Jenna..."

"Do you think I believe her?"

His response is immediate. "It's one of my biggest fears."

My anger from last night returns with a vengeance. I'm also riddled with disbelief that he'd think I'd believe anything she had to say.

"*Everything* she said last night was foul and the furthest thing from the truth." My voice cracks. "I don't need gifts, Graham, I keep telling you this. I'm here because I want to be. Forget the flowers, the cake, the boots. I'm here for you. But right now, it feels like you're pushing me away."

The last word is barely out of my mouth before he's crowding me, enveloping me in his arms. "No. *No.* Fuck. I've spent all night reassuring myself you don't believe her. I panicked after I saw you two talking. The last thing I want to do is push you away, it's just...I don't understand."

I peer up at him. "Understand what?"

He hesitates, discomfort pulling his features tight. "How you can love me."

The splintering of my heart is practically audible.

Since I've met him, I've known he doesn't see himself in the same light as others do. He second-guesses himself, and his words, or worries he's done the wrong thing. With each day we've spent together, he's gained confidence and become more sure of himself.

None of the people who love him want him any differently.

Yet he still can't see that.

"Don't talk like that. Like we didn't just spend the most incredible couple of months together. Take away the gifts and the acts of kindness and you still make me so incredibly happy." I cup his cheek, forcing him to look at me. "Do you remember what you said to me after my mom called? You said, 'You're exactly how you should be; and that is perfect.' I would never want to change you, not like *her.* But if there is one thing I want you to do differently, it's for you to love yourself the way your family loves you. The way..." The tears I've been holding back break through the dam. "The way I love you."

"God, Quinn, honey. No, don't cry." He clutches me harder.

"Tell me you believe me. That you know I love you," I sob into his chest.

"I believe you. I do. We're just so different. All I see is you, and what if one day down the line you realize this is a mistake? I don't want you to regret anything. If you regretted us I'm not sure how I could survive that. I want you to be sure that I'm what you want."

His whispered words might as well be screamed with the way they make my head throb.

"Wanting you has been the best decision I've ever made." I hold onto him like a life raft in vicious white waters and beg my voice to remain steady as I speak. "Do you know what I do regret?"

He doesn't respond.

"Not falling in love with you sooner."

How can I make him believe me? I don't know what more I can give him outside of my words to prove this will never be a regret. I'm so angry at myself for not seeing it sooner. He's become so withdrawn from himself, he's dubbed himself unlovable, despite the small army of people in his life who feel so lucky to be loved by him.

Graham can love, but he doesn't believe he can be loved.

"Tell me what to do? I'll do anything. I don't want to fuck this up," he pleads as his head falls to mine.

"My biggest fear growing up was not being loved. I lived that fear daily. Knowing you love me is the most incredible feeling. Do you know what my biggest fear is now?"

He shakes his head and fresh tears gather in the corners of my eyes. "It's that you feel you have to prove your love to me, and you'll forget to love yourself."

"Quinn. Baby, please. I do..." His words trail off.

He can't even say it.

And that tells me enough.

"You're a beautiful, selfless, incredible man, Graham Sadler, and I'm sorry anyone ever made you think otherwise." The tears are endless now, soaking his T-shirt and blurring my vision. I'm grateful I can't see his face when I speak. "I think we need time. You need time to see what I see every day." I press a hand to my chest, like I can keep my heart from fracturing any further. "I know you don't mean it, but it hurts seeing the doubt in your eyes when all you give me is joy."

"What are you saying?" he asks, his voice so full of anguish.

Even though my next words split me down the middle, this feels like the only option.

"If all you see is me, how can you see yourself?" His grip doesn't loosen when I try to pull away. "The van is ready, and I think a little space is what we both need."

"Quinn, no. Please don't make me say goodbye." The pain on his face is devastating, but he needs this. *We* need this. There's a lot we've both left unresolved for too long. Me with my mother and him with Jenna. I worry that with me here, he won't address them and his fears will eat away at him, day by day.

"This isn't goodbye." I try to smother my sob with my hand, but it's no use as it rips through my chest. "I'm doing this because I love you so much. Sometimes we have to do things that cause us pain to get to the best part. *Us.* We are the best part, Graham. You are one-half of us. Please love every part of it. I need you to try."

At that, the fight leaves him. I miss him the moment he releases me, scared that I'm the one pushing him away now.

"I think I need to work on myself too." My hand cups the back of his neck, begging him with my eyes to understand. "After my mom turned up I realized I was still letting her control me. We have to stop the people from our past thinking they have a say anymore."

He nods his head and takes a step back. The small space feeling so much bigger than it is.

Never did I see the last twenty-four hours ending like this. A piece of me blames myself for ignoring all the times he's talked badly about himself or downplayed the incredible things he did for me.

How long has he felt this way about himself?

For years, all I knew was hate, and it took time for me to love myself again.

As I drag my suitcase out from under the bed, I remind myself that this isn't over. I need him to go on that same journey I went on. If it takes half a decade or more, he's worth it. But it's up to him to realize that.

He stands there, staring at the spot where I just vacated. I fold the lavender blanket we made love on last night and breathe in the scent of *us*.

"Graham," I whisper gently. He manages to drag his gaze away to look at me. "I-I can't pack if you're watching. It's too hard."

His face crumples but he nods as he backs toward the open doorway, only to pause.

"Can I keep that?" He nods toward the knitted blanket balled in my hands. "I'm going to try. For us. I don't know what it looks like, but while I search for what you—we need—can I keep something of yours?"

I don't know how my tear ducts haven't dried up yet. My lip wobbles as I place it onto the bed, not brave enough to give it to him because I'll end up in his arms. "You have my heart. That's what you'll keep."

"It's my most prized possession," he says hoarsely before swallowing. "What if I can't love myself the way you love me?"

"Then I'll wait."

CHAPTER THIRTY-FOUR

graham

Silence was a friend
That quickly turned to a foe
All because of her

IF I THOUGHT LIFE WAS LONELY BEFORE SHE WALKED INTO IT, I don't know how to describe the aftermath of her departure.

It's like spending your days basking in endless sunshine, knowing nothing different, for someone to then lock you away in a windowless, barren dungeon, one hundred feet below ground.

I'm glad she didn't make me watch her pack, because I certainly couldn't watch her leave.

I heard Johanna's quiet voice consoling Quinn as she helped her with her suitcase. Just before she closed the door, she said, "I'll look after her, Graham."

That's my job, was all I could think.

Curly whines and scratches at the door now. Every minute that's passed since she left has sent me deeper and deeper into a world of regret. It's dark here. But I swear, in the distance, there's a speck of light.

My living room still holds traces of her. She said this wasn't goodbye and I believe that. Seeing her yellow rain boots still lined up next to my running shoes feeds that hope.

After thirty minutes of taking in all the things she left behind, I can't stand to be trapped in here for a second longer.

With Curly clipped into his harness, we find ourselves on the same bench where Booth convinced me to ask Quinn to be my fake girlfriend not that long ago. The bite of the cold air means I can feel something other than utter misery.

My dog jumps onto the bench and lays his head on my thigh with a sad noise.

"I miss her, too, buddy."

I'm angry for spiraling the way I did and for making Quinn think I was trying to push her away. When I paid for the repairs on her van, I knew there was a chance she'd leave, but I also know how important her freedom and independence are to her.

After the worst night's sleep, I exhausted myself on a run this morning until I started to think logically again.

Quinn never gave me any reason to doubt she would change her mind about our future together. I was the one who allowed Jenna's words to burrow into my brain and distort everything Quinn and I have built.

Her opinion shouldn't matter, yet I let it. That should have stopped the minute she walked out of the door and into the arms of my cousin. This agreement with Quinn was about proving to Jenna that she doesn't hold power over me any longer. Something I failed miserably at.

As the chill sets in my bones, I take in the white bluffs across the bay. The somber sky above drowns out any color, making everything look solemn—an accurate depiction of my mood. Even the choppy waters smashing against the hulls of the boats mimic the banging of my heart against my ribs, screaming at me to see this—myself—differently.

I lose track of time until a voice interrupts my thoughts.

"Can I join you?"

The sudden appearance of my older brother as he slides onto the bench has my head jerking up. The usual insult or jab I'd throw at him for scaring me is too much effort. So I just nod.

"Quinn's at our place," he says as he settles next to me. "I thought I'd give the girls some space and come find you."

Knowing Quinn has a friend like Johanna to turn to is a small comfort.

"She's okay." He takes in my slouched posture and grim demeanor. "Looks about as gutted as you are though. Are you going to tell me what happened, or do I have to piece it together myself?"

Patrick sighs at my resounding silence.

"Do you remember those few months I was struggling with managing the restaurant and raising a newborn? You pushed and pushed me to take a break. To delegate tasks to other people. Even slept at my house for an entire week so I could sleep. You pissed me off because you wouldn't leave, and I was so grateful to you for it. So we can sit here all day until we're frozen, but I'm not leaving, you surly bastard."

The corners of my mouth twitch.

"You can't keep living with the regrets of yesterday. That's what Dad would have said to you. You also can't keep regretting your relationship with Jenna. It's done. Over. Quinn is *nothing* like her. The fact that she's putting you above your relationship, and her happiness, says that."

"I told her I couldn't understand it." My voice is strained after not speaking for so long.

"Understand what?" He leans forward to hold my gaze.

"What she sees in me. How she can love me. My head was fucked after her and Jenna's conversation."

"Gray—" My flinch cuts him off. "What did I say?"

My fingers flex in my gloves but I know I need to be honest with him. "I hate being called Gray."

His head rears back, brows furrowing underneath his hat. "Since when? We've called you that for as long as I can remember."

"Jenna. The last thing she said to me before she walked out was, 'There's a reason everyone calls you Gray. It's fitting: dull, boring, and emotionless.' Last night she pretty much said the same to Quinn."

"Fucking hell, she really is something. It's a good thing Quinn wouldn't believe a word that comes out of that snake's mouth."

My shoulders droop and I slide down the bench.

He groans and scrubs a hand down his face. "Why on earth would Quinn ever think that? She loves you so much. It's what she kept saying as she sobbed her way through our front door. Christ, Graham, are you really that blind?"

"Yes!" I shout, the sudden outburst causing a flock of gulls to scatter as my voice ricochets around us.

Patrick doesn't ask me to clarify, he just waits. Like Booth, he knows not to rush me.

"She stood up for me, which should be mortifying. I regret how I handled it, but I was so fucking scared after Jenna said those things to her. I hated how I couldn't stand up for myself, or see past Jenna's words, that I clammed up."

"Do you believe it? What Jenna said?"

"Up until this fall, yes." I swallow. "Not anymore."

"I don't know how to help you fight those demons. Quinn is crazy about you. I'm so happy she's in your life and sees you for who we've always seen. Me, Booth, Florence, Mom. Maybe we should have told you more often." He grabs me by the shoulder and pulls me into a hug, the sudden act bringing on a whole new wave of emotions. "We love you, for exactly who you are. And if Dad were here today, he'd say the same. *Believe* that Quinn loves you for you." We break apart. "If you don't, you're going to lose her. Trust this from the guy who spent years dancing around the woman he loved. When you have her, you don't let her go."

"I don't know what to do. I can't change how I feel about myself overnight."

"It's not about change. If anything, you need to show Quinn you understand why she loves you. Prove to her that you're working on it."

He makes it sound so easy.

We settle with our backs against the bench, the cold bite of the wood seeping through my jeans. He stays with me, though, as the minutes pass.

"Dad would tell me to write this all down," I eventually say.

"He was smart. Knew what we needed to hear at just the right time." He shuffles back and pulls out a wad of envelopes from his coat pocket and looks at them longingly. "Right after we found out about the restaurant being sold, his words turned out to be exactly what I needed to read. I planned on giving these to you all at Christmas. I don't know what it says, but something tells me you need his words right now."

He presses the papers into my hands. "The other two are for Booth and Florence. I think you should be the one to give them theirs—when they need it the most." He stands and brushes the snow from his pants. "Do you want me to say anything to Quinn when I see her?"

So much. But she needs assurances now, not excuses. "Tell her that when we see each other next, it's going to be one for the record books."

SOMETHING IN PATRICK'S TONE TOLD ME THIS LETTER SHOULDN'T be read in public.

Which is why I'm sitting at my desk, pulling away the seal of the envelope to reveal my dad's familiar writing. It's been so long since I've seen his curly C's and dramatic Y's.

With a deep breath, I read.

> Graham,
>
> I don't know where you'll be when you read this, but as I'm writing this you'll be landing in New York, to start your first semester of college. I wanted to let you know how proud your mother and I are of you.
>
> There hasn't been a day we haven't been, and I know sometimes you fail to see that.
>
> It can be hard to feel accepted or heard when you're not loud or outgoing. Getting lost in a sea of voices that tend to be our own as we navigate our feelings. As well as our good looks, we share something else in common. Self-acceptance.
>
> Growing up, you tried so hard to be outspoken like Booth or bossy like Patrick or goofy like Florence. You said you were desperate to be liked. You failed to see how your thoughtfulness helped calm Booth; your rational thinking allowed Patrick to take a step back and look at the bigger picture; and your patience gave Florence a new perspective.
>
> You quietly but fiercely cared for them all in your own way.

You, my boy, are and will always be exactly who you're supposed to be.

Your mother helped me realize that about myself and so did you. Since becoming your father you've taught me so much. Patience. Forgiveness. Joy.

All I ask is that you're kind to yourself and that when you find the person you want to spend the rest of your life with, they love you for exactly the man you are.

You always called me your hero, when really, you're mine.

With all my love,
Dad

"Fuck." My glasses clatter to the desk and I bury my head in my hands, letting the raw emotion rock through my body.

Fifteen years. Fifteen years ago this was written. His advice has just been sitting there, waiting for me.

It's not lost on me that his advice is so similar to the words of comfort I gave Quinn after her mother's phone call.

I'd do anything to hear my dad speak these words to me. Reading them is a hit in the sternum with each letter and syllable.

He's right though.

I laugh into my palms, knowing he'd love hearing me say that. There's no point in dwelling over whether things would have turned out differently had I read it sooner. Before Jenna. His death. Meeting Quinn. This letter found its way to me at precisely the right time.

Quinn would still have walked into my life 249 days ago and turned it upside down. Or perhaps, the right way up.

I've known she was the person I wanted to spend my life

with since the day of my mom's accident. I know she's nothing like Jenna and it shouldn't have taken me until this morning to realize that.

It should have been her serenity in my silence. The way she wants to hear me laugh or make me smile. That anytime we kissed, she shined brighter.

Her love for me has been there all along.

My leather-bound journal sits on the corner of the desk. I slide it toward me and read through all the entries since I've met her. There's a change in my tone from that first day I spoke to her; a hint of hope and wonder. And maybe that's it. She needs to see I don't question her love, but I also need to show her how without even knowing it, I've slowly started to accept myself again.

These pages will allow her to see that.

Being apart from her is going to kill me.

But the reunion will be incredible.

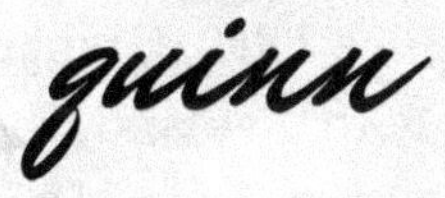

CHAPTER THIRTY-FIVE

THE TEARS FROM WHEN I SAW THE FRESH PAINT JOB HAVE SINCE dried, but new ones streak my cheeks when I open the sliding door to my van.

Ricky showed me the new parts under the hood, and I accepted his word that it was fixed. I should have asked some follow-up questions, but I was too eager to see inside.

"Oh, Graham." My voice cracks with a sob. "I still can't believe he did this."

Johanna stands outside while I turn into a blubbering mess.

The cabinets have been painted in an off-white, brightening the small space. The faded green vinyl flooring has been replaced with a dark-oak-effect laminate. Small spotlights decorate the ceiling. He's been in the van a handful of times, yet he's managed to transform it into my very own vision.

"Acts of service is definitely his love language." Jo's eyes shift to the left, biting her lip as she looks at me. "You should check out the bed."

I drag back the partition curtain he's had installed to reveal a brand-new mattress. Gone is the old, lumpy one. I'd cannonball on top of it if there wasn't a bouquet of yellow dahlias and a crisp white envelope with my name on it sitting in the center.

"Is he here?" I gasp and turn to Jo.

It's Ricky who answers. Poor guy witnessed my whole breakdown. "He came by this morning and dropped that off." He nods toward the items on the bed.

It's been one day since I left Graham's apartment. Jo was adamant I could stay with her and Patrick for as long as I needed, but if I wasn't with Graham, I wanted to be within the familiar surroundings of Nelly.

When we first took my van to the garage almost two months ago, I was so sad to say goodbye. This will always be my first home. I'm hoping that after this time apart, my new one will be with the man who gives me flowers like it's going out of fashion.

My butt hits the mattress with a bounce, and my finger traces over the neat, block lettering. "Have I made a mistake?"

Jo joins me, wrapping me up in a hug. "No. I don't think either of you saw yourselves ending up here, but time apart might be good." With one last squeeze, she stands. "I'll meet you in the truck. Take your time."

I bring the arrangement to my nose. Dahlias are mostly fragrance-free; it's his scent I'm trying to get a whiff of.

With shaky fingers, I open the envelope.

Hi, honey,

How was your day?

I'm sad I can't hear you tell me all about it. I hope you found something to make you smile today.

You probably don't know this, but it's been 250 days since we met. Even during the days I was too nervous to talk to you, seeing you through the bakery window made my days better. Getting to know you like I have these past two months has been the best time of my life. I can't promise I'll stop spoiling you with gifts, but not to make you stay. It will be because your smile brings the sunshine to the darkest of places.

I hated that I was stormy gray while you were sunshine yellow. So different. But now I see it's not the flowers, rain boots, or even the cake I failed so miserably at that has you loving me. You chose me. I see how I make your smile shine brighter. Make the melody of your laughter ring sweeter. You turn to me for comfort when things don't go as planned.

When you look at me, you see me.

It frightened me to death to think you'd wake up one morning and see me differently. I hadn't realized how much Jenna had torn me down. She found it so easy to throw me aside and I was terrified you'd eventually see what she did. Losing you isn't something I would recover from and I'm sorry for letting my fears take control. I should have trusted you like you trust me.

Just one moment is all it took. And every single moment after that has helped me realize I don't have to be someone different.

For you, I want to be me.

Our differences are what make <u>us</u> beauti-ful. Thank you for seeing them when I couldn't.

There's something in the envelope I want you to keep next to your heart during this time. I'm going to try. Not just for us, but for me.

I love you so much.

Forever yours,

Graham

Scrambling to grab the envelope, I tip out its contents. What falls out is tiny, but I'd know that face anywhere.

A photograph of Graham looks up at me, cut into an oval shape. A perfect fit for my locket. The cold metal is cold to the touch, but once I slip the photo inside, it feels warm against my thumping heart.

I fall onto the mattress, clutching the letter to my chest.

He's trying.

"Quinn!" Booth hollers as he walks through the door of the bakery.

I haven't reopened yet. The new display fridge should arrive later this week and Dex is refitting a new glass pane tomorrow. The board covering the front does an awful job of keeping out the frosty morning air, but I wanted to bake something to distract me, even if I can't sell it.

"Hey, Booth. Coffee?" I raise a cup toward him.

"Would love one. Thanks." His smile is bright. It's good to see him, but I'm grateful he doesn't share Graham's eye or hair color.

I fix us both an extra-hot drink and we settle on one of the tables, quick to avoid sitting at the table I once declared as *ours* to Graham.

It's useless avoiding reminders of him. He's everywhere.

"Thanks for meeting with me. I'm sorry to rush this, the restaurant is slammed today. I looked at your prices and honestly, they're too low." He slides a printed version of the price list I emailed him after Thanksgiving, now annotated in messy red handwriting. He jabs a finger onto the paper. "*This* is what I'll pay you. I'm keeping our current supplier on until the new year. Get back on your feet, but then I want a regular order of sourdough and brioche buns. Sound good?"

I blink at him slowly. "What do you mean it's too low? You don't want a trial run? Or...?"

Why am I arguing with him?

"Your accountant put in a pretty good word with me. I've seen how hard you work. I'm sold. Plus, we're going to be family one day, so why would I want to work with anyone but my future sister-in-law?" He stands abruptly and shivers. "Fuck. It's cold in here."

I'm still blushing from his comment about me being his future sister-in-law. "I did offer to meet you at the restaurant."

"Yeah, but I didn't think you'd want to read this with an audience." He pulls an envelope from his pocket, and in the next beat, I'm pulled into his arms. "Thank you for helping my brother see himself. For loving him for the exact reasons we do."

He releases me and I bite my lip to keep the tears at bay. "Is he okay?"

"He is. Misses you like crazy, but he's working on himself." After another charming smile and quick hug, he dashes out of the building, shouting, "See ya, Quinn," over his shoulder.

I tear through the paper the moment the door closes behind him.

The date at the top of the page reads *October 13*. After some quick math, I realize what day that was and what I'm holding.

It's a torn-out page from Graham's journal.

Yesterday she told me her favorite color was yellow. How no one has ever given this woman flowers before is a crime, but I love that I was the first person to do it. I hope she likes flowers because she's going to be getting a lot of them now.

I was sure she was weirded out or angry at how we left things last time. I wish I'd just told her that I'd saved her number and had spent months typing out a message to her.

It's funny how after just a few interactions I feel comfortable around her. She makes me nervous, but maybe it's a good type of nervous.

I love the random things that come out of her pretty mouth.

There was no controlling the blush when she said I was handsome, but what surprised me the most was that I smiled. That's something I haven't done a lot of with people outside of my family.

I'm still shocked she's even considering being my fake girlfriend.

I really hope she agrees to this, but if she doesn't, I hope I can find a way to keep seeing her.

Tears spill onto the pages, so I bring the paper to rest against my lips, not wanting to smudge his words.

I remember that day so clearly. The bizarreness of it all. How he timidly told me about buying flowers for his mother and sister after his dad passed.

That tidbit of information let me know of his caring nature. And something told me he wouldn't share that information with just anyone.

Seeing this side of him is fascinating and I can't imagine how vulnerable he feels knowing I'm reading it.

But from this small insight into his mind, I feel closer to him than ever before.

"Aunty Quinn!"

Chestnut brown pigtails are the last thing I see before I'm attacked by a tiny human.

My heart squeezes like it did the first time she called me

that name. I drop a hand to the little girl's head. "Hey, Lottie. What are you doing here?"

I'm standing outside the bakery, admiring the stencils I applied to the new window Dex fitted the other day. Wreaths of holly and tiny snowflakes now sit around the edge of the glass.

"I have something for you." She smiles up at me, with the same green eyes as her uncle.

Florence, who is wrapped up in layers of clothes, jogs up behind Lottie. "I've been away for a year and already my body has forgotten how cold these East Coast winters can be." She ruffles Lottie's hair. "Hey, stinker, did you give Quinn her letter yet?"

"There you go!" The little girl thrusts her arms toward me, with a little white envelope clutched between her mittened hands. "Daddy told me to say that, umm...Oh! 'Thank you for making Uncle Gray smile like a creeper whenever you're around.'"

I snort and Florence rolls her eyes before speaking. "I also have a message. We don't know each other that well. *Yet.* But the way Graham looked at you when you stepped out of that car at the wedding, it was like seeing a love story unravel before my eyes. My brother has never shared his feelings with many people. With you, he can't seem to contain them. Most of all"— she steps up and hugs me tightly—"you didn't try to change him. You allow him the space to think; to exist in his quiet thoughts. Graham was the person I turned to when our dad passed. Sometimes we'd just sit there in silence together and it was the best company I could have asked for."

"I'm not sure I can handle many more visits like this," I say as I dab at my eyes. "But thank you."

"I'd keep some tissues close by." She laughs before they both wave goodbye and head toward Our Place.

We've been apart for five days.

I hadn't expected anymore letters after Booth's delivery, and

I'm not even through the door of the bakery before I'm shredding through the envelope. My smile grows wider when I see it's another journal entry.

November 15

My worst nightmare came to life today. The second I heard the words Mom and hospital in the same sentence, I thought the worst.

She's fine, but she will not be leaving the house. Ever again.

The last time someone I loved was hurt, the person I expected to see me through the pain let me down. Not Quinn. She stayed with me. Consoled me. Gave me time to collect my thoughts.

For the first time in a long time, I opened up to someone who wasn't my family. It scared the shit out of me but I felt lighter after it.

She said something that rocked me to my core though. "I don't want you to be anything else."

When I held her in my arms that night, I played those words over in my brain. Have I been too worried about what I should be, rather than what I am?

I read the last part over and over. This is dated weeks before the night of the wedding, but his words tell me he was slowly starting to see himself clearly. And also what damage Jenna did to his self-esteem.

When I get back to the van that evening, I add the letter to the pile beside my bed.

The newest David Attenborough documentary airs tonight, but I can't bring myself to watch it without Graham.

He's respecting my wishes for space, but I so badly want to text him about his day and to hear his voice.

I remind myself this is about *both* of us working on ourselves and I need to do my part.

Picking up my phone, I dial the number Jo gave me this morning. After a brief conversation, I have an appointment booked for January to meet with a therapist. It's going to take time, and I know that Graham's own journey isn't going to happen overnight.

But we're both trying.

And I'm so proud of *us*.

CHAPTER THIRTY-SIX

quinn

Two weeks.

That's how long it's been since I've seen him.

I'm not sure how we've avoided running into each other in this small town.

Day after day, a new entry from Graham's journal is delivered to me.

One of his siblings has come in for a coffee or pastry and left me with an envelope I'm always so giddy to receive.

Reading each one is emotional, especially the ones early on when we were trying and failing at faking anything around each other. It was the entry from our first meeting in the bar that opened my eyes the most. Such a contrast to the last one I received, declaring his love for me in ink.

It's been beautiful to see our relationship bloom from his perspective. Having these pieces of him is monumental, and it's clear that his opinions of himself slowly stopped being so negative and doubtful.

Does he see the differences?

When I turn to the clock on the wall, my heart sinks when I

see the time. It's almost five p.m., and no one has come to drop off a letter today. *Maybe there are no more?*

All the chairs are stacked on top of the tables and just as I go to flip the light switch, a knock on the window draws my attention.

Claire waves at me through the glass, with Booth standing at her side, both their cheeks pink from the cold, and I run over to let them in.

"They weren't kidding when they said a snowstorm was coming." Claire shakes the snow from her hat and turns to her son, who is hovering behind her as she wobbles into the bakery on crutches. She's slowly becoming more mobile, and I bet she's itching to get the cast off. "That'll do. Now, run off and stop treating me like I'm made of glass."

"Gee, thanks, Ma. Good to know I'm just your butler." Booth rolls his eyes.

"Oh, sweetheart, you're so much more than that." Claire turns to me and winks. "He's also my private chef."

He scoffs, flips two chairs over for us to sit on, and plants a kiss on her cheek. "I'll be outside. Text me when you're done. Later, Quinn."

Apparently this is a conversation between Claire and me.

After Booth leaves to wait in the truck, I flip the sign on the door to *closed*, lock up, and keep the lights on, casting a warm glow on the snowy sidewalk outside.

She scans my face as I sit across from her before smiling warmly. "How are you, sweetheart? You look well."

I haven't seen Claire since the wedding, and up until now, I was worried what she would think about my and Graham's "separation."

"I'm doing good. Busy since the bakery reopened last week. How are you? Let me get you something warm to drink." I go to stand, but she holds up a hand, stopping me.

"Don't worry about that. Let's talk for a moment." She must

see the worry in my eyes. "Nothing like that. Graham has told me what's going on and I'm not here to berate you like some justice-searching mother."

Chuckling, I settle in my seat, my flustered state slowly easing off.

"As a parent, you want the best for your children. All four of mine are very different. While my love for them is unconditional it can be hard to juggle so many personalities, but that's just part of the job description. I like to think I'm a good parent to all of my kids, but I'd be lying if I said I always got it right. Ted, my husband, was much more pragmatic than me, so when the kids needed that type of parenting, he would step in. When we lost him, they lost that person, but I think it impacted Graham the most. It turns out I've failed Graham a lot recently."

I frown and she shakes her head. "I know about Jenna."

My spine goes ramrod straight, hackles up at her name, and Claire doesn't miss it.

"That's exactly the reaction she deserves. Graham came over this weekend and told me everything that went on between them, and how her relationship with my nephew started *well* before they ended things. Now, don't go giving me excuses and telling me I couldn't have known, because in my stubborn head, yes, I should have. The fact Graham felt he had to protect my feelings like that makes me proud but also tells me we both failed.

"I should have opened my eyes more and not allowed him to brush me off whenever I questioned their breakup. He's a silent protector and I think that's what he was doing, but he shouldn't have had to do that. He knows that now. And we had a good talk—emotional, but good. I can't replace his father, but I'm going to try to see things from his perspective more. In return, he's promised to not hide things from me, even if it's hard to hear."

How the hell do I have any more tears left?

She hands me a tissue and wipes away the moisture in her own eyes. "I don't know if Graham told you about my childhood, but, Claire"—my hand wraps around hers—"you're a wonderful Mom, and they're all so lucky to have you. Thank you for sharing that with me."

She bats a hand at me. "Oh, I should be thanking you."

"For what?"

"For loving my sweet boy so thoroughly and not giving up on him."

The agony in my chest that's been there since I left his apartment threatens to send me toppling sideways. My arms ache to hold him. To hug him and tell him how proud I am that he spoke to his mom.

She reaches into her pocket and pulls out two envelopes. "Graham asked that you read the smaller one first."

I'm around the table and bending to hug Claire in the blink of an eye.

"I'll leave you to it." She pats me on the cheek. "Christmas isn't far away. I hope you'll be bringing some of that carrot cake with you."

With a teary goodbye, I wave to Claire and Booth as they climb into his truck.

My eyes fall to the envelopes. Having his mother hand deliver these ones has nervous-excitement churning in my chest.

Slowly, I break through the seal of the first envelope and a small Post-it note falls to the table.

> This entry wasn't dated, but it was written the night Jenna and I broke up. -G

A shaky breath flutters the paper in my hand.

"There's a reason everyone calls you Gray. It's fitting: dull, boring, and emotionless."

That was how she ended a decade-long relationship.

Relief is the last thing I should feel. Where's the sadness? Regret? Hope that we can try again?

I'm not sure when it ended, but it was long before tonight.

She's wrong for so many things, but I can't find any reason to disagree with her.

Had I been a different man, this would have ended differently. And sooner.

But I'm just Graham.

Gray.

It takes every modicum of restraint not to crumple up the paper in a fit of rage.

I don't recognize the author behind the words.

The other envelope burns a hole in the table and before my anger worsens, I slip the second letter out and cast my eyes over Graham's handwriting. At first I don't notice it, but then I realize this isn't a journal entry but another letter.

To my Quinn,

I'll keep this one short and sweet—like you.

I don't share this entry with you searching for pity, but to show you how I was before you. I know you asked me not to change, and I haven't, but being with you has allowed me to see how Jenna's betrayal and cruelty left me branded with so much self-doubt that I forgot who I was.

Because of you, I found myself again. I'll continue to search for the parts of me I lost or still question.

Last week I took a new step in that journey and reached out to a therapist.

To love you is a privilege. To love myself is fundamental.

I'm still learning, but thank you for teaching me that.

Hopeful to have you in his arms again soon,
Graham

What are the odds?

I know Jo wouldn't have told him about my upcoming appointment, so knowing he's taking this step on his own is big. Even though we haven't been together in weeks, it feels like he's been with me every step of the way.

I'm desperate to have my hand in his for the rest of this journey.

And hopefully, our paths join soon.

CHAPTER THIRTY-SEVEN

quinn

I HAVEN'T EVEN ARRIVED AT THE BAKERY, YET I'M ALREADY itching to receive today's envelope.

Each entry has been a roller coaster of emotions. But I can see it. The way he slowly started to see himself differently. How I've always seen him. As much as his words have comforted me during our time apart, I need *him*.

For now, I cherish his handwritten words until he's ready.

"Please tell me you're going to save me one of those spiced apple muffins?" Jo asks beside me as we walk down Robin Road together, both wrapped head to toe to fight off the blistering cold. It's six a.m., and the sun hasn't risen yet.

We're halfway through December, and the bakery looks like the festive season threw up on it. Holly, bells, wreaths, and ribbons decorate the walls and tables.

"I make no promises. The people love them."

She huffs, but when I turn toward her, she's staring down the street with wide eyes.

"You're telling me." She points in front of her. "Looks like people *really* love your muffins."

There's an innuendo somewhere there, but it gets lost when

I find a line of people already halfway down the block outside the bakery.

"What in the world." My jaw hangs open and we increase our pace, until we stop next to Mrs. Stewart, the grumbly council woman, who is at the front of the line. "Mrs. Stewart. Hi. Um, we don't open for another couple of hours."

She gives me a stern look. "As much as I love your pastries, I'm not stupid enough to wait out in the cold. We're all wondering what's going on in there?"

"In where?"

"Your bakery. Are you a florist now? I think it's unhygienic to have all that pollen and dirt near food." She purses her lips as she waits for me to respond.

"I'm sorry, but what are you talking about?" My eyes bounce down the line of people, who are peering through the bakery window, and blocking my view. *Damn my short legs.*

"Let me through." Jo pushes her way to the front and gasps. "Quinn, I think you should go in. Everyone else…go away!" She flaps her hands, dispersing the crowd.

Panic sets in.

"Oh my god, is it flooded?" I shout as I fumble with my keys. Fire? Burglary? Every terrible outcome passes through my mind as I barge inside.

Only, it's not terrible.

It's yellow.

Lilies, sunflowers, tulips, dahlias, daisies, roses. All different shades of yellows. Flowers I don't even think are in season decorate the room. Everywhere you look, there's yellow.

Excluding one spot.

Our table.

And in the very chair he sat in almost two months ago; I find him.

A sigh of relief escapes us both as we lock eyes.

We slowly take the other in, savoring the first look as if it's been an eternity.

I want to push up his glasses as they slide down his nose. The hair I love to mess up is styled perfectly. He's in a beige, knitted sweater I know is soft to the touch, and his hands rub against his jean-clad thighs, giving away his nervousness.

Seeing him for the first time in weeks sends my senses into overdrive. I need to feel the scruff of his beard against my hands. To immerse myself in his warm, spicy scent. To watch his blush creep up his neck. To hear him whisper my name. To taste his kisses.

From the impatient, craving look he's giving me, he's missed me just as much.

"Hi, honey."

"Hey, you."

We both smile.

Suddenly, I don't know what to do with myself. My hands feel strange when they're not touching him.

Chair legs scrape against the floor as he pulls one out from the table. "Will you sit with me?"

In a flash I'm next to him, and he chuckles at my speed.

What does it mean that he's here? There was never any timeframe to our separation, but from what he's shown me so far, he's taken a lot of big steps in the right direction. We both have.

"How are you?" He takes my hand in his, weaving our fingers together.

"I'm good. The van. Graham, the van. It's amazing. I should have texted. All your letters. Oh god, I'm going to cry again." I drop my head, taking deep breaths to stop the shaking in my voice. "I've missed you so much."

"You have no idea how much I've missed you." He tucks a strand of hair behind my ear. "Curly misses you too. It's been awfully quiet without you."

"I didn't think anyone could miss my endless babbling."

"Quinn." He sighs my name. "I miss you when you're sleeping."

There's a lightness to him. A subtle credence. He's still my Graham, though.

My fingers curl around his bicep and squeeze. "You're looking for a therapist?"

"Yeah." He nods. "I don't know if the first one will stick, but I hope I find a good fit."

"We're really not that different. I meet with one after Christmas."

His eyes widen before filling with pride. "That's good. Really good, baby." I squeak in protest when he slips his hand from mine, making him laugh. "I have another letter for you."

He pulls out a folded piece of paper, and like I've been doing all week, my fingers unfurl, and I wait for it to be handed over.

The tips of his ears go red and there's a slight tremble in his hands. "Today, I thought I'd read it to you. Is that okay?"

My palms press to my cheeks, and I nod. "I'd really like that."

He clears his throat, flashes me that rare smile, and then, like rich coffee, he speaks, "'Date: December thirteenth.'"

Today's date.

"'Sunshine and rain clouds. So different and not often seen together. I couldn't understand why one would want to be with the other. It's after meeting Quinn Jackson that I know why gray clouds and sunshine work so well together. When done just right, they make something beautiful and rare. A rainbow. That's what we are; inexplicably beautiful. Without one, we don't get all the beautiful colors that make up the world around us.

"'I see now that you need both. You brought the beauty and warmth of the sun with you. And I bring the rain that helps the yellow flowers I love to give you grow. Just one moment, Quinn. That's all it took for me to know that I want to spend the rest of my days showing you how beautiful we can be. Thank you for helping me see the good I bring into the world, that I'm worthy of love. I'm sorry it took me so long to realize how incredible we are together. I will love you through all our moments. Thank you for loving me, for me. Now please let me kiss you.'"

He doesn't falter once. Each sentence and word was strung together so eloquently, I could almost see them floating and dancing between us.

I laugh through the tears, feeling so incredibly honored that the man in front of me is mine. So ridiculously happy that he chose himself. "You wrote that last part down?"

A whoosh of air leaves him and he turns the paper around.

It's blank.

"My feelings for you are memorized. You will never have to doubt a single thing on my mind. If you need to know something or I struggle to communicate, ask me." He takes hold of my hand and rests it over his heart. "I'd never forget how deeply I love you. Because it's all in here. This is yours."

I fly off the chair and crash into his arms. He catches me, like he always has. The feel of him finally is so wonderfully overwhelming.

"I'll cherish your heart forever. I love you so much. Thank you for being exactly what I needed." I pull back to look deep into his eyes. "I can't wait for all our moments together. You're a beautiful man, with a beautiful heart and soul. And I'm so happy you asked me to be your fake girlfriend."

He presses his face into my neck, breathing me in as he stands and perches me on the edge of the table. There's no hesitation, no warming up to do as his lips meet mine. We don't need to savor the kiss. We'll have years to do that.

Our lips crash together like we've been starved. Only

coming up for air long enough to take in the other before diving right back in.

It's Graham who has the sense to stop me stripping us both bare for the whole town to see.

"You let me give you so many firsts, but I can't wait until you give me one of my own." He presses our foreheads together, and I can see the reflection of my wild, unfiltered happiness smiling back at me in his glasses.

"What will it be?"

"One day soon. You'll be the first *and* only person I ever call wife."

CHAPTER THIRTY-EIGHT

quinn

I've been staring creepily at Mr. Willis from across the bakery for almost half an hour.

Just do it, Quinn. Rip the Band-Aid off.

"Are you talking to yourself again?"

My eyes snap to Graham. He's leaning against the counter with Curly at his feet, who is snuggly wrapped up in the vest I bought for him. It came with a friggin' hood. Plus, Graham can't be mad—I got him a matching one.

"I'm giving myself a pep talk. Didn't you say you were going for a walk?" My voice is antsy, and I haven't stopped rearranging the display fridge all morning.

"Honey, the worst that could happen is he says no. You've got the preapproval." He leans over the cash register, crowding me as he holds me with a look that says, *You've got this.* "Call me after and I'll walk back to meet you."

I deflate with a big sigh. "Gah! Okay, okay." I smack a kiss to his lips and playfully shove him toward the door. Not before a quick slap to that perfect ass. "Now get out of here. You're very distracting. I love you. Tentacles and all."

Rolling his eyes and laughing he stretches over the counter and gives me one final peck. "Love you."

That will never get old.

A couple of minutes after Graham leaves, I steel my nerves. Armed with a free blueberry scone, I walk to where Mr. Willis sits by the window. As usual, he's people watching with a melancholy look on his face. The town looks like the inside of a snow globe right after being shaken silly. Snowflakes the size of my eyes have been coming down since this morning and large drifts are quickly forming along the sidewalk.

The weather forecast says this is just the beginning of the storm headed our way.

Five days before Christmas.

"Hey, Mr. Willis." My voice sounds confident, but I hope he doesn't catch the shaking of my hands. "I made way too many scones this morning. This one's on the house."

He pats his belly, and his thin lips pull up into a smile. "I'd never say no."

I place the sweet treat in front of him and then stand there, awkwardly.

"Did you need something else?" he asks.

"Can I sit? I'm gonna sit." I'm already pulling out a chair. It's now or never. "I hope this isn't inappropriate of me, but I know you've mentioned about cutting down on the number of properties you manage. Maybe even selling...I wondered..."

I think back to the last couple of months with Graham. How we both unknowingly brought out the best in each other and said good riddance to the toxic ghosts of our past.

He's helped me let go of those old insecurities I still carried from my mom's abuse. I was so sure I had to do everything alone, that I was holding myself back. But I don't. I have an amazing group of friends who wouldn't bat an eye at helping me out. It's not cheating. It's not laziness.

It's family.

Which is why today, I'm finally asking Mr. Willis if he'll consider selling the building to me.

My shoulders drop from where they're hunched up to my ears and I straighten. "What I'm trying to ask is, if there's a time when you decide to sell this property, maybe you'll consider selling it to me. I've been preapproved for a mortgage, but I'm sure if we spoke to the ba—" He raises a hand, halting me.

"I had considered it." His face is unreadable. "I know the interest rates aren't kind at the moment, and I wouldn't feel right putting you in a position like that."

Disappointment seeps into my limbs, weighing them down, but I hold steady, not wanting to show my reaction when he tells me no. I get it, I'm a young, new business owner.

"I totally understand. Thank you for at least listening to me." I smile and go to stand, but he continues.

"How about a rent-to-own agreement?"

I'm frozen, standing halfway out of my chair in shock.

I had to have misheard him.

"I'm sorry, can you repeat that?"

"Please, sit back down." He gestures to my chair, and I collapse into it. "I paid for this place in cash almost thirty years ago. I've had no problem making a return. As much as I love being your landlord, leasing out commercial properties is draining, and at my age, I don't have it in me. Think about it, and if you're interested, I'll have my attorney draw something up. Your rent would stay the same and a percentage of it would go toward the purchase price."

I know for a fact that I'm paying well below what I should, and his generosity has allowed me to put some money aside for a deposit. I'm not close to having what I need, but I thought showing Mr. Willis I'm prepared would make me look responsible and someone he'd be happy to sell to.

I did not expect this.

And it's a good deal. So good. Monthly mortgage payments

would stretch me thin, but this would help my revenue stay in the green.

"I am...well, I'm a little shocked." I laugh nervously. "I thought you'd turn me down."

"I know I'm a grumpy old man, but you've been kind to me. A lot of people in town stopped trying with me a long time ago..." There's a sadness to his tone. "I don't need a response today. Speak to that smart boy of yours. You know where I am."

"I will. Thank you." I bite back my grin so hard, my cheeks ache.

Chuckling, he wraps the scone in a napkin before standing. "Have a good day, Quinn." He tips his head, pulls out a ten-dollar bill, and leaves me standing in the middle of the bakery, speechless for once.

graham

CHRISTMAS MORNING

"One more, honey. Give me one more." I pant into the softness of Quinn's inner thigh, before biting down. Her breathy gasps and the pull she has on my hair have been driving me crazy for the last forty minutes. My hips thrust into the mattress when I dive back into her soaked pussy, thighs bracketing my ears perfectly. "Let me feel you come apart on my tongue again and I'll give you your Christmas present."

"I can't. It's too much," she cries, yet the way her walls quiver around my finger says otherwise.

"You can. You're doing so well." My voice is calm despite the ravenous need to be inside of her.

"Oh god, Graham," she shouts as I pinch her clit. "Only for you. Do that thing I love. I'm so close."

I look up the length of her body. Her supple stomach. Full breasts, heaving with each thrust of my fingers. The rosy-pink nipples she's rolling between her fingers. Her sexy, buxom figure is a damn masterpiece.

"So greedy for both your holes to be filled, aren't you?"

Considering she thought herself as inexperienced when we first got together, she's always willing to try something at least once. This, she loves. I coat my index finger in her slick arousal, before circling that tight ring of muscle.

She clenches around my fingers, pulling me deeper as she turns her head to bite down on the pillow.

"God, I can't wait to take this ass one day." I thrust both fingers deeper, causing her back to arch off the bed. "Now let go. Let me hear you, honey."

As soon as I pull her clit into my mouth, sucking hard, she doesn't have time to warn me, not that I need it. I'm well versed in Quinn's pleasure. With a raspy cry, she detonates, fingers clawing at my scalp as her taste fills my mouth.

"There we go," I praise her through what is her fourth orgasm. "Perfect, so perfect for me."

She collapses onto the mattress, and I kiss her thighs and belly as she comes down from her orgasm.

"Graham, how on earth am I supposed to turn up to your mom's for dinner now? You've fucked me senseless." She tries and fails to sit up, but there's a humor to her exhausted voice.

I crawl up her body, trailing my lips across every dip and curve, until I reach her flushed face. "I haven't fucked you yet," I say with wicked smile.

"Keep your monster tentacle away from me. I. Am. Done. I'll give you a blow job later, but"—she glances at the clock on the bedside table—"we have one hour until we need to be there. And I need to shower."

"I'm holding you to that," I call as she climbs off the bed, squeaking when I smack her round ass.

When she returns from her shower, her skin a dusty peach color from the hot water, I'm already waiting for her on the edge of the bed with her present clutched between my hands. I'm mostly shaking from excitement, but there's always a nervousness when being vulnerable.

It's been almost two weeks since Quinn and I reunited. I'm still working on not overthinking or doubting myself. Quinn's trust and belief in me has helped me see myself in a different light. We're both due to meet with our therapists for the first time next month, but at least we're not doing it alone.

We're not perfect, and there will be hard times, but whatever we face, we'll do it together. On days she needs a quiet, strong pair of arms to bury herself into, I'll be there. When I need a shot of serotonin and a boost of confidence, she'll give me that.

Opposites don't just attract. They come together so uniquely and magnificently, you'd never know they weren't the same.

My striking other half stands in front of me now, naked, and looking so devastating, it takes a tremendous amount of effort not to fall to my knees and beg her to be my wife.

Soon.

We're in no rush. And I want Quinn to fully experience all of the amazing things happening with the bakery.

Her van is still parked on Martin Willis's land, and we stayed there the other night. Never again. I woke up twisted like a bagel and still can't get the knots out of my back.

She hasn't moved back in, but she never fully moved out. Something I hope we discuss soon.

I'm now wearing my Christmas Day sweater—one she picked out. And not only does Curly have a matching one, but so does she. She laughed when I said we needed three girls and three boys to be the modern-day *Brady Bunch*.

She's wrapping herself in a fluffy robe when her attention falls to my hands, and her eyes sparkle. "I thought you were kidding about another present. We said one gift this year."

I love how she says *this year*. Knowing full well this is one of many.

"We did agree to one gift. This is more of a thank-you."

Quinn got me a monogrammed, amber-colored leather journal. *The color reminded me of the leaves we saw up on the trail,* was what she said when I tore through the gift wrap.

"A thank-you for what?" She settles on the bed next to me, resting her temple on my shoulder as her finger skates down the spine of the small notebook.

I press my lips to the crown of her head. "When I shared those journal entries with you, it was a way for me to show you how much of an impact you have on my life." I slide the notebook onto her lap. "I've always loved writing. You once said words hold a lot of power. The ones in here, while short, show the power you have and will always hold over my heart."

Her warm palm rests against my cheek. "I love your words. Spoken or written. Thank you, for being you. And for this." She holds up the one thing I've never shared with anyone. Not from a place of diffidence, but because I wanted to keep this for myself.

Now that I have my person, I want to share this final piece with her.

"Should I read it now?" She looks up at me eagerly.

"I'd like that. Read them to me." I drag her onto my lap and settle us against the pillows.

We're definitely going to be late for dinner now.

She opens the book and I see her cheeks pull up in a smile as she traces the letters. We drift into our own world when Quinn begins reading out each haiku, slowly and softly.

My words, spoken by her.

The way I would describe my love for Quinn Jackson goes beyond the twenty-six letters of the alphabet. All the languages in the world aren't enough.

Yet, from the day I met her, I found myself writing poetry again. Something I hadn't done for almost fourteen years.

Just one moment was all it took for me to see a new future.

Every moment after, has been beautiful, life altering, and

allowed me to not only find the love of my life but the old me again. I have the woman tucked against my chest to thank for that.

That's where she'll stay, in my arms, until the end of my days.

There's no pot of gold
At the end of the rainbow
You'll only find us

epilogue

GRAHAM

The probability of my heart being any fuller: zero.

But then I look down at my wife.

My wife.

Just hours ago, the woman whose smile can't be dimmed by a solar eclipse, weaved her fingers with mine as we shared promises to each other to keep for the rest of our lives. We might have been surrounded by our family and friends, but she was all I saw.

I guess not much has changed since the day we met.

When everyone stood and she walked toward me, time stopped. Even on the arm of my big brother—who most definitely shed a tear when she asked him to walk her down the aisle—it was just the two of us. Her simple, white satin dress was molded to her exquisite body, the material rippling like pearlescent water.

Each step she took, brought her closer to becoming mine in a whole new way.

I didn't attempt to hide my tears and neither did she. Without saying it, we both shared the same thought. This was the moment we had been waiting our entire lives for.

We agreed the ceremony didn't need to be extravagant, and after saying our vows at the town hall, we went back to my mom's house to celebrate. Quinn—*my wife*, because that's never going to get old—wanted just two things. A bouquet of yellow flowers and a wedding cake made by her.

I've never been one to say no to her and she really outdid herself with the four-tiered, half-naked Victoria sponge.

We're all crowded in the kitchen, laughter from our loved ones filling the air.

A tug on my pant leg has me peering down to find my niece staring up at me with a gap-toothed smile.

"Uncle Gray. Now that you're married, will you be having a baby like Daddy and JoJo are?"

Quinn squeezes my hand, curling her lips around her teeth to stop her laughter.

"Also," Lottie continues, "How are babies made? No one will tell me. Well, Uncle Booth said they come out of your butt."

I almost choke on my saliva, and thankfully *my wife* comes to the rescue.

Quinn squats down and bops Lottie on the nose. "I think the bigger question is, what is your little brother going to be called?"

Lottie scrunches her face in deep thought before shouting, "Butt-face!" and running away.

Shortly followed by Patrick chasing down Booth for encouraging his daughter.

"That did not go the way I thought it would." Quinn laughs as she loops her arm in mine and we walk out into the yard.

My mom and sister went to great lengths to turn this space into something special. Fairy lights are strung up inside a small marquee and heaters are dotted around to fight off the cold. Similar to Quinn's bouquet, stems of yellow flowers sit in little mason jars on all the tables.

It's cozy, quaint, and perfectly us.

I pull her away from the small crowd of people, out of earshot, and tug her into me.

"What name would you pick if we have a boy?" I ask as my hand snakes between us to rest against her lower stomach.

"Shh," she hisses but does a poor job of hiding the ear-splitting grin that takes over her face. "It won't be *Butt-face,* that's for sure. Anyway, I think it's a girl."

This is one of the many reasons my heart couldn't possibly be fuller.

We found out four days ago, and she's too early to show yet. It was a surprise, to say the least. But the best surprise we could have ever asked for.

Day after day, she gives me something I hadn't dreamed would be a part of my future until her.

My lips brush her ear as I bend down. "How about we get out of here? You said something about lingerie earlier?"

There's a roguish glint to her caramel eyes, but she shakes her head. "Later. For now, I want to dance with my husband."

Fuck. Now *that,* I will never get tired of.

I tilt my head toward the sky, taking in the canopy of moonlight and stars above us, so similar to the last time we slow danced together. That night was the domino for a lot of things, but ultimately, we reunited stronger than ever. Every day since then, we find new and beautiful things that make us, *us.*

I was lost before her. Now with her light in my life, it's impossible not to see our future paved.

The song playing from the speakers changes to "First Day of My Life" by Bright Eyes. Everyone watches on as we hold each other close to rock slowly with the music.

Her arms are looped tightly around my waist, with her head

on my chest, while my hand rests at the small of her back and the other runs through her silky brown tresses.

"Thank you for trusting me with your heart, Quinn *Sadler*." I feel her smile against my chest. "Even before we met, I think deep down, I knew you existed. Had you walked into that bar ten years later rather than last year, I would have waited. There isn't any length of time I wouldn't wait for you, honey, but I thank all the stars above us now that I didn't have to."

She props her chin on my chest, eyes shining bright, and the only sweetness I'll ever need filling my mouth as I lower my head to kiss her.

She pulls away just an inch and whispers against my lips, "Never in a million years did I think that a dart aimed at a map would find me my everything. We were always meant to be, Graham. I cannot wait to share the love I have for you with our children and watch them adore you as much as I do." She brushes away a few tears that fall freely down my cheeks and gives me a smile I'll remember well after we leave this earth. "This day is for the record books."

"It is. And every day, after today."

****

Thank you so much for visiting Sutton Bay! I hope you enjoyed Quinn and Graham's story.

Want more from them? Read their bonus chapter on my website. www.ronniemathews.com

****

Up next? Sutton Bay's resident head chef. You can pre-order Booth's story now! **All We Need** will release in June 2025.

***

If you haven't read #1 in the series, **Those Two Words** is Johanna and Patrick's childhood friends, second chance love story. Which is available to read now!

acknowledgments

Holy moly, I wrote another book.

After I finished writing my debut, *Those Two Words*, I hadn't expected to find myself releasing a second book less than half a year later. I was always going to give the readers Quinn and Graham's story, especially after all the little bread crumbs I left in *TTW*, but now that they're out in the world, I still can't quite believe it.

This story was a lot more challenging for a few reasons. I wrote this one while publishing my first book, trying to maintain a heavy social media presence to help promote Johanna and Patrick's story, and also, life is hard sometimes. There were some days when I was so close to burning out. Quinn and Graham's story was a difficult one, because I wanted to do them justice, but also show readers how perfect they are for each other while fighting the battles of their past separately.

I couldn't have done this alone, and as always, my husband continued to be my biggest supporter. Thank you for doing extra dishes, making me cups of tea, and always telling me how proud you are of me.

To my family and friends, thank you for seeing this as more than a hobby. For buying my books, telling your friends, and being in my life.

To my early readers, Albany, Christana, Courtney, Jules, Katie, Kerry, Lauren, and Tabitha. Thank you for being patient with me. For sending me voice notes and listening to my rambling ones. For caring about this story just as much as I do. And for being honest, lovely humans.

It's so refreshing to find an editor that cares about your stories as much as you do. Paisley, I'm so thankful to have you with me on this journey, and I know if my characters could thank you in person, they would.

Caroline, a pleasure as always and so grateful to have you as the last set of eyes on my book babies before they enter the big wide world.

Mel! Thanks for putting up with my indecisive brain and helping me take this series in a new direction. This cover lives and breathes the essence of Maine.

Shout out to my Street Team for hyping me up from day one. What a wonderful group of cheerleaders I have in my corner.

To the readers. Without you, I wouldn't get to share my stories. Having you visit my fictional worlds and love them as much as I do means so much to me. Thank you.

about the author

Ronnie Mathews writes small town, swoon-worthy stories with lots of feels and delicious spice. If she isn't writing or reading, you'll find her in the kitchen or out with friends and family trying to balance being an ambivert. She lives in the North West of England with her husband and black Labrador, Jake.

www.ingramcontent.com/pod-product-compliance
Lightning Source LLC
Chambersburg PA
CBHW072201130726

47910CB00011B/1768